ALSO BY
GINA GIORDANO
Strange Eden

ISBN Paperback: 13 979-8-9869834-2-4
Cover design by Coverkitchen Pte. Ltd.
Author headshot by C-Allyssa Reckley

KÄFERHAUS
PRESS

For my mother –
thank you for endlessly supporting my creativity,
and for being my BUNNAY.

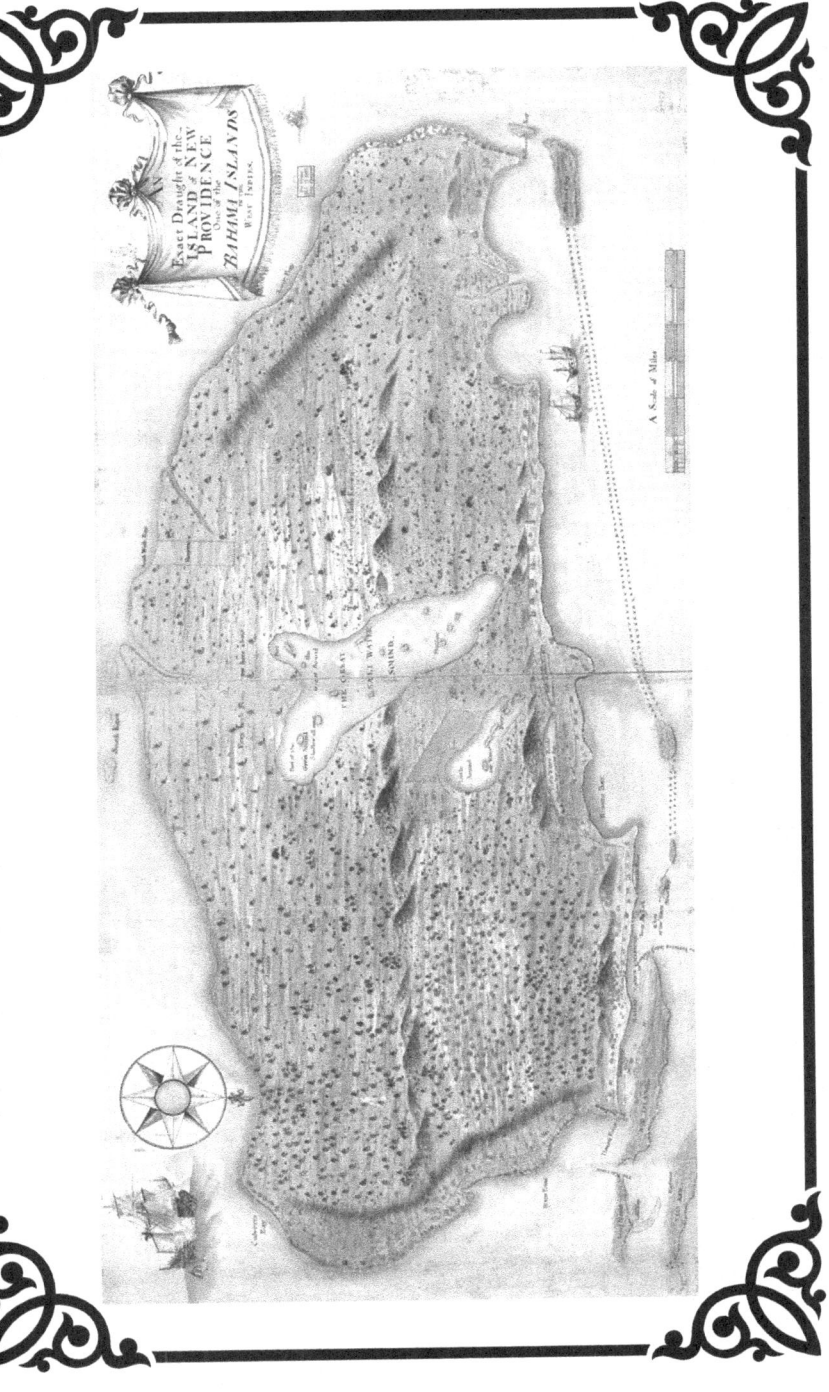

Exact Draught of the
ISLAND of NEW
PROVIDENCE
One of the
BAHAMA ISLANDS
West Indies

A Scale of Miles

CHAPTER I.

– August 1st, 1792 – Nassau, Bahamas –

Cleo awoke with the unsettling feeling that eyes were watching her. Her dwelling was dark and musty, accompanied by a rush of humid air that descended into the space in heavy swathes. Thunder rolled through the clouds across the water in the distance. She wondered if lightning had served as the cause of her disturbance, but she soon found its true source.

A tall, hulking mass appeared at her doorway, hastily ducking underneath the scratchy palms that lined the roof. Cleo did not move, only watched as the shape slowly revealed itself to be a man. Sometimes, it was difficult to tell man and spirit apart.

His breathing was haggard, and his white shirt was soaked to transparency.

"I've killed—I've killed him. I've killed the one man most like a brother to me …"

Once she understood what was happening, Cleo

stood up as Charles dropped to his knees. A slave did not have the luxury of privacy, and she could immediately feel his despair as if it were her own. A whisper of a memory floated through her mind, and she recalled the expectation she had carried of this very event. Cleo had not been present yesterday morning, but she had seen what had taken place.

In a dream many, many months ago, she had seen an innocent man dragged to the gallows and hung, but the rope did not kill him. She had seen Charles standing there, still like a statue, his emotions roiling inside him as he watched. There had been an air of helplessness in the dream, as if he yearned to move, to act, but could not. And when he did finally free himself of his immobility, he did the one thing he did not want to do. He snuffed the life out of his friend. He finished the deed the executioner had failed to.

Charles knelt on the floor, his breaths coming out fast and hard. Cleo moved closer to him, and he embraced her in his strong grip, pressing the breath out of her. She could smell whiskey on him, and she wondered how much of it he had consumed. It was a strange sight to witness someone usually so reserved and composed finally lose control. His sobs shook her body.

"He was suffering. The man was suffering, and you helped him," Cleo began to say. "This was not your doing."

"No!" Charles suddenly shouted.

Cleo was struck by the memory of the little boy who had clung to her skirts all those years ago. When she saw his vulnerability on full display, she could not help but want to stop his pain. A part of her was surprised to see him like this, and she knew it would be a final glimpse into the pieces of him that she had defended so staunchly. He had not come for her aid like this in many years.

"He should have not died today. I should have seen what this was. He tried warning me, and I cast him aside. I called him a liar. And a traitor. I disparaged his name. I helped those who would seek his end. I caused his downfall! He was working for the king, and I obstructed him. And when he could have sought his escape, he chose to ride here to try to warn me one final time. What have I done, Cleo? *What* have I done?"

He released her from his grasp. His breathing grew heavier, and he clutched his forehead in his hands.

"You did not understand. You did not know. How could you know? That man's business is not your own."

Cleo reached for a stubby candle and lit it. It cast the space in quickening flashes of shadow.

"No ... but I should have believed him," Charles answered in a whisper.

"Is a man a fool for not believing a liar twice? Three times?"

Charles readjusted his stance on the dirt floor and leaned against the cool limestone wall. The fact that she shouldn't have been privy to such knowledge caused no anger within him. Charles was either used to her manner of speaking, or he was too tired to protest such an intrusion into his thoughts.

He hastily wiped his wet face and closed his eyes. Thunder crashed right above them as the storm crossed the shoreline. He would not acknowledge what she had said, and so Cleo brought it up again.

"Charles, this is not the first time he has brought conflict to you. You have dealt with enough. Do not clean up another's mess. Focus on your own."

"I find I have become the very thing I hate. An unthinking, unfeeling creature, bound only by my commander's orders. Unfree to reason. To loyalty."

"He has betrayed you. How easily you forget! A man's death does not erase his crimes. This way of thinking will not help you, and it certainly does not help him where he stands now."

"Can you see him?" Charles' eyes grew huge, and his lip trembled.

"Yes." She did not want to say that she had seen him beside Eliza earlier that day, the moment when Charles and Eliza had stood tense on the porch in the midday heat. It was not a good sign. Cleo did not usually see spirits return that quickly. The man's soul should have traveled to his intended destination, but his ghost clung to her shadow. And Cleo had watched her strike Charles. She understood her pain as well, but Eliza was not in front of her now.

Cleo sighed.

"You welcomed him at your door. And what did *he* do?"

Charles looked up at her, and she recognized the return of anger within his eyes.

"That is a separate matter."

"It is not that simple. This man entangled too many paths. He wanted something that was not meant for him in this life. A man is free to do as he wishes, but when he strays from his path, he will have to deal with the new consequences he has chosen. He—"

"I did not come here to discuss that matter," Charles interrupted tersely.

It was apparent that he considered loyalty to his friend and the betrayal he suffered from what this supposed friend had done to his wife two very separate matters. But one could not divide the truth into pieces, accepting only the parts one preferred. That was false thinking.

"But you did come here for answers. And sometimes you must hear things you do not want to," she said.

"Do not speak to me in riddles. There is only one truth."

"Exactly …"

"And the truth is that I betrayed my sole friend, and I hastened his death. I did not put the rope around his neck, but I provided his enemies the rope. And then I finished their wicked task."

Cleo's face grew stony.

"He could have told you that first night, Charles. He could have revealed his purpose that night you reconciled. The night he brought her back to Pleasant Hall. But you were mistaken. He did not return her to you. In fact, that was the night he decided to keep her."

"I am not here to discuss my wife."

"But she is the center of this all. What I mean to say is that if Jean had not followed his impulses, he would not have been here. I saw a ship when I first looked at him. He was meant to leave sooner than he did. He stayed because of her. He made a mistake. Not you."

That was the first time Jean's name had actually been spoken. She could not gauge Charles' reaction to it, but she was beginning to feel the first trembling pangs of wrath return to his energy.

"I tend to drink and to forget, but the whiskey only reminds me of thoughts that are unbearable."

"Yes," Cleo answered. "It is unbearable to be so misunderstood."

Charles shook his head in disagreement.

"I have made countless mistakes. Principally, my marriage. My return to this godforsaken island. I should have stayed in England. I should have—"

"Can you feel this? What do you feel?" Cleo's wide hand patted the ground.

Charles looked at her strangely and then acquiesced. He rubbed the dirt between his fingers.

"It's mere dirt."

"Ah, but it is more than that. You are *here*. Not there," she said as she reached and tapped his forehead. "Your mind is the biggest prison you can ever be trapped inside. It is a waste of time to think of the past. It is done. This isn't some hell. You came from this dirt. Your first steps were on this dirt. And when you die, you're going back into this dirt. If you can't feel the dirt anymore, bend down and touch it. It's always here. The only hell you know is the one you made. You created that. And *you* can undo it, child."

Charles' eyes narrowed with suspicion in the shifting light. The wind began to pick up again, battering an uneven rhythm against the small hut.

"I want to be free of all this. I have known nothing but pain. I understand nothing but pain. And in doing so, I have brought nothing but pain to the ones I love."

"You cannot blame yourself too harshly. You have known nothing but the instinct to survive. A weaker man would not have made it this far. Now, you need to learn to live beyond survival."

Cleo had to utter such words slowly and carefully. She wanted to mask her own emotions. What he needed most now was strength, and in this asset she was rich. This almost gave him solace for a moment, but then his eyes darkened again with self-disgust.

"I cannot stop seeing her," he said quietly.

"Who? Eliza?"

"No," he said with irritation. "Celia's mother. Tabitha." He exhaled sharply, trying to steady his breathing as a new surge of pathos took hold. "I am no different than my father. I am a monster. He had taken an innocent life more than once, and now so have I."

Cleo said nothing and only watched him. Sometimes it was wiser to let a man wander through his feelings without any soothing words.

"I remember it all now that I have returned. Their fighting, the yelling, it woke me up. But Tabitha was there; she gripped my shoulder and told me to go to bed. And then, and then when he did that ... I thought she was merely sleeping. I thought my mother was sleeping! But I had looked upon death itself. When we ate together the next day, she was not there. For any child, death is a burden, but to not speak of its existence? When her chair sits empty, day after day? No one came to look for her. And if I ever dared to speak up … who would come to look for me?"

He glanced at Cleo, his eyes heavy with a lifetime of pain.

"I had to learn to protect myself. I never truly felt safe. I convinced myself it was a bad dream. But when I walked the grounds and I saw her grave, it was a cruel reminder. It did not offer me any solace. I did not see paradise on this island. There was only suffering."

Charles continued in a low tone, "This is no Eden. It is a living hell. The devil does not entice you with brimstone; he deceives you with beauty."

Cleo came closer to him and rubbed his arm.

"You are stronger than you know. We are not given what we cannot endure," she said softly.

"Something is missing inside me. I come to you, begging for relief in the middle of the night. What right have I to ask anything of you?" He gulped down the moist air, steeling himself for his next words. "And she hates me. She ha—*hates* me. I could have suspected as much but today I saw it in her eyes. I cannot be redeemed now. I have destroyed every possible chance of ever attaining her affections. Her trust. Her love …"

His breathing grew more intense again until it dissolved into a loop of sobs that shook his entire frame. He was so loud Cleo knew that the other slaves could hear. What would they think of their master now?

"Shhh …" Cleo said as she rubbed his quaking back. "That is not how it ends."

She knew it wasn't right to think ill of the dead, but she could only feel disgust when she thought of Jean. She thought of the shadow that had trailed behind him in life, the shadow that signified he only brought chaos and destruction wherever he went. How Jean had naturally gravitated towards Eliza when the light around her shoulders was so bright. She represented creation and potential. New possibilities. And now, when it appeared that matters concerning Jean were over, Cleo recognized her role in dealing with his troubled spirit had only begun. She would need to do her work fast and pray that it stuck. She returned to the present and focused on the man lost in his emotions before her.

"I am here by your side. Remember, the color of your soul is all I see. It will not be easy, but you will get to where you need to be. And part of that is being here. On this island. You have great things laying ahead of you. You only need to see it. Not all is lost."

"I have nothing laying ahead of me. I have ruined everything that means anything to me."

"Not everything. There is one avenue you need to follow. Your uniform. That red color you look so bold in. I look at you in it, and I hear a beating heart. It is in your blood."

"And what am I to do with that? What good does loyalty serve when the foundation is rotten? I am lost. I have squandered my life ..."

"Not the foundation. A root. A root that needs to be cut down like Josiah cuts the bushes in the yard."

"I cannot do anything. I serve a tyrant who is as

corrupt as he is rich. Lord Dunmore is not the man I thought he was. My loyalty is misplaced."

"I do not speak of loyalty. I speak of revenge. He fears you because he knows he cannot stop you. Prove that he is right."

In the distance, a crack of thunder resounded around them. Cleo took his hand and squeezed it.

"I was glad to see this night so long ago. Not to witness your pain, but because it told me that you would return home from those battles. Now you must prepare yourself for your final one."

The boat gently rocked with the current. The heat of the sun was intense, but Eliza was relieved of it with an occasional breeze. She desperately wanted to distract herself, and sketching a seemingly tranquil scene brought her some measure of forced comfort. At the very least, it cleared her mind with every stroke of graphite she brought down upon the paper. Even she could admit that Pleasant Hall was a charming, if not beautiful, sight from the water. Its white, symmetrical construction sat on a small slope of powdery sand, framed by wild palm trees and the occasional pine, and the glowing ripples of tropical water enhanced its appearance even further.

If she had been a stranger, or perhaps her younger self, she would have gazed upon such a sight and been easily fooled. This house was an oasis tucked away in private, rugged wilderness, where a young, charming family lived, working hard each day to provide for themselves, to eke out a living in this small part of the vast world. She could picture a strong husband and a devoted wife, with little ones running through the sand, playing a simple, nameless game.

But she knew better now. There was no happiness, no unity to be found within its brightly colored walls. Only division and discord. Rage and bitter jealousy. There was no husband or wife, no children, no family. There was only a man and a woman, complete strangers in affection and love, yet intimate in the darkest parts of themselves—parts so terrible, polite society would not tolerate them if they were laid bare in the blazing sunlight.

How deceiving appearances could be. A stately home, hiding a secret worse than the overt cruelty to those it enslaved. A worthy soldier of the king, incapable of true honor; his young, naive wife, harboring infidelity. An old slave, possessing more power than either of them, even if such powers did not rightly belong to this world.

Then he appeared in her thoughts. Jean: intrusive, loud, unmistakable. Eliza looked back up at the house, picturing the last time she had seen his white horse race inside the yard and the terrible feeling that had followed. Now it seemed strange to her. As if all along she knew somewhere in her heart that their future together was nothing but a mirage. It was as lasting as a wave of heat striking the hard ground. Their plans of escape, of another life, were never properly rooted in reality.

An all-consuming shame returned. Her breath caught

in her throat, and she felt the presence of tears beginning to tingle under her eyes. With a sharp exhale, she
closed her sketchbook, pushed it towards the other end
of the skiff, and lay down. A handkerchief covered her
face from burning in the sun, and she tried to steady her
breathing underneath the fabric. A comforting warmth
penetrated through, and the filtered light danced over
her closed eyes.

A few days had passed in an inconsequential sequence after his death. The stifling monotony of events
had resumed, much like the way she had spent her days
before he entered her life. The idea that a week would
soon arrive, a precise, ruthless measurement of time, terrified her. She inevitably knew that soon Jean's absence
would consume a greater part of her life than his brief
presence ever could.

She slowed her breathing and tried to focus on nothing but the steady swaying of the boat, its occasional
creak, and the breeze coming off the water. She forced
her thoughts in a new direction, the only one that inspired any hope. She wondered if she could take a boat,
perhaps the very one she lay rocking in, and escape. Eliza
had the money to do so, but she didn't know whether
such a plan could work. She doubted she could row herself across the rough waters of the reef to the open ocean.
Once that feat was accomplished, she would encounter
more danger; even experienced sailors had difficulty nav-
igating the waters of the Caribbean Sea. She lacked the
knowledge and the strength. She could take passage on a
ship, but she would surely be stopped or questioned. And

where could she go? Where could she possibly return to now? She was a ruined woman.

These thoughts were too heavy a burden, and just as Eliza realized this with a certain degree of panic, she could also feel a strange yet calm presence around her, beckoning her into softness. It was as if all these troubles only existed within the darkness of her mind, and if she could find a way to quieten it, then she could tap into the soothing rhythms of the sea, where nothing but a ceaseless current existed. She drew in her breaths to march alongside the endless rocking and almost settled into sleep. She was hungry for it. She was the most tortured with grief during the night, and sleep would not come. But here in the open, on the water, where she was perhaps most vulnerable, she felt more comfortable. Here on this skiff, the hands of her husband could not touch her. No ghostly visitation from Tabitha could interrupt her dreams. It was simply her, the sun, and the sea.

Until a new interruption invaded. A precise bump collided with the left underside of the boat, near her ribcage. She sat up, pulling the fabric away from her eyes, and looked wildly around her. She wondered if the boat had somehow drifted into a piece of coral before she saw a remarkably tall dorsal fin angling back and forth. Eliza leaned over the boat to catch a closer look.

There was no mistaking what swam in the water next to her, although she had never had the privilege of seeing a live one before. It was a large hammerhead shark, its stout body a dusky grey and its length longer than the skiff itself. As its dorsal fin cut through the glassy surface of the water, its tip appeared a flushed pink in the sunlight. She watched it in awe as it slowly swam, marveling at its unusually shaped head and wide-spaced eyes. It was most likely on the hunt for a stingray, and its tail steered it forward on its mission over a watery garden of mottled grey and green hues. She wondered how it had gotten through the rough rocks of the coral reef that marked a boundary between this and the more untamed waters further out. It served as a small reminder that safety was always fleeting on this fledgling island.

Eliza had the urge to draw its outline, but she cherished the sight of it more and did not want to look away for even a moment. She considered the shark a companion in a strange way, and she felt honored to sit beside a king of the ocean. She had always found more in common with the fish and creatures of the sea than with her fellow man. This hammerhead was a friend, one who did not judge her, only gifted her with its silent yet powerful presence. Eliza knew with one movement, it could eliminate her from this earth, but its motives for doing so would be unmistakably pure, stemming either from hunger or defense of itself. Animals were transparent in that way, unlike the human relationships she was forced to endure on land.

She watched until it drifted too far from sight to fully appreciate it as the shark approached the horizon line edged with a bank of dark clouds. It was August, and the storm season had fully arrived. Pleasant days like this would soon become less frequent. But here on this small patch of water, the sun still shone on the dazzling waves.

The threatening clouds farther off warned that this could all change in an instant, but she did not smell the rain or see its wavy outline descending from the sky yet. She was still safe where she sat.

She watched the activity on the shore, of the slaves carrying baskets of fruit on top of their heads, of Julius, the groom, leading a horse back to the stable. And then Charles appeared from the back of the house, coming from the direction of the slave dwellings and fields. His countenance was troubled, his brow furrowed deep in thought. One look at him walking around the house made her stomach drop. She threw herself back down against the bottom of the boat, keeping still. Eliza wanted him to only see a boat on the water's surface, nothing more.

They had not spoken more than a customary "yes" or "no" in passing, and this was the only arrangement she could tolerate. A sharp sigh left her body as her predicament reared its ugly head again. Every time she thought matters between her and Charles could grow no worse, she was proven horribly wrong. Their marriage was in the eye of a hurricane; this shaky truce was only an unstable illusion. It was one brought on by the violence and unexpectedness of Jean's death, and she knew the raging winds and rain would return.

CHAPTER II.

"Lady Sharpe! Lady Sharpe!"

Startled by the frantic banging on her door, Eliza went to it and opened it. The howl of the wind of the storm outside made Lucy difficult to hear.

"What is it?" Eliza asked, fully aware of how annoyed her tone sounded.

"Lord Sharpe wants you to come downstairs at once. Josiah says it's safer. Please hurry!" she said frantically, putting an arm around her.

Eliza pulled away just as the frame of the house moaned and shifted with a gust of wind. Charles was clearly using the weather as a pretext to gain a forced audience with her. The very thought of such a design infuriated her.

"It's just a storm; I do not see any reason to be so panicked—" she said bitterly.

"This is not just a storm, Lady Sharpe. This one is bad, like the one we had five years ago. We lost our stable in that one. It even tore down the church steeple in town! A stone church!"

Lucy directed her out of the room and down the stairs as the wind battered the outside of the porch. Eliza sighed as the parlor came into view. Charles was sitting in a chair, pensively watching the flame of a candle. He lacked the smug satisfaction she might have expected and looked no more amused than she. He quietly directed Lucy to prepare tea.

Eliza had avoided sharing his presence since Jean's execution, but it appeared that she could not navigate her way out of this interaction. It was inevitable that, at some point, they would have to occupy the same space. She regretted that the weight of her grief had not lessened nearly as much as she had desired; her nerves were still raw and exposed. Lately, when she opened her eyes in the mornings, and she recalled that Jean was indeed dead, it drove her to sickness. This was no time to share a room with the very man who took his life.

"We should stay here until the winds cease. We didn't have time to board the windows upstairs. The glass casements may burst. I question whether the very roof will hold," he remarked without looking at her.

"You've experienced a storm like this before?" she asked.

She felt the words leave her mouth with regret, but she hated the awkwardness of their uncomfortable silence more.

He seemed surprised to hear her ask him a question. His green eyes glowed in the light of the shifting firelight.

"Yes, I'm afraid. Once. A very long time ago." He reached for his glass of wine.

He looked at her now as if he wanted to speak of something else, but he remained silent. Lucy returned with a tea service tray, placing the delicate teacup down with a shaking hand.

"I will be brief with you, Eliza. You may lie on the chaise. I will not perturb you. In fact, I'll even turn my chair to enhance your privacy."

He shifted the chair on an angle to fully face the fireplace, but it did nothing to ease the sensation of being trapped. The covered windows and the shrieking wind only made the atmosphere feel more tense.

She took the steaming cup of tea and forced herself to sip it slowly in an attempt at relaxation. The fact that they didn't have to look at each other helped a great deal. His back was a lot less infuriating than having to look directly at his arrogant face.

Eliza tentatively pulled her legs onto the chaise and raised them up slightly. Laying on her back made her feel exposed. To make matters worse, the glass of wine he had been drinking was nearly empty. Old fears returned to the surface. He did not appear drunk, but he had indulged in spirits much more than he usually did. She had no clear indication of how much alcohol he had really consumed, and it seemed as though her sobriety was a disadvantage. A blanket or a sheet to cover herself would have eased her mind, but she dared not speak to him.

The warmth of the tea helped settle her after a few more sips. She left the room to use the chamber pot across the hall. When she returned, she was disheartened to see that the clock had barely moved. After some time, the assault of the wind and shifting of the house became a familiar sound. The low lighting of the room and the uneven tempo of nature made an eerily soothing lullaby. Against her best efforts, she felt herself slip into the deliciously heady space of sleep even as her mind yearned to stay alert.

The parlor had been quiet for some hours. He wanted to look at her again, but he dared not. Now was not the time for an argument. He marveled that she had even entertained the thought of joining him in the parlor. The idea of them remaining in the same room other than to hastily eat a meal or briefly acknowledge one another's existence was satisfying. Her presence sometimes made him feel powerless: powerless to keep her in front of him and powerless to control himself. Now matters between them were more tense than they had ever been. And what was worse, he did not blame her.

He swirled the remaining Madeira at the bottom of the glass. This bottle had not lasted long. The storm had forced him to slow down and had given him time to think. Perhaps her willingness to occupy space with him was a good sign. Maybe soon she would even be open to a conversation, although the very thought of such a venture was daunting. At times their distance was tolerable; in a misleading and evasive way, the lack of fighting seemed better than what had transpired before. Charles knew there could be no simple way to mend affairs between them. But the uncertainty of their future tortured him, and he wouldn't be able to tolerate it much longer.

His career seemed to offer a remedy for this. It would bring him the gift of both time and distance and allow Eliza more opportunity to return to the way she had been before. Strong dislike was preferable to the utter hatred she now viewed him with. But something about Lord Dunmore's latest proposal made him hesitate.

Charles had been ordered to Harbour Island to help oversee the construction of a new fortification there. There were inexperienced men to train, new foundations to be laid, and bandits to defend the island against. At any other time, he would gladly accept the change of scenery, but something did not feel right. He had lost faith in Lord Dunmore, and he questioned the timing of the order. Why was it necessary for him to be sent from New Providence now?

But he had to follow orders; there was no questioning that. Most of all, he would regret leaving Eliza. He knew that their marital relations had soured to a point of no return, but he still hesitated to leave her side. Her silent and restrained presence tested his patience now, but he feared her absence would serve as an even worse torment. Charles turned towards her, first leaning, then moving his position entirely when he realized that she was fast asleep.

He eagerly drank up the sight of her. After spending the last year with her, he had come to one conclusion: Eliza was fiery and beautiful, maddeningly beautiful. So much so that she herself didn't quite realize it. She could not possibly understand the effect that she had on others, and this type of wild beauty was the most dangerous. She held complete power over him, whether she knew it or not, and the only thing he regretted was the hurt he had delivered to her time and again.

He focused on her face, finally at peace, the hatred and contempt that usually flashed from her dark eyes now replaced by tranquility. Charles watched her chest rise and fall, contemplating how different people appeared when not awake. He wondered what she dreamt of when her consciousness left her. He knew it was not of him. It was probably of things and places she loved. The sea, her escape from reality, and the people who helped her endure her new life. It was certainly *not* of him.

Further down her sleeping form, his gaze stopped near her midsection. The shape of it seemed strangely curved. Usually, her abdomen was flatter and tighter, and it was even leaner when she was on her back. He knew because he could not forget the sight of her naked in his bed.

It seemed ridiculous to assume she had gained weight from eating. She barely ate in front of him. Her mannerisms had sharply changed since Jean's death, and he wondered if he would ever again witness the intrepid optimism of youth she had once possessed. Either way, she had always been in too much of a hurry to sit and enjoy food in the way that he did. If it wasn't for his constant need of movement and exercise to clear his mind, he would be a much heavier man by now. But he knew Eliza well enough to mark the difference in the shape of her body.

Charles carefully put down his glass and approached her, minding which floorboards he placed his weight on. The image he had seen from a distance did not improve at a closer range. He stopped by the side of the chaise, wanting with all of his might to touch her. He missed her on a level he had never experienced before. The wave of emotion that rose up in him was not lust but a heavy yearning and a deep sadness.

He ached to go back in time and change matters between them. He had never felt such happiness as when they had first arrived at Pleasant Hall. Their endless conversations, her excitement of exploring her new home, her fascination with the water—her very presence brought the house back to life after so many years of dust and decay. Their future had seemed so bright and full of possibility once. But that moment had long since evaporated, and his regret and desperation clung to him like a sweat-dampened shirt.

It troubled him because he knew that matters could never be rectified. He would never know a loving glance from her or a softly spoken word. He understood that he deserved it, but being in the same space with such an unfathomable distance between them was nothing but devastation.

Now he could see that the sight of her swollen stomach was contrasted by a sharp drop in her hips. As he stood over her, he at once understood what he was looking at. She was carrying life within her.

Charles tensed up, a hand almost daring to touch her for confirmation, but he hesitated. He did not want the truth of what he saw to become reality. Then he found a safer option. Lighting and the wicked tricks of shadows could easily explain it all. Clearly, this was the only cause. He slowly retreated back to his chair, slugging the tepid liquid back. The fireplace and candles had cast unusual illusions tonight. He needed to stop drinking; it was only fogging up his mind.

As if directed by an invisible cue, he heard her stir behind him, switching her position on the chaise. The wind still raged on, but strangely enough, he had forgotten about the noise until now. Despite his desperate attempts at control, he felt a single tear break free from his eye. He brushed it away with disgust, focusing on the dying fire as his face was overcome with emotion. At his side, his fist clenched in anger and frustration. Those were always the undercurrent of any disturbance that seized him. But despite his proclivity for coarse reactions, the softness of misery now crested over his temper.

He had felt these depths of despair only a few days before, and he had buried them deep into his core. He detested their reemergence now, with her present right behind him. Knowing that Eliza would never love him was simply unbearable. He had tried to be a better man than his father. He had tried a hundred times and he had failed at every turn.

Eliza felt herself clinging to the edge of consciousness, but she was drawn into a deeper layer of slumber. She was aware that Charles' presence was still around her, but she was draped into a sense of false ease.

The water around her is not very deep. Taller than most men, but a depth that offers security. Her favorite height of water in which to swim. She feels her fingers, bleached white by the sunlight, grasp the wooden chest as best she can despite the pull of the current. She cannot open it, and she cannot view the treasures it surely contains. She stops resisting and allows the current to pull her back. As she does so, a rush of white speeds past her and seizes upon the box. As the water settles from the movement, she realizes it is a group of men, nearly four or five of them. They swim madly against the pull of the water, their woolen undergarments clinging to their limbs.

Another color flashes into view. It is a menacing grey, but in the way that dreams seem to work, she understands its danger without feeling any threat herself. It is a large shark, its skin darkened with the faintest stripes like a cat. It hones in on the men, striking swiftly with deadly precision. Clouds of red bloom in the greenish-blue water, and she admires how beautiful it appears to be.

In a detached way, she knows she is witnessing a scene of terror, yet it strangely calms her. She does not see the men's faces nor who or what part the shark has claimed. Perhaps the lack of detail is what makes the violent scene seem soothing. Perhaps it is because the shark carries no prejudice, and answers to no master but its instinctual drive. Like with the smaller, yellow-tinted shark she swam with in her waking life or the large hammerhead from before, she feels no fear with this one either.

Two of the men who had lagged behind now seem to real-

ize the felicity of their timing and hold back. A second shark approaches from the left, striking one of the men, while the remaining man turns his body around and dashes to safer waters. The sight is blurry, then clear again, much like the streams of rainwater against the window glass or the blotchiness of filtered light streaming to the sea floor. In a moment of clarity, she finally sees the face of the remaining man and recognizes it.

It belongs to Charles. She has a sinking feeling, although she moves no lower in the water. But it is coupled with a curious sense of reassurance. She floats there for a while, and he watches her in the water. She knows she needs air, yet she does not reach for the surface.

Eliza woke up with a quiet gasp and returned to the same wind-battered house. The light was dimmer now as the fire died away. She sighed and turned on her side to face the wall. She briefly considered that perhaps she had fallen asleep on her back for too long and feared Charles had noticed the newly formed curvature of her body. If he ever questioned her, she would claim ignorance. It wasn't that far removed from the truth. She was still uncertain. The back of his chair remained facing her. Charles was focused on the fireplace if his eyes saw anything in that miserable room at all.

Cleo burst into her bedroom, pulling back the curtains. The brilliant light of midday flooded the still space.

"It is past noon now; you have to wake up, Miss Ellie!" Cleo said as she prepared Eliza's washbasin. "Lord Sharpe leaves today. Do you think I will allow you to miss his departure? You can give a few minutes for farewell when he will be gone for over a month. You have had enough of not speaking."

Eliza groaned, pulling the sheet over her face.

"No, that will not do. You must get up."

Eliza heard her pull the chamber pot from beneath the cabinet, and then her frenetic bustling ceased. Cleo rushed to the bed and pulled the sheet back.

"Are you ill, Miss Ellie? I can see that you have been sick. Miss—"

Cleo gasped. The angle of the light and the curve of Eliza's posture betrayed the secret she had concealed for the past few weeks. The contents of her chamber pot only served as further confirmation. The slightest bump was beginning to form at her navel.

Cleo's face paled, and she took a step back. Eliza quickened her movements as she sat up and covered herself fully with her shift. Eliza had known she was with child, but her lack of experience had given her the slightest hope that she had misjudged the changes in her body. Now, the look of horror on Cleo's face erased all her fleeting doubts.

"No, no, no …" she muttered, looking at Eliza wildly. "You are carrying a child!"

Eliza looked at her briefly, then down at the floor.

"You know about these matters. I am not entirely sure," she said.

Cleo sharply exhaled and placed her hands on her hips.

"I supervise the laundry. I see your dirty clothes. I make your unkempt bed. I know everyone's business and what goes on in this house. And I know you have not spread your legs for Lord Sharpe in over a year. We both know this."

Her words hung in the air, heavy like the humidity they both breathed in.

"I am not with child. My stomach is hardly swollen," Eliza said with a scoff.

"Your stomach has been bothering you the last few weeks …"

"It was the fish. It was a bad catch."

"That is why you have stopped swimming! To conceal your shape! That is why you row yourself out there on that old boat!"

"Things I once loved no longer catch my fancy. I find my sadness overwhelms me."

"And you have not bled for months."

Eliza's dark eyes rocketed upwards in fury. Cleo was right, and she hated it.

"I must inform Lord Sharpe!"

Cleo turned on her heel, but Eliza raced towards the door, blocking her path.

"You will do no such thing!" she exclaimed.

Cleo pursed her lips and pushed past her.

"I beg of you. Please …" Eliza said, her voice quivering.

Cleo sighed, placing a firm hand over her shoulder.

"You cannot hide your body, Miss Ellie. And you cannot hide a baby. That man is going to find out, one way or another. He must know. This is not a game."

"He might not have to. He might be detained at his post on Harbour Island. The weather is changing; the storms will be frequent now. Don't you see? This is an opportunity! He might never return …"

"You cannot keep that man's child."

At first, Eliza did not react. She moved now to a bowl of water, and washed her face and began adjusting her hair.

"You hear me, Miss Ellie?"

Eliza slammed her brush down.

"Who said it was *his* child? I never uttered those words."

"You haven't laid with Charles in over a year. You know it, I know it, and Charles knows it!" Cleo hissed.

Just then the door flew open, and Charles stepped in. He was entirely oblivious to the fact that he was indeed unwelcome by both women. Cleo shifted her body in front of Eliza in an attempt to block her torso from his view. An awkward silence dominated the scene.

"I know what exactly?" he asked, his penetrating green eyes surveying them.

Eliza was the quicker liar.

"You know that this could prove to be a wonderful opportunity. It's the chance you've been waiting for since our arrival. Surely Lord Dunmore will have no choice but to promote you when you prove integral to the establishment of yet another fort. And the men enlisted there could not benefit from any other commander …"

It was the most Eliza had uttered to him in weeks. Cleo's eyes were close to bulging from their sockets. She looked steadily at the floor and then the wall.

"Yes," Charles said, looking at Eliza with a strange glance. He quickly recovered and straightened his posture. "That is indeed the end I presently hope to achieve. May providence seek to reward us with such an outcome. I take my leave now. Cleo, please ensure that my wife is well taken care of. Her safety and ... health ... are of paramount importance to me."

Cleo responded with a nod and a curtsy.

"Farewell, dear husband," Eliza said, extending a tanned hand.

Charles pressed his lips to it.

"May you return safely to us," she said.

He looked at her with a softening glance. He seemed as if he was on the verge of speaking further, but then he bowed and left the room.

The women remained fixed in place until they heard the sound of Alastor galloping away from the house.

Cleo whipped around, her wide eyes narrowing in disgust.

"You are a liar ..." she said with malice. "You better hope he returns. Sending him off with false cheer and manufactured emotions!"

"At present, I can scarcely afford a moment longer in his company. I think you would agree. I did what needed to be done. And now we have our privacy once again."

The troubled silence barely lasted a moment longer. Both women were equally stubborn.

"You cannot keep that baby."

"I will carry this child, and I will have this baby, and

then I will consider what to do concerning the matter."

She looked wistfully down at her evolving abdomen.

"I have the constitution to handle it," she added with a disturbed cheerfulness.

"That may well be, Miss Ellie, but you do not know anything. You do not know anything about carrying a baby, and you do not know anything about children. You are forgetting about society. This will be your ruin. You are ruined, Miss Ellie!"

Despite the grimness of Cleo's words, Eliza's eyes now sparkled with a new idea.

"No, it won't. Because you will help me."

Cleo sat on the bed, her hands rubbing her forehead. Then she finally spoke.

"We may have to take you away. You will have to hide your shape, and when that baby comes, you will have to give him to me."

Eliza did not seem to perceive the seriousness of her tone.

"Do you think it's a boy or a girl? Oh, Cleo, you must have some way to tell. What do you think?"

She received no answer. Then a huge smile crossed her lips.

"You said when the time comes, I will have to give *him* to you ..."

"That is what I said. You cannot change the way it will be. That is how it must work. You cannot keep that child; I will say it again. You cannot keep him."

"So, it *is* a boy ..." Eliza said gleefully.

Cleo's face paled. Eliza was not listening to the right

words. She was distracted with a fantasy of a future that could not exist. Eliza spun around in a slow circle, quietly humming a song.

"You know my meaning, Miss Ellie. Do not put words in my mouth."

"I have not felt such happiness in days. Do you see what that man's absence can do for my mood? And in such a brief time, it is a wonder! He will be gone for weeks. It is nothing short of a miracle. I was thinking of names for a girl and names for a boy. But now that he is a boy, I can think of no other name but Philippe. *Philippe.* And what a precious boy he will be. What a balm to my hours of loneliness; can you not see it, Cleo? I am to be a mother! The mother of Jean's child. I will finally have some measure of joy after such suffering …"

"Cease your blabbering, Miss Ellie. You are not thinking. Not even a little. And do not say that man's name again. He has brought nothing good to you."

Eliza simmered with anger.

"How dare you. I loved that man. And he loved me."

"He had no right to love you! And you gave yourself to him despite all my warnings. You did not listen!" Cleo shouted.

Eliza immediately froze. She had never heard Cleo raise her voice before. It was not a slave's place to act in such a way. But Cleo was so much more than a lowly servant, and they both understood this fact.

"Well, it does not matter now. He is gone. He's left this world," Eliza said, the sadness returning to her voice.

"And he left you with a burden."

"Mark me, this child is no burden. He is a gift. And I will see it in no other light."

"It will not be easy. You will bring him into this world, and then I will have to send him away."

"Send him where?"

"To the foundling hospital by Christ Church. That is where all unwanted children go."

"But he is not unwanted. It is so very strange to love someone you have never laid eyes on, but now I can recognize the feeling just the same. You saw this happening. You knew. So, it is fated. It will resolve itself. I know it will. I will not turn to despair."

"They will call you names, horrible names. People will not understand. They will speak your name with disdain. And Lord Sharpe, Lord Sharpe is a formidable man."

"I am only too aware. Do you finally admit that he is a monster?" Eliza quipped.

"Any man forced into his position would be. We know he has wronged you, Miss Ellie. But now you cannot hide that you have wronged him. This child and all that it means will wound his pride, and to that man, his pride is everything ..."

"He could stand to lessen it."

"—so he must never know."

A chill descended Eliza's back.

"When the time comes, you promise you will release him to me?" Cleo asked.

She watched her carefully. Eliza bit her lip.

"I cannot help you without your word."

41

When she did not hear a response, Cleo stood up and began walking to the door.

"Yes ..." Eliza finally answered softly. "I cannot do this alone."

"Then you have my help, Miss Ellie. Come with me downstairs, and I will prepare some food."

CHAPTER III.

Eliza felt incredibly nervous about her predicament despite her best attempts to appear collected and firm in her resolve. The first week, she started at any sign of a fast horse entering the yard, and by the second, she hung close to the windows, preferring to keep a steady view of who arrived and who left the property. But by the third week, she began to settle into her new condition and abandoned her supervision of the yard to enjoy more entertaining diversions. Then, when it appeared evident that Charles would not be immediately returning to Nassau, she grew even more at ease.

The storm season had surged brutally as it reached its close in November, and as she had predicted, Charles soon wrote to inform her that his assignment on Harbour Island had been protracted. A hurricane had nearly flattened all construction progress made on the fort, and the men would need to rebuild at least four months of work. Supplies would have to arrive by ship from other islands. It promised to be a slow and frustrating process, and only once the construction halted could the regiment begin its training in earnest. It was tedious work, and that was exactly what Eliza savored about it.

Charles wrote to her more frequently than she expected, his letters long and winding, but she read the first few lines and then nothing at all. She only cared to learn details about his return. A dubious homecoming that hinted at improbability was all she needed to know. And so, as each month passed and her abdomen steadily grew more swollen, she felt secure in her secret. It was a secret that nearly everyone working in Pleasant Hall had knowledge of, and the one person who simply could not become aware of her dramatic shift in health was decidedly absent. His departure emboldened her.

Eliza spent her days swimming and walking on the shore, collecting sand dollars during the low tides early in the morning. Soon her room was crowded with them, but she continued her new hobby nonetheless. There was something marvelously pleasing about their shape, the whiteness of their surface and the intricacy of the flower patterns emblazoned on every shell. And when it rained, she would sit on the porch, a book in hand, listening to a singular dove cooing near the porch.

Now that she occupied the house by herself, she began to notice small details about it that had missed her attention before. The green shutters needed a fresh coat of paint, and the bougainvillea shrubs along the porch desperately required pruning. The violet, papery petals sprawled along the house, hugging the porch with a relentless creeping, blooming vine. For the first time she noticed the small white flowers that hid inside the bursts of color, realizing that the magenta petals she had walked by so many times were not petals at all but acted as a secondary leaf to the plant. The colored leaves fell to the sand-covered ground, and she watched the wind carry more and more of them away.

The plant would only bloom again in the heat of the summer months. By then her stomach would be flat once more. She shuddered at the uncharted quality of her days only months from now. The summer seemed an unreal and obscure possibility, and so she hesitated to let it occupy her thoughts.

The calm, glassy surface of the water vanished, and the sea grew more chilly as waves disturbed it. The ocean appeared rough, as if gripped by an invisible wintery hand. The nights were likewise cooler, but even in the months of January and February, the island offered weather more akin to the springs she had known in her childhood. A Bahamian winter was like an English May. The trade winds coming off the sea made the days comfortable, and life was pleasant and simple by all appearances. But it was nothing but a tranquil deception.

Time quickened around her, mimicking the unseen internal vibrations in her body, and every smoldering sunset that brushed the horizon brought her closer to an unknowable future. Eliza had resisted the idea of childbirth a year ago. The idea of rearing children with Charles' mannerisms, reaching out towards her with sticky hands and loud voices, was far from appealing. But what she faced now was entirely different.

It was Jean's child. She had counted the small number

of years he had lived on this earth, and she'd wondered how much longer she would have to endure life herself. But now she had a new purpose. Jean had lived life as exuberantly as any man could hope to, but his presence had been snuffed out all the same. And yet, hidden from the eyes of the world, was a part of him growing within her, concealed and yet alive.

She wondered if the child would resemble him, if she could ever see blue eyes like his again. If the baby shared his looks, she knew it would constitute some form of a bittersweet miracle. A new person would be brought into the world, but it would bring remembrances of Jean. In this way their love, a formerly unobservable and elusive figment that had only lingered in her memories, would be transfigured into a tangible, permanent reality. A living, breathing child, created with equal parts of him and her; such a thought warmed and enchanted her. Jean's life was now extended in some way; an echo of him would surround their child, and his memory would be made eternal with every innocent coo and giggle released from the newborn's lips.

As her belly stretched, it was difficult to envision her body splitting open. The baby grew with every passing day and week, and while she relished the progress they made together, she also feared its natural consequence. She became afraid of the pain, and of the omniscient presence of death that seemed to linger in the quiet corners of Pleasant Hall. There was no guarantee that either she or the child would survive the ordeal of childbirth. And while she ruminated on her own death in a detached and numb way, she could not tolerate the idea of the child not surviving. That idea was the most terrifying thing she had yet to face.

She tried to distract herself with sunrises and shells, with watching the small green parrots in the trees, and in idle conversation with Cleo and Lucy, even sometimes with a stony Celia, but the phantom of anxiety always drifted back to her thoughts. There were so many hopes invested in the birth of this baby, and it anguished her to no end when she considered that once she had surpassed the alarms of giving birth, she would only be forced to begin a new, unsettling path as she handed the child over to an unknown future.

Memories of the past would take turns and visit, each one threatening to turn her pleasant daydreams into palpable nightmares. Her thoughts roamed over the gold coins she had found beneath the waves and how their shining luster had dimmed into a distinct threat as time wore on. She had once thought of their discovery as her salvation, but her elusive plan of fleeing the island was now made inconsequential. She could never leave the island in her current condition. And to wait and try to escape with a child in tow was unthinkable. The baby only anchored her firmly in place, and as a consequence, the coins slowly lost their seductive quality. Instead, they served as a source of trouble, one she decided was not worth the security of her already unstable future.

When her worries threatened to overtake her, she feared that she was trapped in the house. That a convoy of men on horseback, with Hiram Bruin at their helm, would arrive in the yard, trampling over the silent peace of her solitude. The sight of the ship captain's face, glaring at her with righteous indignation, was real enough to make her dread *two* arrivals to Pleasant Hall. It was not only her husband that she needed to be wary of. It was also the thieving captain who was convinced she had stolen from him.

"Are you attempting to negotiate with me? With my stolen property? I warn you, I am not a man of negotiation," Bruin said as he eyed her.

The elated happiness she had felt days earlier swiftly deflated in his presence. What if the discovery of the coins was not a blessing or an answer to her prayers? What if it only spelled more trouble? Had she been foolish to assume it was a fortuitous accident?

She reassured herself that the matter had been forgotten. The coins were buried, and the matter would remain likewise. In truth, she did not even know if the pirate was still in Nassau. She refused to think of him as a privateer like everyone else did. She knew the truth of the governor's dealings with him. But one thing he said to her when they had been alone in the house stayed with her:

"And you heed this warning: watch yourself on these beaches. You never know who you will run into," Mr. Bruin said with a glare. "My men are everywhere."

Perhaps the man was no longer even alive. Maybe he sat chained in some dank jail cellar after crossing the wrong person. These fleeting thoughts gave Eliza hope.

After some time, she would push thoughts of Bruin away, only for the governor, Lord Dunmore, and his mistress Charlotte to take his place. She dreaded seeing a servant donned in livery whenever a messenger arrived. The governor was the richest man on the island. He was also the most arrogant, and only he expected his house slaves to wear such outlandish costumes in the tropical heat. She did not think she could ever tolerate a moment in their collective presence again, yet she knew such a meeting was inevitable. New Providence was too small an island to avoid confrontation entirely. Eliza had no doubt that she was the subject of gossip in their lavish parlors. She had already heard it all once before.

"At this rate, I wouldn't be surprised if she missed an entire season only to re-enter our society with a little one in her arms. Her poor husband. I doubt the child will share his looks. I wonder who it will resemble. I gave her a word or two of womanly advice, but mark me, I did not realize she would take it to heart!" Charlotte said.

Catty laughter sounded behind Eliza.

"Charlotte, you are louder than you think with drink on your tongue!"

"Drink? It is only tea."

"Tilly-tally."

"Have you seen how dark she lets her skin get? How unrefined."

"I heard she goes swimming every day. Have you ever heard of such a thing?"

"*That is most likely how she's cultivated this crop of admirers, Miss Shelley.*"

Admirers that included the governor himself. The man had propositioned Eliza at the very first opportunity. An innocent conversation the night of her first ball in Nassau revealed Lord Dunmore to be nothing more than a calculating predator.

"*I cannot tell you how much I appreciate a fine English import,*" *the governor said.*

The mosquitoes were ruthless on the lawn. She watched as one landed on the rolls of his neck and then another. She grew itchy watching the assault.

"*The wine, sir? I thought it came from Loire.*"

He laughed again, his eyes narrowing down on her.

"*No, my dear, you.*"

She felt a grubby hand wrap around the small of her back. His breath reeked of alcohol and the sour smell of tooth decay.

"*I have a quaint guest house near my Tuscan garden,*" *he said, a smile revealing the source of the stench.* "*We can discuss your husband's promotion to colonel. Alone. Away from the noise.*"

"*With all due respect, sir, I do not find this a suitable time for such matters. I really must return to the house,*"

She felt him hold her tighter.

"*I know you have recently arrived in Nassau, and perhaps you do not quite understand the workings of this colony. I will not take slight at your refusal. So, I will try once again. I can make it worth your time, Lady Sharpe. Come, follow me.*"

That was when she had realized the truth about the pristine gardens and the intimidating house that sat on the hill in town. The man who ruled over the island was not honorable. He was a monster. Whitehall had sent him to the Bahamas as a gracious form of banishment from greater English society, and while he never made the mistake of considering his appointment as some kind of honor, he made use of it all the same.

Pirates had been cast out of the colony decades before. But now, the threat of danger and corruption crept back across the sand, washing over every crest of the waves that crossed into the harbor. Lord Dunmore had illicit dealings with thieves and smugglers. He erected massive fortifications like Fort Charlotte which the Crown neither wanted nor approved funding for. He concocted wild plots of retaking the lost colonies in America by invading Florida. And he executed whoever stood in his way.

The more Eliza thought of the people she avoided in town, the more despondent she grew. There was a certain irony to enduring loneliness out of selection. Connections to others in this place could be fostered, even endured, but she refused. She considered these people nothing less than her enemies.

The white house was empty, its halls quiet. This is exactly what Eliza had wanted. Yet it was not as satisfying as she thought. Isolation overshadowed her every mood despite the fact that she knew a child was wrapped within her. And as her thoughts turned to her current situation, sadness invariably crept in and stole the light from whatever hopes she carried for tomorrow. It seemed a crime to envision it without Jean. She would stop whatever she was doing, feel the familiar pang of grief and the quivers that raced through her cheeks. Then her world would dissolve in watery, moving waves.

How could he die without her? Who could she turn to now? Now that her mother and father had left this world, now that the only man she had ever loved was gone?

The weight of her seclusion was crippling. The people she loved no longer existed. They no longer occupied the same space as she did. Instead, they only drifted through her mind, like the infinitesimal fragments of dust that floated through the afternoon sunlight in her room, borne by a tide of painful memories. She could never speak to any of them again. Did they somehow see how she spent her days now? She had only the company of herself, burgeoning with a foolish optimism yet petrified by her every perceived inadequacy.

She did have Cleo. Yet Cleo and she possessed very different visions of what had to be done. She knew Cleo was right. She could not keep this baby. Yet the smallest doubt gnawed inside her. What if Cleo was wrong? *What if?*

How could she live knowing her child would never know her? How should she live? What if other children came after, never knowing a sibling, never understanding the bond of blood? And this baby would share blood from someone who only now lived in memory. This made the child a treasure in her eyes and ensured the eventual parting would be more unbearable.

The weight of it all threatened to suffocate her on some days. How could Jean go ahead of her? How could he quit this life, leave all this behind, and go without her? She knew such questions were useless. He had clearly not wanted to die. Yet he seemed to be in a much better place than she. Her thoughts mused of writing a letter to him. Of wanting to be wherever he was, to travel to him with the ease of a posted missive.

"*Please take me where you are. My sorrow knows no limit,*" she would write.

Where could she put her heart now? How could her heart survive the pain of knowing their child would miss him as well? And that she had released the baby to the mercies of the world? Would the child ever know it was done unwillingly? Her mind was wracked with endless questions and inconsolable torments. She would do anything for the baby growing within her. Yet she could not do the one thing the child needed above all. She could not be his mother.

She begged Jean to come to her in her dreams. He would have the answers she could not find. Every night presented another opportunity for some divine encounter, some otherworldly reunion. But her dreams were disturbed and chaotic, and upon waking, she would curse her weak memory when she could not recall seeing his face. Who would this child call its father? Its mother?

Eliza walked up and down the beach collecting the sand dollars, bitter and mournful in her steps. Could anyone fathom how she felt? She reasoned that there was no tragedy quite like this. At a time when any other woman would feel absolute bliss and the happiness of impending motherhood, she instead bore the weight of knowing that the child's birth would result in a blindsiding conflict of forces. There would be pain, there would be life, there would be joy, and then she would be left with heartbreak.

Jean was in another place, absent from the grief Eliza carried. She feared the child could absorb her pain, that her sorrow could reverberate like the beats of her heart that pumped ceaselessly for two.

There was no limit to what she wanted to say to the baby. She only ever pictured a baby boy, confident in Cleo's accidental revelation. She cradled her growing womb and whispered tidings of love and reassurance to him, knowing he would never remember a word she said. She walked and walked, up and down the white powdery shores, moving constantly to ease her despair, pacing until her mind was briefly quieted again.

Eliza stood respectfully in front of Jane's grave and placed a set of yellow elder flowers by it. The grave of Charles' mother was sad in its singularity, but now it appeared more charming with its new adornment. She sighed, taking a step back while lost in a reverie.

"You are not the only one who comes to visit our Miss Jane."

Eliza was startled but then quickly recovered with a smile. Cleo walked up to her, rubbing her hands on her apron. "Why are you stopping by here so often?" she asked.

"I am not sure," Eliza said slowly. "I suppose I feel some kind of kinship with her. Her story. I am in her place now."

They stood in silence, looking down at the stone. But Eliza's mind wandered to other images of the dead. Of the spirit who had visited her on more than one occasion.

"Cleo, you never speak of Tabitha," Eliza suddenly said.

The quiet between them now grew an edge to it. Eliza looked her squarely in the eye.

"I know you understand whom I speak of. I cannot help but feel there is a gravestone missing."

"Slaves do not get tombstones."

"That does not mean it cannot be done."

"There is no body to bury, Miss Ellie. No one knows what happened to her."

Cleo sighed, placing a wide hand on the stone. She looked upwards as if in deep thought with the heavens.

"Tell me what you know," Eliza urged.

She knew the story in her gut, but the manner of her knowledge was so unsettling. She wanted confirmation. She wanted someone else to tell her the things she had only seen in dreams. She did not want to feel mad any longer.

Cleo's fingers drummed the surface of the stone, and then she shifted her stance.

"Jeremiah Sharpe was a mean man. He never treated anyone right. Not even his own flesh. He found Jane through his cousins, and they came here. He built the house, bought the slaves, and had a vision of what he wanted to plant here. Cotton. But it did not work the way he thought. He did not know the land, Miss Ellie. And even though they made some profit, it was never enough for him. He was greedy. Miss Jane was beautiful, and she was young, and she was kind. She was nothing like him. When they walked, I saw a deep, dark line between them. They had no business getting married, but what choice did Miss Jane have?

"She had the children quickly; she wanted the distraction. She loved the boys. First came Charles. Then Elias." Cleo paused with a shake of her head. "Now that boy was trouble. He always had a cloud hanging over him. But Charles was more like Miss Jane. They were close. The firstborn and the proud mother. I can see them now. He followed her everywhere, even if she came out to the fields, to the slave dwellings. Jane did not like the way the old Master Sharpe treated us.

"Tabitha was her personal maid, and every so often, Master Sharpe would yell at her because they spent more time talking than working. Tabitha had a beautiful girl, strong-minded like her, and Charles and her would play in the yard sometimes. That is why this world is cruel, Miss Ellie. We let the children be free to see the world with innocent eyes. Black children and white children playing. They do not see a difference. And that is the way it should be. Then they grow older, and soon they realize there are rules, man-made rules, and they lose the laughter inside. They reach a certain age, and they start to smile less and less."

Cleo heaved a sigh and then continued.

"Anyway, Miss Jane had an idea one day. And I do not think she meant anything by it. She only wanted to help. Tabitha and her husband, Jones, they wanted to learn how to read. And Miss Jane was the perfect teacher. She did not know that there were rules against that. Tabitha and Jones, they lied to Miss Jane. They told her they wanted to learn things, but they really wanted to run. They wanted freedom."

Cleo pondered her next words very carefully.

"Tabitha was smart. I think she was going to tell Miss Jane at one point. But that day never came. Miss Jane got yellow fever right after she birthed Elias. She got so sick we feared she would die. But Tabitha knew how to heal her. She is the one who taught me what I know, and even though Miss Jane was weakened from the ordeal, we all knew she would recover.

"But the old Master Sharpe did not like that. He was upset with Miss Jane. He found her teaching them how to read. He thought Miss Jane and Jones were lying with one another. I do not know if he really believed that or if the whiskey rotted his mind, but he was angry enough to end their union. He had someone else in mind, an heiress from the Carolinas. But Miss Jane was in the way."

Cleo looked down, her face still troubled even though years had long since passed.

"He went up to Miss Jane's room one night when she was resting, and he took a pillow to her face. He smothered her. He told us all she died from the fever. But we knew it was a lie. That fever had left her bones nearly a week before! They said Tabitha had seen it all. Tabitha knew, and she was going to tell someone. But no white man would listen to a slave. We are witness to their secrets. They cannot hear one man's slave confess his sins without the risk of the same thing happening to themselves. So the white men mocked her. And then the old Master Sharpe found out she had tried going to the magistrate.

"No one ever saw her again. We all know he killed her. Some say he threw her body in the mangroves; others say he buried her in the cellar. We never saw her again. She was a powerful woman, that Tabitha. Some feared she was a witch, but she was like me. She was an Obeah woman. There are less and less of us now.

"Some say she cursed this family. That every generation will know some tragedy, that no son born into this family will know happiness."

Eliza smiled a wry smile, glancing down at her stomach. It was only more confirmation. If such rumors were indeed true, her boy would somehow live a happy life. He did not carry any Sharpe blood within him. But Cleo did not find anything amusing. She continued speaking.

"I do not know about *that*. When people are afraid of something, it is usually because they do not know a single thing about it. I do not think Tabitha would waste her talents on something like that. But people will still talk. Elias was found not a day past twenty-three lying face down in a gutter in London, his pockets empty but full of debt. And the old Master Sharpe drank himself to death in this house. He locked himself in a room and left nothing but empty bottles and a property full of problems. Most people cursed when they heard Charles would return, but some of us were happy. We knew we would get new clothes and food and that this place would be running again the way it should. People get unhappy when they have expectations. I try not to have any. I do not have that indulgence."

Her face changed from the warmth of a past reverie as she noticed Eliza's tears.

"Miss Ellie, why are you crying now? This all happened many years ago!"

Eliza sputtered, unable to stay quiet any longer. She hated the wild swing of her emotions lately, but she was comfortable enough around Cleo to not hide it. She understood that it was finally time to disclose the troubling dreams and visions she had seen since her arrival in the Bahamas.

"Charles saw it happen. He saw his father kill her. He was there. He was hiding."

Cleo's eyes were wide, her mouth open.

"And Tabitha, Tabitha is in there …" Eliza uttered in a low whisper.

She turned and pointed to the ocean. The confession broke down her resolve even further. She erupted into sobs, and Cleo embraced her at once, nearly squeezing the air out of her.

"Miss Ellie, it is going to be all right now. Take a breath, Miss Ellie. Maybe I have said too much; maybe it is too hot for you just now. Sometimes when you are with child, it is very easy to cry. I know. It is all right."

But then Eliza pulled back in an attempt to steady herself.

She took a deep breath and continued. "Cleo, I cannot contain it a moment longer. I have seen her. I've seen Tabitha. I have been having dreams, these terribly vivid dreams that do not fade from my mind when I wake up. They linger for days and days, as solid as my own memories. And I have seen terrible things take place here, Cleo. I now understand what you mean when you argue with me. Charles is not who I thought. It pains me to admit it, as I cannot stand the man. But I cannot help him. I cannot change him. I fear he will become his father yet."

But Cleo was fixated on her earlier remarks.

"What do you mean, Tabitha is in the water?"

"I have seen her, the bones, there are bones, and a chain and a large weight, close to the limestone rocks that lead further into the water. I know it is her. I saw what Charles' father did in a dream, and there is a hoop earring there, the very kind she would wear—"

"Miss Ellie, you are getting the sight," Cleo said breathlessly. "I did not know it could happen so fast ..."

Cleo watched her with curiosity as Eliza continued to cry.

"You know, I am thinking, Miss Ellie. When you made those offerings many months ago, where is the place that you made them?"

"Here, on the beach, of course. I love these waters."

"On the beach?"

Eliza nodded, confused by her need to ask.

"I always go in the water. That's the only place I truly feel peace."

Cleo took a long, hard look at her, then laughed.

"What is so amusing?"

"Miss Ellie, I do not think Erzulie Dantor answered your prayers."

Eliza's eyes darkened. "I don't need someone with your abilities to tell me that. I am still here. Chained to a man I do not love. Now I carry another man's child. I hardly find my situation entertaining. I must have done something wrong. Now matters are even worse."

Eliza cradled her stomach and looked upwards at the palm trees with exasperation.

"No, no, not Eruzlie Dantor. But Yemaya ..." Cleo continued.

"Yemaya?" Eliza repeated, the sound strange and musical on her tongue. "Who is she?"

"She is a mother. She is beauty itself. She is of the sea. She oversees creation, the world, and all that flows through it. White men report strange things in the ocean. Mermaids, they call them. Yemaya is like that. But she is the mother of *all*. And most importantly, she is the mother of Shango, the King. She uses her hands, her long slender fingers, and she claps them together underneath the waters of the world. And she makes the waves like this, you see.

"Now I am sure some book you have offers some other explanation, Miss Ellie, but I was told that when I was young by my mother. You see, some generations later, even two or three from now, they will never get told this, and it will all be forgotten. Lost. Like it was swept to the bottom of the sea. Once a people's myths are forgotten, they die. Like the wick of a candle that is blown out, there is smoke that still lingers, but that light, that flame is not going to return." Cleo gave Eliza an intense look, the kind that signaled one of her premonitions. "I tell everyone I know, and I am telling you now. Maybe you will tell someone else and tell them our stories. But she has been helping you this past year. I do not doubt it."

Eliza's mind flashed to the afternoon she had jumped ship and nearly drowned. To every moment she had sought comfort from the warm, lapping waters. To the infinite, tiny, dancing rainbows on the rippled sand bed below the waves. That she had kept company with sharks and other creatures of the sea and had never been harmed. She thought of all the beautiful shells she had collected, of the countless treasures she had found in the sea. Always in the water, beneath the waves. The sound that lulled her to sleep every night and helped her rise in the mornings.

"It is so very strange. You've confirmed something for me just now. I feel a presence when I'm in the ocean. I see things, marvelous things. Small rainbows and the sweetest voices. I thought it must be the water playing tricks with what my eyes see and the sounds I hear beneath the waves. I check to see if I am alone in the water. I always am, and yet, somehow, I also know that I am not alone. Not truly. I believe you, Cleo."

Cleo nodded. "Water is a powerful thing, Miss Ellie. It is a veil between worlds. I think she has been calling you since the day you were born. That is why you desire to go to places, to distant shores, to sail over foreign waters. She is the one calling you."

"But I am confused. I am baptized in the church; how can I be a daughter of Yemaya? I am not like you," Eliza said. She searched for the proper words. "Do I have to be initiated in this ... in what you do?"

Cleo laughed as if her question was too absurd to control herself.

"The spirits do not care. They choose who they want, child. And if anyone who looks like me tells you otherwise, tell them they are wrong. Unless they can speak and divine with the *orishas*, they know nothing. Do you think these mighty spirits care about such things?"

"I do not claim to understand any of this. But you are the only person who can give me answers, Cleo, and I thank you for that."

Eliza wiped her eyes and looked at the vibrant waters ahead of them. And then a different thought occurred to her.

"Cleo, I think I've finally realized the meaning of the riddle. From the Obeah man, the one I met on my arrival here ..."

"There is no Obeah man on this island; I have told you that once before."

"'*one will strike from the sky, his mother ... the sea.*' Shango will strike from the sky like a bolt of lightning, and his mother, Yemaya, as you've just told me ... she comes from the sea. That is the meaning. Now why would that man tell me that? Perhaps he saw my future ..." Eliza wondered aloud.

"I will tell you about that man, as you call him. But

let us save that tale for another day, Miss Ellie. It is getting late."

Eliza was astonished by the sudden resolution of so many mysterious occurrences. She found solace in the idea of divine protection, yet something still gnawed at her inside. She still did not know what to do about Charles. He would return home soon. And all of the problems she had evaded for these few months would come crashing back.

She looked down at her round stomach and rubbed it, anxious to feel the baby move or kick within her. It had only happened once so far, and she was unsure whether she had simply imagined it. She yearned to feel the movement again. Like the mysterious spirits and forces around her, this child, too, remained unseen. But that did not mean its presence was not just as real as the tales Cleo told about the *orishas*, the unseen but powerful emissaries of God Himself. Or the strange spirits she encountered in the dark.

"Come, let us go back into the house now. It is almost time for supper. And I am going to make sure you eat," Cleo chided her. "A mother must stay healthy. What I mean to say is that you have someone besides yourself to worry about now. Everything will fall into place, Miss Ellie. I promise."

They walked slowly back to the house along the forgotten path that hardly saw footsteps.

"And between you and me, I was happy that Charles came back. Because I saw you were coming with him, Miss Ellie. I was excited to meet you before I ever saw you."

Eliza's fingers absentmindedly brushed her stomach again as she considered that she knew exactly of what Cleo spoke, albeit in a different sense.

CHAPTER IV.

Eliza clutched the letter before her with trembling hands. It now appeared she had less time than she imagined. The day she had dreaded for the past several months was seemingly upon her. She reread the letter's contents again.

My dearest Eliza,

As I am within a few minutes of reviewing the day's progress made on the fort, I could not think of departing without trying once more to drop you a line. I have not received any letter from you except your letter of the 8ᵗʰ, but that was nearly four months ago. There are many days you do not write. What do you do, then? I have had the pleasure of writing to you many times but not of hearing from you. I keenly feel the loss of it. Tell me all you do and how you pass your time. What does this silence mean? It makes me uneasy. Surely you have not forgotten your husband.

I am now in such a place which brings me to mind each and every day I had the pleasure of sharing your company. And how the loss of that light stings me so. For you are such a light, my Eliza. I fear providence, which has been more generous to me than I deserve, has seen fit to punish me now. This island is desolate and its beauty hollow without the grace a woman like you can bestow.

How strangely you work upon my heart. Ever since I left you, I have been sad. Ceaselessly, I recall your kisses and tears. Forgive me; my soul is racked by conflicting forces. I have wronged you so terribly. I cannot think of asking for forgiveness. Even at such a distance, my heart is obsessed with you and filled with fears that make me prostrate with misery. Your very being robs me of reason, and the vicious things you have said out of anger, nigh even hatred, inflame my blood. And yet, it is not within my power to have a single thought that is not of you. My regret at parting has been greater than I can bear.

The governor is confident of my return to Nassau in March, and I count down the days until you are in front of me once more.

Ever yours, Charles

Eliza lowered the letter as she inhaled sharply. She put a hand on the small of her back to brace herself as she took another breath. It was harder to breathe these last few weeks, and reading his latest note left her with even less comfort. She felt a wave of nausea creep up her stomach, but unpleasant digestion was nothing new to her now. It was the middle of April, and March had passed by without his return. For some reason, it had taken nearly a month for this letter to arrive.

She knew it was foolish to wish for another event to delay his arrival any further. Eliza had been only too fortunate with the number of storms this past fall. It was as if some higher force was ensuring her privacy by a week, a month longer each time. But she was still carrying Jean's child, and soon, it would be impossible to hide such a fact from him. This was the moment she had dreaded and put off for far too long. It was only inevitable that her husband would return to his own house. And when he saw her in her condition, everything would change. He would arrive home to a wife unrecognizable.

It seemed as if the distance between them had escalated his affections towards her. It was difficult to trust the lines in the letter. They were no substitute for the living, breathing version. More troublesome still, she could never return such feelings. And now the extent of her betrayal, justified as it might be, would only sunder any promise of amity between them. The unwanted sweetness he portrayed in the missive she had just received would turn into a bitter rage. The damage this baby would cause would surely be permanent, but this mattered little to her.

She lovingly caressed her stomach, pausing to wait for some movement, some silent confirmation from her child of their unspoken bond. This baby was her only connection to Jean, her only connection to some measure of joy in her life.

The thought of him and their child that he would never see brought tears to her eyes, and she waddled to a chair and slowly lowered herself down to sit. Her stomach was heavy and swollen, and she did not think she could tolerate it much longer. The lack of sleep and the swelling of her feet irritated her very last nerve. She desperately wanted the baby to come, and now she needed him to finally make his appearance. Eliza cast a despondent glance out to the darkening yard.

This time of year presented the island in its least lush form; the leaves and ferns always seemed wilted, exhibiting the smallest amount of beauty they were capable of. The days were, however, growing longer again, and the constant sun offered a more gentle heat than on summer days. The sea grew steadily warmer to the touch, and soon, the land would grow frantic with tilling and planting. The cycles that governed the rhythm of Pleasant Hall had not changed, yet she carried a small revolution inside her that would alter her life forever.

The door creaked open as Cleo came in bearing a tray of food.

"What is wrong now, Eliza?" she asked, setting down a plate of tidbits.

"Another letter from him," Eliza replied.

Cleo's dark eyes narrowed. "And what did I catch you casting into the fire earlier?"

Eliza scoffed.

"That was an invitation to a ball at the governor's. It is not important. They most likely sent it by mistake. I am no longer wanted in their society."

Both women observed her midsection, nearly bursting from her dress. But Cleo was not satisfied.

Cleo put her hands on her hips. "And?"

"And what? You yourself know I can never show my

face in that house again. Not after what I've done!" Eliza's voice rang out across the room.

The very thought of Lord Dunmore and his immaculately powdered mistress made her lose her appetite. She glanced at the food Cleo had brought with sudden disgust as a memory from that terrible night resurfaced. The night she had failed to save Jean from his fate.

"You cannot do this. You are corrupt beyond all measure, you—" Eliza cried.

"I rule this tiny island, and it would serve you to remember your place on it," Lord Dunmore roared.

Spittle flew from his rotting teeth as his fury bubbled to the surface. He slammed the door closed just as Charlotte threw herself on Eliza.

"You whore! I knew you had designs on His Lordship! You conniving …" Charlotte seethed, her arms flailing at her.

Cleo stepped closer to her, bringing her back to the present.

"I do not care about those foolish people, and I never did. I ask about Charles, your husband!" she said.

The tone was intended to present annoyance, but Eliza could tell she was also nervous.

"He prattles on about his conflicting feelings and his regrets of our separation. That his very heart is obsessed with thoughts of me," she said, rolling her eyes towards the ceiling.

"You do not think his words are true?" Cleo asked.

"Not a single line."

"Have you written to him since that one letter you read to me?"

"No!" Eliza exclaimed. "To think that the man would seek any further clarification from the vitriol I spewed forth. I was perfectly clear in my feelings. I will *never* forgive him. I struck down any notion of reconciliation the moment he spoke of his desires. He is a fool to keep writing such errant nonsense."

"I never thought any woman could get Charles to write love letters …" Cleo replied slowly.

"Love letters? Mind you, they are not four pages of praise and charm. It is but a few lines, hastily written. The product of a man stuck on an island with soldiers lacking any female companionship. Such an environment has evidently tinted our disastrous marriage in a more favorable light."

"I cannot read, and I cannot write, but I know one thing. This is a mess. A terrible mess you have me involved in."

They were silent as Cleo started to prepare Eliza's bed for the evening. Eliza sighed.

"He was expecting to return home last month …" she said, looking out at the window again, tears welling up in her dark eyes.

"So it could be any day now. He could arrive tonight," Cleo said apprehensively.

"Perhaps he will realize a divorce is the best course," Eliza said quietly.

"I'm going to post one of the men out on the road, they can warn us if he comes through, that could give us time …"

"Maybe he will only strike me. I do not care. As long as he does not touch the baby."

"Brutus and Josiah can wait on the porch; they can distract him when he arrives."

Eliza was surprised to hear Cleo involve more people in their grand scheme. She had exchanged some conversations with the slave named Josiah, most notably about the stories he shared from his homeland, but she marveled that the other man, Brutus, would be willing to help her. She had barely ever spoken with him. These slaves owed her absolutely nothing. In fact, the reverse was true. The thought disquieted her. Would she have been willing to do the same in their position?

"I don't know what I would do without you," Eliza said, locking eyes with her.

Cleo offered a bittersweet smile.

"We have to focus on the child, Miss Ellie. That is the most important thing. You and the baby. We must focus on that. We will see it through."

"I need the child to come now. Is there anything you can do? To induce the labor?"

Eliza's eyes were frantic and pleading.

"No. Matters do not work like that. The only one who knows when this child is coming is the child itself."

Eliza sighed and shifted her weight uncomfortably on the stiff chair.

The pangs of labor came on without warning in the still, grey hours of the morning. What started as a perceptible shift in her body soon turned into wave after wave of slow and deliberate pain, a kind of pain that she feared meant her very bones were splitting. It never became more apparent to Eliza in that moment that violence brutally took men out of the world, and it was the same force of violence that ushered them into its folds.

Waves of excitement and fear came over her, and in the hazy intensity of her suffering, she firmly believed that the baby had understood her recent panic. Now, as she pushed to no end and tried to temper her breathing, she felt as if they were working together towards a common goal. She was surrounded by a handful of women, with Cleo at the helm directing them. Two of them were slaves she had never seen before, and even though she was apprehensive about them keeping their silence, she was grateful for their help.

Propped with pillows, her legs spread wide, she had ceased to care about indecency hours ago. Cleo had urged her to move forward and try to deliver the baby in a squatting position, but she could not muster the strength to raise herself up. In between her strained breaths, she feared hearing the ring of the yard bell, but it did not sound, and the newfound tumult of her previously quiet and still world continued.

Eliza breathed with deliberate breaths, in and out, and she tried to tell herself that surely the pain, the tension that wracked her limbs, could not last forever. She envisioned the baby in her arms, the ordeal ended—anything to keep her trying. She was growing weaker and became light-headed, a continual pulse drumming in her ears.

And then, after a particularly desperate push, she felt herself crack open. The baby slipped from her open legs. And even as she felt bloody and broken, the relentless pain that had gnawed into her very bones had ceased. Perhaps it was because she could only focus on seeing the child. She stopped crying and watched as Cleo and Lucy took the wet infant, his dark hair twisted into a curled mass from the pressures of his journey, and rapidly dried him off. Now his tiny, raspy cries filled the room, and Eliza was in awe at the simple fact that an extra person now held a presence with them.

She was rendered speechless as Cleo quickly put the baby in her arms. Philippe was perfectly formed, and he looked up at her through long dark lashes. She was mesmerized by the familiar blue eyes that now gazed into hers. For the past nine months, she had formed a bond with a small being she had never seen and never held, and now he was undeniably real. She was a mother. She felt relief that the baby was alive, that he was safe, and she was even grateful for his small, grating cries.

But a new fear embedded itself into her, and in her exhaustion, it threatened to overwhelm her. An indescribable mixture of love, recognition, and sadness flooded her faculties, but the fear she felt was stronger. She was responsible for him, and an urge to protect her baby raged within her as a new set of motherly instincts she had never previously experienced took root.

His dark hair was straightened now that it had dried, and his body was warm against her chest. He gazed at her as her shaking, sweating arms held him close. Cleo was talking to her now, and the words left her mouth faster than Eliza could comprehend them. She did not understand what Cleo wanted. All she could see was her small Philippe. She was exhausted, and she was sore, but none of this mattered now that he was finally here.

The full gravity of what had just occurred began to bore down on her. She watched his eyes look at the world for the very first time, and she understood that this was right. That some form of justice had occurred with the birth of this child. She recognized and knew him. She had caressed her belly every time he had kicked, and she had softly sung to him when she could not sleep. But she also understood that this was all a mistake. What had she done? She was not ready for this. Cleo reached for his tiny form, but Eliza continued to hold him.

"No, no, no …" she whispered, clutching him tighter.

Cleo's strong hands came a second time, and in her weakness, she felt Philippe leave her grasp. She watched, stunned, as Cleo brought him towards a basket intended to carry produce or the dead leaves she watched the gardeners collect every so often. It was not made to hold a living, breathing child. The women around her shouted now—they were frantic, and they were afraid.

"Wait, please …" Eliza stammered.

Their backs were turned to her, and it seemed as if she could not command their attention. Lucy drifted perilously close to the bed, and Eliza grabbed a piece of her skirt.

"Get me something from him. Please! For Oya."

In her panic, Eliza could only recall what she had seen the slave women do when Lucy was sold off the plantation. It had seemed so simple and unbelievable at the time that a handful of sand from her footprint could change anything, but Lucy stood before her now. Cleo's prayers to the deity Oya had clearly worked, and this name rang out repeatedly in her mind, like a set of constant, soft drumbeats.

Eliza was desperate, like a cornered animal. Lucy's eyes widened. The request had surprised her. That her mistress could utter a sacred name in a moment like this caught her off guard. But she did not have time to question it further. She dashed to Cleo's side, ripped off a portion of the swaddling cloth, and handed it to Eliza. But the gesture failed to soothe her. Cleo and Celia whisked the baby out of the room.

"Wait!" Eliza cried out.

Her voice was raw and unrecognizable to her ears. She held the fragment of cloth with confused fingers.

Lucy's sense of sympathy, more forthcoming with the youth of her years, made her stop once more.

"The bell. Didn't you hear the bell? The bell rang out," Lucy said quietly, her eyes full of terror.

The two women stared at each other in tense silence for a moment, and then Lucy spun around and began collecting the blood-soiled linens around the bed. She spilled a basin of water and nervously tried to clean away the mess. Eliza did not see her panicked actions. Her view wavered under the weight of her tears as a primal fear stilled her heart.

She had not heard the bell. In the swell of her elation, the one sound that she had dreaded for months had finally eluded her. She knew without asking that Charles had returned home.

The yard erupted into chaos and then maintained a thin facade of stillness. Black boots crunched through the line of trees, and a flash of red appeared.

"Josiah? Brutus? Is that you? Why are you skulking about in the bush?"

The voice was demanding but flustered.

The slaves stopped with a hesitancy of not wanting to linger. But they also knew that they could not ignore their master's inquiry any longer. Charles had called out their names twice now. Josiah's eyes darted to the black horse that had suddenly appeared in the yard as if the animal was the only surety that they had truly been apprehended.

"Are you taking something to market?"

Charles withdrew his pistol, making his intentions clear as he cocked it. He was in no mood for games. He had endured a long journey home, and this was not the welcome he expected. Josiah stared at him in terror. Brutus nodded in silence.

"Then why are you not on the main road?"

The metallic ring of his saber unsheathing sounded next. He pried a verdant branch out of his line of vision to see them better. The men understood they were trying his patience, and they left the bush with reluctant steps.

Charles' eyes fell on the basket. Its contents were covered with a white sheet.

"I only follow what Cleo say, sir, I only follow, I don't know—" Josiah stammered, raising his hands.

Brutus, who held the basket in his powerful grip, looked at Josiah with a glare.

"What is in the basket?" Charles asked, impatience rising in his voice.

Silence was the response, intermingled with the unmistakable energy of trampled nerves.

"What is in the basket? God damn you, and will you answer the question—"

"Sir, I cannot—" Josiah said.

"Damn your insolence! What is in the bloody basket? Put it down at once, or I'll blow your thieving hands off!" Charles exploded. "Is this what I am to expect when my return is delayed by a few months? Outright thievery because there is no management left in this damned estate? If I so much as see a glint of silver underneath that sheet—"

Josiah took the basket and gingerly placed it down. A small cry issued from inside. Brutus rushed forward at once using his body to block the range of Charles' pistol. Behind them, Cleo came out on the porch, her face pale. Her apron was covered in bloody streaks, but her presence went unnoticed. All eyes were on Charles and the basket.

"What is this …" he now said as he sidestepped Brutus and used the tip of the saber to lift the sheet away.

He kept his pistol fixed firmly on them. The mounting pressure was unbearable between the men. The sheet was moved, and the secret revealed. Charles froze, confronted with the reality he had feared the most since the night of the storm back in August. The weight of it was too much to bear. He found himself kneeling in an instant, his hand covering his mouth. The baby's cry was a jolting surprise, but when he saw the infant's face, he needed no explanation.

A false and unwelcome commentary came regardless.

"Lord Sharpe, it a baby. We found a baby, and Cleo say to bring it to Reverend James because he take care of the orphan children and—"

Charles was fixated on the child. His face was struck with horror, and then his green eyes darted upward.

"You said you found it?"

"Uh, yes, sir, yes. I found it, and I uh, I ..." Josiah replied, speaking quickly as the words tumbled out of him.

"Why would you bring this baby to the reverend?" he asked, still staring at the basket as he lowered his pistol.

"'Cause, sir, he ain't got no mother, no father. He a orphan boy. I just do what Cleo tell me; she the main domestic, sir, I—"

Charles raised his hand, shaking his head.

"No, no. He has a mother," he replied, his voice faltering, "And ... a father."

His words were slow, solemn, and painful to utter.

The two men stared, their eyes huge, looking from Charles back to Cleo gripping the railing on the porch. A hand was covering her mouth, and she watched them helplessly.

Charles stood up, brushing the dust from his breeches. He understood what needed to be done. He could not deny it.

"Bring him to a wet nurse. To the cottage next to the kitchen. Clean up the inside first. Make it suitable. Make it decent. Is Mary still feeding her girl?"

"Yes, Lord Sharpe, I think so, Lord Sharpe."

"Tell her she is to tend to this baby. Immediately."

His voice was cold and distant.

"Yes, sir, at once, Lord Sharpe …" Josiah answered dutifully.

Brutus rushed to pick the basket up, watching his master with a wary look lest he change his order. Charles turned on his heel, marching his way up the stairs to the porch. Cleo came to him in a flurry, speaking near nonsense until she slowed her speech.

"Lord Sharpe, it is not what you think, it is not—"

He stopped in front of her before entering the shadows and coolness of the house.

"I know, Cleo."

"Please, sir, please, I beg of you, think—"

"You will speak no more of this matter, and I will follow suit."

He stormed to the hallway, unsheathing his saber and holster, and plied the sweat-soaked jacket off of his back. He started for the stairs as Cleo pleaded for him to wait. Lucy rushed to another room carrying bloody sheets just above him. Despite Cleo's protestations he bounded up the stairs and made his way straight to Eliza's room.

He flung the door open, seething at first, and then

stopped at the sight of her. Her hair was damp and stringy, her eyes swollen from crying. She gathered the sheets around her as she looked at him with frenzied emotion.

"I have returned," he said, somewhat awkwardly.

"Yes," she said, her voice flat and distant.

Tears spilled out of her eyes. In her hand, she clutched a narrow strip of cloth.

"Cleo tells me you have a fever."

It was not a question, and she gave no answer. She turned to the window. She refused to look at him.

"I wish you a speedy recovery."

Neither of them spoke for a while, and he sensed that he was not wanted. He left the room, his boots thundering down the hall to his door. The door slammed shut behind him, and she let out a piercing wail that echoed throughout the house.

CHAPTER V.

Eliza watched an orange crab with purple limbs scuttle close to her foot, its black eyes framed with spots of yellow, cautiously watching for any sign of movement. A breeze swept by, and the crab scurried further into a bush. She leaned against a palm tree, staring listlessly at the moving water. In her hands, she held the strip of swaddling cloth that she had begged Lucy to take.

She had not said goodbye. She had never told Cleo that she wanted to hold her baby one final time. These two thoughts repeated endlessly in her mind, rolling over and over like the white foam that frothed at the shoreline.

She spent her days with a blanket and a book, and she would only venture to the porch to retrieve water. She did not rush back in the evenings because she no longer came to dinner. With a sense of detachment, she was surprised to find that Charles attempted on more than one occasion to bring her a plate of food. She recalled earlier days when he had forbidden such a thing. Now, it seemed that he was desperate for her to return to some degree of normalcy.

It was a task lost in futility. The woman Eliza had once been no longer existed. She was only a fragment of her former self. Her diet subsisted of crackers and fruit that she nibbled on from time to time, whenever she could keep even that meager fare down. Her body was returning to a measure of normal function, but her mind was not.

Eliza watched as her body slowly changed back to the way it had been before she carried Philippe. There was a time in her life when the child had not existed. The idea seemed strange and disturbing to her now. She had not seen him since he was brought into this world, but yet she could not picture her world without his presence. This was a dilemma she could not soothe away, even as more ordinary, mundane problems came and went. She had gotten over the pain of urinating, the tenderness she felt in her breasts, and the dull but persistent aching of her muscles as she slowly returned to her former body.

Even as these matters relieved her, they also disturbed her. The only reminders that the birth had happened, that her boy indeed existed, were rapidly disappearing. And the days after his entrance into the world where she no longer knew him were only growing. When the bright red stain appeared weeks later, accompanied by a dull pang in her lower abdomen, it confirmed her body had completely resumed its normal cadence. It sealed with an aching finality that she had accomplished something marvelous more than one month ago. Time slipped past, and her sadness only increased. She had never realized that healing could be so unwanted a thing.

A detached sliver of her mind was in awe of her body and even of fashion as she truly understood the usefulness of a dress' silhouette. The cut of her clothing could hide her shape, even as it underwent the most dramatic of changes, and remain just as useful as her stomach flattened once more. Cleo was a witness to all that had happened. In this way, the two of them were bonded by the affiliation of experience. She owed her everything, yet she felt betrayed. It was an occurrence that should have been marked by celebration but was instead greeted by dismay. A baby boy who should have been held with tears and love was handed from one pair of hands to another, driven by the coldness of reality, a miracle reduced to a mishap.

It was not Cleo's fault, and Eliza knew this with a measure of bitter acknowledgment. The blame lay only with her. She had been foolish to lie with a man who was not her husband, to carry the baby those many months, to bring him into the world in a whirl of agony and determination. But she did not regret her love for Jean or her instinctual desire to raise the son they had created. Eliza wanted it all.

She had trouble organizing the multitude of observations she collected in her silent hours. She felt isolated, yet she continually rejected any conversation from Charles or Cleo. Her bed, a once quiescent chamber to rest, became a poignant reminder of what she was missing. The bed had transformed into a sacred yet violated space where she had first held the child to the very same place where he had been torn from her arms.

The past few days, she had found solace sleeping on a blanket in the sand, the warmth of the sun and the shifting shadows of palm fronds more comforting than the cold, hollow darkness of her room. It was nothing but an empty chamber, much like her childless body now. She cried and slept, preferring to escape into the softer world of dreams. Reality was a cold hell, and despite all of her attempts to distract herself from it, she could not erase one particular nagging thought that haunted her stronger than the rest.

Eliza could have held on to his tiny form longer, but she had not spoken up. She had not asked. She had not fought for him. She had not uttered a single useful word. Why had she not done so many things? *Why?* That terrible question tore at her insides. It was a cruel and most persistent inquiry, unanswerable and boundless in its malice.

But today, as she arched her back against the rough bark of the palm, a faint sensation of resolve returned to her. Philippe was on this island. Why should they be separated a moment longer? Her mind knew the reasons why, but her heart only yearned to hold him.

Eliza could see Philippe. The connection did not need to be severed as sharply as Cleo judged it. She knew where the baby had been taken. Cleo had told her many times as she reiterated the awful plan to her. Eliza would go, she would tell no one, and then she would return to her other life here on the beach. It was a daunting task, but it was not impossible.

Julius, the groom, brought her mare without delay. He seemed confused that she would want to ride again so soon, but they both knew they could not speak the obvious, and so he remained silent. Eliza bracingly lifted herself onto the saddle, cringing as she arranged her legs in a sidesaddle position. The pain was intense, but her desire to see her child was stronger.

"There you go, Lady Sharpe. And where are you headed today?" Julius asked nervously.

It wasn't his place to question her like that, but she felt bound to answer. He carried her secret like all the rest, without anything returned in kind.

"I have a sudden desire to speak with God, and so I am going to the church."

Her cryptic answer offered no explanation.

"I can bring the carriage forward; it won't take any more time."

"No, thank you."

Julius sighed.

"Careful now, Lady Sharpe. Just ride her nice and slow now …"

Julius looked behind at the house, worried that Cleo would notice and stop the entire enterprise. Before he could grow more anxious, Eliza took off in a trot. She wore a square kerchief over her chest and a day cap, two dainty dress accessories she only ever wore to Sunday service. Today, she felt as though they comprised a kind of feminine armor. Now she needed to remain emotionless as she sought answers to a question that caused her tears on most occasions. If she made one mistake, she knew she could never return to see her baby.

Eliza had a singular focus, and she did not see the silk cotton trees or the wandering slaves carrying machetes and hoes. As she moved closer into the town, she did not notice the stares from the white men. Women did not generally venture out at midday, and they most certainly did not travel without a chaperone.

She saw the church steeple appear in the distance and followed a quiet path until she found herself in the back of Christ Church. A modest limestone dwelling stood behind the larger church structure. The foundling hospital had glassless windows, and its rough, cracked exterior was covered in dappling shadows. She could see no one near the building, and she dismounted with a jolt of pain. Composing herself and adjusting her dress, she took a deep breath and went inside the disheartening building.

The caretaker was a short, portly woman and she appeared startled at Eliza's presence. She rushed up from a creaking mold-covered chair.

"I am requesting to view a child, one that was brought here nigh a month ago. Discretion forbids me to disclose my lady's name, and while she regrets that she cannot come in person due to her station, I have volunteered in her stead," Eliza rattled off.

The woman looked incredulous.

"We only have three babes here, my lady; I am not sure of what you mean."

Eliza swept past her and walked to the cribs, her breath shortening with every step. The majority of them were empty, and the three babies she saw were not Philippe.

The longer she tarried, the more the dilapidation of the building pressed on her senses. The dank smell, the buzzing of flies and insects, the near constant drip of water from the ceiling. This was no environment for fragile new life.

"No, no …that cannot be right. I am looking for a boy with dark hair and blue eyes. I assure you he was taken here."

"My name is Ann, and I have tended the babes for over five years. I have never seen a babe with such a description come through these doors. Not recently at any rate."

"There must be another room, another place where you are keeping him."

Ann shook her head, her pudgy face red and sweltered.

"Perhaps there has been a misunderstanding. I would ask your lady again and return another time," she replied.

The woman displayed a less than genuine smile, and Eliza seized her rotund frame with an impulse that surprised even her.

"Where is my baby?" Eliza shrieked.

Ann gasped.

"You are delirious! Unhand me!"

"Show me where you've put him. I know he is here!"

Ann did not respond, and Eliza shook her.

"Where is my child?" she shouted.

The woman leaned to the side and grabbed a bell and rang it violently. Eliza would still not release her, expecting the second person who had arrived to fly to her assistance. When she looked up and saw Reverend James' horrified face, she returned to her senses.

"May I help you, Lady Sharpe?" he asked.

His question was polite, but his tone was guarded. Eliza clutched the sides of her skirt, looking down at the dirt floor as if its earthen presence could help defend her.

"Yes," she answered slowly, "I am looking for a child who was brought here, and it appears he is now missing."

"When did this occur? What child? Where was he taken from? Who is his mother?"

His last question hung in the humid air.

"Where is my child?" she repeated, oblivious to reason and propriety.

"Lady Sharpe, please take a seat," the reverend offered, indicating the rotten chair in the corner.

"You keep these children in here like this? Subject to the humidity and the insects? The mosquitoes are merciless; do you not offer netting for them? This is inhumane! This is barbaric!"

The reverend's face grew irritated.

"These children were forsaken by society, and we are ensuring they survive."

"I do not see how they have a single chance against tropical fevers in a place like this. The air stinks and is wet! There are leaks in the ceiling!"

"As you can see, Lady Sharpe, we even take in the Negro children. Is not a home like this better than enslavement? A great many men will pay for such a baby but not to raise it. They desire a baby like these to throw shackles on it when it comes of age. Pray, tell me how you would improve their lot?" His thin lips slowly curled into a smile. "We offer them the greatest gift, the gift of salvation. They will be saved, Lady Sharpe. If not in this world, then in the next that awaits us."

"I will complain of these conditions! This is not charity. This is negligence. How dare you collect money for them and not ensure they at least possess dry linens?"

"Please, Lady Sharpe. I will send for your husband at once. You are unwell. You are very unwell."

The reverend began to direct her to the chair, and she moved away from him.

"Do not lay a hand on me! You will do no such thing; this does not concern him."

"Curious. It does not?" Reverend James asked, his beady eyes watching her.

She felt his judgment fall upon her like a slap to her face.

"You took in a child on the seventeenth of April, and yet you claim he is not here. I want to—the lady who sent me wants to inquire about the child, and it seems you have misplaced him. It seems to be a mercy when I look around me. I will be sure to tell her of the conditions in this miserable hovel."

"Lady Sharpe, who is the mother of this child?"

Eliza glared at him, not caring if he was a man of God. This was not God's work. She saw the money they collected on Sundays. Charles himself donated extensive funds to the church.

She knew she had said too much, but she did not care. She let anger flood her system. It was better than the slow, sinking feeling that bubbled up, ready to replace her flash of rage at any moment. The truth was unbearable.

"You are a disgrace, Reverend."

Eliza knew she was burning every possible chance of redemption in this forsaken colony, but she did not care. She only wanted one thing, and she had prepared herself to see her child. And now that it was clear that he was not here, that he was indeed lost to her forever, her fury knew no bounds. Reverend James and the woman would not help her, and so she set off again.

Her movements were mechanical. She tried to bury her panic, her desperation, the wave of acid that roiled her stomach. She saw no person, no trees nor flora. Her eyes were glued to the waves of her horse's mane as she dutifully carried her back to Pleasant Hall.

The horse stopped moving, and in confusion, Eliza kicked her again, only to realize they had returned home. A pulsing beat grew in her ears, and her face felt flushed with heat. She moved to undo her seat from the horse, but she slid off and into wiry arms.

"Lady Sharpe!" Julius exclaimed.

"He was not there. He wasn't there ..." she whispered to him, tears flowing from her cheeks.

She felt him pat her head and then looked up to see Cleo and Charles step onto the porch. The blasted bell must have alerted them of her arrival, but for a second time, her ears had not heard its solemn toll. The yard swirled in maddening circles, and her heart throbbed against her ribs. Every intake of breath clouded her vision with more darkness. She was exasperated and enraged. She wanted to shout loud enough for every person in earshot to hear, but she knew she could not utter a word.

Eliza stood on an invisible border between dizziness and cruel alertness. The man she hated cried out her name and ran down the porch, taking her by the arm. She wrested herself away from him, but he clamped down again. They proceeded up the stairs, and Eliza spoke to Cleo from the pain in her eyes, but Cleo offered no response. She could not answer her. She must have assumed what she had just tried to do, but yet her expression lacked any criticism.

Cleo had warned her of this time and again, and Eliza had not believed her. She had refused to believe that her heart could ache so badly after Jean. There could surely be nothing left, no amount of feeling tissue, after his death. But this was incredibly worse. She had denied time and again that a person so small could leave such an exposed hole in her heart. She had only known Philippe for a day. But in truth, it was much longer than that. She had carried the baby for nine long months, and now he was gone.

Charles seemed afraid of her, surveying her reactions as if she had gone mad. She relished in his disturbance. If she cried even louder and pushed all remnants of her self-control away, perhaps this would drive him from her forever.

They were in her bedroom now, and he lifted her to the mattress. Cleo was busy preparing some liquid in a small brown bottle and lifted it to her lips.

"Here, Miss Ellie, you will feel better now; it is all right ..." she whispered to her, but Cleo would not meet her eyes.

The tonic was bitter and hard to swallow when it mixed with her grief. Eliza turned to her side, crouching in a fetal position. Charles would not leave the room. She closed her eyes, willing some invisible force to make him depart. Her body was tense with the expectation of a falsely reassuring touch from his hand. She knew she needed some reason for her excursion, some excuse for why she had left. She dismally wondered if it even mattered. She had revealed her secret in the orphanage. It was only a matter of time before word reached Charles' ears.

She did not care. She hoped it would crush him. She hoped that when he found out, he would be so hurt he would finally leave her. She prayed for release. *Why is this happening?*

Eliza thought about the scheming duplicity that revolved around this colony. She had been welcomed because she had been viewed as a pawn and nothing more. Her value had only been measured in her usefulness, and the one man who had tried to put an end to it all no longer walked this earth.

Cleo had given her the gift of hope; she had believed in nearly everything she had told her. Cleo had promised that she was supposed to be here, on this plantation, on this island secluded from the world. Cleo had said she was meant to be Charles' wife. She had believed that matters would improve, that a blissful future was nearly within her grasp. She was meant to be Charles' wife but another's lover.

Jean had held the answer to all of her problems. Even after Jean's death, despite every wound to her body, to her heart above all, Eliza had continued to fight, knowing that relief was in sight. This child was an extension of the hope Jean had almost delivered. She could feel it. If it had been a substance made of air, she knew she could draw it into her lungs—it had felt that tangible to her. But now her last hope had been extinguished. Her intuition had been horribly mistaken.

No one would tell her the fate of her son. As long as Charles was the master of Pleasant Hall, she understood now that the secret would not be revealed. It was possible he already knew about the baby. If so, it was doubly certain that he had something to do with Philippe's disappearance.

She shuddered to think of it. Cleo would never cause harm to her, this much was true. But even Cleo answered primarily to him. Perhaps that was all that she had ever been. She was limited in her allegiance. Perhaps her words of reassurance were nothing other than an order, and as an enslaved person, Cleo had no choice but to follow his command. Perhaps their unnatural alliance was nothing but conjecture. There were no ancestors, no ancient spirits, or subtle guiding hand. Eliza had feared Jean was spying on her for Charles, but she had never realized that perhaps Cleo was the Judas in her circle.

Maybe Celia's anger was justified. Celia had never pretended to hold a claim of friendship with her, yet she had helped her in her most urgent hour. Eliza looked at Celia with different eyes now, but it was too late. She needed to speak with someone, anyone, and she also understood that there was no one.

She was alone.

A war had raged inside this old house, and she knew she had been sorely defeated. In all her studies and academic pursuits, she had never taken the time to comprehend battle stratagems and war tactics, and her sheer naivete had been her final downfall. Charles was a hardened officer with a sharpened mind; she, merely a foolish woman with a desperate heart.

The realization was bitter and stinging. Eliza felt Cleo tuck the sheets around her, but she could not shake her utter mistrust now.

"You have betrayed me," she said bitterly.

Cleo hesitated to answer. Eliza waited, hoping within the strained bounds of hope that she was mistaken.

"Forgive me, Miss Ellie. Forgive me."

She felt Cleo's warm hand squeeze hers, and the knife sank deeper into her chest. Cleo shuffled out of the room, slowly closing the door behind her. A renewed wave of grief descended over her. The tincture burned in the back of her throat, and she tried to swallow it away. In a moment of disgust, a new idea settled upon her—a gradual smoldering ember that evolved into a single flame, fanned by the heat of revenge and retribution.

The familiar ringing in her ears sounded, and she knew if she opened her eyes that Tabitha would be there, sitting without weight on the edge of her bed. It brought her a sense of twisted comfort, either in knowing that she truly was not alone or that she was truly mad beyond redemption. All of this was madness. She had fallen, and her display of hysterics was the final awaited confirmation. In her mind, she implored the spirit to leave and did not care if it displeased her. Fear no longer had any effect on her. Eliza only wanted peace, and she welcomed the darkness. It was the only thing that held her without judgment.

CHAPTER VI.

Eliza's mind dwelled on the past now, to days when peace still seemed an obtainable objective. She thought of Jean and when she carried his child, but she also remembered the wonder she held for this beautiful island. She recalled a time when everything she had seen fascinated her, from the fish in the ocean to the trees around Pleasant Hall. One of these older days that remained prominent was when Cleo had given her instruction about the various plants that grew around the gardens. But it was more than a cherished memory; the information she had been given that day had never faded from her mind. They had walked together in deep discussion, and the countless plants Eliza had passed a dozen times without notice suddenly took on new significance and meaning.

The gardens and natural vegetation around Pleasant Hall were not only charming to behold, they were useful, some even essential to living on this island. Some plants could heal, acting more beneficial than any medicine derived from continental knowledge. She had learned that if she burned the husk of a coconut in her room, it would keep the biting insects away and ensure a peaceful night. Cleo had advised the use of the tobacco leaf for the same purpose, although the coconut husks were easier to procure. Oil made from crushed fever grass could be applied to the skin so insects would not swarm when she walked on the beach at dusk. Fever grass tea would soothe away any sickness if consumed at the first sign of a sore throat. The fruit of the soursop plant could strengthen the body's defenses and ward off disease.

But some plants did not serve a healing purpose; some could indeed take life away. They had passed by a long-leaved bush dotted with bursts of stunning pink flowers. Something was pointedly different about the oleander plant; its leaves were sharp and unwelcoming, like daggers. Cleo had warned of the toxicity of the bush and stopped Eliza from picking a flower. All parts of it were poisonous; even clippings of it burnt in a bonfire could be deadly if inhaled. Two of its leaves could kill a horse within the hour.

The admonition had never left Eliza's mind. Every time she had passed that bush, she had gazed at it in a much more attentive way than she did any of the other flowering plants in the yard. The oleander tempted her, and she could not erase Cleo's words from her mind. At times, she pictured utilizing its pointed leaves on herself. But as of late, there was only one person she envisioned when she looked at that bush. There was only one person who caused her an unspeakable amount of pain.

Shortly before dinner that evening, she plucked the

leaves of the oleander and left them stewing in boiling water. The slave working in the kitchen had asked no questions, unaware that Eliza had slipped anything into the water. After all, Eliza was not a typical plantation mistress, and they were used to receiving strange requests from her: an extra bowl to rescue a lost crab from inside the house, a shell that needed scourging to remove the algae from it. When the water cooled, she took a portion of it and poured it into a carafe, mixing it with red wine. The rest she dumped unceremoniously into the sand and urged the kitchen staff to scrub the kettle vigorously.

Charles believed that she had finally returned to the dining room because of his recommendations, that she had finally adhered to his guidance, the caring counsel of a concerned spouse. But in truth, she had only returned to sharing a meal with him for one purpose.

Exactly on cue, Lucy took the wine first to Charles and then to her. She declined it with a throw of her hand and began to eat her soup, gripping her spoon tightly. Waves of queasiness hit her as he picked up the glass, giving the wine a swirl. Eliza wondered if he noticed its lack of saturated hue.

Despite all her efforts to remain emotionless, she knew her ears were flushed red. She wondered if he could hear her panicked heart prattling inside her chest or if he even noticed the sweep of crimson that danced across her tanned chest. Time seemed to stall; the arms of the grandfather clock had never moved slower.

But Charles would not drink it. He left the glass neglected for longer than she could bear. Her legs tensed like the hard limestone rocks dotting the surf, connecting to the wooden floors, anchoring her over a bottomless hole of anxiety and dread. A few more moments passed. But still, he would not touch the damned wine.

Then a new feeling came to her, one that she couldn't ignore. She no longer saw a brutal, unfeeling man sitting before her but a scared child, crouching into a wall underneath a bedside table, tears covering his trembling cheeks. A boy whose childhood had been robbed from him, a boy who had watched his mother's life stolen from the world. This recollection of the dream, the most disturbing of all the things she had seen in her sleep since her arrival, flashed vividly before her.

"No!" she shrieked, standing, her chair violently scratching the floor.

Charles looked up at her strangely.

"There's a fly. A fly—in your, your wine ..." she said dumbly.

She rushed to him and took the glass from him. She knew he didn't see it. But she carried on, embarrassment and fear goading her performance. Lucy appeared from the pantry, taking the glass with a scrutinizing eye.

"I don't see a fly, Lady Sharpe," she said, utterly confused.

"There is a fly," Eliza said, false confidence holding her chin upright.

Lucy swirled the red liquid with squinting eyes. She wouldn't leave the room. Eliza could feel Charles watching her very carefully.

"There *is* a fly. Now take the glass and get rid of it,"

Eliza said angrily. "In fact, take the entire thing away. How long has this been sitting out? You know the insects savor the sweetness of it!"

Lucy apologized and slowly left the room, still staring at the drink. Eliza wasn't sure if her ears could get any hotter. She regretted speaking so severely to her, and she knew her aggression was suspect. She never spoke to the slaves with a harsh tongue. But she had done so now for one simple reason: it had occurred to her that her success depended on Lucy's ruin. If Charles were to die under her service, no one would look at Eliza. But they would all too easily blame someone, anyone, with dark skin. She thought of her and Cleo's welfare and of how foolishly stupid she had almost been. Eliza returned to her seat at the table, attempting to eat her food. She wanted to cry at the folly of what she had almost committed. But she was alone in this endeavor. Charles sat stock-still, rigid, glaring at her.

"A fly is not poisonous," he finally said, his eyes un-flinching.

Lucy returned with a new glass, pouring wine from a different decanter. Eliza swallowed. He knew exactly what she had almost done. He looked at her like she was a feral animal. Like she was a threat that needed to be eliminated.

"No, husband, but it is unpleasant."

She swallowed a new surge of fear, desperate to re-main collected in front of him. The silence was stifling.

"I find your lies unpleasant," he said.

Eliza tried a new tactic. She refused to glance in his

direction, busily stuffing her mouth as if this alone could change the subject. The quicker she ate, the sooner she could leave and the incident be forgotten.

Charles scoffed, his hands coming together on the table as she looked up.

"You are malice in its purest form, my dear."

"That is unkind," Eliza replied with a contrived smile.

"I suppose all malice springs from a natural source. A righteous source, one would say. Indeed, one must have a cause for such malice. I find myself to be a great source of it, whether I comprehend the reason for it or not."

Eliza looked at him, lost in his critical gaze. She was not in the same place she had been when she entered the room that night. She had crossed a line, but despite her panic, she also knew that she had nothing to lose now. The truth came bounding out of her.

"I was wrong," she began. "This entire time I assumed you capable of the utmost cruelty. I saw a darkness in you, Charles. But I was mistaken. *You* have been subject to the worst atrocities."

"I do not catch your meaning."

"I know what your father did," she said plainly, a weight lifting off of her. She searched his eyes for any trace of recognition in him.

Denial met her first.

"My father left me a grand estate. Land. A title. For which I am very grateful."

She tried again. "You were so young to see such horror. Then you lost Elias. I know now why you did not want to return here. It is far from a paradise for you," she said softly.

Eliza timidly reached out to touch his rough hand.

"You are deluded with the heat—"

"I know that your father killed your mother."

Charles stopped, his eyes flashing up at her. There was a warning concealed within them and something darker. Hardness was setting over his features as he bit his lower lip. He ripped his hand away from hers.

"My mother died from tropical disease. She was nothing but a wanton whore who didn't understand her place. I barely remember her."

Her stomach began to twist again, emotion making her eyes water. He was going to fight her over this. He would deny the truth; it was too great a challenge to endure.

"Those are your father's words, Charles, not yours. You know the truth."

He was quiet. She knew she was treading through treacherous territory. Eliza sat on a blade's edge between a brilliant epiphany and a descent into a bottomless abyss.

Charles took a deep breath.

"Who have you been speaking with? Hmm? Cleo? Lucy? I'll see to it that they are removed from this house immediately. The past is long gone and dead. It is the least appropriate fodder for your latest ruse. You mean to distract me. You threatened my very life, but it is not enough. No, you come a second time to attack my childhood—"

"Charles, no, please, listen. I know what you have experienced. I saw—"

His temper surfaced, ignited like gunpowder in contact with a flame.

"Who told you? Who told you!" he spat.

His hands gripped the curved edge of the table.

It was clear to her that he could not comprehend the dreams she had experienced in the house, but he would recognize one name. If she could only speak it into the air, perhaps he would finally understand.

"Tabitha," she finally answered.

His face paled.

In a flash, his arm shot across the table, grabbing her by the throat. There was the loud metallic clatter of utensils hitting porcelain and glasses of water being knocked over. He stood up, towering above her, her hands struggling to remove his grasp on her neck.

"She has been dead for years! You are wrong. You are so very wrong. You have made a deadly miscalculation, my dear."

Her breath came out in broken rasps, her eyes watery.

"Please, I am sorry for …" she managed to say.

She heard a scream behind her and knew that Lucy had returned.

"Get out!" he shouted.

His thumb dug even deeper into her throat, an excruciating pressure following it. Her head felt like it was going to explode. She fell from the chair, still trying to free herself from his grip.

"I have given you everything! Everything!" he shouted as he continued to strangle her.

Her vision was spotty now, and her focus was rapidly fading. She tried using her legs to kick but felt her strength leaving her. It was useless. She could only focus on the pain at her throat.

"I was trying to start anew. I was trying to make something for us in this colony. But you have been nothing but a betrayer and a deceiver to me. And now you mean to poison me!"

Eliza was failing to struggle anymore, her face red with exertion, her eyes glassy. The world was quickly reduced to a small circle, darkness encroaching on all sides until she could only see his eye, animalistic in its rage, boring down on her.

"Do you know how many lives I have taken?" he fumed. "I can destroy you! I can kill you with my bare hands! I could squeeze the very life out of your body!"

She felt saliva flecking against her cheeks as he seethed. With no other recourse, Eliza started praying. She knew she was on the verge of passing out.

Charles cried out in despair and frustration, moving away from her line of sight. She felt suspended in the air, her body rigid and racked with pain. The remnant of the room she could still see was dissipating. She feared what the darkness meant, but she was also desperate for the pain to stop.

And then he released her. She gasped for air, hitting the floor with a thud and rolling onto her side.

Realization that she was still alive swept through her, and a cracked laugh escaped from her lips. Her ears were ringing, and it hurt to swallow. But she was still there, in the room with him, lying on the hardwood floor.

Then she heard it. A single sob. She struggled to a shaky stand, her balance unsteady. Charles sat in his chair, his face red with torment, crying. She tried to say something, but her voice was too hoarse. Eliza lost her footing and collapsed to the floor again, a wobbling forearm propping her up. He rose and grabbed a sharp knife, pushing her back down.

The fight for survival ignited again as her head rushed. Her now-raspy voice protested as she saw the blade descend towards her torso, and then she felt a sawing motion as he hacked and cut at her stays. His aim was not intended for violence this second time but for relief. He must have realized that her stays were only further constricting her labored breaths. She felt his strong grip pull away at either side of her chest as he ripped open her garment. She breathed in a rush of fresh air, making her head even more dizzy.

Charles left her, backing away as he dropped the knife near her arm. She coughed and wheezed. She heard him take a seat again, his hands running through his hair, his head downcast.

"Charles ..." she managed to say, her voice thin and grating.

"I did not want this."

"I am trying to help—" she said slowly and painfully.

Eliza's eyes were bloodshot and pleading as she lay there. Charles looked up towards her, his eyes full of sadness and lingering fury.

"I am fortunate to have a wife who cares so much about my well-being. I'll be sure to take similar precautions with you," he said with a faltering voice.

He wiped his face with a linen napkin and stalked out

of the room. Eliza lay there, motionless. There could be no redemption for a broken man like him. She had seen terrible things but had also seen a glimmer of promise. Every time she had doubted their future together, Cleo had managed to bolster it.

"I raised that boy. He is a good boy," Cleo had told her, a *deep smile growing on her face.*

Now that idea had been violently extinguished. Eliza had nearly killed him tonight; and he had returned the favor. She was grateful to be alive, but now her ragged breaths seemed more fraught with danger than before. Their battle was unfinished, and the uncertainty of its conclusion chilled her bones.

CHAPTER VII.

Cleo was beside her dwelling, tending to the meager patch of land allotted to her and picking weeds one by one, when she heard him. His furious steps crashed through the bush, and his powerful hands pushed through the giant swinging leaves of the banana trees.

"Did you tell her? Did you?" Charles shouted.

Other slaves that had idly strolled by took one look at him and fled in alarm. But he only saw Cleo. His long hair was disheveled, sweaty with agitation.

Cleo did not respond, and she would not answer him in his current state. He was livid with emotion, but his presence was not enough to rattle her. Instead, she continued separating weeds from the vegetable leaves. She did not want these intruders to choke off the sunlight and nutrients of her younger plants.

"Cleo, look at me! Did you tell her?"

His voice was louder. A parrot scuttled from a nearby tree, shrieking into the distance.

Now Cleo turned and looked at him, her eyes simmering with a passive anger. She was not pleased with what he had done.

"Did you tell Eliza about Tabitha? Did you tell her what my father did?" he demanded.

"No."

The answer was simple and plain and seemed to infuriate him further with its finality. His face flooded with exasperation as if he would lose all control.

"No, come inside with me."

Cleo tossed the weeds into the distance and brushed her hands off. Charles followed her sullenly into her house, and he sat on the dirt floor, covering his face with his hands. She began to arrange some bottles and containers on the small wooden table and selected a few leaves to add to a kettle over the fire. She looked up at him, studying his posture and analyzing his distress. It was clear that he held combat with his inward agony.

"Are you sitting?" she asked him.

The answer was obvious and did not require a reply.

"Do you feel the ground beneath you?" she asked again.

He shot a glaring look at her. She shuffled closer to him, seizing a hand and brushing it on the sandy floor.

"Do you feel it now?"

He muttered a half-audible "yes."

"Good. Then we can start," she said.

Cleo stood over him, gazing intently at the space around his figure. She sighed, shaking her head, humming a curious tune. Her wide hands grasped the air around his shoulders and his head, and she began a pulling motion like she was cleaning unseen cobwebs from around his body. Her hands moved faster and faster, and then she went towards the door, tossing the invisible mess outside into the sunlight. Finally, she exhaled sharply as if this gesture would keep it away. Charles looked at her without seeing her, his mind still stewing with turbulence.

Cleo returned to the table, checked the kettle, and poured him a cup of tea.

"Here, drink this."

He waved a hand away in disgust.

"Drink it."

It was a command. He shot her a look of silent rebellion, but then, with a long sigh, he acquiesced and slowly sipped it.

"It's tea made from the Moringa leaf. It will help settle you. Your nerves, your heart. Make you feel steady."

Cleo folded her hands in front of her face and closed her eyes, preparing herself for what she would say next.

"You will not touch her again," she said gravely. "I am not pleased. *They* are not pleased."

She looked up as she said this, as if for emphasis.

"She tried to kill me, Cleo! She tried to—"

A hand stopped his diatribe.

"Shh! Drink! Slowly … and breathe."

He reluctantly listened, and the internal battlements he had so carefully constructed to contain his thoughts began to fall away, piece by piece. But that was partly why he had sought her out, and Cleo knew it.

"I have ruined everything." His voice faltered into a

whisper. But then, a wave of defense returned. "She tried to poison me, Cleo. She knows! She knows …"

"And how do you know that she tried to kill you, Charles?" Cleo's voice was devoid of passion, flat like an inquisitor.

"I smelt it. That curious, earthen smell. It's metallic. Acidic when mixed with wine. It was the same smell I remember when I infused it in my father's drink. You know of what I speak …" His green eyes were darkened, smoldering, the rage of the past finally boiling to the surface. He had an aversion to yielding so completely to his feelings. "She has tried to do what I once did. I have become a figure of hatred in her eyes. She wants *me* dead."

"Where is she now?"

He took a moment to think, to brood over the terrible scene he had departed from. And then his more rational senses began to return.

"My God, I left her there. On the floor! I should go back, I should—" he exclaimed as he started to rise.

"No! You will stay here. Leave her. You will only make it worse now. She will be frightened. You let your hands speak for you, and you will have to reap the consequences."

He rubbed his fingers through his hair, lost in sullen distraction.

"She spoke of Tabitha, Cleo. If you swear you did not share that name, how can she be privy to it? That witch. There is something foul and wicked happening on these grounds."

"That is certain," Cleo said with a wry smirk, although she knew her full meaning was lost on him. Instead, she was thinking of the father of Eliza's child. "Tabitha was not a witch. You know that. She cared for you and your mother. She was an Obeah woman. Like me."

Charles shook his head.

"No, you are nothing like her."

"I am simply older. Tabitha did not have that opportunity."

There was an unsettled moment of silence.

"The truth will eat you from the inside, Charles. You must speak it. It will be revealed one way or another, and it should be you who does it. No one else. You cannot hide the things you have done."

"I had no choice, Cleo. You know this. There was no other way."

"And do you regret it?"

"No."

"You already know my feelings. It was not wise. You will live with the consequences of your actions for the rest of your life."

"What else was I supposed to do with that child? *His* child? You think I only speak from wicked selfishness; I am certain of it."

"This will change everything."

"I pray to God that it does," he said, his voice light with hope. "That it finally brings her a return to reason. I cannot have trouble like this, not for one day longer. It must stop."

"You are playing a dangerous game." She shook her head and clicked her tongue, reaching for the stained brown bag that held the pig-knuckle bones she used for divination. She murmured something to herself, shook the bag, and let the contents spill over the wooden table. But her silence was prolonged.

"What does it say? You are quiet for far too long. Tell me! For God's sake, speak!" Charles urged.

"She has free will. She has the right to choose ..."

Her dark hand waved over the fallen shapes.

"I have nothing good to say. She challenges you. You must be careful with her. One misspoken word, one cruel glance ... Charles, you *must* be careful with her," she warned.

"What have I done?" he said to himself.

"You use force against her when you shouldn't. You take when you should give. They are saying a woman does not forget. No, she does not forget. What they mean to say is ... you have broken her trust, and that trust was not given cheaply," Cleo's face grew troubled. "She would have let you. But not that night. Or not that day. You stole from her."

He realized that the conversation had taken a different turn, and the meaning was not lost on him.

"I have not touched her in that way since. I thought all women feel discomfort at first. She never said anything to me; she never told me it was unpleasant. I know we have discussed this before, but I did not know. I did not *know* ..." he said, his voice breaking.

"She said *no*. You did not listen." Cleo sighed, clicking her tongue. "A woman does not forget."

Charles was about to protest in defense, but she would not hear it.

"You picked the flower before it had a chance to bloom. You trample its petals, and then weep over its destruction," she continued. "They can see *all* you do …"

"Cleo, I listened to you. I did everything that you prescribed! You confirmed the troubling visions I had seen, and I did as you asked. Nothing more!" Charles cried.

Cleo raised her hand in agitation.

"I never told you to do *that*," she said firmly. "You did not hold back. I never told you to treat her so roughly. Men and women have very different ways of solving the same problem, but you did not have to act so bold."

Charles scoffed, casting a sideways glance out into the yard.

"At least I didn't make her a swimming costume. You enable her far too easily," he said.

"Do you want your wife to drown in a dress?" Cleo asked.

"I want her not in the damned water at all!" Charles shouted. "You astound me with your carelessness, Cleo. Why should we even take the risk?"

"You cannot control her. She has free will."

Charles let out a long sigh and bowed his head.

"What do I do now, Cleo? How do I mend this? Is there anything I can do after today?"

"Do not bury your pain. Look what it has done. Look where it comes out. It pours from your hands as destruction. But those hands are capable of creation as well. You can create a better life with those hands. Tell her your secret." Her tone changed to a more somber one after she took a deep breath. "Is it true? Have you made your decision?"

"Yes. This can fix it all! This madness must end. I must do it, but how? And when? I fear I will only wake a domestic storm. I do not want to disturb her any further; I must tread carefully when I tell her. She is in a more delicate state than ever before."

Cleo looked displeased.

"It may not have the effect you desire. She has the freedom of choice. She wants you to hear her. She needs to be seen. And I will state it once more. Eliza has free will. She can leave. Do not be surprised, they say."

"I will not allow it! I cannot allow it. She doesn't understand ..." he started to say.

"Take her to church," Cleo answered.

"Beg pardon?"

"Take her to church. Take her this Sunday."

"Yes ...yes, we'll go there. Surely only God can save this marriage—"

"Show her the grave. Show her Jean's grave," she added.

Charles' face paled.

"You spent enough money on it; you might as well tell her what you have done."

"She will think my intentions are suspect. She does not need to know. There is time enough for that. Her heart is so attached to his memory I fear she will sleep alongside his tombstone," Charles said. "I am not a perfect man. I fear she will never understand me."

"This will help her see. To see the man you truly are."

"I did it only for Jean. So that his soul may rest in peace. I pray he has found it now ..."

Cleo scoffed.

"But I still do not understand how Eliza possesses knowledge of my past. It is unnatural."

Cleo's lips curved up into a smile.

"She has the sight," she answered.

Charles' face tightened with dread as if the sudden explanation was worse than not knowing.

"She can see Tabitha too? Oh, what have I done bringing her here to this cursed island?"

"She is protected. And that means against you as well. If you touch her again, they may not stand by. Yes … she has seen them. Legba. Shango. Yemaya surrounds her constantly. She offered prayers to Erzulie Dantor. To Oya. But they did not answer her."

"Legba?" he asked with the faintest recognition.

"Papa Legba. Did he not come to you as well? The night that you screamed in terror? Did he not come to your bed when you were a boy? The dream you had of Elias and how he would leave this life …"

"That is a childish memory. A fever dream."

Cleo gazed at him with an unflinching, ferocious stare.

"The only reason you are alive is because of the *orishas*. Do not think you walked off the battlefield on your merit alone. That dream terrified you because it was not a dream. It was one of your first visions."

Charles stared up at Cleo. "I saw Eliza in the pitch of battle once. She came to me amidst the blood and the frenzy. Walking in a shift, her stays visible to the eye. That is how I knew we would end up here." He looked up at the wooden beams in the ceiling and sighed. "This is a poor conclusion, is it not?"

His words ended with a half-whispered laugh.

"This is not the end. By far. But you must be careful. They are repeating it in my head."

"I recall your earlier warnings. I tried to keep her safe. I forbade her to swim. I tried to keep her away, to occupy her with pastimes in the house. Why did I repeatedly see her without her dressing clothes? I was fraught with worry the entire journey here. I feared the night of the storm on the ship that my terror would come to pass, but we arrived safely.

He sighed. "All of my dreams, all of the times I have seen her in my mind, she is in nothing but her shift and her stays. I fear for her safety, Cleo, even now as I become the sole monster to threaten it all. I was not gentle with her. I was harsh beyond measure, and I did not care if she saw me as a tyrant. At least then she would stay alive."

"You are not meant to control her. You must let her be free."

Charles did not appear to take this piece of advice in. He was preoccupied with other thoughts.

"Has she ever spoken of her dreams? I do wonder … has she ever seen me? Before the day we met?"

Cleo paused, not wishing to offend his sensibilities.

"Her dreams began once she arrived at Pleasant Hall. I suspect the waters here made it easier for her. Although we both know Tabitha can be demanding."

"She must think herself mad … to see such horrors, such frighteningly wonderous things."

"As you once did."

"I still do." He sighed again. "Only God knows where we will end. I should have drunk the wine tonight and ended both our miseries."

"That is not the way you go, child."

"Then by all means, enlighten me."

"You know my rules. They have never changed. I cannot tell you," she said sharply.

"Then let that part of my life remain in suspense. It is so very strange. I come to you with seemingly insurmountable problems, and then I leave feeling a changed man. I know now what I shall do."

He stood up and walked closer to Cleo, grasping both of her hands in his.

"I cannot thank you enough for all that you do. All that you have done. I owe you a great debt, Cleo. I will find a way to repay you."

His face seemed pained as he said this, but Cleo only offered a smile and squeezed his hands in return.

CHAPTER VIII.

They waited outside Christ Church, the heat smoldering on their shoulders. Eliza wondered why she had fussed so much with her appearance. Sweat was already dampening the edges of her hair and darkening the crevices of her dress. The church behind her was constructed of heavy cut stones, and although no stained glass adorned the windows, it did possess a steeple. The church yard was modest, dotted with crooked graves and wild, unkempt grass that mixed with palm trees.

From what she had read, the church used to be a wooden building, but the Spaniards had burnt it down on two occasions. Since then, Christ Church was a proud limestone edifice, complete with pillars and massively thick walls to withstand hurricanes and enemy fire. Sage green wooden shutters slanted in downward angles above each window opening, and the painted color of them neatly matched the walls inside.

She toyed with the petals of a fuchsia bougainvillea sprawled along the wooden fence. They had arrived nearly an hour ago but could not proceed to their pew until the governor arrived. It was bad enough that Charles had convinced her to come today, but she had entirely forgotten about the other unnecessary aspects of the service. He suggested that she take a stroll among the gravestones in the church yard to distract her from the monotony of waiting. But she remained where she stood, wiping the sweat from her brow. The decaying ruins of past islanders did not catch her interest on a sweltering day like this.

Lord Dunmore's expectations of attending church on Sundays were various and included that the service would not begin until he arrived and that the congregation would stand as he and his retinue entered the small building. Charles, as one of the highest-ranking military officers in the colony, not only occupied a space in this select group but also felt it an honor to participate. This unspoken rule did not dictate the governor's timely arrival, although the rest of the community was expected to fulfill their duty, no matter how long it took for Lord Dunmore's carriage to finally arrive.

Eliza believed in God, but she also believed that the Lord himself would find this weekly presentation to be nothing more than a mockery. This island and most of its well-to-do inhabitants that frequented the church were drunk and debauched on Saturday, then miraculously made devout the following morning. It was merely a display without any real substance, and she consequentially found it to be utter nonsense. Eliza had complained about the superfluous tradition of waiting on Lord Dunmore, but her remarks had fallen on deaf ears. And now she unwillingly returned to take part.

The situation and the sun had become nearly unbearable just as a team of the finest horses on the island came around the bend. The carriage stopped, a groom opened the door, and then the obese body of Lord Dunmore wiggled to the ground. He looked irritated, but this was the mood he customarily exhibited. He briefly nodded to the small group awaiting his arrival, and then he began his march towards the church.

Eliza said nothing to them as he and Charlotte passed her. She refused to give respect to a man who was not worthy of it. Then Charlotte stopped walking and turned behind her.

"Lady Sharpe, what a pleasant surprise! We have not seen you these ... nine months at least. Yes, surely it was *nine* months. I do believe so," she said, her tone like ice.

Eliza wanted to quip back with something vicious. She wanted to crush Charlotte like a small and meaningless ant on the blistering walkway. But she only smiled and nodded.

There was a unanimous stamp of people standing at attention, then they made their way towards the front of the pews. The interior was high roofed and furnished with an organ, but the rest of the church was quite plain. She wondered how any of the people they walked with could withstand the clear frustration of the rest of the town as they passed by. Ahead of her, a row of five pews remained vacant. Family names inscribed in brass plaques adorned every row, and she mournfully walked into the one marked *The Sharpes.*

The organ began to play, the priest appeared from a side door, and the congregants began to sing without proper tune or rhythm. Eliza was immediately lost in a reverie. When they returned to a seated position, Charles lightly brushed her hand, but she retracted it. Time passed by painfully, and she considered whether waiting outside in the sun was a more diverting option than the captive role she now endured.

"The text reminds us today that we are charged not only to be hearers of the gospel, but doers also. For every one of you shall be known by your fruits, for every good tree bringeth forth good fruit, but an evil tree bringeth forth evil and corrupted fruit ..." Reverend James began.

"I know you do not find the reverend's sermons particularly impressive, but I feel that we should return on Sundays," Charles had said the night before.

"The more we search the scriptures, the better able we shall be to judge of the frailty and weakness of human nature and to make such observations, that during our short and transitory passage in these earthly regions, that very often unexpected storms and tempests arise. We are surrounded with approaching misfortunes and insurmountable troubles, and may compare the present situation to the mariner, who, for a series of years must go through dangerous scenes of chance and be tossed in the troubled ocean."

"It would be good for you to see people, to interact with the other ladies. You are not yourself, Eliza. I have been thinking at what has transpired between us, and the fault is entirely mine."

"I will not feign amicability, especially where it never existed," she had replied.

"Perhaps there is a new face, a new friendship you can cultivate. It does you no good to never leave the house."

Eliza barely stifled a yawn and looked down, studying the curves of her fingernails. Someone in the back of the church coughed. She looked up at the altar, adorned with depictions of the Ten Commandments, the Lord's Prayer, and the Creed. The lifeless eyes of Moses and Aaron looked back at her, and she found herself bothered by the artist's clear lack of proportion to their limbs and bodies. A fly buzzed near her and then assaulted a woman on the other side of the pew.

There were no friendships to be found in a place like this. Everyone sat upright, rigid with attention, but ultimately false in their intentions.

"If you so desire, we can continue to the bookseller. I believe he still keeps hours on Sunday morning. Or perhaps attend a meal with Lord Dunmore."

"If you mean to entice me, you are miserably failing," she had retorted.

"I only mean to start anew ..."

Reverend James' voice grew louder. "I look upon our small and humble congregation, and I am reminded of recent events that have transpired in the colony. There is no need to acquaint any who are here present with the sad occasion of what occurred on this island nigh a year ago. The earnest prayer and endeavor of all good men and loyal subjects ought to be that no such wickedness may hereafter be committed among us to the reproach of our nation and of the holy religion which we profess."

Eliza's dark eyes looked around the congregation, her mind desperate to wander.

"For which reason I have chosen for the subject of my following discourse, this solemn charge of the wise King Solomon to his son: 'My son, fear thou the Lord and the King: and meddle not with them that are given to change.' In which words are bound upon us three rules of life, very necessary to be observed by all who would not be deemed enemies to the public peace and tranquility."

The reverend cleared his throat.

"The first is, 'To fear the Lord.' The second is, 'To fear the King.' The third is, 'Not to meddle with those that are given to change.' Government, it is clear, cannot subsist where there are none who will submit to be governed and own their dependence upon their governors: there can be no sovereign where there are no subjects; no commanders where none will obey. To call anyone king and at the same time to rebel against his authority, what is this but to mock him with an empty title? We can rightly say that the governor, as acting agent of the sovereign, is likewise due the same respect and obedience."

Eliza's spine grew tense as she leaned forward in her seat, her heart beating in rapid strokes. This was not material she expected from the reverend. It spoke of political duty, not a celestial one. Lord Dunmore sat in the first pew, and from the quiver in his rotund shoulders, she could tell he was pleased.

"The unparalleled treason committed before us this past year and all the confusions and miseries consequent upon it may be ascribed to the neglect of this most necessary caution. Indeed, it can hardly be doubted that from the beginning of those unhappy troubles, there was a desperate man, one who held the lofty office of secretary to our royal governor, who had in view the utter subversion of the established government on this island and was resolved to stick at any villainy that might conduce the accomplishment of his end."

He continued and raised his nasally voice even louder.

"By this artifice, multitudes of undiscerning and unwary people, ye even some who are in attendance today, were drawn into his assistance, and to a criminal union with them, indeed even an intimate friendship at times, betraying all other oaths to king and country and even the most sacred institution of marriage. For where there is no loyalty to God, nor to the King, nay even his appointed ministers on this island, can it not be expected that no such loyalty is even observed with one's own spouse? Can we not observe how the sin of one man multiplies into the sins of the many?"

Reverend James had looked directly at her as he had said those words. Eliza shot up from the pew, her ears burning with anger. She stared with incredulous shock as the priest continued his sermon.

Charles yanked her back down to her seat.

"Would you sit and let the man finish his speech, my dear?" he whispered harshly to her.

Speech? Speech, indeed. This is no sermon, her mind raged.

Charlotte slowly turned her head to look behind her,

revealing the slightest smile behind her wavering lace fan.

Reverend James surveyed the room and then continued his pace.

"I have weighed my decision to recount the following encounter before you all, and I remain steadfast in my mission to promote the truth. For we are told that a time will come when the secrets of all hearts shall be opened and disclosed. Ezekiel 33:6 tells us we are responsible if we do not sound the trumpet when confronted with the truth, and though the sword may strike them down for their sins, it is we who will be accountable for their blood lest we fail to do so!"

He pounded his fist on the lectern. "I have witnessed a most tragic scene, of an individual who through the grace of God was afforded all of the privileges of wealth and prosperity, of domestic happiness even, and yet was still tempted beyond reproach to cast these luxuries aside and commit the sin of adultery. I call on this person now, repent and beg forgiveness of our God before it is too late."

Eliza's mouth hung open, the bottom of her eyes tingling with disbelief and shock. Charles' hands could not stop her this time. She rocketed upwards, deaf to the outburst of gasps and admonitions that sounded around her and raced to the back of the church, escaping into the bright sunlight outside. She looked around desperately for Julius to bring the carriage forward to take her back.

His booming voice rang out in the chapel yard. "— Man that is born of a woman hath but a short time to live, and so fast, so fleeting is the wing of time, that we are all soon brought to the same dust from whence we are sprung. 'For unbelievers, the corrupt, the immoral, and all liars—their fate is in the fiery lake of burning sulfur. This is the second death ...'"

She saw the groom then and signaled to him. Moved by the reaction on her face, Julius took off running. Charles now appeared through the doorway, sweat already beading on his brow. He looked flustered, eyes scanning the incoming carriage as it rolled up.

"Eliza, for God's sake, return inside. You incriminate yourself needlessly with your flight!" Charles said.

"Needlessly? Is it not obvious that he is set on embarrassing and shaming me at Lord Dunmore's directive?"

"Please find some measure of restraint!" he said.

Charles cast a helpless look at the silent tombstones as if the dead could bring him some form of aid. But Eliza had already set her mind on leaving.

Julius opened the carriage door, and she stepped inside. To her surprise, Charles joined right behind her and closed it. He banged on the frame of the carriage to begin their journey. As Christ Church receded into the background, her eyes welled up with tears of frustration and anger. She thought of all her past encounters with the reverend, the unfortunate aspects of their most recent encounter, and how she had first seen him at a ball, publicly intoxicated and in the arms of some lewd woman.

"God does not instruct us to pass judgment on others. God does not praise such arrogance. Is this man to be universally respected merely for his education, that he can read the antiquities, that he alone should interpret the gospels? Is he not also a fallible, corruptible man? I myself have seen no justification for treating him as anything else. Must everyone be expected to turn a blind eye to his behavior at every social event? What example does he set for his supposed flock?" she demanded.

Charles listened to her with wide eyes as the carriage rocked and rolled on the uneven road. He was focused on the diminishing outline of the church and its lonely, cluttered graveyard.

"Are you not a thinking man? Do you not carry emotions like any other person? How can you stand for this? He is so miserably confident of his own righteousness while passing judgment on the congregation he has sworn to protect. The man uses fear as instruction, just as the governor uses fear as the rule of law. They are well suited for one another. If Reverend James finds himself intolerant of any behavior, he dooms that person to damnation and hell without so much a cursory glance. Does he not see his *own* reflection in the mirror? How false he is! It is unheard of to draw attention to the actions and behaviors of individuals so clearly and distinctly; it is not Christian. It—"

"He failed to call you by name," Charles interjected.

"Do not waste time; we both know he was describing Jean and me. You are not a stupid man. Do not pretend to be one now."

"Still, I do not think it aided you to flee so abruptly."

She shook her head. "There is no turning back. Do not seek to comfort me with such foolish notions."

"I do not think we can return to church for quite some time."

"Damn him," she spat, "and may he burn for eternity in his perceived hell."

She thought she observed the slightest smile on Charles' features, and it did little to temper her anger. Of course he was pleased. She had been shamed in public, her secrets laid bare to the community, and all the ways she had wronged him brought to light. It occurred to her for a second time that he was involved with the disappearance of Philippe. Cleo had instructed the others to bring him to the orphanage, yet the boy had never made it there.

Eliza had always felt favored that she and Cleo had somehow accomplished the most perfect timing. After hours of unimaginable labor pain, she had finally delivered her son. The baby had been taken from her and swiftly removed from the house, and a few minutes later, Charles had finally returned home, none the wiser. What if he had run into Brutus and Josiah along the way? Cleo had told them to take the bush trail and to not use the main road. But what if he had seen something? He sat now, a hand to his chin, gazing out the window, the natural light making his eyes seem to glow.

She couldn't look at him without feeling defeated. She had tried to eliminate the threat he posed, and she had failed miserably. Now the score he made against her seemed even more abhorrent than before. And if she was wrong in her suspicions, if she ever uttered the truth about why she was ill that day, and he truly had no knowledge of it, then she would be ruined regardless. The calamity she had tried to evade would descend upon her even swifter if she ever questioned him. Eliza was beaten, exhausted, and rapidly drowning in despair.

She wanted to stop fighting, to stop struggling, to stop seeking another plan. She needed to find silence and peace. There could be no possible path for her future happiness here. She saw that clearly now, and in an odd way this thought alone brought her solace. She had come to a realization, and the effect of it had the power to change her life.

As they sat in silence, she watched the shifting clouds roll against the sky and was once again reminded of the beauty of the island. The carriage moved past tall grasses, banana trees, and fields of guinea corn. The sky was so brilliantly blue, and the palm fronds so vividly green. Life abounded in this place, and in all of its vibrant magnificence, she found her troubles temporarily diminished and soothed. She yearned to leave the small sphere of mankind and escape into the domains of nature, where neither the constraints of time nor society could threaten her. She wanted to stop feeling; she wanted to achieve a way of existing that was free from attachment. She wanted to truly escape.

CHAPTER IX.

Eliza heard Charles' boots thunder down the staircase, pause, and then he made a request of Lucy. She drifted into a drowsy state once again until she heard the sound of Alastor's gallops fading down the lane. The eerie feeling, that buzz in the still air sounded, and she sighed, forcing herself to wake up. She knew what that sound meant, and she did not want to deal with Tabitha that morning.

As she sat upright, the shrill electricity in the air slowly quieted, and she left the bed and gazed out the window. It was like any other morning, yet she knew that this day would be unlike every one that preceded it. Today was the first day she had not worried about her future or what the next day would bring.

The waves outside were growing rougher and the sky was darkened with heavy storm clouds. She had written a note last night, blotchy tearstains blurring one or two hastily written lines. The act of transcribing the message had nearly made her change her mind. But she had awoken with an unexpected sense of determination.

Her fingers grasped the folded note, and she reread the contents once again.

"Dearest Cleo,

Thank you for all you have done and for all that you have endeavored to teach me. I cannot bear the pain that I hold inside me any longer. I've resolved to quit this place once and for all. I have no desire to remain in a world without love. I have failed, and miserably so. By the time you read this, the ocean will have taken me. Thank you for making my stay here more tolerable. You were a constant solace to me."

Eliza laid the note on the unmade bed where she knew someone would find it. She made her way downstairs and left the house, waving away Lucy's offer of breakfast. The wind was picking up, and it blew her skirts about in an almost playful manner. Celia walked by her next, and the two women smiled at each other in the garden. Despite the beginning of their relationship, Eliza respected her. Celia had never lied to her. Celia had never promised her a glittering future and then sat passively by as it was stolen away.

Eliza gathered flowers alongside the white porch railing. In her pocket, a small glass vial of rum jingled against some coins. She would make one final offering today to Yemaya. The word sounded strange to her, yet familiar; the inexplicable yet comforting presence she had always felt in the water remained the same, only now it carried a name. Tears streamed down Eliza's face as she headed to the beach. She had faced so many fears and so many obstacles on this sand. She had found love and new hope, but those days were long past. A part of her cried that she wouldn't gaze upon its brilliance in the full sunlight again and that only a duller, stormier version of it loomed next to her.

The walk to the Black Reef seemed to pass by quickly with her focused footsteps. She felt more detached now and filled with silent purpose. Before, she had nearly been smothered from the sorrow and despair.

She was whole before she had met Charles. She had been filled with girlish hopes and the promise of the unknown. But now, the betrayal she felt only caused her unending misery.

She had done everything Cleo had said. She had wished so strongly with her heart, and she had made daily offerings of colorful petals and rum. She had felt it beginning to work, only for everything to so hideously fall apart. She had first lost Jean, then their child. She had tried to forgive Charles. And she had tried to make a final connection with him, the same man who had burned every possible opportunity for healing between them.

She oddly did not even spend much time thinking about him the past few days. They were merely two people who shared a house. She returned to eating her meals in solitude and had not exchanged any words with him since Sunday. She had achieved a perfect measure of seclusion, but in her isolation her feelings only pressed upon her mind relentlessly.

Eliza was about to leave this place, this endless cycle of insurmountable problems, the constant suffering, a place where the only glimpses of happiness were fleeting, and the sorrow weighed more. She was tired of pain, of being buried under sadness, of waiting for change. She once looked forward to the sunrise. It was a new start, and the most beautiful time of day on this island. But it was merely a distraction, and now distractions were not enough.

Yes, there could be change, but *when* and *how*? Events more terrible than the last continued to slam against her consciousness, and she was wise enough now to understand that there would be no reprieve. No one was coming to save her. Neither a messenger from the world of spirits nor a handsome stranger riding a brilliant white horse would come to her aid. The only person who could help her now was herself, and it was a painful lesson to bear.

She had disappointed her family and her parents. The people of this island looked down upon her with scorn, although their opinion caused her the least amount of turmoil. There was someone worse she had wronged. Eliza had failed herself. She had accomplished nothing since her arrival two years ago. She had become a woman through hardship and brutal force, not by merit or growth. She counted the birth of Phillipe as one of her greatest accomplishments, but it also served as one of her greatest failures. She couldn't even protect his future. And in doing so, she had destroyed her own.

The wind picked up as she walked closer to the edge of the rocks. The Black Reef was not black but a rough grey limestone outcrop that raced to the edge of the land and formed a sharp cliff face. Here one was reminded of the perilousness of this island. There was no beautiful beach or gentle slope of sand caressed by soothing water. The dark waves of the Atlantic thundered and slammed into the side of the rocks as if it was angry that this island interrupted its wide, unbroken vastness.

The Black Reef was more resemblant of a portal to a watery underworld and true to its nature, it had served such a purpose. The number of slaves who chose freedom on the other side of the cliff was untold. Charles had shared this sordid tale on her first night in New Providence, and like the sinister nature of the oleander leaves, the story always stayed in the back of her mind, waiting for an opportunity like today.

The pounding of the water overpowered any other noise, and occasionally, when all the waves aligned in one direction, their combined might would cause a burst of surf to shoot sky high. The front of her dress was already splattered with the remnants of such an explosion.

Matters in her life had grown worse than ever, and she could measure this by the absence of wonder as she stepped closer to the edge. The height was not very great, but it would do. If the water did not claim her, the sharp rocks and coral reef would help. It was the mixture of these forces, the deadly collaboration of nature's tools, that would finish anything trapped below, whether it be fish or man. At the Black Reef, the ocean was on display in all its formidable glory. The placidness of any other long beach on this island was not to be found. Instead, one encountered the very thing that made all men fear the sea, regardless of whether they eked a living out of it or not. Its energy was all consuming, like its relentless striking.

Things that once brought her joy no longer had the same effect on her. Nature only reminded her of the rawness of life now. Eliza thought of how excited she had once been to journey to this place, how Charles had promised to bring her to this spot after her arrival. Now he had driven her to it.

That first night always lingered in her memory. Why had it all gone so horribly wrong? She and Charles had finally united together after the strained journey by ship. This island held so much promise and possibility. Why had she said no to so many other men but chosen him that young summer day? What was the point of it all? What was *this* for?

There was something calling her to the edge. Eliza had someone waiting for her on the other side of this brutal world, and she only wanted to be with him. With Jean. He was an elusive source of happiness in her waking hours, but that could all change in an instant. This would be no end, but a reuniting. Eliza used to dread death, but now she viewed it not as a finality but as a transition.

She could feel him around her in some invisible, unknowable way, and this feeling had only grown stronger in recent days. She wished with all her heart to see him the way she could see other unexplainable things. She felt betrayed by the utter irrationality of it all. To lose sleep and keep company with ghosts who were unknown, yet never be visited in the same way by the one she loved racked her mind with cruelty. But every time she felt tired of surviving another day, the idea of this cliff she now stood on brought a degree of comfort. There was a way to quiet her lower emotions, once and for all. And it only required one single step.

Eliza walked barefoot to the edge, the sharp, piercing path nearly jarring her from her goal. The pain was distracting. Some of her steps were free of discomfort, but then, when it returned, it felt brutal on the soles of her feet. She looked down at the swirling water, allowing herself to become mesmerized by its power. A dull light flickered and danced on the surface.

She first released the rum into the water, followed by the coins and the yellow petals of the flowers she had picked. A few got stuck on the rough rocks of the cliff. She took a deep breath as a gust of wind enveloped her.

"Yemaya, I feel your presence. I always do. If I have offended you, if I have wanted too strongly, if I have asked for too much, forgive me."

She slowly untied the stained strip of cloth from around her wrist and held it aloft, the wind making it dance in the air.

"I have focused on the wrong things entirely and only realized it too late. I should have prayed to keep him from the moment I knew he grew within me, but I did not. I am a fool, and I do not ask for protection for myself any longer. It is a waste of breath. I instead ask that one day I will see him again in some unspeakable way. And I ask you, Yemaya, as a mother yourself, to ensure that my child knows nothing but love and protection in this life. That is all I ask. Please ... protect him. Let him find a truly loving home. With a father and a *mother* ..."

The last word was heavy and bitter on her tongue. Tears welled in her eyes, and she blinked them away.

"I have committed the gravest of mistakes. The greatest love is a child. I did not know my heart could be so consumed by love, a love without expectation. He filled a void within me whose depth was unknown before I held him in my arms. I mistakenly let him go, thinking I had made the right choice, but it has never felt right. In fact, he will never know me. And I can no longer stay here."

She released the strip of cloth then, and it was carried away, far from her eyes, red and streaming with tears. The wind whipped her hair around her face with a furious gust. She could feel Yemaya's presence in her bones. In an incomprehensible way, she knew that every word that had left her mouth was weighted and that her utterance had been heard.

She slowly undressed so that she was only in her shift, and she did not care when the buffeting wind began to slowly blow her crumpled dress away. The feeling that she was not alone came back stronger, and she could just see the darkened silhouette of a presence standing across the way in the edges of her vision. Tabitha must have followed her here.

The familiar, unsettling ring in her ears came next. Eliza could not do what Tabitha wanted, and she knew that the world would still turn and revolve on its own.

It was simply self-important to think that it needed her. The tides would still come in, and the moon would still rise without her presence. She shook her head as the ringing grew louder, then stepped off the ledge.

Eliza's surroundings seemed to blend into a painfully slow standstill, and in that moment when her feet left the ground and she descended, she looked up and saw Jean. He was as dimensional as a living man, his hand outstretched as if to clasp hers. The sight of him was an impossible phenomenon. She would have more easily believed that he had never died than comprehend what she saw now. The reddened ligature around his pale neck was the only signal belying how unnatural his presence was. He would have terrified her if it had not been so incredible to witness. He still looked so striking, his eyes beautiful from a distance, even without the necessary spark of life. His pale lips curved into the slightest smile. Jean was still everything she had ever wanted, and she yearned to go to him as if his form was still made of flesh.

"Water is a powerful thing, Miss Ellie. It is a veil between worlds," Cleo had once warned.

Eliza's arms flailed helplessly as she plummeted down into the water, his spectral outline still visible from below the surface. She heard disembodied voices next, but it was not the usual melodious sounds that soothed her. These voices were yelling.

She had made a mistake.

The water wasn't as cold as Eliza expected. Perhaps it was due to the shock coursing through her body and the instant pang of regret that circuited through her mind.

She had made a grievous error; she wanted to live. She closed her eyes as if to force herself to stir from some terrible dream, but she remained where she was. It was no dream. She floated weightless for a moment from the buoyancy of the water. The sea tried to hold her up, embracing her form in its invisible hold.

Then a wave pummeled her into one of the sharp rock walls. She instinctively pushed away from it and tried kicking back up, only for a swell to throw her to the other side. Even though she was a strong swimmer, she was no match for the force of this tide. There would be no peaceful surrender into oblivion. Her body knew better. She knew how to conquer water, how to hold her breath. She was conscious, and she could feel it all. This would be a fight against nature, a desperate urge to return to dry land, all the while knowing the odds were against her.

Eliza struggled to raise her head for a breath of air. Seawater burned down her nose to her throat, and she sank again. She was starting to lose focus. A wave hit her and knocked her back into the coral, cutting her thigh. She started to try to swim away from the rocks, but her attempts were fruitless. The current towed her under, and her legs struggled to kick but grew entangled in her shift. She tried to hold on to a wall, but her fingers could not grasp it.

The current ripped her from her would-be anchor, then mercilessly slammed her into it again. She spun around like a piece of sea grass, helpless with every fluctuation and turn. Each assault from the churning waves tore at her skin. Her gasps for air did not suffice; water only seized the opportunity to rush down her mouth. It filled her ears this time, and she lost her orientation completely. Down appeared up until she regained sight of the light grey sky and twisted herself towards it.

She prayed for relief, cursing her situation and regretting her stupidity. Eliza kicked as hard as she could, desperate to control her own body and make for the open water. She struggled and made no further progress, the surf swallowing her whole once more.

It was then that she realized she would never leave the water. That the haven she had once sought would become her final torment. The sea had been her one comfort, but now it would take her life.

A surge came, and her head crashed against the wall behind her, and she succumbed to a roaring, swirling darkness.

Charles dismounted from his horse, his nostrils flaring with irritation. He could not afford to be late to his meeting with the governor. He had not been briefed as to its purpose, but he knew enough to surmise it concerned something urgent. He marched up the steps and into the house.

"Lucy! Lucy!" he called, searching the parlor. "Where is that damned slave?"

She came running from the back, wiping her hands on her apron.

"Yes, Lord Sharpe?" Her dark eyes were huge.

"I asked you to retrieve my saber from the smith's yesterday. You did not return it to its rightful place."

"Oh, I'm sorry, Lord Sharpe. Yes, Lord Sharpe, right away, my pleasure."

She took off running to another room and returned with the saber.

He grabbed it from her and was just about to step outside when Cleo and Celia rushed towards them.

"Lord Sharpe! Wait a moment!" Cleo cried.

He stopped, his hand retracting into an angered fist. "What is it, Cleo?"

Celia's voice took over when Cleo's faltered.

"It's Lady Sharpe, sir. She is in trouble! She went down to the Black Reef! She intends to end her life!"

Cleo waved the note in the air, a hand on her chest trying to steady her breath. Charles said nothing. He knew from their joined reaction and the sinking of his heart that it was not a ruse. He dropped his saber on the floor. He was out the door in moments, Alastor galloping as fast as the rough road would let him.

As Eliza's body was pulled one way and then another, suddenly, her vision returned. She was hovering near the bottom of the pool, her skirt wedged in a crevice. A sharp pain flooded her chest as her lungs burned for air. She kicked and kicked, the banging pressure of her heart nearly unbearable. Above, she saw a figure looking down at her. At first, she prayed that it was Jean, but then a mottle of red peered over the edge.

She knew it was Charles. She still wanted to reach the surface, but she also feared him. She wanted to hide in the rocks, to become unseen. If she did not die this way, she feared what end she would meet in his company.

But then, a hand was extended like a branch, and her instincts drove her to reach for it. There was no time for past grievances or sore feelings, only the need for survival. The rock on the bottom that posed an impassable obstruction shifted ever so slightly as she struggled. One more kick, and she felt herself freed. A huge swell ploughed into the reef, pulling her upwards.

In that moment, Eliza rushed higher with the water as it surged, and she grabbed hold of Charles' hand. She felt herself ascend towards the edge of the drop, the fringe of rock grazing her abdomen. Charles was leaning on his stomach, and in one movement, he stood, pulling her with him. They made contact, and she was returned to level land.

They stood in front of each other like two strangers. He was breathing heavily, his green eyes panicked and dilated. She looked incredulously down at the ground, her torn shift clinging to her skin, translucent in the light. Then, as if she was not truly in possession of her soaked body, she felt herself take one more step towards him and embrace him.

He stiffened up at first. She couldn't tell if it was from the dampness of her skin or from the shock of her actions. They stood there without words as she clung to him in the wind. Then she weakened, her muscles shaking and unsteady, and Charles used his arms to support her back. Eliza buried her face in his red jacket and started to sob. His frame was a strange and steady relief after the incessant movement of the waves. Pink spots of watery blood began to appear on her shift where the limestone had cut her. She waited for the anger and reproach she knew all too well from him, but it did not come. Rather, his other hand moved up from her lower back to her shoulders to cradle her. She did not cringe or recoil from him. She allowed his touch and remained there. His uniform was soaked from the rain and the sea, but the heat from his chest made it a comforting refuge.

It began to pour in earnest now, the wind blowing the raindrops at a painful, biting angle. Charles scooped her up, carried her back to the beach, and helped her onto his horse. From this height, the reef looked even more menacing. She felt the warmth from Alastor underneath her hand and marveled that she was still alive.

She looked across the way for Jean, knowing that he would no longer be there. The sad knowledge that she would most likely never gaze upon him again filtered over her. They belonged to two separate worlds, and unlike the hours that passed before, she knew now that she wanted to remain here. With a baffling sense of purpose, Eliza knew that she belonged. She could not explain why or what precisely had changed, but she knew her place was not with death.

Charles urged Alastor into a gallop, and the dark horse carried them away from the slippery rocks.

CHAPTER X.

The dappled light danced on the hallowed stone floor. Eliza looked up from her contemplation to see Charles standing motionless beside her, his bearing as composed as a statue, his heart hardened like rock. The organ played a hymn unbearably loud as a memory she had tried to banish from her thoughts haunted her.

"May the Lord mercifully with his favor look upon you, that ye may so live together in this life, that in the world to come ..." the old minister droned. His voice, twisted and distorted, turned deeper and darker, transforming into the more recent and judgmental tones of Reverend James. *"The secrets of all hearts shall be opened and disclosed, Eliza. Eliza ... what are you hiding?"*

The notes of the organ expanded in grandeur, a fiery blast of air, full and heavy as it resounded through her ears. She tried to move away from the noise, but she was planted in the spot. A feeling of weight pressed down on her arms.

"Eliza ... Eliza!"

The pressure did not relent, and she finally opened her eyes.

The stark light of the cloudy sky blinded her as she awoke in a bed that was not her own. She could hear the waves again, but this time the sound came from a more distant place. Eliza took a sharp breath as she realized where she was and recalled what she had tried to do. What she had *failed* to do.

A sharp pain like a knife in her side jabbed her into further consciousness. She realized the pain occurred every time she took a deep breath, and she panicked, fearing she had broken something. She tried to raise herself up and saw that Cleo had lightly wrapped a strip of cloth over her breasts but that her torso was exposed, riddled with red and plum-darkened patches along her sides.

"Your ribs are not broken, thank God, but they are badly bruised," Charles said.

Hearing his voice only caused Eliza to try to rise up further. She had not anticipated his presence quite so soon. She recalled what she had done on the rocks and how, in a moment of weakness, she had clung to him. She started to cough from the panic and couldn't steady her breathing. The deep ache that spread from her ribs to her lower back was pervasive and spiked with intensity whenever she moved.

Eliza feared she would have to cough again, so she kept her breaths shallow. The rest of her body felt stiff and sore from fighting the waves. The noises around her sounded distorted, and when she tilted her head, she could feel the water inside her ears. And now that her skin was dry, she could feel every cut on her body. The pain from her legs touching one another was unbearable. Scrapes like red marks from an unseen paintbrush marked her calves and thighs. The broken pink flesh stuck to the other parts of her skin, and she found it hard to lie still comfortably. This ordeal was made no easier with the present company she kept.

Charles hovered over her again, a bowl in one hand, as he dabbed a scratch on her forehead. She winced.

"Do you require more laudanum?" he asked, his green eyes studying her face.

"No!" she exclaimed, remembering her first encounter with that tincture. She knew she was being irrational; the laudanum would ease her pain. But she had never forgotten how Lord Dunmore had once tried using it to force an intimate acquaintance with her. She tried to brush those disquieting thoughts away.

Eliza allowed Charles to continue dressing her wounds despite the protest that burned within her. He was treating her skin very gently, but she wanted to recoil from his attentions. On the rocks, she had succumbed to a whirl of raw emotions and desperate gratitude. Now she only felt foolish and awkward beside him. She no longer understood the place they occupied in relation to one another, and she still feared delayed anger from him.

Eliza wondered how long she had lain in this bed and why she had been placed here. A shrill whirring noise racketed along the clapboards of the house outside as if in answer to her queries. There was still a storm raging over the island. Charles observed her take notice of the situation outside.

"I brought you up here because you needed to lie down. If the storm worsens, my room should be the least affected. It's connected to the strongest wall in the house. We do not want to have to move you multiple times. You need to rest."

All she could think about was moving. She wanted to flee from the room. His words did not make sense to her. In past times, they had sought shelter downstairs. There was a chaise in the parlor she could recline on. Moreover, it was an open area with multiple entries and exits. Here she felt undeniably trapped.

She waited for a conclusive reaction from him with dread. Charles appeared calm for the moment, but she knew better than to trust his outward display of concern. She knew only too well that an explosive current ran through this man. His fury was all-consuming when ignited.

Charles worked his way down towards her neck with the damp rag, then moved her hair.

"This will hurt," he said as he examined the area and then carefully wiped it. "Cleo crafted this poultice. She said it would help your wounds heal much quicker."

Eliza wondered why Cleo wasn't administering this medicine herself. She found it hard to lie still in his bed when it only conjured unpleasant memories. The longer she remained on her back, the more vividly her reasons for seeking the Black Reef returned to her. The unsteady pendulum of her emotions was making her queasy. Her nerves were wracked with anxiety, and she wanted to be left alone.

"You press too hard!" Eliza whimpered as he navigated between torn flesh and bruises.

"I hardly press at all …"

"I fear something has happened to my neck," she said as she reached to feel it.

"It is there, I assure you." Charles reached for a bowl. "Your collarbone is bruised and tender. That is the sensation you feel."

He continued applying Cleo's potion, his presses growing more gentle as he moved to her chest. She lay there staring at the ceiling, occasionally stealing a glance at him when she knew he was not looking directly at her. He had removed his jacket, but his clothes remained the same. She could tell from the brown streaks of blood on his shirt. His face seemed haggard, his eyes small and lined with exhaustion. The usual hardened expression he carried seemed rattled now.

It was clearly morning. Had he slept at all? She looked over to his side of the bed. It appeared untouched.

"You weren't wearing the clothes you usually wear for swimming," he said abruptly. "Nor did you have your hair braided."

His perceptive eyes were fixed on her. It seemed clear that the reaction she was waiting for was nearly upon them.

"I was not trying to go swimming."

He stared at her for a moment; then he moved to treat the lower part of her legs. She seized up immediately, clamping her legs shut, but he waved a hand of reassurance. He waited for a moment, then continued dabbing her shins.

"I do not recommend leaving a farewell note to a slave who cannot read. Although it seems I have miscalculated Celia's talents," Charles said, his voice slow and measured.

Eliza did not respond. She found it easier to focus on the cuts and scrapes he tended than on the words that left his lips. Perfect red lines ran in one diagonal shape and then another on her skin.

"I won't ask you why you did it," he said, rotating a bruised ankle.

Eliza remained silent. She felt wildly uncomfortable lying in his large bed, injured and helpless, while he stood up and walked about. She wanted Cleo here instead. Perhaps if she kept talking, Cleo would hear her voice and come back into the room.

"Your meeting with the governor ... how did it go?"

She had asked the question without fully realizing how false she sounded.

"I think we both know that I was preoccupied with other matters yesterday."

His tone bordered on the edge of annoyance. Eliza instinctively raised herself up on the bed, then grimaced from the effort.

"Don't move; stay as you are. You are lucky no bones were broken on the rocks," he said, returning to the side of the bed. He gently pushed her shoulders back down.

"I bruised my ribs on a campaign once. My horse was

shot out from underneath me. It took nearly two weeks to heal. I do not envy you," he said, placing the bowl on the nightstand.

She wished her silence would make him leave. Tears began to well in her eyes. She had not resolved anything by her actions. Indeed, it seemed that she had placed herself in an even worse situation.

"Would you like some brandy?" he asked.

She paused, her stomach twisting at the idea of feeling more incapacitated. He seemed to perceive her thoughts.

"For the pain. To help ease the pain," Charles clarified softly.

"No."

"Then you should take the laudanum," he said, reaching for something next to her pillow.

"No, no, I am fine. Thank you," she said.

A spoon appeared at her mouth, and the act was done so quickly she could barely register a protest. Now she began to cry in frustration.

"You must take something for the pain, Eliza. It is for your benefit," Charles said.

The door creaked open, and Cleo appeared.

"Lord Sharpe, you should rest now. You stayed up with her all night. Let me watch her," she said, her presence enough to dominate the room.

"Yes, thank you, Cleo. I think I will. I'll rest in the parlor downstairs."

Eliza watched him walk out of the room. He seemed to be acting differently, and it made her uneasy. Once he was gone, Cleo locked eyes on her.

"Miss Ellie," she said as she shuffled to the chair beside the bed. "I always have words for you, but this time, I do not know what to say."

"I cannot do this any longer; I cannot—" Eliza said, sobbing.

"If Celia did not read that note, if he had not left his saber here … madness. Madness, Miss Ellie," she said, her dark eyes bulging with vexation. "You are too smart for that. I never want to see you do something stupid again. Do you hear me?"

Eliza gingerly shook her head. "I am the most wretched of beings. I would willingly bear whatever catastrophe would leave me no room to feel. This sadness, it is unbearable. I am torn in pieces by the force of my grief. What difference could limestone do to my flesh? I foolishly thought I could kill myself, but even this task I could not accomplish.

"I tried to be strong, Cleo, I have tried. But I failed. And now I am more at his mercies than I ever was before. I saw him," Eliza cried.

"Saw who?"

"I saw Jean. I thought I wanted death. I thought there was nothing left for me here. My thoughts revolved around Philippe. But in the last moment, the very last moment before I took my final step, I thought I could be with Jean again, and as I stepped off the edge, I saw him. He had his hand raised as if to touch me, but it was too late. I had jumped off already. The water was so violent, I was afraid …"

"Now listen, Miss Ellie, you *must* stop talking about

that man. No good ever came from him, and no good ever will. Stop talking about him. Stop asking about him. Let him rest. He is not a part of this world any longer, and you can never join him. You *cannot* do that," Cleo said, her voice stern.

"I love him," Eliza sobbed. "I love him, and I didn't even realize it until I saw the life leave his eyes. Do you know what that feels like, Cleo? To realize something and to lose it all in the very same moment? I cannot bear it, but I did it a second time. I willingly gave you my son. I let him be taken from the room to a fate unknown, and now he is gone."

"You cannot talk about that anymore. Do you understand? You cannot think about that man anymore. Look at what it has made you do. You do have something to live for; you only need to find it," Cleo said.

It seemed as if her eyes dampened with emotion as well.

"I want to believe you, Cleo, I truly do. I made the offerings for Yemaya, I made them every week. I spoke to her before I jumped. I believe it all, but I cannot fathom it. It makes no sense."

"And what did you ask for?" Cleo asked.

"I prayed for him. For, for Philippe. That he will find love, that he will have a father and another mother ..." Eliza replied, her voice cracking. "He was so beautiful, and I let him slip through my hands. I cannot forgive myself. I wanted to escape this terrible life. I couldn't stand this existence for a single day longer. But once I was in the sea, I regretted what I had done. I was so scared; I thought the waves would never stop tossing me. I wanted to drown to be done with the pain … but then I so desperately wanted to be above the water again. I truly cannot comprehend how I lie here now."

Cleo looked at her, her eyes huge.

"Even you are speechless. Why am I still alive? There is nothing for me here. That is what drove me to the reef to begin with. I have lost everything. I have lost my home, the love of my parents, Jean, my son … I have no virtue, I have no honor, I have nothing, Cleo. I am *nothing*."

Her voice trailed off as she felt the laudanum take command of her body. Time lengthened and moved on. Muffled voices in the hallway revealed that Cleo had left her side. Eliza worried that Charles would return. The conversation was too distant to hear clearly, but the voices were heated.

She heard Cleo's words, a harsh whisper: "You need to tell her!"

The conversation was drowned out by the wind battering the house and then the slow, dull thudding of her heartbeat as Eliza drifted into a stiffened sleep.

She awoke to a booming noise so loud it could not possibly be thunder. Charles and Cleo were gone, and her candle was burning perilously low. In the dim light, she could just make out a shape through the dark windowpane, and what she saw caused her to rush closer to the window. As soon as she did, she recalled why she was bedridden in the first place, and she cursed. The pain she'd initially felt when she woke up hours before had now doubled.

Charles was right; the laudanum was indeed a comfort. It seemed as if any sort of movement caused her agony. She had taken the art of breathing for granted before, but now she was acutely aware of every rise and fall of her chest.

Eliza steadied her breathing and held her posture in a careful, deliberate way. She fixed her eyes on the ocean beyond the house as an invisible, whirring sound cruised through the air and blasted apart a tall shape in the distance. The glowing burst of flames reflected in the wavy pane of glass, and Eliza stood spellbound by what she was witnessing.

It was a merchant vessel. The terrible noise resounded again and again as the burning ship loomed closer to their shore. Flames engulfed its frame, and then it issued a dire moan as it foundered on the reef. She watched as the men inside it began to flee like rats escaping a trap. Another cannonball wrecked the main mast, and it creaked and toppled into the sphere of fire beneath it.

In a daze, Eliza slowly put on her shift and descended the creaking stairs, wincing when a pungent smell assaulted her nostrils. She looked around the bottom of the staircase in disbelief at the strength of the sour odor when she saw a dark puddle. It was blood. When she looked down the hallway toward the side porch, she realized she was not alone. Wounded men leaned against the walls of the main hallway, moaning with anguished cries. She gasped and then gagged at the stench, the motion a severe blow to her bruised ribs.

A wet, sticky hand latched on to her ankle.

"*Aidez moi!*"

Eliza retreated in horror. A man a few years older than her, with blood streaming down his face, was fixated on her. He clutched his side and gnashed his teeth in pain. It did not seem to matter to him that she was horrified or that she was wearing only her shift. He needed help, and he expected her, or anyone for that matter, to give him aid.

Eliza pulled away from his trembling hand and kept walking, stepping over huddled masses, each man seemingly more disfigured than the next. Shells exploded in the distance outside of the house. A man with blonde hair watched her, and as she passed him, she noticed a wide hole where his cheek should have been, his gums stained with blood and vacant of teeth. Across from him, a boy no older than sixteen gripped his right thigh, but that did nothing to stop the torrent of blood spurting from underneath his breeches.

The men in the hallway were writhing in agony, a jumble of curses and prayers to Mary the Mother of God constant on their wounded lips.

"*Je vous salue, Marie, pleine de graces, le Seigneur est avec vous ...*" one voice said.

"*... et Jesus le fruit de vos entrailles, est beni. Sainte Marie, Mere de Dieu, priez pour nous pecheurs ...*" another whispered in agony.

Eliza approached the end of the hallway with confusion. The scene beyond the door presented an even more bewildering sight than the one within. The smell of acrid smoke and sulfur now assaulted her nostrils, the air harsh on her lungs. The ship was completely ablaze. A wall of scorching fire reached nearly ten feet high, crawling up the shrouds and consuming everything in its path. A giant cloud of black smoke billowed out to the west. The popping of glass and crash of wood drew her notice to the back of the ship. The captain's quarters and every single gun port was bright with orange flames. Vivid flashes signaled more explosions as the heat consumed the stores in the hull of the ship.

The wailing of shells deafened Eliza, and she covered her ears. She did not know if the artillery fire could reach the house, but the ceaseless bombardment seemed so close. Another group of sailors lay waiting outside, in front of the porch. The sand beneath one man was darkened with gore as he shrieked in pain. The person next to him did not fare much better, his body racked with the agonies of the dying. She watched dumbly, helplessly, fearing that these mortally wounded men would continue to live for far too long as they writhed in agony on the ground without the possibility of easing their suffering.

Eliza was so transfixed by these two men that she at first did not realize the gravity of the display before her. The piteous screams of crippled and dying men sounded further down the beach as well. There was a crawling effect of the ground, of the sand moving, filled with forms of the dead and dying. Eliza reeled, clutching the railing of the porch. Every blast of cannon made her heart feel fainter, and she began to detest the sound. The fear and panic in the air made it impossible for her to think clearly. She wanted to be far away from this. She thought of what she had tried doing to her body, that she had elected to throw away the one thing that now proved so elusive to the quivering men around her.

A wave of nausea rolled up her chest. Chaos surrounded her, and she felt so very alone. Her life flashed before her mind in static and shaking pictures punctuated by the whirring of shellfire. Eliza felt an astounding urge to live, to stay alive, to survive this debacle. She scanned the property for a single familiar face, someone to keep her fear from paralyzing her completely.

She saw now with squinting eyes that field hands were stacking a heap of corpses on the dune to the left of her. Some bodies were recognizable forms, others only mutilated pieces. These men, alive only minutes before, were now rendered as inanimate as cordwood by the merciless rain of shells. Or perhaps they had drowned in the waves. Men's heads bobbed in the water; some able to swim, others taken under by debris and the current.

And then she saw him.

Charles was shirtless, the water up to his waist as he pulled victims of the shipwreck to shallower depths, where Josiah handed them to a second slave. She could tell he was shouting, giving commands to those around him and generating some form of order in the pandemonium, as if he alone was capable of controlling the commotion. She watched what she imagined he had been like on the battlefield during the war in America, and for the first time, it appeared to her that his coarseness, his commanding presence, his bodily strength, and the fury he barely contained within himself was balanced in a fiery environment like this. She saw a benevolence in his strength that she had once thought inconceivable.

Charles shouted again, directing both the slaves and one of the sailors who was able to walk. She could not understand what they were attempting to do now, but one thing was abundantly clear. He was a voice of reason when logic seemed lost. He was leading. He was being selfless. He was keeping men alive.

These men were French. They were not his own soldiers. He had no duty to fulfill here, and yet he seemed blind to this fact. One man reached with outstretched hands towards him, struggling to stay afloat. Charles dove under the water and put his arm around the man's shoulders, pulling him to safety.

A shattering crash made the earth tremble with a blast so loud she felt the reverberation in her body. Eliza hit the porch on her knees as she instinctively ducked away from the final blinding explosion. She covered her face with her hands, cowering in fear. An eerie quiet followed, with only the flames audible as the breeze carried some of the latent heat to her.

A strange sensation, one that she had previously thought impossible, rose inside of her. This singular thought rang out in her mind against the unnatural stillness around the house. Eliza slowly rose to a painful stand, gritting her teeth, her eyes focused only on the spot where Charles had stood before. No men stood there now. A slow, sinking feeling of dread overtook her. The sky grew thick with black smoke. There were no more men left struggling in the water. The ship had completely keeled over the side, and only a small portion of one of the masts was spared by the fire. And now, in the distance, she could see the dark shadow of a second ship, a familiar ship. A ship that flew their colors.

One of His Majesty's vessels prowling the turbulent ocean.

Tears welled up in Eliza's eyes. The beauty and the peace of her small section of the island, her haven and sanctuary, had utterly been destroyed. And for what purpose? Her mind returned to the unintended and confused thoughts that swirled in her head. She looked back to the spot where Charles was last seen.

Concern burned through her gut. It was unfamiliar, and most of all, it was unwanted. She had always been so convinced of her feelings that it seemed a cruel joke to suddenly be in possession of anything but hatred towards him. Everything around her seemed disorienting, from the lingering dullness of the laudanum she had swallowed to the violence and tumult on her doorstep to the peculiar feelings for him she now harbored.

He was still nowhere to be seen. Eliza's anguish doubled. She steadied herself on the railing, suddenly realizing her right foot was covered in someone else's blood. She hadn't even noticed until now. Shaking in disgust, she went to move to the water bowl on the porch when a group of men rushed the stairs. A hand was on her shoulder, and she turned, her heart seizing up in terror.

It was Charles. His breeches were soaked and stuck to his skin, and his hair was wet and sticky with salt. He too was covered in other men's blood. She gaped at him.

"Don't be afraid," he said, looking at her square in the eyes.

Relief flooded over her, but she refused to speak it aloud.

"They need assistance; why isn't Josiah going to them?" she said instead.

Charles looked to where she pointed but did not react.

"These men, these men here!" she exclaimed, looking to the two men who had been closest to her.

"Eliza, they are dead," he said quietly.

She looked again for confirmation, her lower lip trembling. Their lack of movement seemed to confirm his words. She started to cry again.

"What does this to men?" she asked, speaking to herself. "To their bodies ... what kind of artillery ..."

"Other men," he answered bluntly.

"I don't want to die."

"You don't?" Charles asked, wryness escaping from his voice.

She knew she made no sense to him; she barely made any sense to herself.

"Here," he said, fumbling with the belt around his waist. He handed her a flintlock pistol. "Go back upstairs and have this ready at your side until I return."

The gun was heavy in her shaking hands.

"When you fire do not get scared of the flash, and leave it on your target for a three count."

Eliza did not want to hold the gun, and she certainly did not want a lesson in firing one. But after what she had just witnessed, it did offer some measure of security. Even if she couldn't fire it properly, she could at least intimidate others with the sight of it. She sighed and lowered it.

"What happened? I don't understand ..." Her voice was a barely audible whisper.

"It seems as if our navy had orders to fire on this ship," he said darkly. "It fired back in defense. There was a volley between them. The French ship sunk on the reef."

"Why are you saving them if the French are attacking us?"

"These aren't French soldiers. They are merchants, and the navy damned well knows that," he added bitterly. "Anyone can tell by the rigging of the ship. It is a merchant ship. In fact, you are already acquainted with them. These are your acquaintances from the cave."

He offered a dry half-smile and bounded off the porch to where Josiah and Julius were waiting for him on the dune.

CHAPTER XI.

Eliza lost track of time. She only understood that something terrible had happened on this island, something much bigger than herself or the dark pathos that had driven her to the Black Reef, and she struggled to comprehend it all. The night had come and passed, and with it, a new day began, but it did little to lessen the horror outside the windows.

A series of loud steps rushed up the top stairs. The door swung open, startling her, and she reached for the pistol. Its weight was strange in her hands, and it slipped in her grip as she struggled to hold it straight. Charles' face appeared, stained with the blood of strangers. He offered a disarming hand gesture.

She dropped the gun.

"May I sit in here with you?" he asked.

Eliza did not answer and started pushing the pistol across the bed.

"No, hold it a while longer," he replied, pointing to the firearm as he sat down in the chair across from the bed. "You may need it yet."

There was a pause in the conversation amidst the sound of men shouting outside. A relentless metallic scrape of shovels against crystalline sand followed it.

"Where did you learn to do that?" she finally asked, her gaze shifting from the blurred glass of the window to his haggard face.

"What is your meaning?"

The old wooden chair creaked as he shifted his weight.

"Retain your calm when the world around you is on fire ..." Her voice trailed off into nervousness, unsure of how he would react. His gaze bore down on her, then he softened into a laugh.

"Indeed, it is the only time I feel such calm," he said, rubbing his jawline. "I, of course, am usually alone in this sentiment."

"Was that a battle?" Eliza asked.

"You could give it that name."

"I thought battles were planned in advance, with due preparation."

"Formal battles in this age are few and far between. Chaos is a better name for it."

"I did not know we were at war with France," she whispered.

He nodded. "Yes. On paper, officially by decree, we now are. But you could be forgiven for not realizing it, for this has been an ongoing struggle for quite some time. There has been no trust between our nations for centuries, I wager."

"And it has come all the way to our small island."

"That is the cost of empire. Without it, we would not be here," Charles responded, his voice growing louder.

"Civilization," she replied faintly.

Having finally seen every side of such an empire firsthand, it seemed to Eliza too great a cost to bear. To think that she had spent the majority of her life sheltered in ignorance and seclusion seemed a cold and hollow thought. She had never spent much time pondering the meaning of British rule. That she, as a subject of the king, had some stake in all of this. She had not thought about the human lives that fueled it, some by choice and others under duress. That the rule and wealth of a select few determined the fate of many.

A day ago, ideas of sovereignty, duty, and glory would have served as immediate and nearly thoughtless answers to what empire consisted of. It was not only land; it was dominion. It was measured by colonies marked with colorful flourishes on a map in all corners of the world. But dominion meant much more than that, and now a singular thought captured hold of her mind.

Perhaps the idea of greatness she attributed to British supremacy had all but supplanted ideals like freedom and natural rights. How could the elected members of Parliament possibly know the goings-on of colonies across the seas, thousands of miles away? What force of providence could limit the greed and selfishness innate to mankind when ordinary men, ill-suited for the task at hand, were given power over tiny kingdoms in the ocean? What could be an empire's fate when it was built on the blood and sweat and backs of others? Men whose voices and ideas had no surety of ever being heard, and some men whose voices were housed in enslaved bodies?

Eliza realized it was not only *this* empire that caused her distress. There were other empires willing and eager to take its place, the results of that struggle literally sat huddled a floor below them, caked in blood and misfortune. But if Britain herself sat on a thin rope between annihilation and greatness, between the destruction and the glory it so desperately sought, what measured steps would it take to reach the latter? Every empire had to ascertain the imperceptible boundaries of nature, to contest its own unknowable yet looming mortality. How bright could the flame of the Crown burn before it sputtered into darkness?

The sun had disappeared behind a bank of heavy, violet clouds. Eliza watched the figures of the field hands working and tending to the men as they silently moved up and down the sand dune. What if this empire took a step in a different direction? What if it worked to abolish the one thing that it stood to profit the most from? What if instead of espousing freedom for a few, it granted freedom to those whom no country would yet set free?

It was a juxtaposition that haunted her, a moral dilemma she could not soothe. She knew that others shared her thoughts, but this island's isolation was a damning circumstance. The abolition of the slave trade seemed to exist only through the optimistic words of enlightened men and women on paper. At its worst, it seemed an impossible ideal.

As she pondered the bleak reality of her society, she

was reminded just as intensely of the pride she carried in her heart for Britain. Britain was a beacon of ingenuity, of progress, of stability. Her subjects left their familiar confines and chose to cross dangerous waters bringing ideas and inventions to foreign shores.

Eliza thought of the lost colonies in America. She did not understand everything about that conflict, but she knew enough now to see that they had once been Englishmen and had diverged to a different path. Britain had sown seeds of freedom, of common law, of natural rights. It seemed only fitting that under such prosperous beginnings, under such benevolent guidance, a new nation could be born. One that took a step further than its predecessor in its quest to banish injustice, throwing off the shackles of a constitutional monarchy for a constitutional republic. A land where the power rested within its citizens. A government that served the people. It was a radical and dangerous idea, a noble experiment at best.

Yet America also faced similar trials. How would that fledgling nation, birthed in the fury of freedom, administer independence to its people? The newly formed states, fringed by the Atlantic, would serve as a stage to the world in lessons of liberation and self-governance. Its success was far from guaranteed. A new century beckoned in the distance, and she wondered how the world would fare.

"What if they were right?" Charles suddenly asked, breaking her reverie.

"Beg pardon?"

"I spent nearly seven years destroying men who

thought like me, with the same principles as me ... in the name of honor ..." he said, his palms extended in thought.

Eliza was taken aback by his comment, at the strange appearance of having just speculated such similar concepts. It was as if their internal dialogues had serendipitously merged into a single stream of connected thought. She knew exactly what he was speaking about; she had wondered the same thing herself many times before. Her heart began to pound, anxious for him to continue speaking.

"You were fulfilling your duty for King and country. Surely there is honor in that," she said.

Her statement was intended as a slight. She wanted him to continue in the epiphany she so desperately wished he was having. His subsequent scoff was confirmation that she was on the right course.

"Would to God I were. I fear the honor is theirs. Lord Dunmore ... that man ruled over them too. Virginia was a nest of seditious serpents. I understand Massachusetts. They lit the spark; their rebellion was barbaric in nature. But Virginia ... all that landed wealth. Men not unlike me. Their rebellion was formulaic, philosophic, poetic. They took the animalistic urges of Boston and fashioned them into a campaign for *freedom* and *liberty*. They sustained that spark from the north, and it spread like wildfire. Why did such rage spring from there, spreading like a contagion to the other colonies?" Charles shifted his weight in the chair, then continued.

"I did not see it. I did not wish to see it, but it was in

front of me time and again. Do not mistake my words. I do not blame the king. I can see it all so clearly now. How could he possibly choose the right course when he was advised by such incompetent fools? The lies of Lord Germain, spineless Lord North ... that man singlehandedly lost America. How could a divided cabinet and a multitude of departments work to win a war when they could not be united by a single policy? When our government was stalemated by inadequacy? Our system is faulted, and it is severely so."

"I am not as well-versed in politics as you are. I was a young girl when that war occurred," she replied quietly.

"It was always a matter of balance. Diplomacy is like tuning the pendulum of a clock. If only our leaders had been wiser. What if we had simply redressed their grievances?" he demanded. "We met them with fury and bayonets and slaughtered them as if they were foreign enemies, tearing father from son, brother from brother. Allegiance. Loyalty. We had to not only conquer a foreign land and keep it in our possession, we needed to restore amity between ourselves. How miserably we failed.

"They told me it was an unhappy country, destined for endless anarchy and bloodshed. Are they not saying the same now of France? Our leaders told us the rebels were not even worthy of the conventions of war. We were to go in and rescue our fellow subjects from despotism, from the cruel yoke of congress and committees, of arbitrary tyranny. What if the Americans had the foresight to clearly see the ills that riddle *our* government?

"The more years that pass, the more it all seems a chimera," he confessed. "We were told there were swathes of loyal men who needed our protection, only to find time and time again that it was not so. And when we *were* fortunate to find them, we did not trust the allegiance of those who came to us! We did not restore civil government in our strongholds; we ruled over them like they were recalcitrant children.

"We jeopardized our security in our other colonies to wage that damned war, and when France allied with them, we could have lost it all. All those lives wasted, all the money squandered. Only to lose our objective so spectacularly. The Americans were here once, you know; they captured this island. That governor handed them the very keys." Charles scoffed once again. "This colony could have so easily fallen. Its fate is precarious at best, and it only gives me cause to ponder one question. *Who* is the better man, Eliza? Who does the hand of providence truly guide?"

She sat in the bed, breathless, as he finished his torrent of words.

"You told me that once the decision to go to war by king and parliament has been determined, the private sentiments of every man should give way to service in times of crisis," Eliza responded.

She could tell from his face that it was a bitter reminder and that perhaps he had never fully believed that himself.

"Yes, but it now appears to me that my duty as an officer and my duty as a man are no longer compatible. I do not often speak, Eliza; indeed, I hesitate to speak, if only to stop the flow of incongruous thoughts spilling from my mind. They torture me. For unlike other men, I cannot subdue such thoughts with drink or the promise of riches. They run ceaselessly through me, again and again, and I am confronted with my weakness. I hate myself for my inability to act. I curse the clarity of my conscience. And I rue the day I chose the gratification of others over my own happiness. I fear it is too late to remedy."

Eliza was rendered mute by the sharpness of his words. Irrationally, she feared his anger was also directed at her; the intensity of his wrath was palpable in the air like the sticky humidity that surrounded them.

He sighed. "I fear I have spoken too much. I so rarely speak my innermost thoughts that it is like a deluge springing from my mind when I choose to do so. But you require rest. I will take my leave of you."

Charles exhaled sharply and stood up, stretching his tall form. She nodded in silence, gripping the sheets of the bed, as astonishment coursed through her.

The bitter, metallic smell of blood still hung in the air the next day. The injured men were quieter this morning, having been made silent from either exhaustion or the rawness of their throats.

Eliza and Charles stood on the porch facing the ocean in a rare moment of inactivity. They had not slept well that night, and Charles had tended to the men's needs for hours. Eliza could not help much. Her own body still ached, but she did what small tasks she could. Now a merchant whispered in French to his comrade, but otherwise, a thin, barely perceptible sense of calm surrounded them.

The bell in the yard tolled, and Charles sprang into movement again, his eyes scanning the distance to spot the rider. A stout man dismounted, his chest heaving from the effort. Charles seemed to recognize him.

"Lieutenant-Colonel Sharpe, good day, sir," the man said as he strode up to Charles.

Charles nodded, presenting an otherwise icy demeanor. Not only did he know the man, he did not seem to like him.

"I trust that you and your slaves have salvaged the remnants of the cargo from *La Vierge*. His Lordship, the governor, would like to see it promptly delivered to town so the customs officials may inspect it and place it in the appropriate storage house."

Pieces of the ship were still smoldering, and yet here was a government official eager to collect any profit from its destruction.

"Salvage? Are you mad?"

Eliza began to shuffle towards them with weak, slow steps. When Charles noticed the official staring at the bruises on her chest, he offered a hasty explanation.

"My wife assisted us in pulling men from the wreckage," he muttered in a low voice.

The man nodded at Eliza but otherwise continued with his quest.

"You heard me properly, Colonel. Lord Dunmore would like to retain the salvage immediately. The guns must be rescued from the submerged ship, and any profitable goods like wood or rum must be removed."

Charles placed his hands on his hips and turned away for a moment. He then scoffed and clenched his fists slowly.

"After the same man illegally ordered it to be attacked and blown to the heavens?"

The man seemed surprised by his reception.

"You go too far. It was an unfortunate accident, nothing more. A simple matter of mistaken identity. I would urge caution with your words if I were you. You never know who is listening."

"I believe that you and I and my wife are the only people who are here unless my eyes deceive me. If my reception of your message were to spread to other ears, I do not consider it presumptuous to assume its source. The blame would fall on your head, Mr. Jennings. Your warning is useless to me."

The official sighed and gazed out at the water. The charred remnants of the skeletal ship were still moored on the limestone rocks in the distance. The usual brilliant turquoise water had disappeared in favor of a darker, soiled hue. Fuel and burnt wood had made the bobbing waves slick with debris. Flotsam was strewn all over the otherwise pristine sand, and it was clear from the few particles that had washed ashore that nothing from the ship was salvageable.

"May I remind you that in my duty as Receiver of

the Wreck, you must report any findings to me at once. Lord Dunmore has filed a claim for this ship, and you are therefore not legally allowed to retain any of its cargo," Mr. Jennings said.

The man sniffed dismissively and crossed his hands behind his back.

"It was a French merchant ship. Or is the sunlight rendering you blind?" Charles asked, stepping closer to him.

"I speak of the art of *salvage*. An ancient practice which you, an old Conch citizen, must clearly be well-versed in."

Eliza looked at Charles, well aware of the anger slowly brewing beneath his features. She had never heard anyone refer to him as Conch before. He did not seem to take to it kindly.

"Let me speak plainly. Nothing was salvaged except for the dead and dying men we managed to recover from the waves. Do not speak to me of cargo again. There are bodies that need to be buried, and still more dying men around my house."

"Men? What men?" Mr. Jennings asked, his interest peaked.

"Forgive me, but did you presume they had all blown skywards in the blast? They were men on that ship when it was attacked. Seventy or more, by my estimates."

"You mean to say they are still here?" Mr. Jennings asked with horror.

"My slaves and I saved what men we could. We are tending to their wounds."

The official wheezed in disbelief.

"You are sheltering them? *French* men? May I remind you that we are at war?" he questioned.

He raised his eyebrows at the lack of response.

"Lieutenant-Colonel Sharpe, I will not ask again. There are very valuable items missing, and I am here to facilitate the collection of such wares," he said.

"You are free to roam the beach at your pleasure, Mr. Jennings."

"That is not my meaning, and you know it. Where are the missing items?"

Charles shook his head. "Do you think I stole them? You are welcome to go to the bottom yourself. I daresay the sharks are the only scavengers in the water now. The blood and noise attract them from miles. I wouldn't dare step foot in the sea, but you are free to. By all means, sir …"

Charles flourished his hands and bowed and then turned on his heel and walked away.

"I will tell Lord Dunmore to call up the militia and aid in bringing the prisoners to the fort. They will need to be interrogated. I am speechless that you have not already taken the prerequisite measures. Surely, you have erred, Colonel!"

"No men will be leaving here. They are wounded. This is not a military matter. It is a civilian one."

"These men are wanted, and they will be questioned. Make no mistake."

Charles stopped and faced Lord Dunmore's man again. He stood inches away from his face, peering down at the short man with disgust.

"*You* make no mistake, Mr. Jennings. Those soldiers obey my commands, and they will not step foot on this property. No one is being taken away. Now remove yourself before I have Josiah do so for me."

The man was offended. His mouth opened to speak, but no noise came out, and that was how they left him in the yard. Eliza slowly followed Charles back to the house, returning to the scene of subdued horror that awaited them. She watched her husband with widened eyes.

"Damn him and damn every official he sends over here!" Charles seethed.

She knew he spoke of Lord Dunmore, but she could scarcely believe her ears. Charles called over Josiah, Brutus, and a few other men.

"I need you to prepare several long boats. If that man sends my soldiers to come and take these wounded men, they will find no one. They can wait on the water, around the bend, unseen. I will make further arrangements for them to leave this island. You are to obey no one's command but mine. Is that clear?"

He gave the instructions to them, and they did not question him. Only Eliza watched in shock. Charles meant to disobey Lord Dunmore. She was now a witness to his once faithful trust in the governor unraveling like a loose ribbon in the wind.

CHAPTER XII.

Charles and Eliza descended the porch stairs in strained silence. She had managed to avoid the congregation at Christ Church for the better part of three months, but now she could not excuse herself any longer. The island was beginning to talk, and her lack of presence at nearly every town gathering did not help matters. Her eventual return was inevitable, and this inconvenient fact was not lost on her.

Eliza had agreed to accompany Charles today, but she had not agreed to be pleasant. Fortunately, he did not seem to expect any amicability from her. Matters between them had improved slowly, but general cordiality was still the most she could afford to offer. Julius stood there with the carriage, and he smiled, although she did not return it.

Yesterday, Charles had ordered the surviving men to board two boats, and she caught one final glimpse of them as they rounded the corner on the beach. He would not disclose any details about where they intended to go. He claimed she would remain safer in ignorance, but she had overheard pieces of their conversations in the hallway. One of the survivors was a nephew of a French financier by the name of Desprez, and from what she could gather, *Le Vierge* had been no ordinary trading convoy. The merchants had been en route to the Spanish colonies with the aim of exchanging their goods for precious metals desperately needed in France.

She prayed that Lord Dunmore had finally made a fatal mistake, that he had ordered the Royal Navy to fire on the wrong vessel. But as with all matters on this faraway island, time seemed to still, and consequences never made their intended arrival—especially in regards to crooked earls whose deeds never fully caught up with them.

It was an entirely different matter for Charles. He was a mere baron, a planter, a Conch. His standing in the army as a lieutenant colonel awarded him some merit, but now the foundations of his once-coveted position were untenable. He had disobeyed a direct order from the governor. He had lied to officials when they came to Pleasant Hall searching for the men. And Eliza had watched it all unfold beneath her bedroom window.

She questioned whether Charles had turned into a reckless fool or if he no longer cared about the opinions of others. She prayed his disloyalty to Lord Dunmore would prove permanent. It might become the sole matter they could finally agree on. Eliza took a quick glance at Charles. If he was nervous about encountering the governor and his contingency at the church, he did not show it.

She was about to step into the passenger seat when she stopped at the recognition of an unusual sound. It was a noise she had heard only once before, and when she heard it for the first time, it had utterly changed her life. She could not forget it. Charles' eyes were on her, hot like the end of a poker. She heard it a second time. All hesitation left her body, and she took off. She no longer cared about anything else. Her mind focused only on where she was headed.

The source of the noise sounded past the house and towards the kitchen. She ran and ran, feeling as if her feet had never moved as fast as that moment. She flew past the cottages, stopping by the third. It was a roughly hewn limestone dwelling intended for the slaves to handle laundry. She paused by the doorframe, breathless and anxious, her eyes searching every inch of shadow. When she saw a slave holding a babe near her breast, her heart dropped. The baby's skin was too dark to be her own. Confusion flooded her features; Eliza had possessed such surety and faith. Her chest heaving, she leaned against the opening of the room, trying to regain her breath when it sounded again.

Philippe. Her son.

She pushed further into the room and, on seeing her child in the bassinet, she sank downwards to the dirt floor, her skirts pooling around her. Philippe had grown so much since she had last laid eyes on him, but he was still such a tiny being. An immaculately crafted boy with beautiful eyes that she had seen once before on the man she loved. Even still, Philippe's eyes were different—they sparkled with freshly minted innocence.

Charles had caught up to her, and he stood panting behind her, observing in horror as Eliza sat on the ground in shock.

The wheels turned in her mind as she finally understood what had transpired. But she could not possibly understand it all.

"Eliza ..." he began to say.

She had her hand covering her mouth now as tears streamed down her face.

"I must offer an—I fear I owe you an explanation. I feared your reaction, Eliza. Truly, I did not know when to tell you."

"He's *here* ..."

The woman lifted Philippe from the bassinet and handed him gingerly to her. She took him with careful hands, her eyes welling up with tears, and she clutched the baby to her chest. He watched her with wide, wet eyes, shining with the density of new life. She shook her head.

"I should have never let them take you. I should have fought harder; please forgive me," she said to the baby, sobbing.

"I am sorry, I could not afford to tell you until now, Eliza. This is my doing," Charles said.

"It is your doing that he is still here? Oh, my baby boy, my sweet boy," she said, her lips trembling with emotion.

Charles slowly walked over to her, and she clasped his hand, not fully aware of her actions. His touch felt like an anchor. Her thoughts were spinning, the reactions and conclusions she had felt so sure of even this morning flipping over entirely in her mind. It was overwhelming her with bliss.

"Philippe is so beautiful, just as I remember …" she said, oblivious to the room around her.

"Please forgive me, Eliza."

Now Eliza looked up, her face troubled. She rose to a shaky stand as Philippe began to cry. She bounced him and tried soothing him. The slave looked on nervously, fearful that she could be blamed in some way for keeping the secret.

"I will leave you. Please, give me time to gather some possessions, and you will see no more of us," she said.

"No."

She looked up with bewilderment just as Philippe began to grow quiet. Her face paled with fear.

"I do not intend for this child to leave these grounds," Charles said, his voice filled with the authority she found hard to bear.

"No," she said, shaking her head. "No, I will not leave without him. You cannot do this. Why have you done this? Can you be so devastatingly cruel?"

She charged towards him, and the slave came and took Philippe from her arms.

"You do not understand. I am not doing this for your sake alone. Nor do I act within my own interest. Certainly, common sense urges me in a different direction. But I have no choice."

"I do not understand," she said, her sudden happiness consumed by anger.

"It is the least I can do. For his father's memory," he said quietly.

Shock coursed through her as she struggled to understand his meaning.

"You mean to, you intend to—"

She was unsure of how to react. She wanted to trust him. She wanted his words to be true, but she knew it was impossible.

"I will act as a father to this child. Honor requires nothing less. I regret that I could not tell you sooner. I admit that I was unsure in the beginning; I only knew I could not bear to have the child taken away from here. Once I made my decision, I kept it from you. Forgive me, Eliza. I feared disturbing your sensibilities beyond reprieve."

He appeared anguished with his confession, and she knew he was telling the truth. She wanted her son, but she was also not entirely sure she wanted this arrangement.

"But such a thing cannot be. People will talk. There will be vicious rumors, and they will destroy your standing. You have not thought this through. Let me leave with him. I will return to England, and I will exist as a different woman," she pleaded.

"Mary has been ordered to silence. Only she and Cleo know among the house. No one else need know who his father truly is. You were with child during my absence, and you bore this child. And he will be my son. *Our* son, Eliza."

She shook her head as her eyes grew blurry with tears.

"No ... no ... they all know. They *all* know he is not

yours!" she shouted.

Nearly all the slaves had participated that day or heard about what had happened after it occurred. They had helped her during the pregnancy. They had pushed her to deliver the child; they had concealed him in a basket and taken away the blood-soaked rags from her bedchamber. They had done all this and more because they were loyal to Cleo and, above all because they feared Charles' reaction.

He walked towards her with outstretched arms, speaking words incredulous to her ears.

"This child can offer us a new beginning. I know your burden is heavy. Lay it in my arms, Eliza," he said.

"You cannot possibly show him any measure of kindness. It is not within your heart," she said as she looked around the room.

They had created a kind of makeshift nursery. Philippe looked healthy and thriving. She could not deny that the child had been tended to.

"I know the shock of my words must be immense."

"I will leave with the next ship. You can forget about all of this and take another wife. She will bear you the children you seek; only do not try to force this distortion further. This is not the family you desire. *We* are not a family."

"I cannot let you leave. I forbid it."

"So, I am to live here as a prisoner? To live out a lie? To have the man who caused his father's absence act as his living father? To raise him with the same hands who snuffed the life out of … Jean?"

Her voice cracked as she said his name.

"I read his papers," he said, something unrecognizable darkening his features.

The veins in his temple pulsed, and his lower lip quivered. Her heart sank in her chest as she watched him slowly unravel. The display before her went against all her inner objections.

Charles finally regained command over his voice. "He was the better man. I have only shame within me."

She gawked at him in astonishment as his eyes grew watery.

"I ask you to forgive me, Eliza," he whispered.

She swallowed, hesitant and unsure of his motives.

"And what do you require of me in return?"

Then a clenched jaw seemed to retract his sudden display of vulnerability in front of her.

"To mother the child to the best of your abilities."

Eliza had no immediate response. She turned and watched Mary swaying with her son.

"What did you call the boy?" Charles asked.

"Philippe."

He smiled and looked down at his boots.

"That name suits him. Philippe Sharpe."

The boy's newfound name made her gut turn. So, he was to carry the name of the man who had betrayed his father. She looked away, lost in a hundred unspeakable fears. But the once-impossible opportunity of never having to leave her baby again was foremost in her thoughts. The greatest pain she had ever felt in her life, worse than even losing Jean, would dissolve from her heart. Relief began to trickle through her.

"I do not expect to receive any forbearance from you. I do not deserve your affection, and so I will not pressure you. I will not make demands of you. I only ask that you stay with me to raise this child," he said.

His usual steady voice sounded distraught.

"I will never be separated from him again," she whispered.

A sob escaped her lips, and her body bent over, wracked with a fresh onslaught of crying.

"I looked for him. I truly did. At the orphanage. I thought—I thought he was lost to me forever," she said in broken gasps.

"I could not allow Jean's child to be cast aside. Besides, the child will look like you; people will know on this island, and they will talk. This is the only way."

"I will never be parted from him again ..."

Charles sighed. "Cleo advised I tell you sooner, but I could not bear the idea of putting you through further agony."

She was torn between the idea that the man in front of her had hidden her son for months and the idea that this same man had found some inconceivable way for her and Philippe to be reunited.

And what had Cleo's involvement been? She had also been so confident of his fury if the baby was discovered. What if they had brought the baby away before Charles had found him? What if she truly had lost Philippe? The thought was unbearable, and it reminded her that possibilities of the future hung from the thinnest of cords.

The baby began to cry again, and Mary moved to nurse him.

"No, let me, let me," Eliza said to her.

"Please don't fuss, Lady Sharpe. I can tend to him. It is no trouble," Mary replied.

Eliza was not satisfied with her reaction, but then she realized her meaning.

"I want to feed him ..." she said, then looking down at her chest, "Oh, it does not work in this way, does it? I cannot ... not any longer."

Fresh tears sprang to her eyes.

"I can take care of it; please don't worry, Lady Sharpe."

"Yes," Eliza said dejectedly. "You are capable; you have your own child. Yes. I need to—I need—"

She walked towards Charles again, her eyes wide but unfocused. With every step, she felt herself grow weaker, and then she collapsed without losing consciousness entirely. He rushed to her, raising her to a full stand.

"I cannot give you what you want," she mumbled.

"Shh ... there is no need to speak. You must rest now. The shock is too great."

Eliza had started her day ruminating about the consequences of Charles disobeying orders and aiding the French merchants. Now she felt panic as she considered the silent rules governing society that he intended to break next. The boy would grow up, and people would whisper as they looked at his features and mannerisms. There would no doubt be troubling times ahead of them, and with her acceptance, she was choosing to endure it by his side. But even in the muddled chaos of her worries one thing was clear. If she wanted to keep Philippe and raise him, this was the only way.

She felt Charles take hold of her arm as he began to walk her back outside, but she turned, wanting to see Philippe one more time. She balked and refused to take another step.

"Come, he is not going anywhere. He is safe here," Charles said in a vain attempt to soothe her.

"I am not leaving him. Not again. Let me take him!" she protested.

"I fear you will drop him. You can barely stand, Eliza."

"I want him to be brought in the house. I want him to be with me. In my room."

"Yes, yes, of course. This can be arranged. Please do not trouble yourself."

She covered her mouth with her hand, shaking her head in disbelief still. How could he remain so calm, so unerringly rational? Did he judge how her legs quaked, how her tears would not stop flowing? Charles said nothing, merely walking her to the house and up the stairs as if she consisted of delicate porcelain and not mortal flesh. Yet Eliza allowed him to lead her to her room, too distressed to speak. A tumult of thoughts and emotions coursed through her body, and while she was stunned and dismayed at what she had agreed to, she had undeniably never felt purer elation before now. She was concerned for the days ahead yet comforted with a remarkable sensation.

She had not lost Philippe. They had been reunited, and now she could have the opportunity she had so feverishly prayed for. She would be a mother. The mother of Jean's only child. They would forever be connected in some way, the baby a testament of their love and commingled blood.

The room wavered as tears crowded her eyes. Eliza had only ever cried this intensely one other time in her life—the morning she had lost Jean to the brutal hands of fate. But now, in her solitude, she knew she had found some degree of peace, of the tranquility that she had lost before.

Yemaya had heard her prayers.

CHAPTER XIII.

"Lady Sharpe, it is quite refreshing to finally enjoy some company that is up to my standards," Charlotte said with a deceitful smile.

The sweltering afternoon heat pressed upon them as Charles and Eliza sat in the governor's mansion among a small group of people. Lord Dunmore had sent an invitation a few days ago, but Charles had interpreted its cold tone as a threat. The shipwreck had not proceeded according to the governor's plan, and Charles would finally be made to account for it. Pretense had expired after many weeks, and the topic could no longer be avoided.

Eliza accompanied Charles today in the spirit of newborn reconciliation. But she abhorred the present company she was required to keep. She had once looked forward to opportunities to socialize, like Sunday service or the balls held in this mansion, but those days now belonged to the past. And the fault for this volte-face in sentiment was entirely Lord Dunmore's.

Now his spiteful mistress Charlotte fussed with her

skirts in a manner all too symptomatic of her self-importance, impatiently waiting for her to speak.

"Yes, this afternoon is quite pleasant," Eliza replied, her tone betraying her true sentiments.

She had not been in the governor's house since the night before Jean was executed. She could not fathom why Charlotte would even exchange niceties with her after their last encounter. She had been prepared to not speak to her at all, and the woman's friendliness took her off guard. She could not imagine how someone could be so stupendously false.

She was not even aware if Charles realized the extent of her desperation that terrible night. She had boldly offered herself to Lord Dunmore to save Jean's life. It had been a venture that disgusted her beyond measure, but she had seen no other recourse. Now it was an exercise in sheer mortification to sit in the same room as that man, without even the mercy of the pews separating them as they had in church. She inwardly hoped that Charlotte would take offense at her brevity and leave her alone.

"Come, won't you take a turn about the room with me?" Charlotte asked eagerly.

Eliza knew better than to trust that polished countenance. Charlotte appeared to be scheming. The men's conversation grew louder.

"It is puzzling; we have never found any survivors from the wreck near your lands. Despite reports that several men were spotted," Lord Dunmore said as he blotted away excess sweat from the folds on his face.

"Early reports can often be misleading in number, my

lord," Charles responded.

"Mr. Jennings here claims to have seen men, but when the soldiers arrived there were none to be found."

She was anxious to listen to the rest of the discussion. She wondered whether Charles would finally speak his mind, but Charlotte's presence was distracting and relentless like a fly.

"No, I'd rather not," Eliza finally answered without disguising the bluntness in her voice.

Charlotte looked sullen for a moment. Then she perked back up.

"No, I don't think you quite understand. You see, I'd like to discuss something of a *personal* nature with you," she explained. "It would hardly be polite to discuss it here in front of the others."

Charlotte took a careful sip from her teacup, her eyes never leaving Eliza.

"Whatever you would like to say you may say it here. I'm sure that the gentlemen will not mind," Eliza said tersely.

Charlotte's teacup clattered in the saucer. Eliza gripped her cup so tightly she wondered it did not crack. By now, the governor, Charles, and the other officials in the room were beginning to focus on them. Even they could tell that this was not the usual stock of mindless feminine chatter. Eliza regretted the reversal.

Charlotte cleared her throat.

"If it pleases you …" she said, a gleam in her eye. "What is this going about the town that you jumped off the cliffs by the Black Reef?"

Eliza's cheeks colored for a moment, surprised by Charlotte's audacity. She had always assumed that she cared too much for propriety to cause a scene in polite society. A deep-seated anger she had once thought buried rose up in her throat.

"I am not sure I know of what you speak," Eliza managed to reply.

The flush of red on her chest and around her ears betrayed the facade of stoicism. Charles swirled his punch and watched them. Humiliation began to cover his features as well.

"Oh, but you see, I think you do, Lady Sharpe," Charlotte said, goaded on by the clear dissatisfaction on her face. "You see, I heard that you purposely threw yourself into the ocean. That you tried to end your life. Isn't that, how do they say ... a bit histrionic?"

Eliza didn't have time to respond as Charles leapt into the conversation.

"It was an accident, a terrible accident," he said with an air of indifference.

He took a swig of his drink, then smiled disarmingly at them.

Eliza began to say something in retort when Charlotte cut her off.

"Peculiar. All very peculiar, to say the least," she said. "It is quite a strange story from what we heard. You see, try as we might to control them, these slaves all divulge things to one another. Apparently, your house slaves told my slaves that it was all due to that criminal. That spy that was hung last year. A certain De Longchamp, if I recall. The French one. He was French, wasn't he?"

Now the entire room was listening with a silence so awkward it begged to be shattered.

"I'm afraid this conversation is over," Charles said.

His tone was still level, but there was a dark fire simmering behind his eyes.

Charlotte did not heed his warning. "The story making its way around town is that our lovely Eliza here had a certain weakness for the Frenchman. She fell in love with him, I daresay, but it was unrequited. And then the wretch died. I remarked at the time that it was a kindness to the kingdom to hang him. Not even the devil welcomes spies into his lair. And so, she threw herself to her death, or at least tried to, and then *you*, of all people, actually saved her! How very noble. The one person she was trying to rid herself of. But do tell me where I am mistaken, Lord Sharpe," Charlotte said, demurely sipping her tea.

"I will tell you where you are wrong. I will repeat myself. It was an accident, nothing more." The growl in his voice was unmistakable. "And I will not tolerate you speaking of my wife in such a manner."

"I had not the faintest idea she took to fancying other men. Of course, I caught her trying to seduce the governor on multiple occasions, but I still found it quite appalling. Why, look around the room, Eliza. Do you see any men that strike your eye? Who can tell, maybe even the servants aren't free from your snares. Or do you prefer the field hands? They're likely much stronger than any man here. Perhaps that's what you crave in your bed.

I took you into my confidence once before, but I never dreamed of the result. Mark my words, I would have trodden more carefully!"

"Charlotte! For God's sake, woman, shut your mouth!" the governor said, his wig moving in agitation. "We are trying to conduct business here, something you women would not understand!"

The governor's displeasure was surprising but not effective enough to curtail her entirely.

"John is a very Christian man. More so than my natural tendencies are capable of. I told him it would lower our standards to admit you into our society again. But I suppose even a cuckolded bridegroom and his slut of a wife can find their place in this backwater colony," Charlotte said adamantly. She took a sip of tea and then added, "And I believe congratulations are in order. Tell me, does the baby more resemble you or his father?"

Eliza flew from her seat and lunged at her. The tea cups toppled down, bursting into pieces as the dark liquid sloshed along the polished floor. When she saw the horror in her enemy's eyes, it gave her more hellish satisfaction than any act of God could bestow.

She wanted Charlotte to fear her. She wanted the blood to recede from her cheeks and her tongue to be silenced. Her surroundings were dark, and it nearly made her forget that they were indeed spectators in the room. Someone cleared their throat, and it brought her back to the present moment. In their newfound proximity, Eliza finally regained control of herself and lowered a trembling fist. Charlotte's terror receded, and she was thrilled with her narrow victory.

Eliza backed away, looking at each person in the room, their eyes following her. They expected her to flee from the scene, but she remained where she was. She refused to give them further satisfaction.

"It was no accident," Eliza said.

"If you would excuse my wife, she is not feeling well of late," Charles said, also standing up, militant in his bearing.

He reached out a hand as if this simple gesture could tame her.

"If this isn't the strangest arrangement I've ever seen. We are fortunate to have our afternoons enhanced by such entertainment. Who needs the theater—" Charlotte replied with a sharp giggle.

She kicked away a shard of porcelain with a slippered foot.

"I did attempt to take my life," Eliza started, her voice a low shudder. Then she regained her volume. "It is true. I did it for reasons someone as vapid and self-possessed as you could never possibly understand. What do you care for anyone's troubles unless they threaten your own coveted position? You are Lord Dunmore's mistress, and we are all trained to not see it, but *you* are nothing but a whore. We all know it. You do not love the man; you love his power. His riches."

A man's glass clanked against the table as he muttered something to himself about decency.

"Ah, how the viper strikes …" Charlotte replied adamantly.

"We are only on this island because England has refused our presence in one way or another. We belong to a colony of liars and thieves. We are unwanted. I will not deny my past conduct. I have joined your ranks. But I will never let a man take me to bed for money or jewels, as you so plainly do."

Eliza gestured disdainfully at Charlotte's glittering bosom and then continued.

"Perhaps the scene in this house would seem less ludicrous if you did not share the same name as his lawful wife. I cannot blame her for her absence. I too would remain in Sicily if I were shackled to the likes of a man like him. That *you* would willingly lie with him for petty baubles makes you the lowliest of creatures. My actions were spurred by love, and laugh at that as you may ... my sins will never stem from greed."

There was a pall over the room as the group waited for Eliza's next move as if she was a wild cat unleashed from a crate. She knew she had crossed an invisible boundary, and it only pushed her bold actions further.

"Charles, manage her; this has ceased to be amusing," Lord Dunmore said dryly as he rose to a slow and unstable stand.

The governor looked enraged, but this had little effect on Eliza.

"My wife is very unwell. I executed poor judgment in the matter; she should remain at home until she has fully recovered," Charles said.

Eliza rushed to the governor next.

"I do not fear you. I do not fear any man. You are

a deceiver, Lord Dunmore. You are the king's servant, but you so easily accept bribes from the very criminals our king is asking you to apprehend. If this is not your underhanded intent, then you possess a capacity below mediocrity. You are clearly so little cultivated by education, you are ignorant of the rights of the king's subjects. You may feel yourself to be ruler of this small island, but you are not my king. Not now, nor ever. You are not fit to serve as governor."

Audible gasps filled the parlor.

"Treason! This is treason! Take her from the room!" Mr. Jennings shouted.

Lord Dunmore held out a conciliatory hand to soothe the witnesses of her tirade.

"This is why no man takes a woman's interest in politics seriously," Lord Dunmore grumbled.

"Because I speak the truth? I do not slight you for this stance. It would be your undoing."

The governor stepped closer to her and lowered his sweaty face. Charles sprang towards them.

"But you fail to realize that I will be *your* undoing. And I will relish in every moment of it, you vulgar witch," he hissed in her ear. "I never had quite so much satisfaction as when you came to me, offering yourself, begging for his life. I would advise you to grow accustomed to that position, for you will revisit it shortly."

Lord Dunmore moved away, a self-satisfied grin curving his pudgy lips. Nothing that had transpired instilled fear in her. This made her dangerous and senseless. Charles took her by the arm.

"You are no better than the pirates raiding ships in the cays," she called out. "I daresay they possess more decency than you ever will. For they at least are honest in their thievery! Deception and hypocrisy are the only currency you deal in. You are tyranny in the flesh!"

"For shame!" Lord Dunmore shouted, slamming his foot down. "You will not slander my name in my own house! I am the representative of the greatest monarch on earth, whose majesty you affront by treating me in such a contemptuous manner! Leave at once, you wicked woman!"

He motioned to the footmen lined against the wall, earless and mute to the chaos unfolding in the room. Two men came up to her, but Charles withdrew his saber.

"You will not touch her," he said in a low tone, blocking her from them.

"Good God, was I ever a witness to such bedlam!" a minister remarked.

Charles turned back to the others. "My deepest apologies, Your Lordship, Miss Charlotte, gentlemen," he said quietly, as he bowed his head.

"If you cannot manage her, how can you possibly manage this motley excuse for a regiment? This is inexcusable," Lord Dunmore seethed.

Eliza did not wait for the servants to open the door. She flew to it, and using all her might, she pulled the heavy wooden door open and released herself from her torturous surroundings. The governor and Charles continued their strained discussion, but she no longer cared. She was so absorbed in her success that she rushed out into the darkened hallway and did not see who was waiting there until she nearly collided with him.

Captain Hiram Bruin stood before her, and by the way he smirked, she understood that he had been privy to the entire affair. He had most certainly heard her rant about pirates. She cared little if she insulted a person like him.

She quickly avoided his eyes and made for the stairs, but he blocked her in an instant and latched on to her wrist.

"Unhand me at once!" she snapped.

Her venomous tone of voice had little effect on him. In fact, he hardly seemed bothered. His skin was swarthy like he had just returned from a voyage. He grinned and held on to her.

"I am fairly surprised to catch you indoors on a day like this, Lady Sharpe."

She attempted to wrestle herself free and failed. Her rush of excitement from confronting Lord Dunmore and his mistress was quickly diminishing into a sense of inopportune timing. They both understood why he had stopped her flight, yet the words remained unspoken. She did not want to volunteer any vulnerability to someone brash like him. The gold coins she had discovered two years ago in the water were the last thing on her mind.

Loud and determined footsteps approached behind them, and Eliza was grateful for the sound. Charles would serve as a useful intrusion.

"A word before we go our separate ways. You may not see me very often, and I doubt you will return to this house, but that does not mean I am not aware of your every move. And your frequent afternoon swims, now that the little one has been born. I would caution you to be wary, Lady Sharpe," he said, his voice sly and menacing.

"You are a lowly criminal and nothing more. If this is an attempt to frighten me, you are wasting your breath, Captain."

Her words demonstrated bravery, but she inwardly felt disturbed.

Bruin issued a quiet laugh. "Indeed, a lowly criminal headed to receive a royal pardon from the governor himself. Take care with your words, Lady Sharpe. I would hate for you to regret it." Captain Bruin released her and smugly sauntered into the chaotic room.

Eliza's ears burned. This wretch was to receive a royal pardon? The one salvation that had proved elusive for Jean, a truly innocent man? What had Bruin offered to secure such a mercy? Her blood coursed through her with more heat and anger than before. She heard Charles acknowledge him with an obligatory good day. She was of a mind to shout after the captain, but her welcome in the mansion had steadily evaporated. She cursed. There was nothing good about this day.

Charles began to question her about the terse exchange that had occurred with Bruin, but she seized on him with renewed anger.

"You disgust me," she said, glaring at him. "I marvel you did not let the footmen drag me from the room on my hands and knees."

Charles said nothing, his lower jaw tense, his fists

clenched. He sheathed his saber with a sigh. She descended the stairs with him in pursuit, her feet careless of how many steps she took at a time.

"I confess I have lost control. But I suffer no regret nor offer any apology. I pity you," she continued as they reached the ground floor. "Your soul is enslaved to the passion of ambition. Your very life and happiness depend on the breath and nod of another. A watery grave seemed to offer more to me than standing a moment longer in your company ever could. How this has ceased to make an impression on your mind even to this day confounds my comprehension."

Eliza could faintly hear Charlotte and the rest clapping in celebration. She sharply exhaled and walked out to the carriage. The irony of how sinners gladly welcomed other wrongdoers in their company was not lost on her.

The journey home was filled with an air of agitation, but her flurry of enraged thoughts made the time pass mercifully by. Charles did not say a word. His gaze was locked on the woods and dunes of sand that rolled alongside them.

When they arrived at Pleasant Hall, Eliza's temper had not subsided. She stormed down the hallway, past a bewildered Lucy, with Charles following in her wake.

"Eliza …" he started.

"Do not speak to me. I have had enough of this day," she said, removing her plaited straw hat. "I cannot bear to withstand your rebuke." She tossed it on the side table. "I could have spent my afternoon in the company of Philippe. Instead, it has been squandered."

Charles watched as she furiously tore open a package and revealed a rattle the local blacksmith had made. It was crafted with silver, and its end was finished with a twist of red coral to serve as a teether. The instant she saw it, the storm raging inside of her quieted down. She had only left Pleasant Hall for a few hours, but she already missed Philippe. She seldom left the house these days, and after today's events, she scarcely believed she would have a reason to do so again.

"This should capture Philippe's attention," she said to herself with a smile as she inspected it.

But her husband interrupted her momentary solace.

"I always knew you would make an excellent mother. You are fascinated by the smallest of creatures," Charles said, as he approached her cautiously. "You radiate such joy whenever you think of the boy."

"He is brilliant, I can already tell. The way he looks around him, he is so observant. I can hardly wait until he speaks. He is so like his father in every way," Eliza gushed without much forethought.

She had said too much. Such an obvious and brutally painful aspect of the child's new situation had yet to be discussed. And now, uttered for the first time, it seemed as if the enormity of their newfound domestic arrangement threatened to extinguish the air between them. The subject had been avoided, and it was evident to her that this had perhaps been Charles' deliberate intent.

Did he really assume they could continue living like this without a single mention as to why Philippe was fatherless? She could understand his reluctance, his silent avoidance, but did he truly intend to have this serve as some diversion to the cold rift between them? Even his current enthusiasm to discuss this rather than the debacle that had just occurred at the governor's mansion seemed suspect.

"Yes, his father was a good man. I hope that I can provide the boy with everything he needs. I owe it to Jean, to his memory. I fear you do not entirely understand my motives, Eliza," Charles said slowly.

"I am afraid I do not," she agreed. "You … you have given me everything. But I still fear there is a cost to your benevolence."

"I only want your happiness, Eliza. That is all I have ever wanted."

Eliza swallowed, her gaze refusing to meet his. She did not believe his sincerity. She had sworn to never feel exposed around Charles again. The thought of that cruel morning by the scaffold worsened her shaking jaw. And here they were, returned to the same mahogany paneled hallway, as more uncomfortable words passed between them. She was so very tired of it all.

"You have also taken everything away. Do not lie to me now. That is not entirely true," she said softly.

Her silk skirt brushed against the floor as she glided towards the stairs.

"I understand you now. I should have never brought you among those people," Charles said.

She stopped her movement and looked back at him, her eyes ablaze with fury.

"You must think me utterly insane," she replied without regret.

"On the contrary, I have always found you the most sensible person in any room." He joined her near the steps.

Eliza shook her head. "Why? You speak like a fool. I have single-handedly ruined your career. I daresay no house on this island will invite me to any function after tonight. I will find it a blessing, but you will surely find it a curse. If you cannot control one woman, how can you be expected to lead an army of men? The governor said as much himself."

She leaned against the wall, ruminating over her words. She feared in time she would come to regret her actions, but at that moment, in the darkening foyer, she did not feel its sting. It was all too fresh in her mind.

"They do not deserve to be in your presence," he said, his green eyes searching hers.

She said nothing in response. But he continued speaking.

"Eliza, you have opened my eyes to things I had not been able to see until I met you. I know now that the way we started was not right—"

He reached for her hands, but she pulled away.

"You care nothing for my happiness."

"We went so terribly off course. I didn't understand that before. I did not see that it was *my* doing. You made me feel so happy in the beginning, I never once realized that you were not. That was my mistake. I failed you—"

"This was always about your needs. It never concerned me. I was just a cog in your wheel," Eliza said, refusing to meet his eyes.

"I never imagined myself with a wife. I feared my days were destined to be solitary and companionless. But you have made Pleasant Hall a home …"

"Yes, I am aware that you are quite content. You have land, fortune, and a woman. What else does any man require?"

She was about to continue up the stairs, but he stopped her.

"Those things alone do not give me satisfaction. It is not enough. I could have married any other woman, but—"

Eliza exhaled sharply. "Then why am I here? Why do you continue to torment me? Why—"

He put his hands on her arms to quell the loudness of her voice.

"I could never be with another woman."

"Why didn't you let me drown? Why did you save me?" she said. "You will regret this. I will make sure of it, Charles. I have only just begun."

As the words flew from her lips, she knew the answer was obvious. She still stood in that house because of Philippe. That is why she had seen the apparition of Jean on the limestone rocks. That is why the *orishas* had spared her. There was no greater love than that between a mother and her child.

She wanted to go to Philippe now, but Charles still held her. She looked towards the banister and remembered how he had not hesitated to tie her to it. Perhaps those days would return. He had not displayed any rage since she had tried to take his life, but he couldn't have so vastly altered his character. Men were simply not capable of such tremendous change.

"The only thing I truly regret is the time that I wasted with you. Of the infinite ways I have wounded you, Eliza."

Eliza wondered if he would ever acknowledge what he had done. The first few nights and days spent with him were bleak in her thoughts. Their union was too utterly divided for well-intentioned words to smooth the course now.

"Stop this! Such sentiment does not sit well with your features," she snapped.

"Mark me, my intentions are serious. I do not ask for forgiveness—" he said, the volume of his voice increasing.

"Nor do you offer an apology."

"I can think of no other person that I would rather spend my days with. You have singlehandedly altered my life. I know I have wronged you gravely. I lay up at night thinking of ways to talk to you. To make amends with you. To restore some measure of peace. I have sat outside your closed door many nights, dreaming that I was on the other side. It seemed no matter what I did, nothing could improve our relations. I want all of you—"

"You already have taken me," she hissed in a low tone. "Nothing is stopping you. I certainly couldn't before."

"You mistake my meaning. Nor do I wish to subject you to that. I was selfish. I presented myself nothing short of a monster, and I do not question that you detest me. I only ask for a second chance. Allow me to show you the man I truly am. I beg you."

He sighed. He appeared to want to say more, but he relented.

"What have I possibly done today to inspire such words? Perhaps *you* have gone mad," she said, her eyes locked on the floor.

"Eliza, you are braver than any man. You have expressed words that I myself have thought over and over again but never dared to speak. Even now, I am tortured by thoughts that I have been eager to express to you … but your presence overpowers me into weakness."

"I did not know a hardened soldier could possess the sensibilities of a poet."

"You have not let me into your mind or your heart. I know I am to blame. You were so innocent, so pure, so full of hope. And I destroyed such a gift … the very part of you that held me captive in enchantment. That day in the garden, I can see you even now. The color of your dress, the freedom of your steps, your smile in the sunlight. Your presence alone beguiled me. I could have had any number of women as my wife, but none of them ever came close to what I have found within you."

"Yes, I am the only fool that ever desired crossing an ocean at your side," she said bitterly.

"No, you are the only woman I ever asked," Charles said frankly. "I am in love with your mind, Eliza. No other woman can fathom the world as you see it. You see beauty everywhere around you. From the smallest insect to the vastness of the sea. You are not afraid of the world; you actually *live*, Eliza. You embrace it. You do not complain at its downturns; you see them as challenges to be overcome. You are resilient. You are incorruptible and fearless.

"No other woman would not only survive here but thrive as you have. You can outmatch any man on any topic of discussion. You understand the works of the ancients, geography, history. You know the stars in the sky and the fish in the sea. You fascinate me." He softly stroked the side of her face.

Eliza wanted to retreat, but he had cornered her. She would be forced to endure his speech.

"I did not make a mistake asking for your hand. I only regret underestimating your brilliance. Our meeting that day, on that bench, was providential. I made the mistake of assuming that you were a vision from the heavens above and not a woman with feelings and a heart. A heart that should have been treated so delicately but instead was met with the crudest and roughest of hands. I do not deserve you. I have flaws which render me utterly unworthy of you. I was arrogant, I was a fool, and for that, I am truly sorry."

Charles took a deep breath; such a confession seemed a weighty release. He waited attentively for a response and watched her with the intensity of one trying to decipher another's thoughts. Her dark eyes flicked up to him, embittered and silent. Minutes lingered on. She refused to answer.

"I cannot undo what I have done. I am in agony with shame. I dread the night when it comes because when it is silent, I am left alone with my thoughts. And I cannot bear the damage I have caused. I want nothing more than to remedy this marriage. I wish we could return to the beginning. To heavens, I would if it were possible ..." Charles said, desperation heavy in his voice.

"But what drove you to do such things may still reside within you, and this thought I cannot soothe away," she finally said.

"I only ask that you allow me to show you, Eliza."

"I have betrayed you. No man of feeling could possibly forget such a fact. How you can bear to be reminded of it daily, I cannot fathom," she said, shaking her head. "I am not a fool. Do not take me for one."

She looked at the rattle despondently, rotating it slowly in her hand.

"I do not see betrayal when I look at Philippe; I only see an innocent child. The son of my friend, my brother."

His words offered such promise, but she did not trust them. She scoffed, shaking her head.

"I want to raise this child as our own. I cannot make you believe my sincerity, Eliza. I can only demonstrate it to you with my actions," he said.

A look of horror crossed with revulsion came over her. Her body stiffened up on the stairs. She searched for some way to deliver her message that would cause the least offense, that would cause the least disturbance to her already fragile heart.

"It is unnatural," she said in a simple tone.

"Unnatural it may be, but it is an issue of honor. Eliza, allow me to rectify this; allow me to show you the man I truly am."

Her chest tightened with the realization that she did

not have much choice in the situation. As much as her mind screamed with misgivings, the man in front of her had saved her child. He had given Philippe back to her despite having every reason to take revenge. Instead, he had done the unthinkable. But still, her mind rebelled.

"As if *you* would rear another man's child! I wonder Jean does not rise from his grave to see you speak such foolishness. You have no desire to assume the burden of Philippe's care. The days will pass, and your rage will return. You will say the child little deserves such a mercy. You cannot convince me that you do not have a bad design in this. The boy will resemble him in person, and you will fear that he resembles him in mind. This is folly, Charles!"

"I swear on my life, Eliza. I have no ill will towards the boy," he urged.

"What I allow for within these walls is one matter, but such a thing can never be accepted out there. They will know," she said quietly.

"Damn the world! Damn them all! Did you yourself not just utter the same sentiment in their very presence? That world ... *their* society is the source of our misery. Eliza, we can find happiness here. Together. This child is offering us a new chapter. I can feel it in my bones! It is palpable in the air. Do you not feel it also?"

He clasped her free hand then, and she did not withdraw it. His touch seemed to steady her just as anxiety crept up her chest, stilling her breath.

"I am owed nothing; I make no pretense here. But allow me this chance, Eliza."

Eliza closed her eyes, listening to the relentless rhythm of the waves crashing outside. She knew he was waiting for her to respond, but she could not find the capability.

"If it pleases you, we do not need to speak about what occurred. We are all capable of indiscretions. I suppose it is only natural to crave satisfaction, to fulfill the pangs of lust. He was the lover I could never be," Charles said.

Eliza ripped her hand away from him, her lips trembling with emotion.

"No ..." she said, "I fear he was more than that. He did not pursue me like a hunter. He did not defeat me like a soldier. He did not make demands of me like a husband. He was kind. Gentle. You fail to understand, Charles. He did not calculate his every action to meet some predetermined end. No. I was only met with restraint in the beginning." She looked past Charles towards the golden light of the setting sun.

"Love, the wildest love, comes and grabs hold of you precisely when you are not trying, when you are not thinking, when you are not even looking. Then ... then it takes you, and it leaves you without mercy. And you are left alone, with nothing but the memory of their touch. And even you, with all of your careful words, cannot replace that," Eliza said.

Charles watched her with anguish. "I only wish to return to where we were ..."

"The girl that arrived on this island is gone," she replied.

"I disagree entirely. I saw her on full display in Lord Dunmore's drawing room."

"I have nothing to offer you nor any other man. I do not entirely understand what you seek from me, but I know that I cannot give it." She shook her head. "I was so excited for our new life together once. I had never reached such dizzying heights ... and I have never fallen so far. I am without redemption, and I have chosen a life of ruin. But I have the surety that it was indeed *my* choice and not that of another."

"There is nothing for you to redeem. You have done no wrong," he said.

"Falsehoods roll off of your tongue so easily."

"Have I not made myself entirely clear? What more can I say?"

"On the contrary, you madden me with confusion."

"I love you, Eliza, dammit!" he shouted. His words were an explosion of frustration that filled the corridor. "I love you," he said again, more quietly.

Both of his hands braced against the wall on either side of her.

His face was flushed with redness, his desperate bearing stripped of all restraint. Eliza's eyes were huge. She appeared breathless; her anger dashed away to nothing. She had not expected him to lower his guard. His words brought an element of surprise to their conversation, but they also disturbed her. She had known it on some level, but now that it had been spoken out loud, it was clear that it was undeniably true. And the knowledge frightened her.

"I felt something from you that day on the rocks. The way you held on to me. I thought for once that our minds were finally one again. Tell me, Eliza. Tell me that what I felt was not wrong," Charles pleaded.

She shook her head, biting her lip. "I have suffered at your hands. And now I cannot give you what you want. It is not possible."

"I am only asking for us to start anew."

He squeezed her arms for emphasis.

"Do not touch me."

"Please listen to what I am saying. Please consider it with the deliberation it deserves. That is all I ask."

"You ask too much," she spat, as she tried to shove him away. "I hate you!"

He did not move. Her hands struck his chest as she tried to push him.

"Eliza, please …"

She hit him again and again. Charles took a step back, but she was ferocious in her assault. She nearly fell off of the step, but he blocked her.

"I hate you! That is the only thing I can offer you. I *hate* you!" she shouted.

He grabbed her suddenly and kissed her hard, holding her face still and stopping her torrent of enmity. When he finally released her, he looked exasperated, as if he had reached his limit.

She wiped her mouth with a shaking hand. The kiss was markedly different than any she had ever received from him. It did not feel the same as she remembered. His lips had always transferred dominance, aggression, and an unwanted invasion, as if he could steal the very air from her lungs.

As unexpected as his contact had been, this kiss had nearly felt gentle. It seemed born of despair and flushed with pain, assigned with conveying something his words alone could not. Charles looked miserable as if he only now understood the depths of his failure. She was stunned to see him like this. She had never seen a man so bewildered, so tormented with heartache.

Philippe began to cry upstairs, and she welcomed the piercing noise. She left Charles and rushed to her room and the baby without another spoken word.

CHAPTER XIV.

It seemed as though all the noises of the island that had charmed Eliza when she initially arrived years ago had been duller and less vibrant. The frogs at night had sounded quieter to her ears, and other inhabitants, like the birds, seemed to have vanished entirely. It was a somber reminder of the capriciousness of nature; even its most regular cadences and patterns were subject to change. The only constants on this island were the ceaselessly advancing waves and the heat of the sun. But now she could hear the parrots again.

Eliza consulted her naturalist book, wondering if the green birds left the area for a particular length of time, but it had not specified any notes on migration. She did learn that the birds paired monogamously and remained bonded until the chicks reached independence. They were social creatures and put the interest of their chicks first in order to ensure survival. There was even an account of a male parrot from one pairing raising the chicks fathered by a male from a second pairing, although she had never heard of any other species behaving in such a manner.

As varied and vocal their calls were, so too seemed their demeanors. Before, she had enjoyed looking for them in the treetops because they were so startling to behold, but now she appreciated them for an entirely different reason. So, when she heard their noisy squawks in the trees behind the house, she felt satisfaction. It was a small and familiar comfort, but a comfort nonetheless, and a reminder that pieces of happiness were slowly returning to her.

Eliza smiled as she leaned against the railing of the porch, a hand shading her eyes from the sunlight. It was unusually bright today. The light didn't seem to affect Philippe. He looked upwards at her, giggling whenever she made faces.

"Can you hear the birds?" she asked him as she swayed.

Her life would never be the same. They communicated with each other with eyes and mouths, with grunts and pants. It was all so simple in these early days, but she knew they would not last, so she savored every moment with him.

Philippe was growing rapidly now. She had to be careful with him because he seemed to relish putting objects in his mouth, and he could even crawl. She monitored his evolving form and delighted in every milestone as if they each measured small victories. She wanted to praise every breath that emanated from his tiny chest; it made her recall the thin and fragile line between life and death. The boy's movements and facial expressions continually reminded her of Jean, but the ache in her heart had not dulled. He should have been there to see his child, and so despite her joy, the child's development was still bittersweet.

The door behind them opened, and Charles and Lucy came outside. Eliza looked twice at Charles. He was not wearing his uniform this morning and instead had donned a plain black jacket with tan breeches.

"My business this morning is not suited for regimentals," he said, gazing outwards at the sea. "But I think you will find it pleasing nonetheless."

Eliza bobbed Philippe in her arms, smiling at his cooing noises, and then looked back at Charles.

"What is on your schedule today?" she asked.

A week had passed since her outburst on the stairs, and time had seemed to soften it into a hazy remembrance. They did not linger on the words that had been exchanged but focused instead on small cordialities and more harmless topics.

"I've been called to a political meeting. Mr. Wylly has organized it."

"I do not know him."

"I think you will find that you and he share similar sentiments to events transpiring in this colony. There needs to be a discussion on the future of these islands."

Eliza bobbed Philippe up and down in her arms again, focusing more on the child than her husband. "Is Lord Dunmore not attending this meeting?" she asked distractedly.

"No. Indeed, he is the subject of it."

Eliza's interest perked.

"I fear that I may have squandered eighteen years of my life in service. I did not fight for this," Charles said in a strange tone.

She studied him with surprise as he watched the waves lap the shoreline. He carried himself differently today. She wondered what had induced him to go to the gathering. Philippe began to cry, and Lucy reached to bring him inside. Eliza looked down and rubbed her abdomen, sighing.

"Are you still feeling ill?" Charles asked.

He took a step closer to her.

"I admit my stomach does not quite feel right."

After dinner yesterday she had felt nauseous, and she had thrown up twice in the night. It nearly reminded her of the mornings when she had carried Philippe, only she had not lain with a man in over a year. The cause of her discomfort had to be attributed to poorly prepared food. She had been fortunate to have not experienced such illness since her arrival.

Charles studied her, but she pretended to not notice his concern. She distantly wondered whether she would ever find his attention towards her charming. His behavior and mannerisms had been less distressful of late, but something about him still quickened her nerves.

"I'm a fool to have not thought of it before, wait here a moment," Charles said suddenly as he dashed into the house.

She considered going inside to escape the heat when he finally returned with two silver cups that she had never seen used before. He handed one to her and retained the other. She looked down at the yellow liquid in the cup.

"You've never presented me with pineapple juice," she said, amused by his behavior.

"No, I'm afraid I have not. It's rather sweet. You will taste nothing else. But it will soothe your gut. I mean to look after you, Eliza. We should guard our health and take every precaution we can. It is so very remote here."

Her thoughts wandered back to her first day on the island in town, when she had tasted the same fruit. He smiled and watched her drink it. A series of splashes erupted a few yards ahead in the sea. A pair of dark brown fins collided and tossed up white water as they circled and met each other.

"Nurse sharks," she said quietly as they watched the action.

"I suppose they are mating or fighting for territory. What other struggles does one encounter in life?"

"They're certainly sedentary the remainder of the time. I've even brushed my fingers alongside one once."

Charles looked alarmed. "It is a shark, Eliza."

"Yes, but these kinds are docile. I am rather fond of sharks. They are so mysterious. And everyone fears them."

"For good reason. If it has the ability to rip a conch out of its shell, surely it can take a pretty chunk out of your arm."

"To be powerful is to be misunderstood."

They took slow sips of the juice and gazed at the beach together. The drink refreshed her, but then she began to feel lightheaded again. The heat did not agree with her today. It seemed to assault her body in increasing degrees, each flash stronger than the last. She rubbed the back of her neck and looked down at the railing. Her slender hand rested only a few inches from his, and she had not moved it away. She raised her head, feeling unsteady.

"Did you manage to sleep well? I did not. The moon was like a beacon," Charles asked, watching her carefully.

His green eyes looked piercing in the natural light.

"No, I did not. I might rest for a bit," Eliza answered.

He took the empty cups and passed them to Celia as she walked to the door.

"I must take my leave now," he said, biting his lower lip.

He paused by the stairs as if he wanted to say more. Eliza slowly turned to him, the faintest smirk appearing across her face.

"If this meeting concerns what I think it does, if its very nature is shrouded in such secrecy that it necessitates you leaving your uniform at home, then I confess I am proud, Charles."

His face paled with the unexpectedness of her remark and then softened with what looked like relief. He nodded in silence, his eyes down on his boots, and then descended to the path.

She walked to the front of the house and watched him mount Alastor and ride off. As he rode further away, she could not help but think of him with a small amount of warmth. It was a foreign feeling. Her thoughts moved next to Philippe, sleeping upstairs in his bassinet. The feeling grew when she considered that such a wonderful feeling of contentment was possible due to the man who now galloped through the lane of silk cotton trees.

He drew his horse to a full stop, and he turned back. Eliza was confused for a moment until she saw him raise his hand in a wave. The unexpected action made her laugh, and she returned the gesture. His smile was fleeting. He urged Alastor forward again and disappeared behind a cloud of bone-colored dust.

A surge of heat took hold of her again, followed by a sharp pain behind her left ear. She clearly needed rest. Eliza coughed, something wet and warm dribbling from her mouth. She wiped the corner of her lips with her hand and looked down to see a scarlet drop of blood on the back of her hand. She observed it, marveling at its nearly perfect hue of red, yet puzzled by its strange and sudden appearance. A second cough came, and with it more flecks of blood stained the inside of her cupped palms.

She looked at her trembling hands with confusion, then the wave of heat returned, and the delirium she felt was so overpowering that she collapsed, feeling her hip and upper arm collide with the wooden porch. In the distance, a single parrot flew from its mate; its bright green body and white-crowned head swooped across the still yard with a brilliant flash of blue peaking from underneath its wings. But Eliza did not witness its hurried departure.

Slow, dizzying circles of black obstructed her vision with numbing regularity, and she felt herself lose the strength to even move her crumpled form. She wanted to cry out for help, but then even this thought was likewise carried away in the constant shifting tide of darkness. The beats of her heart, resilient and scarred, echoed in her ears until even this noise drifted into a ringing quiet, and she felt herself succumb entirely to the silent waves.

"You mean to risk everything to give that man, the one man who has misused your person in every possible way, a second chance? An opportunity?"

The words echoed around her ears, her heartbeat the sole constant marker of time as she drifted further into her suspended consciousness.

Eliza stood in front of the guinea corn fields that bordered either side of the dusty road to Pleasant Hall. The tall grass had grown nearly double since her arrival two years prior. The heavy perfume of the guinea corn possessed an unusual mix of sweetness and damp earth and was perceptible even yards away. She took a slow inhalation; she wasn't entirely sure how she arrived there. She was confident she was still dreaming, but the vividness of her surroundings beckoned with whispers of sharpened reality.

Memories of shouting and gunfire traced across her mind as she recalled Celia bursting through the line of trees further down and how they had desperately tried in vain to hide. The men had found them despite all their efforts. Now something different approached her, and as she watched the lush corn stalks quiver and bend, she regretted her presence. The shape of raffia, of the dried palm found on the slave huts and other outbuildings, surged forward and stopped.

It was a man, his dark arms and legs the sole clues of his true nature. The rest of his body and head were draped in rows of thousands of thin pieces of straw, wrapped around him, forming a conical shape. His face was covered, and it was unclear as to how he could even see in front of him. But it was certain that he was indeed aware of her. It was as if a yellowed, barren bush had become suddenly animated with the spirit of man, and he began to sway in a silent and disturbing dance before her.

She stood breathless, unsure of whether to run and without knowing if she even could move her legs. She was transfixed, her ears hearing nothing but the dry rattling of every piece of straw. She wanted to speak, to say something, but rationality slipped from her mind. With each stiff jerk of his body, she grew more afraid he would lunge out at her.

The figure jumped up and landed on his feet, then pulled himself a few steps back from her. His back was bent as if in a mock bow. No convulsive movement from him ever revealed his face, and when he began to retreat, a channel began to emerge from the parched earth at their feet. Water dribbled into it before her eyes and then filled it completely, forming a small creek through the corn field.

Eliza looked in amazement to her left and right, unable to see the beginning or end of this strange stream. The figure had stopped moving, and without completely understanding why, Eliza felt herself drawn to the man. She crossed over the water and joined him on the other side. Still, he would not move.

"Who are you?" she asked now.

The nervousness of her voice made her feel loud and stupid. They were surrounded by the tall, dense grass, and the milky bronze-colored beads of the corn swayed near her cheeks. A surreal blend of distant voices and the thuds of her heart assembled into a queer melody, and she felt herself grow dizzy. Her vision softened into blurriness and humidity, and an unbearable heat blared inside her. The warmth did not seem to come from the sun, descending from the sky and hitting her back, but rather seemed to emanate from her very core. She could barely catch her breath now, and when she did, the sour taste of grass and dust made her cough.

When the man refused to answer, she grew impatient, the temperature only adding to her frustration. She reached out a hand and was trying to move the raffia to the side in order to see his face when he jumped and rushed towards her. She screamed and lost her balance, falling backwards into the green corn stalks. She felt them bend and crack underneath her weight, and with it came an earthy smell from the strange cushion of broken corn. The light above her was so blinding it washed away the blueness of the sky, and all she saw was a starburst of rays and the now grey orb of the sun. She squeezed her burning eyes shut and, in the static darkness, felt herself sink.

His lips pressed against hers, insistent and impatient. She recognized his presence at once—the fragrance of leather and the faintest waft of citrus, the warmth of his face near hers. The blue light of the moon flowed near the top of the palm fronds, making them appear nearly silver in the darkness. This *was the last night of Jean's stay, the last night they had spent together. The overwhelming delight that had catapulted her mood to the highest of satisfactions had withered away to a somber murmur of strained happiness. A dilemma was slowly unfolding before her, complicating their endeavors and stealing away any mirth.*

"I realized that I was being inherently selfish. Charles would need my help, and so I delayed your journey. Our journey. I didn't know how to save both of you, but now it does not matter. It is so startlingly clear to me. I only needed to save you. I am sorry for the sudden urgency, Eliza, but we must leave tomorrow. The letter I received earlier makes it clear."

If only she had known the days that lay ahead, she wouldn't have wasted time with the words she uttered next.

"You cannot mean that you intend for him, for him to be—"

Jean's face was grave.

"He is not a good man to you, Eliza."

"But he does not deserve this fate, surely. I cannot stand idly by. Not with this knowledge! You must tell him."

Jean took a step back, his face perplexed.

"Do you hear yourself? And what about the wrongs he has committed against you?"

"You said it yourself! Dunmore will strip him of everything, and then he will be treated as a common prisoner. Not as an officer. Not as a noble. They will hang him like a petty thief without just cause. You must help him. You have the advantage!"

"This is not charity; this is some twisted form of guilt. Has he truly warped your mind?"

"It is the right course."

"*You mean to risk everything to give that man, the one man who has misused your person in every possible way, a second chance? An opportunity?*" Jean asked incredulously.

These words seemed the loudest he had yet spoken. They echoed through her, but she could not ignore the feeling in her core, and so she continued her protest.

"*You chose to prevent my departure for his sake only to damn him now. This is wrong! He does not see the corruption as plainly as you and I. He will fall. And from such great heights, it will be miserably so!*"

"*From the first night I encountered you, you spoke of nothing but ill sentiment towards this man. You complained of how you were tied to him. You do not love him! He means nothing to you; you've only said this nigh a thousand times in my presence.*"

"*Jean, you know his nature ...*"

"*I do not give a damn about whether he lives or dies. I thought we were of the same mind.*"

"*I cannot believe that is true. He was a brother to you. How easily you forget!*"

"*We have a history I do not expect you to understand.*" Jean stepped forward, grabbing her hands. "*Why are you fighting this?*"

"*I tried to ignore my conscience, but I cannot any longer. We are sinning, despite how much he may deserve it. Let us not add to this compunction!*"

Jean's face changed abruptly.

"*I know what this is. You're afraid. You're afraid to leave it all behind,*" he said quietly.

"*That is a lie.*"

"The door is standing open, and you can peer through it, yet you dare not take a further step."

He looked at her with disgust, and it made the weight on her shoulders unbearable.

"If you do not do this, you will regret it for the rest of your life," she protested.

"Eliza, you can trust me. I am making the right choice. It is a difficult choice, but it is the right decision. I love you. Please listen to me."

"You hesitated once before out of concern for him. I do not know what brand of fraternity causes one to pause over saving a man while enabling his marriage to be doomed. We have utterly betrayed him in every other way. We have already destroyed one part of his life; therefore he should at least have the chance to live out the latter half of it."

"I find your sudden loyalty remarkable. Only an hour ago, your heart was pure ice concerning him. We have no choice, Eliza. We must do this for us. We must leave this island now before it is too late!"

"I do not claim loyalty. This is his very life! This does not concern our relations."

"You are mistaken."

"I know he is not an honorable man, but you must tell him tomorrow."

Jean sharply exhaled as he realized the depth of her stubbornness.

"He will ruin us."

"He will never know about you and me; it will not fall from my lips. Nor should it cross yours. There are two separate matters at hand."

"And yet you stand here trying to convince me that he must also leave this island. That is your intended meaning. He cannot stay here. None of us can. Do you think this is natural? The gaiety of our dinners? The rhythm of our conversations at the table? He is not a stupid man, Eliza. He is not blind. He will find out at one point or another. You contradict yourself at every turn. This is madness! Please be reasonable. The same troubles will only follow us to England ... we can never be together if he comes with us!"

"England? You told me I would sail to France, that your sister was expecting my arrival. What else are you keeping from me?"

"France is full of hazards. War is coming."

Eliza scoffed and kicked at the sand near her feet. "We always have troubles with France."

"No. This will change the world. This is a revolution fueled by dangerous and violent minds. Someone hungry for power will watch with bated breath as the citizens of France kill each other like dogs and then wait for the opportune moment to strike. You have not seen the papers I have read. Europe will be embroiled in a great, bloody war. It will not be contained to Versailles. I daresay I will never live to see another king of France on the throne."

But then the memory morphed into something new. Something current, present, alive. Jean grabbed her wrist with sudden insistence.

"You must listen to me. No matter what, you must always listen to me. The queen is dead; they've gone so far as to take her life. And they will take her son's. They will lie and say he died of illness. Be careful who you trust, Eliza. The age of chivalry is gone."

The words he uttered now were so pressing in urgency, so immediate. But then the scene softened around the edges, returning to the more muted renderings of remembrance.

"So then we should remain here. Far away from it all," she said slowly.

"Yes, the three of us can continue as we have done."

His tone smacked of sarcasm. The displeasure in his countenance threatened all the joy she had so recently felt.

"I desire to be with you! Do not mistake my intention!"

"And yet not far away enough from him. I do not understand you at all, Eliza. You do no credit to your sex with a sentiment like that. You wish to help him. Why? He offers you no common decency."

His tone was full of anger and arrogance. He had never spoken with so little regard to her feelings before.

"We can arrange matters … once we quit this place. We can go to another island!"

"He will find us, and he will be our ruin. He is incapable of mercy."

Eliza could not deny this.

"Please. At least warn him. At least explain what you are truly doing here in Nassau. Help him understand the severity."

Jean shook his head in disgust.

"He will not listen. And he is not worthy of saving. This is a mistake. You will regret this."

She watched Jean step away from her and walk back towards the house. She wanted to stop him; she wanted to retract everything she had said, if only to lessen the weight of his disappointment in her. But above all, she wanted him to stay.

She knew that if he continued walking away, she would never see Jean again. She opened her mouth to call out his name, but no sound left her lips.

The next few hours danced before her eyes: the yelling and shouting, the pistol shot, the smash of glass from the fallen decanter. How irrevocably wrong she had been. A brutal image of the still, hemp rope followed next, and the knowledge that Jean had died because of her foolishness made her scream, and she fell to her knees. What had she done? The land seemed to shift beneath her, and she jolted forward.

Eliza opened her eyes, the bright light of the parlor making the adjustment difficult. She swallowed in distress and, looking around, realized she was lying down on the chaise. Someone held her hand, and her skin felt wet. Turning, she saw Charles sitting next to her, his eyes moist but now widening with surprise.

"Eliza! Thank you, Lord, thank you," he muttered, bowing his head into her hand.

The normalcy of the setting had the slightest effect of softening the panic she felt from the interrupted dream, but a jumble of other images trickled through her mind. She saw herself rocking Philippe into slumber, waving farewell to Charles on the porch, and heard the slightest whisper from the one man she would do anything to stand beside again.

But then she remembered one dream more in depth—the words they had exchanged on one singularly real night more than a year ago. The regret of her mistake was still bitter on her lips until she recalled one final vision, which was the dancing man covered in straw. Only upon awakening did she realize how analogous the experience was to that night on the beach in the thunderstorm or the serene sense of well-being she felt when she swam in the ocean. Perhaps the encounter was more than a mere dream. But what did it all mean?

At any rate, cognizance finally made her question why she was lying in the parlor and not in her bedroom and why Charles appeared before her in such a distraught state.

"The color has returned to your cheeks," he said, observing her. "How do you feel?"

"Terribly exhausted. Only I sense all I have done is rest."

She recognized the lack of stays on her torso and pulled the sheet higher up to cover herself.

"That is to be expected," Charles answered.

"What happened? I do not recall a thing other than your departure. The meeting with Mr. Wyatt, how did it go? I pray I did not cause you to miss it."

"Mr. Wylly," he answered, correcting her. "It went well enough, although I daresay there is time to discuss that yet. I can think only of your recovery. Lucy found you collapsed on the porch, and with the help of Josiah, they brought you in here. Cleo managed the affair from that point on. Your body was ravaged with malignant fever for nearly two days." Charles took a deep breath. "Your case was severe. You were coughing up blood. There was so much of it. I was on the verge of notifying Mr. Banks in town. I wanted to have him bleed you. That is the customary practice for tropical fever. I was desperate, but Cleo would not hear of it. She made you drink concoctions she had prepared, guava, I believe. No, it was a tincture of fever grass, ginger, and honey, and something she mixed with warm water. I cannot confess to understanding how she managed it, but she was able to reduce the fever. I have never seen such a transformation. Indeed, I feared the very worst …"

"I suppose providence has seen fit to keep me here a while longer."

She laughed as she said this, but his face paled. Eliza looked away, finding his display of emotions too intense.

"Where is he?" she asked quietly.

Charles' demeanor shifted abruptly, and she at once knew that he misunderstood her.

"I believe you experienced some vivid dreams. Fever dreams. There is no shame in it. You said his name countless times."

She felt him drop her hand.

"I meant Phillipe."

Charles composed himself and shifted his weight in the chair. He had revealed a vulnerability and now clearly regretted it.

"Lucy is tending to him at the moment. We dared not bring him near this room. I think we should wait longer still, as a necessary precaution. Infants are especially susceptible to this fever."

"Yes, I understand."

She did not feel entirely comfortable knowing her son had been left in his care. But she could not deny that she was grateful that Philippe was spared from the sickness.

"And your health? Cleo's? Has anyone else fallen sick?"

"I am fine, thank you. Cleo is immune to the fever, and I was taken with it when I was very young. It has no effect on me now."

"I feel as though I have slept for ages. I daresay I wouldn't be surprised if the world had gone utterly mad since I was last awake. Is it still November?"

She laughed as she said this, but Charles' face was solemn.

"I regret to admit that such a statement is too near the truth. I was reading *The Gazette*. Events in France have reached a breaking point. It seems that the fanatics were not sated with the king's blood alone."

Be careful who you trust, Eliza. The age of chivalry is gone ...

"They have killed the queen ..." Eliza said to herself, not realizing how clearly she had spoken.

It was disturbing to say aloud. The idea that a woman, born with royal blood, could fall victim to the whims of a bloodthirsty mob chilled her.

"Yes, they have even beheaded the queen now." Charles shook his head, but he paused, his countenance troubled. "How could you possibly know that?"

Eliza looked away towards the ceiling, swallowing nervously. She was herself shocked to hear the news, although she had known it before Charles had told her. A chill traveled through her as she realized it served as some ominous confirmation from Jean. She had not experienced a mere fever dream. Jean had visited her in some nameless space that was neither life nor death.

"It's no matter. Perhaps you read it somewhere before you had fallen ill."

But the tone of his voice did not seem convinced. He sighed.

They've gone so far as to take her life. And they will take her son's. They will lie and say he died of illness.

"They will come for her son next. They will lie and say that he was taken with illness."

"Indeed, I fear for this world. The French are lusting for blood at any cost."

She had spoken too quickly once again, although Charles had not thought her words strange this time. The more alert she grew, the more she feared what else she had accidentally shared. Charles had intimated that she had called out for Jean. What else had she revealed?

"I apologize for anything I might have said. I cannot recall it clearly," she said, her ears burning with shame.

"If I may be so bold, whatever haunted you in your dreams is but fiction, Eliza. You are safe here. Philippe is safe. We are all safe now," Charles said. He leaned uncomfortably close and kissed her forehead. "I will return later and read to you if so desire it. Rest is still necessary at this stage."

She nodded in polite agreement, but all she could think was one repeating thought.

She had surely chosen wrong that fateful night.

CHAPTER XV.

Eliza squinted, rereading the same paragraph for the second time. She was nearly done with a chapter of her novel, and she needed to freshen up before dinner. She wondered where Charles was and shortly found out as the front door slammed. A series of booming footsteps, precise like a military drill, brought him into her field of view. He looked slightly disheveled. Sweat beaded his forehead, red from the sun, and his pulled-back hair was askew. As he turned, she noticed something else striking about his appearance. A red swollen mark surrounded one of his eyes.

"I'm afraid I've done something terrible …" was all he said.

Eliza placed her book on the side table and slowly approached him, staring at the darkening bruise around his left eye. It occurred to her that whoever had the gall to attack a man like him must be even more intimidating if not a completely reckless fool.

"What has happened?" she asked.

"I find myself in the act of making enemies all around, and these people have sought petty vengeance. I was struck with a rock as I alighted Alastor. I regret that he sustained some damage as well, but Julius is now tending to him in the stable. I'll find a pretty mark on my face tomorrow, no doubt."

Charles removed his black jacket and rifled through his pockets, placing a series of crumbled papers on the table.

"Were they Dunmore's men? I do not understand. To be accosted in broad daylight …"

"No, no. At least, I do not think so."

"Do people lose respect when they do not see a uniform? You are the commander of the regiment!"

"I believe that is precisely the fount of their anger. They harassed me and urged me to better remember my place, as they put it. They said a man has almost as good a right to set fire to his own house, though his neighbors be destroyed by it, than to act as I have done."

He placed himself in a chair with a heavy thud. Eliza's mind raced with wild misgivings.

"And what exactly have you done?"

Eliza stood on edge, waiting to hear the very worst. Charles swallowed, fussed with the papers, and then took a long sigh.

"I have freed Cleo."

The words set Eliza's nerves ablaze. She must have misheard him.

"Beg pardon?" she whispered.

Charles seemed irritated by her reaction and handed

her one of the papers. One side displayed the back of a claims form, the other a hastily scribbled note that read:

December 12th 1793. I manumit and forever set free a Negro woman nam'd CLEO FINDLAY. In witness whereof I set my hand and seal.

SHARPE.
WITNESSES: MALCOM HARRISON. BAHAMA IS.

> *Memorandum this twelfth day of December 1793 personally appeared before me, Malcom Harrison, the subscribing witness to the within written manumission and made oath that he was present and did see Lord Charles Sharpe of Nassau sign, seal and as his act and deed, deliver the written writing.*

She looked at the man before her, his countenance grim and brooding, and back at the paper. Eliza wanted to embrace him, to kiss him even, but she restrained herself. Whatever joy she felt was insignificant compared to the emotions Cleo would feel. *Cleo Findlay.* That must have been the surname of her former owner. And what of her name before she came to the West? Her true and given name? These and other queries sprang up with force in her mind.

Eliza felt tears forming in her eyes, but she held them back. She feared sentimentality would further drive him to regret his decision. And what an extraordinary decision for a man like him. She wanted to ask a thousand questions, but she controlled herself. Only one truly mattered.

"And it is official? Legally ... legally binding?" she asked.

His hawkish glare darted back up at her.

"Quite. The court asked me to describe her only as 'disposed' from this point on. Not 'freed.'" He shook his head. "But freed she is."

Chills cascaded down her back.

"Well ... this is momentous! I am in awe, Charles."

But her jubilation withered away under the force of his persisting discontent.

"My intentions are sincere, but it would appear that the law and the language of this colony is not. It seems as though a law was created but not meant to be utilized."

Now the source of his troubled reaction was beginning to be clarified.

"Surely no one can fault you for making use of a law that exists for such a purpose? You've done no wrong," she countered.

"And yet I can find no evidence of committing any right." He kept his gaze focused on the window before him as the dark shadows of fieldworkers crossed the front of the house. "What makes her truly free? A piece of paper?" He scoffed, taking it from Eliza's hands. "A flimsy piece of parchment. That is all the surety she now has of a God-given right."

His voice was deep and low like a growl. Eliza's heart had remained at nearly a standstill, but it slowly resumed a quickening beat. She had never heard him speak like this before. A window of opportunity appeared, and she burned with impatience. She rushed over to him, placing her tanned hand over his.

"You have done no wrong. Indeed, you have done something wonderful." Eliza studied his face. "Did you get such an idea from your political meetings? Is this what you discuss there?"

Charles had acquired a steady habit of attending these meetings for the last couple of weeks. He rode out regularly every Thursday to the Wylly plantation. Eliza was curious about what the men discussed in these gatherings.

"No, I daresay they tried to discourage me."

Eliza's confusion doubled.

"What inspired such a feeling then?"

His eyes seized on her then with an emotion she couldn't quite place. She yearned for him to place his confidence in her. A change was occurring within him, whether he acknowledged it or not, and she wanted to seize its momentum before it evaporated.

"I will not be the man my father was. I refuse to even resemble him in the slightest, and yet I fear that I have started the process of making this place nothing more than a large, white house. My father groans in his grave."

"That is of no consequence. You've never held him in high regard."

He paused, lost deep in thought.

"What troubles you?" Eliza pressed.

She could almost see him constructing fortifications inside his mind, fastening down the feelings that carried too heavy a weight. He, at times, seemed eager to speak, but his lips remained closed as if he thought better of whatever sentence he yearned to say.

The clock in the hallway gonged for the hour.

"It will never be enough," he finally said. "I thought I would feel triumph, relief even. But I feel pained. I feel remorse. The most incredible, bitter remorse. And nothing can check it. It is like a flood overwhelming my faculties. Ninety pounds … the price of freedom costs the same as a fine silk dress." He bowed his head in his large hands. "I intended to do an act of kindness, of justice, and now I am faced with insurmountable heights. I feel as though I have gone mad. There is a twisted knot before me, and I do not have the power to unravel it."

Eliza's hands grazed the fabric of her skirt. Her mind went to the handful of silk dresses she had stored in the trunks of her room. The idea of putting a price on a human being's freedom was disconcerting. She had been on this island for two and a half years now, and the idea of slavery had never settled into any degree of normalcy. She wondered how a planter, born and raised on this land, inheriting its system of brutality and cruelty, could have achieved the same turn of opinion. And she feared he would swing back to the same frame of judgment he had used before. She needed to tread carefully with her reaction.

"Surely you are free to do with your *property* as you please." The very word was sour on her tongue. "Surely … other men like you have done the same thing. I have heard of planters freeing their female slaves, of freeing children—"

"They free their mistresses, Eliza. The ones who have given them children. They free their wards, made from their own flesh, a continual, living reminder of sin and weakness. They do not free slaves in the name of justice alone."

Eliza's heart sank as she realized another angle of barbarity hidden from her view. It begged an urgent question.

"And what of Lucy? Is she to be freed as well?" She waited anxiously for a response.

The protracted exhalation she heard was not promising.

"The clerk has informed me that they're withholding her case for *'reasons unknown.'*" He examined the piece of paper again as if its meager scribbling could offer some sought after answer. "For ninety pounds, I fancied something more substantial, but the court wishes to conserve paper on the island. For 'more *important* matters.'" He drummed his fingers on the table. "Mind you, it was not my first occasion, but rather my fifth, to see the magistrate. The office had a difficult time in acquiring a witness. At first, I found it an oddity, then I understood it to be deliberate."

"How precisely does one go about freeing ... another person?" Eliza asked, her eyes glued to him.

He sighed. Evidently, he even found the act of explaining it wearisome.

"Custom dictates an announcement in the papers to be made first, and generally, one would bring the slave to the judge and proceed in the standard way. But the law is looser here; the slave does not need to present themselves. I feared I would frighten Cleo to death if I asked her to accompany me to a courthouse, so it is a blessing. Instead, money is paid to the Receiver General and Treasurer. There's a small fee for the filing as well. And a witness, as I have now learned, is essential. The magistrate hands you a written statement that is signed and sealed. And that is all that is required."

"It baffles all comprehension. So, you must return to the court for Lucy?"

"I have no other choice."

"When will you tell Cleo? You should go to her now!"

"I hesitate to. What shall I tell her? You are free to go, but your child remains in bondage?" Charles scoffed and threw his hands on the table.

"You must tell her ..."

"In one sense, she is safer in my hands. Under my control—"

"Nonsense! She is free now. It is a blessing, it—"

He slammed his boot down against the floor. "Eliza! You do not know of these matters. I have spoken to my lawyer. Now that Cleo is freed, she is in more danger than she was before. Do you see this slip of paper? This leaf that can blow away on the very wind? That is the only thing guaranteeing her freedom. Her safety. If she were to lose this paper, she would lose everything. Slavers can come and kidnap her and sell her somewhere worse, to the south, to the sugar islands. A planter can come and say, 'Here is my runaway that escaped last year ...' and clamp her in irons. A crueler man can simply rip up the paper. It would be his word against hers. None of this is simple."

His voice was pained.

"She can remain here. She is protected here—" Eliza offered.

"Is that freedom?"

They were both silent. Eliza's buoyant attitude was beginning to sink, but she desperately wanted to retain her hope.

"I have made a mistake. It was senseless to get the court embroiled in my private affairs," he uttered. "Now I have made more enemies than before."

Eliza crouched down beside his chair, taking his hand in hers once more.

"You have done the right thing."

"It hardly feels like it."

"No, no ... you have done the greatest of things!"

But his unrelenting severity on the subject began to make her feel uneasy. This great house was sustained by one force and by one force only. Would it crumble if its very foundation was removed? Granting Cleo her freedom was one matter, but what of the rest? How would they react to such news? Would they be vengeful?

"It is useless. She has now spent more days of her life unfree. Fettered to one man, and then cast off to another. Inherited like any other piece of property. A mere object."

"One breath of freedom will taste sweeter to her than any nectar..." Eliza urged, squeezing his hand for emphasis.

"I carried other plans before turning to this. I had a mind to slowly train the field laborers in practical crafts. Josiah would make a fine blacksmith, for one. If they have skills, they can better navigate this world. Then—"

The fate of the others demanded her attention again. An unsettling worry grew in the pit of her stomach. She rose to a stand.

"I am afraid that cannot be the answer. You will only create laborers with commendable talent whom you do not have to pay and over whom you still possess the greatest legal control. That will not do."

But she could not bring herself to say what should be done. Because in that moment she realized, much like he had said, that the problem was so much more complicated than anticipated. She had spent much of her waking hours ruminating over the darkness that stained Pleasant Hall, but at the moment of such an important discussion, she herself failed to conceive a practical solution.

"Indeed. I anticipated such faults. I have been thinking about this for some length of time. I had ideas of generating an income from rents and interest. I thought the answer could be found in the law, but now I am not so sure. I am glad Cleo was spared the violent scene as I left the courthouse today. At least I have that for compensation."

Eliza was lost in thoughts of society, of the other plantations that dotted this island. It seemed that a very thin but unbreakable and sinister line connected all parts of Nassau to the trade. Even those who did not directly hold the whip had much to gain from a system of violence and oppression. It was daunting to confront an adversary so embedded into the very sands of the Bahamas. She wanted some reason other than greed to account for the evilness of men.

"I still do not understand why they attacked you so vilely. What do they care for the manumission of one slave? Or two?" When he did not immediately answer, she continued. "I have heard of others freeing faithful servants. Why, take Mr. Harris, for example. This is no different. Who are they to strike you?"

"Mr. Harris was an eccentric old man that no one paid any heed to," he said with a glare. "And besides, the slave he freed was his own child." He paused when he saw horror wash over Eliza's face. He continued in a calmer tone, "I am freeing a woman. A woman that someone could use for some purpose, even if it's simply dusting the portraits in a hallway for the rest of her miserable life. And I am the commander of this island. I am setting a dangerous example."

"And so they attack you in the street …" Eliza said quietly.

"I fear they are privy to my design. I wish to free my slaves now and not on condition of my death. I am ultimately bent on freeing all of them. In my legal queries, I have come across the case of an American in Virginia who has formed a method that unfolds gradually. He is still involved with the local courts."

It took a moment for her to register what he had said, so smoothly and deliberately had he said it. She examined his expression, greatly surprised by the total sincerity she found within.

"*All* of them?"

"Every single man, woman, and child," he answered.

The floor seemed to undulate beneath her feet, and

she felt herself fall back and to the side. Charles shouted her name, but she had lost control.

Eliza awoke on the sofa with his iron grip on her arm. His green eyes were dilated and boring down on her with a curious mix of fury and concern.

"Not a word," he threatened, his tone menacing. "I should not have disclosed that to you. Your nerves are in too tender a state."

His aggression took her off guard, but when she spotted Lucy in the background holding a damp cloth she dimly understood his meaning. The conversation they had just held rang through her ears in a silent loop.

"Smelling salts are no longer necessary, Lucy. Lady Sharpe cannot abide the use of them." He turned back to her. "I remember it well."

The scene of Charles securing her hand in her father's study in Bleinhill Manor now seemed more distant in time than a few years ago. He leaned in closer to her, brushing the side of his cheek against hers as he whispered, "I beg you to keep this in your confidence."

Eliza started up in protest.

"But you must tell Cleo. You must!"

With one hand, he pressed her gently back down on the cushion, placing the rag over her forehead. The pressure from his fingertips caused two rivulets of water to stream down her face.

"I will. In due time."

"Charles?"

"Yes?"

"You have done the right thing."

"We will see."

His tone was disturbing and devoid of any reassurance. He stood up, strode to the table to collect the manumission paper, and left the room.

Charles ducked into the doorway of Cleo's hut. He had stepped outside to walk along the beach and process what he had just done. But when he saw the first line of thatched palm roofs that marked the beginning of the slave dwellings, he felt a sudden urge to tell Cleo at once. It would be cruel to keep such news from her. Eliza was right in that regard.

Cleo stopped what she was doing when she saw him. Alarm washed over her face. He felt a great sense of satisfaction knowing that her expression would soon change. He came bearing news that would alter her life. A heavy burden would be lifted from both their frames soon enough.

"What happened, Charles? Did something happen? Are Eliza and the boy all right?"

Charles was confused for a moment, then adjusted the expression on his face into a more serious one. He had pictured this very moment in his mind dozens of times. He feared he would stammer and blunder his delivery.

"Here," he said slowly. "It is your freedom." He waved the piece of parchment towards her, his face turning redder by the moment. "It is a reward for your service to the Sharpe family," he added.

Cleo looked at the manumission slip and then back at him. Her demeanor was unreadable. She was not reacting the way he had imagined.

"You are mistaken," she finally said with a wry smile. "For I was always free. I do not need a piece of paper to tell me that."

Charles grew hotter, and he clenched his fists.

Does she not care? Does she not understand the hell I endured? he thought.

He steeled himself. This moment was about her, not him. He needed to remain calm.

"Yes, yes, I understand that you may feel that way with your manner of thinking, but this is a legality. You are now legally free, Cleo. Do you understand ... my meaning?" he asked.

"I live by the rules of another world, Charles," Cleo responded as she placed it on a table and returned to her task. She started wiping out a bowl carved from a gourd as if this was any other banal conversation.

"That is not the same. I owned you. And now I do not."

"I am the same person I was before you came to me today," she said, extending her palms and turning them over. "See?"

"Cleo, why do you test me like this? Do you not recall that I sold your daughter when I was short on my debts? Monster that I am," Charles said painfully. "You *belonged* to me! You were my property."

Cleo sighed.

"And is that how you viewed me? In your heart?" she asked.

"No! Heaven forbid … Cleo, you know me. You raised me!" His voice grew louder.

"I do," she said with a nod. "And that is why this was unnecessary. You have brought unwarranted trouble to yourself now."

Charles' shoulder twitched with the slightest frustration, but Cleo ignored him. He looked outside the hut, then back in, feeling more akin to a confused child. He felt nothing like the proud, righteous man he had envisioned. He had believed she would be grateful. He had foolishly thought that his regret would be soothed away by her outstretched arms. Cleo studied him for a few moments.

"But thank you for this … I can see it caused you some trouble," she said, softening her reaction.

She walked towards him, inspecting his bruised eye.

"Would you like me to make a salve for your eye? I can mix aloe with some chili peppers. The warmth will draw the fluids away from it. It looks tender."

"No," he said with impatience. "It is not necessary."

Cleo gave him a questioning look, then returned to the back of the dwelling. A warm breeze entered the space and stirred the paper laying on the low table. He eyed it nervously.

"Be careful with it. I beg you, Cleo. Please be careful with that paper."

"It will sit right here. Where else can it go?"

"Cleo, you do not realize what this means! You are free, but there are people who will try to take it from you. If you cannot show proof of your freedom, they will not care. They will only see the color of your skin, nothing more."

Cleo did not answer. She continued rearranging various bowls and plates.

"You are free to leave here. You do not have to work another day in your life!"

Now she stopped, and the smile left her face.

"I will not leave Pleasant Hall. I will never leave my daughter," she said, shaking her head. "You know that. So, there is no need to worry. Your energy is precious enough as it is. Do not waste it with false thoughts."

"You are acting like a fool! Any other slave would fall to their knees with tears of joy. You carry on as if nothing has occurred! Do you not realize what I have done for you?" he shouted.

His voice was loud enough for the others to hear, but he no longer cared. He felt exasperated. It was as if his trials would never cease.

"You are not upset by today. No," she said slowly, shaking her head. "You are upset over other things. Things that happened a long time ago. You feel guilt. But you should not. You do not owe me anything."

"How can you, of all people, say that?" he said, the timbre of his voice fraying like a worn thread.

"You did not buy me. Your father did."

"Stop with these mindless games and twists of words. The matter is black and white. You cannot convince me otherwise."

"The color of the soul is all I see. You know this, Charles. Now, no more talk of this."

She walked around the small space, putting what few material items she owned in order. Then she stopped, clutching her chest.

"What is the matter?" he asked with concern.

"Oh, it is nothing. Sometimes I get a pain here."

Charles watched her, but he was still troubled by what they had discussed.

"Tell me how to make amends. I thought this would correct the course; I believed that you wanted—" he said, his irritation rising again.

"It is not your place to give it. Just as it is not any man's to try to take it away in the first place."

"Make no mistake, Cleo, this piece of paper that you so carelessly toss away is the only thing these men care about. It is priceless."

"Why? What does it do? Does it make them look at me any differently? Does it make them respect me? That is the greatest gift. And no amount of money can buy that."

Charles slumped against the damp limestone wall.

"I wanted to fix it. I wanted to stop all of this misery. I simply want it all to end—" he said.

Cleo came to him, rubbing his arm with reassurance.

"You know … you live like a man who thinks the gate of heaven can close on him before he ever reaches it. But there is no gate to heaven."

He looked up at her, his green eyes narrowing in disgust.

"I cannot tolerate your meandering talk a moment longer."

"You trouble yourself with the burden of others. And it will break you, Charles."

"I was trying to help," he said in a broken whisper.

"This has nothing to do with you. What I mean to say, child, is that you have no control over it. But it will end soon."

"I wish I had the optimism you so effortlessly display time and again," Charles quipped. He looked down to the floor. "I cannot tolerate the machinations of this plantation a day longer."

"You have before. And you will again," Cleo replied, placing a hand on her hip.

He glared at her slightly. He hated when she was right. He turned to leave the hut, his stomach uneasy with this entire encounter.

"I do ask one thing."

He stopped and rushed to her side.

"What? Tell me. Tell me how to make this right," he demanded.

"Free my daughter. Free Lucy. She has a longer life to live."

"You have my word," he said with a nod.

Charles did not have the heart to disclose that he had already initiated her daughter's case. Cleo wouldn't understand the legality of it all. In truth, he wasn't sure he entirely did either. He wanted to avoid questions. It would lessen the chance of him losing his temper. That was not the way he wanted to end this conversation with her.

He was eager to take his leave, but he heard the pig knuckle bones Cleo used for divination hit the wooden table.

"Better days are on the way. You will end together. Every time you grow apart from her, you come back even stronger. Remember that."

The idea that she was offering him advice at a moment like this did not lessen his guilt. Instead of focusing on her own future and that of her only child, she was thinking about his marriage.

"There is no need for counsel. I did not seek it," he said quietly.

"It does not matter; they urged me to throw the bones," she said, studying their abstract pattern. "You worry about far too many things, Charles."

Her dark eyes, deep like still pools of water, connected with his. But then he realized that Cleo was looking past him, above his shoulders. He didn't like the look on her face.

"What is it?" Charles asked, dreading the answer. "There is something else. I recognize that look."

She sighed. She was troubled by whatever she saw.

"Beware the governor. He is not an enemy you are used to."

Relief filtered over him. This was nothing new.

"I'm well aware," Charles said.

Cleo raised a hand in stubborn defiance.

"No, there is something with a piece of paper. They keep showing it to me ..."

"It must be the invitations I've received. I have turned

down several. I wager he is not pleased with me. I once answered his every beck and call," Charles replied. "But I thank you for the information."

He was not impressed with the message, but it was better than receiving an ill omen.

"You are not listening. He uses other men to wage his fights."

"I could have told you that." Charles laughed in a low tone. "The man can barely strut across his parlor."

Cleo's expression did not shift. Whatever she had seen still concerned her. He wished she would redirect her thoughts. This was not important.

"You told me once before that the man could not stop me. And I'll make sure of it," he said.

Charles smiled at her, but the tense energy she displayed did not waver.

"And I will see to it that Lucy is manumitted. However, I must warn you, the courts are slow and tedious. Especially with a matter like this."

Cleo nodded, but it was solemn, as if she was more concerned for his welfare than her own. Nothing he could say would shift her attention.

Everything on this island is backward, he thought as he stepped outside.

His head ached. He needed a dram of whiskey and a silent room to sort through his troubled thoughts.

CHAPTER XVI.

Charles turned his back to the glaring light of midday and began to rustle through some letters in his folio. He wanted to go for a ride after this. He needed to feel the wind on his face. The heat was unbearable in his small quarters in the afternoon. Fort Charlotte was still not entirely completed, and a cramped, makeshift space served as his office. It had a pressing effect on his senses, and it did not bode well with his current mood.

Anxiety rattled his mind as he pondered over his extenuating legal issues. Manumitting Lucy seemed even more daunting than freeing her mother. Cleo's reaction to receiving her certificate of freedom a week earlier still left him unsettled. Charles feared his sacrifice was lost to her. Cleo lived by the rules of an entirely different world. It had the effect of making her a strong woman, one whose will was crafted from iron. He should have understood this better. Either way, false expectations of tearful gratitude could have never soothed his guilt away.

And now he had prodded the hornet's nest. He feared stirring up more notice; he knew the governor's beady eyes were directed on his back, tracking his every move.

The opinion of a few strangers who were angry with his business in the court was one matter. He cared little for their response. But on this small, isolated island, he knew gossip spread quicker than fire. It would only be a matter of time before Lord Dunmore heard about his dealings with the judge. In all likelihood, he already knew. Charles could well expect an invitation to a private dinner with him, a formal yet thinly veiled threat, when he arrived home later that evening. Indeed, he was surprised one had not yet been delivered.

But Charles was a well-prepared man. He had already concocted a plausible excuse as to why he felt the need to free Cleo. He was duty-bound; after years of serving the Sharpe family so faithfully, the old woman deserved nothing less. Lucy's manumission case was a harder task. She was young and could still provide many years of service. She was an attractive woman, and Charles knew that many plantation owners would not hesitate to use her for other nefarious purposes. Freeing a slave like her made no rational sense to anyone on the island. It did not matter if he had the funds to file her manumission, he also needed a flawless argument for doing so.

In the true manner of worries and the way they spread like a contagion of the mind, Charles' thoughts even strayed to Philippe. He did not want him to be raised in such an environment. Charles knew the effect of that well, and he did not want the same fate for the boy. He refused to subject him to such a cruel world. He knew the child would face enough difficulty as he grew older and his understanding deepened. If he were to raise the child as his own, he could not tolerate the idea of passing on his burdens to him. Charles could not control events outside Pleasant Hall, but he would be damned if he couldn't make the child's home a place of refuge from it all.

And then there was Eliza. The way she had looked at him when he confessed his plan inspired him to move forward, but he also feared disappointing her. She, of all people, understood why slavery was a bane in this colony, but she had little knowledge of how the legal system worked in this regard. In truth, he himself had only recently realized the paper-thin fragility of concepts he had once taken for granted.

As a young man, he had accepted the brutal lesson that freedom was denied to some people because of the color of their skin. But he had also understood that his position in society afforded him the privilege of disposing of his property as he saw fit. Now, the further he was involved in the court system, the more he understood he had little power over any of this. Invisible chains kept tight boundaries over this society, governing people's actions and, as a consequence, their very thoughts.

But it would not stop him. That made him a dangerous man in Nassau.

The slightest scrape against the damp limestone floor alerted his attention. His aid must have returned. It was convenient timing. Charles had forgotten to mention something to him an hour ago.

"Turner? Before you finish the report, is it possible to undertake a second review of the actual figures? We cannot afford another round of errors."

The answer he expected was not forthcoming. Charles turned and saw a man whose face was new to him. His dark hair was stuck to his head with sweat and grime. He stood there holding a rolled scroll of paper. He did not offer a salute or announce his name.

"What is the meaning of this?" Charles demanded. He stepped forward, annoyance at the unwanted intrusion beginning to surface.

The soldier stared at him. There was a sinister look in his eye that seemed out of place in the awkward encounter. And then he lunged, revealing a knife he had concealed inside the scroll. He crossed the distance between them in one move.

This caught Charles off guard, and he could not dodge the flash of the man's blade entirely. His arms flew up in defense while he tried to push the man back. The man slashed his struggling arms and drove the blade down, aiming for Charles' torso. He twisted his body away, but it wasn't fast enough. The knife landed in the soft tissue of his thigh, driving into the muscle, and Charles cried out in pain as he watched the metal leave his body and rise into the air again. A devastating warmth began to flood through his leg, and an uncomfortable heat emanated from the deep wound.

But he tried to focus only on the knife and keeping it far from his body. There was no time for talking or even shouting. The attack was swift and brutal. The archway that led outside revealed no source of help. The men engaged in a wordless struggle between life and death, a match between a knife fueled by anger and struggling bare hands.

Charles caught the man's wrists, holding them aloft, and a contest of strength ensued. He needed to pin the arm that held the weapon down. His mind raced with names as he tried to place the soldier's background. He had seen his face once or twice in the last few days—a new arrival to the island colony. The soldier was wiry, but his rage made up for any physical weakness.

Confusion made Charles slower and more vulnerable than he liked. He looked around for his pistol, but it was too far. His sword was likewise at too great a distance. He had foolishly disarmed himself in the heat of the afternoon sun. A few blocks and a well-placed kick sent the attacker backward, and Charles had only a moment to reach for his firearm when the pain in his leg stopped him. He clutched the gaping wound, trying to stem the flow of blood. That kick had momentarily stopped the soldier, but it also reminded Charles of the precariousness of his new situation. He was wounded, and this weakness could prove fatal.

When he looked up again, the man was inches away from him. He grasped the arm that held the knife, trying to hold it back each time the enraged man swung toward him. They stumbled backward until Charles collided with the cool stone wall. He could not afford to be trapped like this. He needed to recover the space between them, and he used all of his force to drive the enemy back.

The soldier was still trying to pull him down and overpower him. He had now managed to grab the back of Charles' neck to control his target. When Charles felt the blade reach his throat, he panicked, repeatedly using his wounded leg to kick the other man, ignoring the pain with every strike, and then an explosion erupted in the small stone cavern.

Charles' green eyes went huge, fearing for a moment that the bullet had found its way into him. A coup was clearly taking place. His mind raced with possibilities of some devious scheme, but he did not feel the familiar burn of a musket ball. Instead, his attacker gasped and began to slump down Charles' body, the blade leaving a painful trail down his neck to his chest. Charles finally thrust him away, losing his balance as his wound consumed the last of his strength.

His adrenaline was surging, and he was out of breath, nearly forgetting the presence of the intruder who had stopped the attack. He looked up and saw a stocky black soldier breathing heavily, watching the blood pool from the attacker's back.

"That the most dangerous beast, sir," he said simply, shoving the body away from a stunned Charles. His voice was deep, his accent foreign.

Charles was still trying to process what had occurred, that the man standing before him had actually saved his life. That someone who looked like this man had seized the opportunity to help him and not hurt him. He did not like the position he found himself in, lying on the floor, wounded in more ways than one. He recognized from his lapel that the soldier was a captain, and he was ashamed to not know the man better.

"What? Someone who looks like me?" Charles uttered, still trying to gather himself after a whirlwind of chaos.

The new soldier stepped forward as if dismissive of his answer.

"A traitor."

They looked at each other briefly, then Charles cringed in pain.

"This the Derry man. Coulter. James Coulter. He arrived last month, sir. We was ordered to the afternoon drill, but I saw him sneak away. Saw him messin' with some roll o' paper. He walked in a direction he shouldn't, so I followed him."

"What is your name, Captain?" Charles rose to a shaky stand, almost stumbling. The soldier stepped over the dead body and offered his arm for support.

"Drummond Johnson, sir. My one master named Drummond. The other named Johnson. One man sold me. One man bought me. I carry both names now, sir." He realized the difficulty Charles had with walking, and he rearranged his stance so he could support his weight fully. "I remember you for years now, sir. I first saw you in the Floatin' Town. In America. Long time back. Got my freedom when I enlisted, sir. You saw me one day and said I was the only man fit for soldierin'."

Johnson walked with Charles to the desk, securing his pistol in his own waistband and grabbing his blade.

The blood was still flowing fast from Charles' thigh. Charles struggled to remember the captain from the past and regretted that he could not recall a single instance of him in the American war. He prided himself on knowing the men who fought under his command, and for some reason, the very face that eluded any recognition was the same face that ensured he was still breathing now. The irony was not lost on him.

"I think it best we leave this place, sir. I don't know what kind o' plot that Derry man had. And excuse me for sayin' this, but I think Lord Dunmore is a changed man. Derry man, he fancied dining at the governor's. Said as much every chance he got. I don't think anything good came from that."

That line of information sank into Charles' gut. He quickly scanned the space around them. Matters could never be the same. Charles had been in danger since he first discovered the smugglers in the cave. A clock fueled by political corruption was steadily ticking against him, and the future was uncertain.

He desperately wanted to return to Pleasant Hall. To see her face, to hold the boy in his arms. As he thought of Philippe, another face inevitably resurfaced in his mind.

"They will first try to come for me and then for you. I finally have the proof I need to secure the recall of Lord Dunmore. I am leaving for England tomorrow. I must again warn you of the precariousness of your position, Charles. It is not safe here," a pleading voice from the past rang out in his thoughts.

And so it was not. Charles had been proven wrong yet

again, with only a sliver of mercy from a stranger to save him from a violent end. His leg was still bleeding profusely. He began to panic, wondering if the Derry man, as Johnson had designated him, had severed an artery. He comforted himself with the belief that he would already be dead by now if that were the case.

"Tell me the way to your house, sir," Johnson said as they struggled through the doorway.

They were both struck by the eerie sight of an empty fortress. Not a man was in sight.

"This is planned. They might return. We need to leave, now …" Charles' voice faltered. "The road along the beach, take it all the way down."

Charles was in disbelief that the vocation he had dedicated his life to was betraying him in such a manner and that the man who had just become his hero was no different from the men and women he owned at Pleasant Hall. There was, however, one glaring exception. Drummond Johnson was a freed man. And he wore freedom well.

"Why are you doing this?" Charles managed to say.

He had been taught his whole life that violence bred more violence. It was the natural order of things. That people who looked like the captain instinctively harbored some form of hatred against people with pale skin, no matter how deep it was buried or how well concealed. Women were softer, weaker in their resolve. But he had no doubt that men like him could never be entirely trusted. Lord Dunmore had urged the formation of black recruits in the regiment due to the lack of healthy soldiers.

Charles had never questioned it, but he had always retained his suspicions of their loyalty until now. How very wrong he had been.

Charles watched Johnson with a detachment fueled by blood loss and dizziness as he found cloth to act as a constricting band, tying it tightly around the wound. Now his leg felt cold, and he feared he was bleeding far too much. He couldn't understand how they had moved so quickly to the base of the fortress to where the horses were kept. He pointed weakly at Alastor, and Johnson raised him upwards in a painful lurch and mounted the animal behind him. He heard a pistol cocked, and Johnson kicked them forward into motion. The heat and humidity outside felt overbearing, and the light, free from the battlement's shade, was harsh.

"You the only person to see me as somethin' other than a slave," Johnson said as they rode. "You saw I could become someone. You pulled me from the back o' the crowd on that ship and put me up front. Don't you remember? Back in Virginia? I'm a captain now. I'm one o' the few men to survive all the fevers passin' through here."

Somehow the story seemed more reminiscent of fantasy. Johnson's admiration was certainly misplaced; perhaps another officer had acted in such a way towards him, but there was no time to question it now. He briefly wondered if Johnson was in some way involved in this plot, yet he inexplicably trusted this stranger. Indeed, he felt nothing but baffled gratitude.

"You're promoted …"

"Sir?"

"You're promoted, Captain Johnson. After this ends, I shall see to it that you are made a major. *Major* Johnson."

"Don't fuss 'bout that, sir," Johnson said, fixated on something behind them. "Hold on, I not gonna stop 'til we there. It ain't safe in town," Johnson said.

Charles thought of recent events that had transpired. How he had deliberately disobeyed the governor by aiding the French merchants. How he had upset the townspeople by manumitting Cleo. It now seemed that these actions threatened everything he held dear.

What have I done? Once again, Charles' heart sank.

The day of Jean's execution revisited his mind. The day he arrived on the island with Eliza. The many conversations he and Lord Dunmore had exchanged. The mutual respect and yearning for recognition were dashed to meaningless drivel. There was no doubt in his mind that Lord Dunmore had hatched this scheme.

His thoughts next raced to Eliza and her safety. Alastor could not carry them as fast as he desired. The searing sunlight bore down on their backs, and he felt shame in running from the town. Charles wanted to stand and fight, but that battle would have to wait. He eased himself against the horse, feeling himself drift away into a soft monotony of hoofbeats and buffeting wind.

Eliza looked up from her book when she heard the commotion outside. As Celia opened the front door, she stood hesitatingly at first, distracted by all the noise, but when she saw Charles, she screamed.

"Oh my God!" she cried as she looked at him.

His skin was pale, and there was dried blood all over his neck and chest. For a brief moment, she wondered if he was still alive until she noticed his shallow breathing. His normally pristine white shirt was torn in the front, and he could barely register his surroundings. Then his hawkish green eyes locked on hers. His eyes conveyed pain and exhaustion, but he also looked pleased to find her standing there. She immediately looked away, taking a deep breath. She couldn't quite understand if she felt regret or relief, and she didn't have the luxury of time to process it now.

Celia backed away with wide eyes. It was strange to see a normally strong and athletic man, whose presence intimidated those in his company, in such a weakened state. She stared next at the man who was holding him upright in a half-stand. Celia had never seen a man like him wearing the red uniform, but Eliza had. The first time she had seen soldiers like him was when they had been sent to arrest Jean. Both women hesitated and backed away from him.

"Lady Sharpe?" the soldier asked, waiting for some acknowledgment. "There was an attack at the fort. The colonel will bleed out unless he gets tended to."

Celia and Eliza looked at each other in bewilderment. Celia began to move a table to the side, but the man shook his head.

"Wherever he go now, he should stay. Where his

chamber? That where he should rest," he said as he dragged him towards the stairs. "We needin' to dress the wound."

Eliza ordered Celia to fetch Cleo and watched in suspended horror as the black soldier began to move Charles step by slow step upstairs. She waited for an opportunity to slip by them, then rushed to open the door of his room. She watched in amazement as the soldier hoisted him up onto the bed and began to diligently remove his tattered uniform. Cleo bounded up the stairs next and ran to his side.

"Lord Sharpe! What has happened?" She stopped and looked up at the soldier questioningly. "Who are you?"

"Captain Johnson, ma'am. Drummond Johnson. A Derry man came and attacked the colonel; he aimed to kill him. I shot him dead through and brought the colonel here. This some order from the governor. You can't tell me otherwise. He payin' that Derry man."

"Shh, shh … we need to clean this wound before infection sets in. Bring that bowl over here," Cleo said as she began to dress the wound. Her hands were shaking as she cleaned the blood from his skin.

Cleo's lips murmured a nearly silent prayer at a rapid pace.

"Thank you, Shango. Thank you. Shango, keep him alive, Shango help him …" she prayed.

The distraught look on Cleo's face was unsettling. It was clear that this was not something she had foreseen. This was not supposed to have happened. Eliza watched them both tend to Charles and hung in the back of the room like an unwelcome guest. Cleo and the captain were so much more invested in his situation than she appeared to be. She knew she was not acting like a proper wife. This soldier probably assumed she was strange, but she did not care. She was struggling with the wild emotions that raged through her. She did not like the thoughts she had harbored when she thought he was dead, and she was grateful that the moving shadows of the room hid her expression.

She had never pictured an outcome like this. His fate, and hers along with it, had been unfairly upended once again. She quietly left, using Philippe's cry as an excuse to escape.

Captain Johnson's fork scratched against the plate as he devoured his food. Eliza watched him with curiosity, wondering when he had last eaten. She didn't expect him to have the manners of a courtier, but there was something desperate in the way he ate, almost as if he expected someone to take it from him.

Charles had been stabilized, and the laudanum Cleo had given him had sent him into a deep sleep. It was clear that the captain intended on staying the night, and Eliza was grateful for the security. Cleo had told her to send him to the kitchen in the back to take his meal, but sending away the man who had saved Charles and performed such a courageous deed seemed ill-mannered.

She was still confused by the series of events that led up to this. Perhaps only Charles could explain it fully when he awakened.

"I thank you for the hospitality, Lady Sharpe. I don't deserve a seat at this table," he said with a mouth full of food.

Eliza's eyes widened with surprise. She placed her hand on his in a gesture of welcome, but he rapidly pulled it away.

"Nonsense. It's the least we can do. I owe you a great debt for saving my husband's life. Would you like some more?"

Without waiting for an answer, she turned to Celia, who was ogling at him.

"Fetch some more food from the kitchen. He is still hungry," Eliza ordered.

But Celia wouldn't move. Eliza gave her an impatient look. She asked Lucy next but received the same response.

"And stop staring at him. It isn't decent," she said to Lucy under her breath.

"But people like him ... they're not supposed to sit at the table next to you, Lady Sharpe," Lucy whispered.

"That doesn't concern me."

"But if Lord Sharpe finds out, Lady Sharpe ... he will be angry."

"And he has the benefit of such a reaction solely due to the captain's quick thinking," Eliza said loudly. "Lord Sharpe is not here, and he won't find out. Now, to the kitchen, Lucy."

"Yes, Lady Sharpe. My pleasure. My pleasure, sir …" she began to say, looking questioningly at the soldier.

"Captain Johnson, Lucy. Do your best to remember. It's not every day we have a guest at Pleasant Hall, let alone a captain from Lord Sharpe's own regiment." Then Eliza turned to Celia. "And you can take your leave. Your job is to serve, not to stare."

Celia glared at Eliza. "You might need something," she said, her voice capped with an edge of defense. "Perhaps more wine?"

Celia sprang into action, refilling both of their glasses to ridiculous heights. It was clear that her interest was not the same variety as Lucy's. Eliza sighed, slightly embarrassed to witness such blatant reactions from the servants. There had been enough dramatics for one evening. She bowed her head in exasperation.

Captain Johnson looked at Eliza for a moment, then returned his focus to his plate. After Lucy's footsteps faded away and Celia returned to her place against the back wall, Eliza continued their conversation.

"I am still unsure of what transpired. At the fort …" Eliza began.

Johnson's fork clattered to the plate, and he straightened to attention.

"It was the Derry man. He plottin' to kill Colonel Sharpe."

"The Derry man? I do not understand."

"James Coulter his name. He a Derry man. Come from Derry. Folks like him, they Catholic. Don't support the Crown. Din't make much sense that he'd want to defend it. I had my eye on him the whole time. He was boastful. Don't like men like that."

"Why would such a man be accepted in the regiment?"

"Oh, they be takin' anyone, Lady Sharpe. Anyone at all. They needin' the men."

Eliza nodded in understanding, then swirled her wine.

"And what possible grievances could he have against my husband?"

As soon as the question left her lips, she feared hearing the answer. Charles had never wanted her to see the fort or watch the soldiers' drills, and she always wondered if he was a brutal commander.

"Colonel Sharpe never did nothin' to him. I'm not sure the two ever crossed paths," he said. Then he sighed. "Military affairs ain't meant for women's ears, Lady Sharpe. It don't concern you."

"Anything concerning my husband concerns me," she snapped.

She knew if she turned around, she would find Celia smirking at the exchange. Eliza's back grew hot with irritation.

"Apologies, Lady Sharpe. I confess I not used to all this. Sittin' at a grand table in a fine house. Bein' waited on." He seemed to hesitate with his next words. "And I don't speak to many women like you."

Her stance softened as she recognized how uncomfortable he was.

"I am simply trying to understand what occurred. I

fear my nerves won't settle until I do."

"Yes, 'course, ma'am. May I speak the honest truth?"

"You have my permission."

"I think Lord Dunmore did this. I think he payin' that Derry man. He wants Charles dead."

Eliza's face paled, and she looked away. Captain Johnson looked mortified to even utter the words as if a contingent of Dunmore's men would advance on him that very moment. She looked back at him, burning with the urge to say a number of things, but she knew it would be inappropriate. They were only on formal terms, after all.

"There is no need to fear, Captain Johnson. I believe you. Entirely."

She could tell that he was hesitant to speak further, so she prompted the conversation.

"And where do you hail from, Captain? What brings you here to Nassau?"

She began cutting up her sugared fruit, expecting a light discussion to follow. She was wrong.

"I a runaway, Lady Sharpe. From Hampton. Hampton, Virginia. Lord Dunmore proclaimed us slaves free durin' the American war, and I answered."

"The governor? This governor?" she scoffed.

"He the governor o' the Virginia colony then. He made a proclamation in '75, yes ma'am, and he set all us Negroes free. Times was awful that year. He had to flee to Yorktown from his palace with his family, and he took to livin' on a big ship. I reckon there had to be near two hundred ships at one point, near three thousand folks in all. We lived on those ships. Called it the Floatin' Town.

It was a sight to see."

"A floating town?"

"Oh, yes. We had everythin'. A ship for the sick. We had ourselves two Anglican priests and even a Methodist minister, a Mr. Wilkinson. Even had rafts o' poor families livin' besides the ships. Lots o' Scottish folk. The planters in Virginia din't like them none 'cause their properties was ruined by them Scots. The Scots was creditors, and they made lots o' folk go into debt when they couldn't pay. But we all came together there, one Floatin' Town. Hot summer, cold blizzard … din't matter none." The captain's eyes grew moist with remembrance, and Eliza feared she had disturbed his sensitivities. "We always needin' food, and we needin' men to fight, and because o' that, we needin' even more food. Hungry bellies, naked backs, no fuel. Folks got sick. No water, no wood, no food. But we had God, and we had our freedom. We was together, defendin' the colonies."

"I don't understand. Why was everyone converged in one squalid mass?" she asked.

"Fear mostly. We all wanted safety, and that the only way to get it. Times was hard, folks had no money."

Confusion furrowed Eliza's brow. "Fear of what?"

"Those patriots, them was crazy folk. Real bloodthirsty. They was mad at what Lord Dunmore done. Said it was unjust and all."

"Yes, I suppose the trauma of any war starts with the anticipation of confiscated property."

She said it plainly, but the words made her feel sick. She did not know where this story was going, but she knew the man behind it well enough. There was no goodness in Lord Dunmore.

"They mostly mad Lord Dunmore set us free. Thousands o' us answered him and joined the British. Sometimes six to eight men a day, mind you. Even Harry Washington. That's right, the American commander's own slave came. That was real shameful for them, I think. They was ragin' mad then. Don't look good for the cause, you know. We was called Dunmore's Ethiopian Regiment. That made us real proud. They was callin' us *his* men. We was commanded by a white officer, paid a wage for the first time in our lives."

Captain Johnson's voice swelled with pride. "We never got no uniforms but we din't mind much. We was his unit, and we was damn proud o' it. We finally had some dignity. Now, some men was sent off as laborers, diggin' trenches, but the strong ones, the fit ones he used for soldierin', real soldierin'. We was trained, armed, sent into battle. You know they kill slaves if they get hold o' a gun in Virginia land. But now I had my own."

Eliza understood the pride such a recounting inspired in him, but she could not stand that the corrupt governor was the one who inspired such sentiments.

"Lord Dunmore set you all free so he could use you in the war?"

"Yes, ma'am. That raised fury in the Americans. They said it was a trick. He would sell us in the West Indies after, they said. Throw our bodies to the sharks the instant we get sick. But we knew better. Those white men set up slave patrols with their dogs. If they caught any o' us, we got sent to salt mines out in the West. I heared they even refused to let the clergy see us when we died. Makes sense to me; they wanted us to go to hell. They wanted their stolen property back. Was we prisoners o' war or fugitive slaves? Depends on who caught you. I ain't never get caught. I'm fast, Lady Sharpe. With my mind and my feet."

He took a gulp of wine and looked timidly at Celia, who still lurked behind Eliza.

"We built Fort Murray, and we fought there. We was mostly in charge o' stoppin' rebel trade. We caught ships from all kinds o' places I ain't never heared o'. Turk's Island, Rhode Island, Glasgow, Grenadine. We caught smugglers too. French and Spanish men. The rebels called Lord Dunmore all kinds o' names. 'Lord Kidnapper,'" he continued.

The irony of such a title was not lost on her. Her mind recalled the night the governor had attempted to gain intimate knowledge of her by force. The Americans' moniker for him was, unfortunately, accurate, albeit not for the right reasons.

"It seems that the governor prefers to use political outsiders as his bludgeon. He likes to divide people and then turn against those who help him at will," Eliza said with bitterness in her voice.

She was referring to this Derry man who had attacked Charles and to the slaves Dunmore had freed during the war in the American colonies. But she also thought of the pirates he colluded with, like Hiram Bruin and his crew. And of Jean: the secretary everyone on the island had whispered vicious rumors about, the man they had never trusted because of his French blood. The captain continued speaking, interrupting her wandering thoughts.

"Then new ships come. The 14th Regiment. Two companies. And then after that, Henry Clinton came on his *Mercury*. We was gon' show those Patriots British strength, and find the Loyalists too scared to show support. Bring them out o' hidin' and into the fight. And we was gon' win. That was the plan, anyway."

Captain Johnson's glorious portrait of past days spent in Lord Dunmore's company was starting to grate on her.

"Eventually, we 'stablished a camp on a little island. I thought things was gonna get better then, but they din't. We had to leave the Ches'peake Bay. They bombarded us real bad one day—even Lord Dunmore got pieces o' wood in his leg. That's why he walk funny like that. We had to 'vacuate. He told us to leave behind anyone sick. Even if they was only a little sick." Captain Johnson shook his head. "I still see their faces. That's the first time I din't agree with him. That was plain cruel. That was planter logic. These bodies not useful. No need to keep 'em. But they wasn't just bodies to me. They was men, women, children. He lost the Old Dominion. It only existed in the Floatin' Town, and that ended one day too."

Captain Johnson fiddled with his hands, then stared into the darkness outside. He resembled Charles in that he never seemed to be fully still with his movements.

"Why are you rebelling against such a great man?"

She asked it with sarcasm, but she was genuinely curious.

"I found out some things. I din't like it. Can't hide the truth forever, Lady Sharpe. It gon' come out, and when it do, sometimes it bite. I din't know no better back then. Not like I do now.

"You see, there was this one Negro man, he a free man. But his wife and children was still slaves. He joined the Floatin' Town tryin' to fix their freedom. He brought all his property on board, but Lord Dunmore kept it for hisself. Said he needed it. Probably to entertain all the rich folk that came for supper on that ship. When this Negro man found out, he complained, but the other white men din't believe no one lookin' like him could have fine things like that. They questioned why he was there if he was already free. They din't understand him none. But it was true just the same. That man was desperate."

Captain Johnson looked into the candlelight; his eyes focused on something else entirely.

"That is terrible, Captain, but it does not surprise me in the least. Every encounter I have had with the governor has told me he indeed possesses such a character. He is like a great, fat hog, and he'll take anything that catches his eye. It's a shame what happened to that poor man."

The captain nodded, then said, "Lord Dunmore did lose a lot. He had to leave behind his land, over fifty slaves, they said, a great deal o' things. He wrote to the Crown for a new allowance, but they wouldn't give him none. He was always lookin' for new money. At first, I understood. Costs money to have an army, to build a fort.

Folks don't realize that. But then I saw his greed take over. His own wife don't want nothin' to do with him. I ain't seen her once in nearly twenty years. Now that says somethin'."

"Yes, I believe no one has met Lady Dunmore. Not to my knowledge. Some claim to have met his son a number of years ago, but your point still stands. I, for one, hardly blame her." Eliza noticed their wine was running low, so she called for more. Celia was eager to provide it. "But I do wonder what brings a gentleman like you to this island."

"Some o' us soldiers left after the war, but some o' us followed Lord Dunmore here, to Nassau. It's a war zone within a war zone, some say. The Spanish in Cuba and East Florida, the French on that other island, St. Domingo. Pirates on the sea. It needs defendin'." He leaned back in the chair, stretched, and then settled once more.

His face contorted then as if he was dissatisfied with what he had just said. "But it more than that, Lady Sharpe. Nassau is a haven o' free black folk, like me. They ain't as many plantations here like on other islands. The soil ain't no good. Folks here rather harvest salt, fish, go wreckin'.

"Some call this land hell, but I know about hell." He shook his head. "Hell is tillin' Virginian soil until your back breaks. All while some educated white man preach about liberty at the town hall. But he only ever mean his own. Don't give a damn about yours. Plenty o' men like that in Virginia land, Lady Sharpe. Here I'm in paradise, and I got my freedom and my dignity. I a workin' man now. I soldier. I can even read a little. I have somethin' to defend, and I do a damn good job o' it. But now it seems I have to defend it from the man who freed me."

"You're a smart man, Captain. Don't let such thoughts deter you. Lord Dunmore only freed you to deprive the Americans of labor while augmenting our forces."

"No, ma'am. England stands for freedom. Real freedom. I know it. I can feel it. Besides, there ain't no bad countries. Only bad men."

His love for England was admirable. Eliza sighed, studying a chip in the crystal glass.

"I pray that you are right, Captain Johnson. I do. Most fervently."

Philippe began to cry upstairs, and Celia left the room to tend to him.

"Some o' the other soldiers wasn't so lucky when they got here. They stepped off the boat, and they was enslaved just as quick again. Their papers said 'FP,' 'Formerly Property,' so some planters here figured it justified. They was lost property, and the white men took 'vantage. Freedom a vulnerable thing, Lady Sharpe. If you have no certificate, you ain't free. Don't matter what you say, how loud you cry out. They'll take you real quick. But if you wearin' this red coat … you always free. I ain't never takin' it off. You can't steal from the king, can you?"

Eliza's face paled. "But surely such a thing was illegal. Wasn't it the law that set you all free? How could they allow such a thing?"

"Lord Dunmore tried justifyin' it when we complained. Never made no sense to me. He always needin' that money, and he'll do near anythin' to get it. I learned a long time ago that man's promises ain't worth nothin'," he said.

Eliza shook her head with disgust.

Captain Johnson leaned forward, pointing a finger at her. "Now, you listen here. Lord Dunmore ain't livin' by the law, hardly since he step foot in this place. He gave me freedom, and he gave me confidence, but now I'm confident in knowin' that I don't need no thief to help me no more. I do better on my own. You can't make me soldier in your army, and then expect me to betray it. I ain't gon' do it. Don't care what you dangle in front o' me. I won't fall in line for no tyrant runnin' a plantation, and I won't fall in line for no tyrant rulin' over this island. He think he some kind o' island king. Ain't his kingdom. It's God's. And I answer to Him alone."

The passion in his voice was undeniable, and no doubt remained about this man's true loyalties. Eliza was astonished. She could tell he was sympathetic to her views, but just how far did that sympathy go? And did he expect something in return? She couldn't blame him; such expectations were only natural. She had been thrilled at their discourse so far, finding his words such an unexpected source of relief. But she could not suppress the urge to query him further. And now she feared their amity would falter.

"My dear Captain, you are aware of where you sit? You do understand what my husband does here at Pleasant Hall?" she probed.

"The colonel ain't like that. He got this from his daddy. Folks like me talk. He used to cause trouble for his old man. But that man was a mean drunkard. Colonel Sharpe escaped into the army like his daddy escaped into a bottle. And Colonel Sharpe never treated us no differ'nt. What do you do with somethin' like this?" Captain Johnson waved his hand around the room. "He never wanted it, but it's in his hands now. He need to support hisself. Can't say I blame him. I don't like it none. But I can't blame him neither. This life complicated, Lady Sharpe. All I know is what's in men's hearts and that Lord Dunmore don't have one."

"And yet you are so confident about the kind my husband possesses," Eliza said breathlessly.

"Why did you come here?" he asked, turning the focus on her.

"I married Lord Sharpe."

"Well, 'course. But why you pick him? For your husband?"

Eliza swallowed awkwardly, not knowing how to answer. The captain was testing the boundaries of polite conversation, but she had encouraged him to speak freely thus far. It would be false to shut down his inquiry now. She sighed.

"He asked for my hand, and I said yes. I thought it would be an adventure. Beautiful fish, colorful birds ... I wanted to leave England and set off into the unknown."

I did not know him, she thought.

She couldn't shake the feeling that such an idea was still very much true. This unexpected conversation with her guest was more revealing than she had bargained for.

In fact, when they had first sat down, she feared an awkward silence would take root. She had been pleasantly mistaken.

"And you happy? With the choice you made?"

Eliza colored under his question, but she could feel his sincerity in tone. She hesitated, wanting to immediately say she wasn't. But as she heard Philippe chortle with Lucy, her heart warmed.

"Yes, I would say so."

This stranger did not require an exact delineation of her reasons, and so she left it at that.

"Colonel Sharpe a blessed man. Lord Dunmore don't have that. His wife won't even come near this place."

"This island is the most beautiful thing I have ever seen. I cannot imagine living anywhere else now. It's quite strange," she said fondly.

"That we can agree on, Lady Sharpe. And to think what we could make o' it ..."

His voice was burgeoning with optimism, but it failed to catch on with her frame of thinking.

"I fear Lord Dunmore threatens its future."

Captain Johnson scoffed, shaking his head.

"He may think he the king o' Nassau, but ain't. And men like that always fall from grace."

"And to think what would have happened if you had not stopped the attacker today ..."

Worry unexpectedly slipped from her tongue. A strange kind of kinship had grown between them over the course of a meal. The captain had a subtle way of disarming her. She discovered his company was one in which she could freely express her thoughts and vulnerabilities, and it was steadfastly becoming one she rather enjoyed.

"Now don't you trouble yourself none with that. I'm here to protect Colonel Sharpe, and you and the child."

His energy had a comforting effect, and she knew he meant every word.

She smiled, wanting to linger at the table. "Tell me of you and Charles. What was he like in the old war?"

She waited in half-anticipation and half-dread.

"It were like this, Lady Sharpe. He saw me one day on the top deck. And he say I was the only man fit for soldierin'. Out o' fifty somethin' men, can you believe it? I was standin' in the back 'cause I'm tall. They din't want me blockin' no one. But Colonel Sharpe took one look at me and put me in the front. We almost the same height, Lady Sharpe. He never afraid o' me. I ain't never gonna forget that."

Eliza tried interjecting, but Captain Johnson continued. Celia quietly returned to the back of the room.

"He made me feel important. Lord Dunmore may have freed me, but he had his reasons. No, Colonel Sharpe look at me. He *see* me. He see what I could become. He gave me a future. I am a captain, but he said he gonna make me a major today. I can't believe it. If you told me that when I was young, I would have laughed."

Captain Johnson smiled to himself. "I can't tell you how happy I was when I heard he was returnin' to the island. I knew things would get fixed real quick, Lady Sharpe. Colonel Sharpe follows orders, just the way it should be. The fort would get finished. We would get us some real trainin'. Real, serious trainin'. Not what them other officers did with us. They wouldn't drill us none. Only use us for tasks. 'Bring me water.' 'Shine my boots.' That's not soldierin'.

"Colonel Sharpe differ'nt. He my commander. And I'm defendin' him with my life. I will protect that man until my last breath, Lady Sharpe."

Thus ended Captain Johnson's dedicated speech about her husband. His body relaxed, and then his eyes narrowed.

"I intend to stay here until matters get settled. He told me to contact a Mr. Wylly on the ride over here. I can manage tonight on my own, but I'll be needin' more men. And I don't quite know the sleepin' arrangements here, but it's best you stay in the room with him."

Eliza almost sputtered out her wine. The conversation had crossed into dangerous territory.

"No, I'm afraid that's not possible," she said quickly.

"Why? You must, Lady Sharpe."

She paused in awe of his boldness. "I sleep in my own quarters."

"Tonight be differ'nt, Lady Sharpe."

"No, I refuse," she replied, her voice bordering on panic.

She naively assumed this would be the end of the matter, but she did not understand the depths of Captain Johnson's stubbornness.

"Lady Sharpe, you must. I can't be guardin' two rooms. It better if you occupy the same space. Attackers can come in the night. I must protect the both o' you."

Celia pursed her lips as she removed their empty dishes, and Eliza saw a smile escape from the corner of her mouth as she sauntered away from view.

"Now, now, nothin' to be afraid o', Lady Sharpe," Captain Johnson said reassuringly. "I intend to stay here until Colonel Sharpe recovers. You have my word."

She desperately wanted to retort that she feared what the room contained and not what might lay outside it. But she remained silent. She did not see a way to remove herself from the situation.

"But my son, he needs—"

"The baby too, ma'am," the captain continued. "You must all stay together."

She swirled her wine in the glass, downed it, and called for more. It would be a torturous night.

CHAPTER XVII.

Eliza begrudgingly walked up to Charles' chamber, a room she had made sure to never step foot in deliberately. It was strange to willingly walk into what felt like a trap. The captain tailed close behind her with a candle, and when she reached the top of the stairs, she knew she had nowhere to go but onward.

She entered with apprehension, ensured that Charles was fast asleep, then nodded to Captain Johnson. Eliza eyed the wooden chair in the corner of the room. It would make do for a bed tonight, and it was the safest option. She refused to go anywhere near the bed. It only contained unpleasant memories for her.

She noticed Philippe's bassinet had already been moved. Her son lay inside it, peacefully asleep. She was glad to see the sight, but an irrational anger rose to the surface.

"I see you've directed my servants for me," she quipped, losing her veneer of patience.

"Yes, Lady Sharpe. The room is set. You can rest."

Eliza should have been grateful for his thoughtfulness, but she was only annoyed. She was about to close the door when he raised his hand.

"I be stationin' myself out here. That way, I can best be protectin' all o' you. I trust your ladyship not be needin' use o' that chair in the corner. It gon' be a long night."

What he said made perfect sense, but Eliza inwardly recoiled. Her chest tightened as she understood she could not deny him.

"Yes, yes, of course," she answered.

She wistfully looked towards the chair, stepping aside as the captain took it and brought it to the hallway.

"Good evening, Captain." She curtsied and then shut the door between them.

Once it was closed, she stared at it as if it held some recourse for her current situation. But it did not. She became furious—angry that she was placed in this situation, and angry that another man, a man she just met now, had decided something so dreadful for her. And what was worse: he did not even realize the vastness of its consequence. Captain Johnson had broken a silent rule in Pleasant Hall without so much as a moment's hesitation.

She paced with frustration and walked over to where Philippe's bassinet had been placed. He was fast asleep, and she dared not disturb him. Then finally, at the end, she turned towards Charles.

He lay in the bed, dressed in his white nightshirt, his head perfectly rested on his pillow, lost to a laudanum-crafted bliss. Cleo had cleaned the blood off of him, but there was still a deep cut trailing from below his left ear, down his throat, to the start of his chest. His thigh was wrapped in bandages, but it didn't make his figure any less menacing.

She walked to the far side of the bed and sat awkwardly on the edge. The fact that her back was facing him made her even more uneasy. How strong a dose of medicine had Cleo given him? What if he stirred? What if he expected Eliza to nurse him? To administer a gentle, caring touch? The idea disturbed her.

Eliza studied her shoes, noting how stained the sides of her slippers were from trekking outside. She had only briefly stepped into the yard today, but now that she had nothing else to occupy her mind, the difference in color was striking. She kicked her feet out slightly, sighing. She could surely not pass an entire night like this. There was no clock in his room, only a large clock downstairs in the hallway, and the lack of knowing the time threatened to drive her mad.

She looked towards the fireplace. The fire had died down to near embers. The servants had retired for the night, and it would eventually fail. The evening was balmy and mild, but there was a dampness in the air. Then she had an idea.

She rushed towards the door with the hope of an easy distraction.

"Excuse me, Captain Johnson? It seems the fire has died," she called through the door.

The man behind it slowly opened it, looking at her strangely.

"Lady Sharpe, you check for a tinderbox? There should be one."

His voice sounded confused, even slightly irritated as if he had enough social interaction for one evening.

"No, unfortunately, I cannot place it. It should be there, but it is not," she said as she stepped away so he could enter the room.

The captain came inside, but with a respectful quietness of step, lest he disturb his commander. His eyes flashed as he looked up and down, then he located the brass tinderbox in a seemingly obvious place.

"No worries, Lady Sharpe, it right here."

Eliza knew how to start a fire, but it wasn't necessarily a skill she had honed over the years. Servants had always taken care of the task for her. So, while she disdained the feeling of helplessness, she welcomed the time spent in allowing him to distract her a little further. He was doing her a grand service, even if he never quite realized the significance.

Eliza watched with satisfaction, knowing it would take multiple attempts to create a spark. But to her disappointment, it only took him two tries. He struck the firesteel against a piece of flint and let the subsequent spark catch fire inside the nest of char-cloth, blowing on it until it was engulfed, and then he tossed it into the fireplace. There was enough wood inside to absorb the flame. Celia had clearly been careless in stacking the wood and not stoking it properly. But the captain resolved the issue with unexpected speed, much to Eliza's detriment. He was decidedly too useful.

"There you are, Lady Sharpe. Should take to goin' now."

The captain nodded, put the tinderbox back in place,

and left the room.

Eliza was alone with a sleeping Charles once again. She sighed and returned to the bed, but her back ached from sitting still without any support after a while. She rose a second time and made her way towards him, daring to get a closer look at him. The cut from his throat to his chest was long and grotesque; it would most certainly leave a scar behind. He looked almost handsome in repose, although her knowledge of his true self certainly skewed the reception.

She scoffed. No, he was a handsome man, but his inner character blasted it all to hell. She feared his eyes would flash open, the cold, searing green glare she was used to. She feared his lips would call out her name. He looked tired, weary.

It was the same state of being she herself struggled with day in and out. How different were they really? But there was a vast difference. He was brutal and full of rage, and even though his attitude had lightened considerably in the last few months, she knew that tremor of coldness always lurked just beneath the surface. There was a tenseness to his facial features, present even when he rested, that reminded her of a warrior. Yes, a sleeping warrior. Even the hollowness of his cheeks recalled a man who was never quite at ease with his surroundings. And now he had almost lost the greatest fight: the fight for his life.

She looked away, refusing to recall the emotions that had stirred within her when she thought he had died. It had not been immediately clear that her husband wasn't mortally wounded when they staggered through the door earlier that afternoon, and she hated the feelings she had harbored in that instant. It was fear, pure, utter terror—the kind that made the floor beneath her feet drop away to a gaping hole. That she had suddenly lost something, a piece of her life, that had meant a great deal. It was the cruel irony of finally finding peace in the turbulence, only for it to be taken away in one deft stroke. That gnawing she had felt returned now: she truly valued him despite her best attempts to mask such an emotion.

Her hands went to the side table next to the bed, quietly pulling open the drawer. Her curiosity beckoned and promised a distraction from her worrying thoughts. She didn't want to linger on such unpleasantness. As she pulled it open, she stopped with the weight of it. Inside was a flintlock pistol.

She grabbed it without a second thought and ran to the door again.

"Beg pardon, Captain Johnson, but can you see to this pistol?"

She imagined she heard a sigh issue out of him, but he appeared at the door in all readiness just the same. He looked at her, then grabbed the gun out of her hands. She almost felt insulted by his lack of trust in her. He seemed terrified of a woman brandishing a pistol.

"I would like you to ready this firearm. If we are to suffer an attack in the night, it would calm my mind greatly to know we have this at our disposal," she said.

He checked it thoroughly and was ready with a conclusion.

"It already loaded, Lady Sharpe. Nothin' to fear," he

said, slowly handing the cold weapon back to her. "You only need to cock the hammer back like this."

He handed the primed weapon back to her. She made a face of surprise, but she was really mortified. He must have thought her completely unintelligent at this rate. She should have known better. It was only natural for Charles to keep a loaded pistol at his bedside. He was a soldier, after all.

She thanked him and closed the door one final time. It would be a devastatingly long night.

Philippe was still asleep, and she mused to herself about the synchronicity of the two men in her life completely lost to wakefulness. One who was new to this world and completely innocent, and one who was jaded to it and scarred by it—indeed, one who fought against its every current.

She sat back on the bed, pistol in hand, only realizing now that she should have brought a book with her. That would have eased her mind a great deal. But she couldn't bring herself to disturb the captain anymore. Her ears started to ring, making the silence of the room a jarring entity instead of the more neutral companion it should have been.

She knew it was only the wine, but it was inconvenient. She had been too liberal in her consumption. Indeed, she prayed it was merely the alcohol. She was in no mood to tolerate a visitation from Tabitha.

Eliza's head began to feel heavy, as if unseen hands were squeezing either side of her skull. She needed to lie down. This time, when her back ached from the strain of sitting up, she slowly lowered herself, letting her back touch the mattress but keeping her legs at an angle. She took a deep breath. As long as she did not close her eyes … if she did not lose her guard to sleep, she could retain a sense of control.

Her surroundings undulated around her in her drunken haze, and she tried to steel herself against each wheeling motion. She swore the bed had moved, that the man next to her had finally stirred, but it was only a trick of her muddled thoughts. It felt good to lie flat, to finally elongate her spine after remaining tense for so long. The bed, as distasteful to her sensibilities as it was, was far more comfortable than her prior position. Her hands remained stiff, clutching her abdomen; she was ready to fly off the bed at a moment's notice. She took a deep breath and tried to ease her body into rest.

As soon as she managed to relax, her anxiety assaulted her in a vicious stroke.

"Sometimes you must endure a little pain to have satisfaction, my dear."

Although it was nothing more than a memory, his voice was clear, immediate. She rocketed upward immediately, wanting reassurance that he was still asleep. She had not had a reaction on this scale the last time she was in his bed after she had tried to end her life on the Black Reef. Then again, she'd had no say in the matter that stormy afternoon, and more importantly, she had not had to contend with actually sharing the bed.

She gazed upwards at the ceiling, crackled from years of humidity. She refused to sleep. But the more she looked at the ceiling, recognizing familiar patterns and bold lines, she could not help but recall how she had stared at it before, the first night she had arrived. New memories barraged her, one by one.

"I have waited to have you long enough, and I am not a patient man."

Her breath caught in her throat, and her legs tensed up without her awareness.

"I could not restrain myself nor wait for a bed," Charles said with a laugh. *"Such is your beauty, my dear. I have told you once before I think of little else."*

She looked towards the crib. Philippe could serve as a useful distraction. Besides, she was not truly alone. Captain Johnson sniffed and cleared his throat by the door.

Of course, nothing can happen, she thought.

But it already had. And this was the most difficult idea to accept.

She turned her head, her eyes latching on to Charles' sleeping form. Her throbbing head made it appear that he was moving, but it was only the regular flow of his breaths.

Eliza grappled with why she still felt so much horror. He had not touched her in nearly three years. Relations were entirely different between them. But her mind would not be silenced.

She thought of the night she realized his rage would not be contained to the privacy of Pleasant Hall's walls, the night when he had erupted in the carriage leaving the ball.

"You turn your emotions on and off. Like an actress in a theater," he said in a very low tone. *"Like ... A WHORE!"*

Charles had blamed her for merely trying to survive. She had sought freedom: freedom in choice, freedom in love. But he'd refused her such rights. He had not tried to understand her motivations, immoral as her actions had been. He had merely shamed her. It was so very easy for him to blame everything on her.

"Look at me! Do you enjoy it?" he shouted, his voice a mix of unleashed emotions. A whirlwind of rage, desperation, and agony drove him. He shook her. "Do you? Do you enjoy giving him your body? Lying on your back for him?"

She knew she shouldn't have cared what he said that afternoon, the rainy day when he had brought her home after pulling her from the ocean closer to town. She tried not to think of the pirates, of that rogue Captain Bruin. It only increased her panicked flurry of remembrances. She had been defiant that day, ignoring the vicious words he had hurled at her. But she couldn't forget them.

"I know men that would disfigure your face. They would not hesitate to beat you with a stick because it is their right to do so and because you need to be broken."

These words still stung because she believed them. It was a searing confirmation that no man would ever truly tolerate her. The idea that she *needed* to be tolerated, that she was not acceptable to anyone the way she naturally was, cut her deeply. That she could only be misunderstood, time and again, by family, by acquaintances, by mere strangers. By the man who swore he would be her protector on this dangerous island. But the danger did not lie in the wavering palm leaves and bush outside, it lay in the bed beside her.

"You need to be sorely reminded of your place, Lady Sharpe. And that is underneath me. I will have no difficulty reminding you of this. Over ... and over ... again," he whispered in her ear, his tone sickening.

Shock coursed through her as if all of these events were fresh in her mind. Clutching the cool metal of the gun was the only thing that steadied her nerves. As she held it close, a different idea took hold of her.

She could end it all. She tilted the pistol, not daring to point it towards him completely.

No.

Her vision wavered as tears crowded her eyes. She could not do it. She could not even pretend with a false show of bravery. The difference between now and the night she had nearly poisoned him was too vast for her to fully comprehend. She had been a mother without her child that desperate night; now she lay in bed with the very person who had reunited her with Philippe. A man who had no obligation to do so, a man who had every reason not to.

Eliza still feared it was too good to be true. When she couldn't sleep, certain thoughts rotated endlessly through her mind. Charles was a smart man. He could have used the child as a way to trap her, and though this idea had crossed her mind repeatedly, she knew she would fall victim to it regardless.

She refused to be without her only child. And even though she rebelled against the ways of the world, she had to think of someone other than herself now. An illegitimate child walked a much harder path than one deemed legitimate. She refused to let the child suffer any further. He had already lost a father, and as a boy, she feared the challenge would prove too difficult for his pride. Only time would reveal the boy's inner strength and resiliency of character. In the meantime, she would do all she could to protect him.

And it seemed so would Charles. He had spoken of honor, of his reasons for accepting another man's child as his own. If this incident was pure of heart, she feared other recent events proved more calculating. What if his show of abolition was nothing more than a way to turn her? He had tried to earn her affections in so many other ways: force, kindness, a wilting patience.

The way he had spoken of the slaves at Pleasant Hall in the past seemed to prove that such a man could never truly change. He was hardened beyond reproach, disdainful of mercy and forbearance. Yet, some of the people enslaved under his very chains spoke the highest of his character. It boggled her perception.

Then there was today's vicious attack. The assailant had to be formidable to almost conquer a man like him. Charles clearly did not orchestrate this as some cheap ploy to stir her sympathy. This was no plea to soften her affection. This was a result of crossing the governor. He had finally stood up to Lord Dunmore after's Jean's unjust death. It was all she had ever wanted him to do, and now he had reaped the consequences of his defiance.

Eliza studied the pistol again. No, the difference now was that she knew she wanted him alive. And it saddened her because she knew that her acceptance of him also meant her acceptance of more torment. This man did not guarantee any happiness. If past days foretold future ones, he could only twist more pain into her being.

Why? Why did these people think he was a good man? And why was he not good to her? More tears streamed down her cheeks, and she struggled to swallow with a strained throat. She squeezed the gun, lifting it back to the far side of the bed. She refused to let go of it, but she knew it would remain in place now, far away from his body. She already regretted bringing the dangerous thing anywhere near him. His life was in a fragile enough state as it was.

"I raised that boy. He is a good boy," Cleo said wryly, a deep smile growing on her face. "I never said he was without flaws."

Flaws ... no man or woman was inherently perfect, and no single person lived a life free of them. But to her, it seemed their flaws were engaged in a never-ending duel, some ancient struggle whose true origins neither of them could remember. Was Eliza simply a flame to the well of oil within him? Or was Charles more like a wandering moth, looking for the light and the love of a woman?

"What do you do with somethin' like this?" Captain Johnson waved his hand around the room. "He never wanted it, but it's in his hands now. He need to support hisself. Can't say I blame him. I don't like it none. But I can't blame him neither. This life is complicated, Lady Sharpe. All I know is what's in men's hearts ..."

Oh, Eliza had judged Charles only too easily. She had seen everything that Pleasant Hall was and the abject horror it stood for, placing the burden directly on his shoulders alone. It was more satisfying than blaming the ghost of his drink-riddled father, but it was a problem that belonged to the world around them. Even now, as he struggled to free Cleo, the solution was not without a new set of dangers. She knew that he had dreaded returning to the island, yet she had never offered him the grace of understanding how deep his troubles truly ran.

What nightmares stirred him from sleep? In her dreams, she had seen his rebellious youth. She knew Jean and he had bonded as brothers, both men very different from their fathers. Or at least Charles had tried with all his might to take a different path. Had he accomplished the deed? And if not, could he succeed now?

"No, Colonel Sharpe look at me. He see me. He see what I could become. He gave me a future."

He had seen her too. Truly seen her in a way no other man invited to Bleinhill Manor ever did. She had spoken her mind freely, and instead of mocking her, he had sought her hand in marriage. And even as the other men ridiculed her in Dunmore's mansion, he had strode up to her on the veranda when they arrived in Nassau. A wandering, lost moth, seeking out her flame, her boldness, her fire.

And one final hollow whisper.

"He always accepted me, which is a kindness I cannot easily forget."

Words Jean had uttered even when the hope of any reconciliation seemed lost between them. Direct from the lips of a man who should have known better. But maybe there was nothing to adjust in his statement. Charles was a man misunderstood, one whose actions were easily misinterpreted. Perhaps he was not unlike her.

The more she thought about these matters, the more a different impression began to evolve. She saw him as a little boy again, hiding beneath a side table, clutching a damp wall. A boy who needed his mother and would never find relief. The one vision that had stopped Eliza from killing him with the oleander poison.

And was Charles a bad man? He had saved her life and accepted as his own a child born of betrayal. He had finally started to unravel the curse of his family by freeing Cleo. He had stood up to his superior, the governor, disobeying his command to turn over the survivors of the shipwreck. And his actions had achieved near deadly results. At dinner with the captain, Eliza had only focused on the past wickedness of Lord Dunmore, refusing to think of a more tender topic—that the governor threatened something much more dear to her heart than she ever wanted to admit.

Lying next to him now, a new perspective became clear. For once, she and her husband finally felt like equals. His height could no longer intimidate her. His brash movements could no longer threaten her when he was so very still. The room wavered again as a fresh wave of tears rushed to the surface. She could not quite understand it or put a name to what she felt, but she knew a page had been turned. Some momentous transformation filtered over her as she looked at the sleeping, injured man. She didn't have the preciseness of mind to analyze what she felt; she could only recognize its sudden effect on her.

It was the wine. It was only the wine. This torment would subside tomorrow in the daylight, but she couldn't ignore the sudden lightness she felt in her bones. Their past appeared nothing more than a stale night terror now. The sun would rise tomorrow, and she would hold Philippe. And Charles would whisper sweetness to his friend's child, each gesture a vow to protect his every breath. Philippe was fortunate to have two people so deeply invested in his happiness, one whose claim was not even natural, yet stronger than it should have ever been.

And perhaps this was the greatest miracle of all, that the three of them could truly become a family over time. What once seemed grotesque to her sensibilities now warmed her heart. It was what she desired above all. By the time the boy spoke, who knew what their relations would be. How strongly could time soothe such deep, uncrossable rifts? Charles had taken her power from her that very first night, and she had wanted nothing but to return the favor. To prove her value to him, to show him the cost of his grave mistake.

But perhaps there was even greater power to be found in forgiveness.

Eliza reached out and lightly rested her hand on top of his, studying his features. When his lips were not shouting, when his words weren't sharp as a blade's edge, when those eyes did not threaten to see right through her, there was a kind of rugged beauty in his face. She couldn't recall the last time she had seen him sleeping. The only time they had ever shared a bed, she had never turned to look at him. The sight of Charles lying in peace was unfamiliar to her.

Her emotions swung back and forth like the mechanics inside a clock. Jean had taken the forefront of her sorrows this past year, so much that she had failed to recognize a subtle change in herself. To understand that a slow, settling relief had followed her darkest days. She had stopped trying to merely survive on this island. The fiery hatred between her and Charles had softened, softened so much that tonight, when he was dragged into the house by the faithful captain, she had nearly fainted from the shock.

That moment had been an epiphany for her; to see something happen so beyond the borders of her control made her reflect on the things she *could* control. What had she done to improve relations between them? After suffering so great an injury that very first night, did she ever reach out and ask for an explanation? Did she ever try to mend matters between them? No. Instead, she carried her wounded heart like a badge and counted his every subsequent mistake with satisfaction, weighing them on a scale more severe than she would have used with any other person. She had engaged in a battle with him, bypassing any means of reaching a treaty, and had instead launched her own offensive. She had willingly slept with his childhood friend, and perhaps the sin had tasted so much sweeter because she knew it would hurt him. She had wanted to devastate Charles in those days.

To destroy him. But now, the deed had nearly been accomplished by another party.

Not now, not now, please God ... let this pass, she thought as she grasped his motionless hand.

Cleo had tended to him as best she could, but Eliza still feared infection. It was the greatest killer of their age. It did not enter a room in a bluster of bravado, like the explosion of a bullet or the flash of a sword. It crept along silently, and as smiles deepened and hearts eased into the arrival of knowing better days, it struck without warning. Once infection grabbed hold of a person, it never let go. Even a man like Charles, strong and full of energy, could succumb to its merciless grasp.

The idea of losing him seemed even more terrifying in the wild tumult of her pathos. But she could not tell what instilled more horror: to live without him or to question why such a contradiction existed within her heart. She knew she feared the change it would bring, the unknowing, the uncertainty. She had finally achieved some semblance of balance in her life. That was one explanation and a reasonable one at that.

But there was something deeper still. There was a wicked gnawing inside of her, a small piece of her that wanted to return to their very first dinner. The fleeting moment when they had finally settled after a day of travel, and they had regaled each other with stories. They had survived crossing the Atlantic, and that was no small feat. They had been young and excited, and the future blazed with the optimism of new beginnings. Oh, to go back to that moment and stop what had followed.

Her hand traveled to his stomach and stopped there, watching the steady rhythm of her hand as it rose and fell with every shallow breath. His muscles felt comforting to her fingers now. There was something reassuring to be found there, some unspoken message about his resiliency woven into the very fibers of his being.

Charles would survive this night. And there would be hell to pay. She was sure of it. With a slight trace of trepidation, she leaned over and kissed his cheek. She tried to impart her sorrow and regret, her hopes of a better tomorrow. Then she did the one thing she vowed never to do in his presence.

She closed her eyes and let go, surrendering deep into a hazy sleep.

CHAPTER XVIII.

Eliza awoke with a start at the sound of the iron-clad bell tolling in the yard. There was a pleasant, warm sensation over one hand and a cold, metallic one in the other. She turned and saw Charles' hand grasping her wrist. Then she recalled the pistol in her right hand. She slowly pulled away from him, and he stirred in his sleep.

Outside the door, Captain Johnson's footsteps thundered down the stairs. There was no time to process the conclusion her thoughts had reached last night or to analyze the manner in which she awoke. Danger had come to Pleasant Hall.

Eliza shot up from the bed, grateful that she had never undressed. She rushed down the stairs. The weakness of waking made her grip on the gun shaky. She found the captain near the porch.

"What is happening?" she inquired breathlessly.

"Do not fear, Lady Sharpe," the captain replied with a broad smile. "It Mr. Wylly. It time for the meeting."

Her eyes scanned the distance, looking for a horse.

"But Charles needs to recover," she said with worry.

"Your husband requested his company at first morning light. The rest o' the group was alerted by now, no doubt. I expectin' near forty men to come today. I already told the servants to ready the parlor, no trouble for you there, Lady Sharpe."

Eliza watched as a lone rider approached the front yard, and she moved away from sight. She was in no mood for socialization. She would return upstairs, tend to Philippe, and spend her time outside. Her presence would not be wanted at the meeting, and for once, she was glad for it.

A few hours later, she returned from the beach, a shell hidden in her grasp. Now more horses filled the yard, and clouds of fine dust rose in the air, mixing with the suffocating heat. Eliza was intrigued by the spectacle of hosting so many guests, but she did not want to linger. She tried her best to avoid being seen by anyone, and as she approached the stairs, she heard Charles. She was surprised to hear him sound so lively. Then his voice sounded louder.

"Come, join us, Eliza."

She stopped and turned to find him standing in the doorway of the parlor. He was using a cane to support his weight.

"How is your leg?" she asked.

She hated how unsure her tone sounded in front of him. In truth, she was worried about him, but she dared not reveal it yet.

"The pain comes and fades away again. But when it returns, the constant throbbing is nearly unbearable."

"Then you should rest."

"No. Staying bedridden does not suit me. Besides, no position is truly comfortable. We must hold a meeting today. The matter cannot wait," he said with a sigh. "And I would be pleased if you joined us."

She looked down at her damp skirt and sand-covered ankles.

"I have other matters to attend to," she said dismissively.

Charles bit his lip and looked down, but when his glance returned to meet hers, his green eyes smoldered with a curious kind of desperation. She looked away and was about to head for the stairs when he stopped her.

"I insist."

Leaning against the wall, he rested the cane off to the side, then carefully removed his scarlet jacket.

"Here, to cover yourself," he said, rustling the jacket towards her.

Eliza stepped forward, accepting his offering with slight hesitation. He usually did not wear his uniform to these gatherings, but she reasoned that it heightened the dramatic effect. One of His Majesty's bravest soldiers, brutally attacked by a paid assassin. The spectacle of the torn red jacket would inflame the men's senses on sight. She turned to peer inside the brightly lit room.

"This is a meeting for gentlemen. They will not tolerate my presence," she said quietly, looking down at his wrinkled jacket.

"Nonsense," he said, reaching for his cane. "Such a notion never stopped you before."

"I have nothing to offer in this conversation. I do not possess a military mind."

"No, but ideas can deliver lethal blows. I think you know this well enough."

She blushed at his forwardness. She thought of the way they had woken up together, their hands intertwined. He seemed to be referring to many things at once. Either way, he was insistent, and so she slowly put on the jacket. It was slightly damp with sweat, and it smelled like him. The notion disgusted her at first, then the intrigue of wearing a military jacket became stronger. Eliza moved slightly so she could see her new appearance in the gilt hallway mirror.

"Come, it's starting," he said, pushing her towards the parlor.

She stepped inside and found a room transformed. It was no longer a quiet parlor, undisturbed save by angles of sunlight slowly turning in arcs. It was filled with thirty or so men from varying social backgrounds. They were loud and brimming with energy, and they now stared at her unabashedly. Eliza clutched the red jacket closed with a tighter grip. Past hurts resurfaced, and she worried he had done this solely to embarrass her. But she recognized no malice as she looked back at him. She took a seat next to where he sat on the chaise with his injured leg extended.

One man turned to look at her and then spoke.

"Your wife may be better suited to resolving complaints regarding linen stolen from the clothesline than matters of politics, my dear Lord Sharpe," he said.

Eliza's blush flared, and she could feel the heat reaching behind her ears. But Charles defended her.

"She can converse upon nearly any subject," he said loudly for all to hear. He readjusted himself to a more comfortable position. "Her bedfellows are Locke, Hume, Montesquieu, and Rosseau, which I find rather unfortunate as I do not like to share my bed. But otherwise, I must say her taste in men is without flaw."

Hearty laughter erupted in the room, and the rarity of having a woman join them was smoothed away. There was important business to discuss.

One man stood in front of the room, and from the way he carried himself, she assumed he was the leader of these clandestine political gatherings. William Wylly, a loyalist originally from Savannah, appeared to be of a similar age to Charles, but there was something restless and agitated about him that made him seem older. His neck was short but muscular, and his blue eyes flitted from one corner of the room to another, calculating his plan of action.

Eliza recalled that Charles had told her Mr. Wylly was an attorney and had studied in England. He was once Lord Dunmore's solicitor general, but the arrangement had been short-lived. She did not need to wonder why. Dunmore no doubt found this man as threatening to his schemes as he did Charles. Now Mr. Wylly paced the front of the room, eager to start the meeting.

"Gentlemen," he began, his voice much louder than

the size of the room warranted. "To the king!"

He turned to a side table and raised a glass of punch. The men in the room followed suit and took a sip from their glasses. Pipes were lit, and the parlor was soon filled with smoke. A basket of bread and cheese was passed around, and the men eagerly took handfuls of it. Eliza noticed that the fine china stayed well hidden. There was something disturbed and uneasy about their energy. It seemed as if Charles did not trust his finer trappings in their rough hands. One older man passed her the basket of bread, but she waved it away.

Mr. Wylly surveyed the room with a steely glance, nodding at one particular gentleman in the second row of chairs.

"I am glad to see you here James. Oftentimes it seems you dedicate more time to hunting turtles."

The man he addressed sneered and answered with a brief reply, "Some men *need* to make coin."

Their remarks drew attention to the vast differences between the men. Some of them wore finery, while others looked like mere fishermen. Eliza recognized John Wells, the owner of the bookshop and the *Gazette* newspaper. Others she recalled seeing about town included several artisans, shop owners, a few merchants, and an elderly sea captain.

"Now, to return to our purpose. The governor has lost the trust of the people, and it is not to be recovered. We islanders find ourselves in an affair destructive to good order and the liberties of the king's subjects. We have requested the governor to convene the assembly, and these pleas have fallen on deaf ears. Without a legislative body in which to deliberate, we are helpless, and the tyrant is well aware of this. He believes he can deny the will of the people. The king must become aware of this effrontery!" Wylly said.

There was a low grumbling of voices. Indeed, they were a handful of men of different interests and sensibilities, but they were Englishmen, and they were united in one common interest: their hatred of Lord Dunmore. Eliza smiled to herself. The governor wielded a great amount of power, but he was a fool, and power never lasts long in a fool's hands. When she had first arrived, she had never noted so much discontent. Now, after Jean's death and the attack on Charles, the hatred aimed at the governor was unmistakable.

"And now he has sought to rid our island of our very own commander! As you are all well aware, Lieutenant Colonel Sharpe was only yesterday attacked by a man, paid off to finish his cruel deed by none other than Dunmore himself. Our governor is no leader. He is a villain with the blackest of hearts! For we know that if you kill a soldier … you are guilty of both murder *and* treason!"

"Aye, but that Derry man was no match for our most artful, clever fellow Sharpe!" one man with a northern accent exclaimed.

"None but the devil himself can take down this man. No American. No pirate," another said.

There was a round of cheering and vigorous claps. Charles motioned to speak.

"Gentleman, gentleman, I am only present today by

the grace of Captain Johnson. This man saved my life. It is he whom you should thank. If it were not for his bravery, I would be a dead man."

Eliza turned around with the others and saw the captain standing by himself in the back. He stood with them in the room, but some unnamed boundary kept him from sitting in a chair. He would not join them, and he did not contest his position. Even after all he had done for the colony, he was still not truly welcome in this crowd. She wanted to say something, but Wylly's voice interrupted her thoughts.

"Before James Coulter, this Derry man, as he has so been aptly named, the governor dangled a council seat. Coulter arrived on these shores a poor, destitute fellow. His pockets were bare one day, and then he was spotted with a large purse the next. They say every man has his price, but I, for one, can never be bought off by this traitor! I will have *no* footing in treason!" Mr. Wylly declared. "May the colony be relieved of him!"

"Hear, hear!" multiple men cried.

The men stomped their boots on the floor, and the china tucked away in the cabinets trembled.

"Colonial order can surely be restored, and the sovereignty of Parliament upheld!" someone shouted.

"The violations this Dunmore commits are great; I hardly need repeat them," Mr. Wylly said, regaining control of the conversation. "Lest we forgot the many grievances caused by his fat, grubby hand let us consider this. Our very own Warren here was challenged by an off-duty officer nigh a week ago, and he was forced to knock the man down to the ground." The man named Warren nodded, and Mr. Wylly continued. "Lawlessness is rampant on our humble island now. A colony where soldiers can be bribed, where government officials only look to their own purse. By a modest count, our kingdom loses thousands of pounds in revenue to smugglers. And what does our dear Dunmore do?"

"He invites the very smugglers to our shores!" one man answered. His enthusiasm was too great, and his punch sloshed out of the glass to the floor. The alcohol and heat did not portend a calm atmosphere by any means.

"This governor intends to subdue us by artifice with these grand balls and gatherings he holds on the lawn," another man added.

"Aye, he will find a way to water that lawn and keep it green whilst we islanders die of thirst!"

"Gentlemen, these islands need friends who will not remain silent. Friends who do not fear giving offense. We have submitted a catalogue of indictments and abuses of power to our agent in London. We can request a recall with a petition. But first we must make allies inside Whitehall. Our agent will deliver it to Earl Fitzwilliam and the Marquess of Lansdowne. We occupy the very outside of the world, but that does not mean our rights as Englishmen are to be taken away!"

One discontented man jeered. He sprawled in his chair, and Eliza feared the back would crack and not support his weight.

"Whitehall does not care. We provided a list of thirty-two men we identified as the governor's tools, and we have received silence in return," he mumbled.

"The men I have just named have an interest in Dunmore's downfall. They will champion our cause and go to our king. Before him, we will lay our humble supplication, and his heart will have no choice but to be moved by the distress of his subjects. I have confidence that this time, it will be treated with the greatest secrecy *and* receive a speedy reply."

But doubt surfaced among the crowd.

"If the ship does not get lost at sea ..." one said.

"If the king even reads it. I hear he never reads his own petitions anymore. He'd rather read a book about husbandry and tend to his prize hogs," another scoffed.

"Perhaps the smoothest course would be to hand our petition to the Prince of Wales!" a timid man suggested. The minute the words left his lips, he sank low into his chair.

A ruddy faced man turned around to see who had spoken and glared at him.

"For shame! You should hold your tongue if you are that misinformed and let better educated men speak," he said.

"Aye, that is long in the past. The king has recovered fairly well."

"Indeed, that was in '88, shortly after my arrival to our fair island. Let us stay focused, gentlemen," Mr. Wylly concluded.

The men continued in their chatter.

"My compact is with my sovereign alone!"

"The best of kings may be willing to hear our grievances, but I wonder if he *will* ever hear them, thousands of miles away, at so great a remove."

"Indeed, we are separated by a vast ocean with any number of misconceptions ..."

"Hear, hear!" a multitude shouted.

It appeared that Mr. Wylly was on the verge of losing the group's confidence.

"You may find that our dispatches have accumulated in the secretary of state's closet, unopened and unmolested for years. I wonder if he can even find this island on a map. But I can offer some reassurance. I have it on good authority that Lord Grenville himself has taken a personal interest in our affairs," Charles said.

Eliza looked at Charles. He spoke of Jean. He truly had read Jean's correspondences after his execution. At least one of Charles' recent turns of character finally made sense. There was no doubt that Jean's death had converted him, and now affairs on the island had grown darker than before. She gazed at his wrapped leg and then returned her attention to Mr. Wylly.

"London will deliver redress. I hold such a notion to be true," he said, puffing his chest out.

But the squabbling continued.

"The governor will punish us," the timid man said.

But Mr. Wylly's response was swift. "If an inquiry into the administration of a government is a crime, then I am a criminal and a proud one," he simply said.

"Hear, hear!" the room clamored.

"Indeed, we are up against a governor who makes it his business to turn every disturbance into a riot and every riot into an insurrection. To him, idle conversation is likened to treason. We are toying with fire," a new man spoke.

"Aye, if His Excellency Dunmore carries such strong feelings, then we must unseat him."

"That is indeed our present task, gentlemen," Mr. Wylly said.

"I wonder whether his replacement will be any more congenial to our aims," Charles replied in a low tone.

A few men around him chuckled, but the others remained silent with worry.

"We should make arrangements for a team to patrol the streets nightly."

"That is too much escalation; we must tread carefully. It will be seen as treason."

"Treason is a failure to defend our liberty. I value my freedom at too high a cost."

Lucy meandered in-between knees and chairbacks, angling herself to refill their glasses with punch. She received no thanks in return. One gruff man waved her away like an obtrusive fly after she filled his cup. She still murmured her customary "my pleasure" regardless.

"Have you heard these reports, Wylly? What say you?" a man near one of the windows asked.

"What reports, Cullen?"

"Of military stores vanishing? That cannon has found its way burrowed under loads of manure? Secret stockpiles of munitions, buried musket balls?"

"Aye, and our women are melting the pewterware into bullets. Fanciful tale, that is."

There was a snicker of laughter.

"All we have at our disposal are several old chests of muskets," an elderly man said.

"Aye, he is confusing us for Virginians, me thinks. Perhaps Dunmore himself is the source of these rumors, the great oaf."

There was a murmur of agreement.

"I hear that Dunmore accepts bribes for selling confidential reports."

"I heard even the sheriff is bought these days."

"What is worse, I have procured intelligence that he writes odious and false accounts of these islands. Heaven knows what foul lies that man spreads to Whitehall!" The man's powdered wig shook as he spoke.

"Worry not. The king cannot be deceived, nor can parliament be misinformed!" one man countered.

"Both offices are occupied by living, breathing men. It is folly to assume them infallible. We can only hope one checks the other," retorted Charles.

"And what are we to do with how he treats the Negroes?"

"Aye, and how does he treat them? They call him the 'Great Liberator,' yet he keeps his own slaves! He only meddles with ours for sport! Can't you see through his weaselly ways?"

"A more apt title would be the 'Great Deceiver.' This Guinea Town behind his mansion is trouble. I hear there is another settlement springing up near the fort for runaways. No white person dares make his appearance at risk of his very life," Wylly said.

Eliza couldn't help but turn to see the captain. He was tense but kept his face forward and emotionless. He was the very image of a perfect sentinel. She prayed the conversation would take a turn for his and Lucy's sake. It was strange to speak so passionately of freedom and rights while denying others in the room the very same.

"He means to deprive us of freedom and property, and all that is worth living for on earth!" one man passionately said.

"Some in this company would effect to do the same …" another muttered.

A few heads turned to Charles, and Eliza realized the speaker's intended meaning. A clear allusion to the business her husband took up in court had been made. She watched his reaction, expecting his temper to rise, but he remained calm and did not address the man.

Charles cleared his throat and spoke.

"There is no doubt that he has lost the people's confidence. Our authorities malign us in every way," he only said.

"Lord Dunmore possesses no true greatness. Even with all his art, he cannot counterfeit the people's admiration," Eliza quickly added.

This time, when she spoke, fewer heads turned around. She wondered if they were ignoring her or if her presence had finally been accepted in some unspoken way. The complaints carried on without missing a beat in pace.

"That man insults me!" one man said, raising his voice. "He takes the sacrament every Sunday, but it's only to ensure he qualifies for his office. I believe he is entirely incapable of any religious feeling whatsoever!"

"Aye, he's a true devil, that one is."

Their voices quickened, growing in agitation.

"When the Crown pays his salary, what incentive does he have to listen to us?"

"The fault lies within our charter. It is outdated. We are nearing a new century!"

"That is not our business here today; we belong to the House."

"Pray, do tell me what matters you claim responsibility for. Enlighten me, Joseph."

"I feel that our words are too strong. There are practical ways to address this in the House, and we are simply not—"

Mr. Wylly cut off the speakers without hesitation.

"Gentlemen, reclaim your focus! We are not allowed to convene in the House of Assembly any longer. This discussion is useless. I am waiting for Lord Dunmore to declare martial law once again! We are at war with France now; there is no denying it. That pig on the hill grins with every outburst of gunfire over by St. Domingo," he said.

"It is true," another spoke up. "The French are not far off. I fear they will invade our shores. He will no doubt use that to his advantage as well, with that duplicity for which he carries a particular talent."

"He has sacrificed this colony to his own ambition. He is a lurking serpent!"

The group was troubled again by foreboding thoughts

of invasion and property loss. But Mr. Wylly redirected their attention once more.

"Would not a wise leader protect his constituents from such an affront? If he does not care for the rule of law, we have no choice but to assume the task ourselves. We owe no allegiance to a governor who tramples our rights. And God be thanked, in an English government, we have a right to expect it!" He paused as the group cheered. "Man enjoys no greater blessing than civil government. But should a corrupt governor imperil the rights of his subjects, he overthrows the very design of it."

"And the people are thereby discharged from the duty of obedience," Charles rejoined.

"I ask you now ... would a wise leader threaten the life of his commander during such unstable times? I remind you that an assault on the rights of one is an assault on the rights of all! First, he wrongfully executed his secretary. Now, he comes for our dear Colonel Sharpe!"

But not all in the crowd agreed with this sentiment.

"You mean that spy? That scheming Longchamp fellow? Hardly a glorious name for our cause. I myself believe the rumors."

"He was no spy," Eliza said under her breath, forgetting herself.

"He could hardly be guilty of spying; the information he obtained was common knowledge to most of us. His aim was merely to acquire proof," Mr. Wylly countered.

"How can a man be guilty of treason on an island where no civil government exists?" Charles argued.

"I wager Whitehall can say the same of Dunmore then."

"You fool, he is the cause of this misery! He is an evil man who planned to raise his own fortune and advance himself to posts of power and glory at the expense of this forsaken colony!"

"I wish the Ministry would cease listening to those who misrepresent us. These islands will never forgive Dunmore. And the king should not either."

"He looks to fill his coffers, nothing more!"

"Is the man merely indulgent, or is he indeed corrupt?" Cullen questioned.

"If you cannot divine the answer to that query, you are blind, Cullen. Attempting to wheedle Englishmen out of our rights and privileges … we will not have it!"

"There is a larger plot to ruin this island by degrees. Dunmore has not only poisoned the waters, but he has even contemplated subduing us by force if necessary. Let my own experience speak for me. If this is not the way of a tyrant, then tell me what is," Charles said.

One man's voice grew louder and floated above the rest.

"Unless he is to resign his commission, tell him that his house will be immediately destroyed and his life in continual danger!"

The energy in the room immediately shifted.

"May Dunmore burn in hell!"

"I, for my part, wish him a natural early death."

There was a rush of agreement, but Mr. Wylly endeavored to temper the angry crowd.

"No, no, we will not resort to violence! Cease such reckless speech! Our aim is to establish a union that is formidable to our adversaries, and we will use common English law to such a purpose. If you continue to speak this way, I will have you all thrown out!"

The men settled down, a few of them grudgingly. Mr. Wylly's voice drowned out their discontent.

"I know you are concerned, gentlemen. It is only natural. But let us here make a secret pact today that we will vindicate one another should any of us be made to suffer for the noble efforts we have made to save this island," Wylly said in a somber tone. He turned to Charles and Eliza. "Colonel, you and your family can count on our support and our protection."

Charles nodded. "I thank you, Wylly. Thank you, gentlemen. And I, for my part, will not stop until this problem is fully eradicated."

A series of claps echoed throughout the room. The man in front of Eliza turned suddenly, looking at her slightly disheveled appearance up and down. He appeared displeased by what he took in.

"And what does our *fair* lady have to say to such complicated matters concerning our governor?"

Eliza was surprised by the turn of conversation, but her answer was clearly faster than the man expected.

"I find him to be a wicked man who prefers to oppress rather than govern."

"But he is an earl. Surely, he merits the luxury that falls into his lap?"

"No, sir. I believe that government was meant to serve. It is a force to whom even kings are servants, not masters."

"The majority of people would not agree with you."

"I very little regard the opinions of others. What I speak is the truth."

"Hear, hear!" cried the voice of one man.

The man speaking to her glared at her nameless supporter.

"I ask you now … do we as a colony flourish more on account of the king's care or the king's neglect?" he asked in a drawling tone.

Eliza could feel all their eyes on her. To them, she was nothing more than an object of attractive curiosity, and they anxiously waited for her to misspeak one word. She would deny them the pleasure.

"Why do you ask me what your very eyes can attest to yourself? Is that not the point of these gatherings?"

The man exhaled sharply, nearly rolling his eyes.

"And what, my dear, do you suppose we should do?"

"Do you mean to test me, sir?"

"I simply mean to ascertain why your presence here is necessary."

The room went awkwardly silent.

"May I remind you that you sit in my husband's house, Mr …"

"Mr. Rivett. The owner of all those lovely stores you see on Bay Street. Surely you can recognize me," he said pompously. "You possess my wares in this house."

Eliza was neither impressed nor intimidated.

"I see … Mr. Rivett. I find Mr. Wylly's plan to be a sound one. Perhaps our gracious king will intervene; I do think it possible. Shakespeare's Henry VIII delivered his people from unscrupulous courtiers, and he circumvented a revolt—"

Mr. Rivett barked out a laugh.

"A woman praising Henry VIII, how little you must be educated of him. I did not think your kind admired him. Perhaps you should not learn your history from a playwright."

"I do not speak of his private affairs or of his bedchamber, but you cannot refute that he was skilled in controlling those below him. The man understood power. If that king was such a monster, I shudder to think how wicked his ministers and nobles were. Yet he controlled them all and kept them in check."

Mr. Wylly drummed his fingers on the table, anxious to reroute the group's attention.

"Indeed, he does fail to hold a candle to our beloved monarch, but her point is the same. That is the duty of a king. Besides, without such a monarch, we would fail to have a Royal Navy or the church as it stands today," Charles interjected.

Eliza looked at him with surprise. Had he truly defended her in front of all these men yet again?

"But is it not ungrateful to squabble and complain? We may have rights, but we also have obligations to our king, Lord Sharpe," Mr. Rivett said as he turned back to Eliza.

"I find no conflict of duty in the business you gentlemen discuss, Mr. Rivett," she said, her voice confident. "After all, there is no animal that cannot defend its own liberty if it can only fight for it."

Charles gazed at her with an emotion she couldn't

quite place. Mr. Rivett was priming to speak again when Charles interrupted him. He shifted on the chaise, leaning forward.

"You seem to take a keen interest in probing my wife, Mr. Rivett."

Eliza recognized that tone. Charles had used it so many times on herself.

"I simply mean to source her opinions, of which you have spoken so highly," he replied with a false smile.

"If that is your aim, you will be here until the sun sets and it grows dark."

Charles' remark was intended to be light, but the two men stared at each other. It failed to break the tension.

Mr. Wylly cleared his throat.

"Perhaps Mr. Rivett is fascinated as to how the colonel procured such a rare creature for a wife. He forgets himself," he said. "Now, back to the matter at hand." He rustled some papers on the table near him, but the room remained tense.

"I declare that Lord Sharpe be our governor!" a man younger than Eliza shouted.

The young man's words set every pulse racing in the smoke-filled quarters. It was a parlor turned political backroom, and she barely recognized it. Everyone watched for Charles to respond. Her stomach tightened with the anxiety of waiting.

"We should have a right to elect our own governor. A man who knows this island through and through and all its ways. Not some crooked earl whose greed is larger than his belly!"

"Only the king can appoint a governor, you dotard!"

"Aye, but I say Lord Sharpe would be a fine choice. What say you, Lord Sharpe?"

Charles looked mildly uncomfortable, then with a new presence of mind and self-command, he rose. Eliza gathered that he held the men's silent admiration. While they did argue over some matters, there was no doubt that he impressed them all.

"Gentlemen, I do not possess the gift of political design. I set more store in ideas than institutions. I carry an allegiance to principles, not individuals. And I am, therefore, unfit to help found empires."

He looked at the floor after he spoke, and his discomfort with the new topic was evident.

"We find you as vigorous as a man half your age. Besides, you are so clear in your views and abundant in good sense, you surely cannot err—" one man close to Charles said.

"Your idealism gets in the way, my kind man," he replied.

"Only you would know how to best defend this island!" another man chimed.

"It is true. Fort Charlotte is ill-situated for an offensive attack. It is nearly impossible to defend. What are your thoughts on the matter, Lord Sharpe?" the man closest to Charles asked.

"I consider myself relieved of duty. I wish to steer clear of a government that has clearly gone rogue. I have long ago learned to deny myself many of the gratifications in life, even the sweetest, most desirable ones, for the sake of my country. But a governor's post is not my calling."

When he said that, he looked directly at Eliza, unabashedly, in front of all the strangers. She looked away, her cheeks coloring. He continued speaking, his head turning to address the room.

"Liberty cannot long exist in the tumult of a tyrant's grip. It is a commodity more often admired than enjoyed. I find that men happily extol it when they in fact mean nothing by it. I am jaded beyond your comprehension, my dear men. I can only offer my ideas. Nothing more."

"Please, sir, you have remained silent for far too long. I have seen you at every one of these meetings, but this attempt on your life marks you as a dangerous man in Dunmore's eyes and, therefore, a most valuable one in mine," one man emphatically said.

"I thank you," Charles said, nodding to him. He continued speaking to the rest of the group. "The people owe it to themselves to monitor those who govern. There is no crime to be found in these meetings. The only danger is complacency. That can hardly be stressed enough. The foundation of a people's ruin is often laid with the smallest, nearly imperceptible encroachments. Indeed, no people should ever forget their own power."

He seemed to hope these words would suffice. But the crowd longed to hear more from him.

"That is the very reason you should wield it for us! You are from a Conch family. You understand the trials of those who have only recently come to these shores. You can bring true leadership to this colony!" one answered.

"It is too dangerous for him to govern this island. He is afraid," the man lounging in the chair said.

Charles stood a bit straighter. "I do not need to be reminded of the toll that politics takes on my own private affairs. I have personally seen the way this governor can bend the truth to his will. Yet, I do not believe this is to be my role. I will act with prudence and continue to help our cause. I find myself a changed man. I no longer sign my letters. I carry a pistol with me wherever I go, and still, it is not enough. But I will not be deterred. I will continue to contribute to the cause in whatever way I can."

He then returned to the chaise with a sigh. The group settled down, and Mr. Wylly ran over some other matters of business. When he had finished, he quickly made some concluding remarks.

"Every man enjoys an uncontested right to his life, liberty, and property. Our rights may be threatened now, but we are subjects of the greatest government on earth. This bloodshed and any further blood will be on the hands of the governor, and he should consider his very life in danger. Dunmore has awakened this island from its sound sleep, and he will rue the day he ever equated Nassau with an easy profit! To the king! May he come to our aid in our time of need! Long live the king!"

All the men stood up, and Eliza joined suit, clapping and cheering. Charles remained sitting, but his face was pensive. A handful of men walked over to him, offering their sympathy and support. Light discussions followed about crops and the weather. He shook hands with others he only knew by name, and she was impressed to see the number of people who wanted to share a private word with him.

When the room grew empty, Mr. Wylly finally approached him.

"Charles, about what we discussed previously," he began in a low tone. "I implore you to accept a word of caution … not to set yourself in opposition to these men. We must have unity. You know my feelings on your plans. I beg you to tarry a moment. They will never understand what you intend to do. You must cease this business of setting them free. One can go unnoticed, perhaps, but more? It is unthinkable. They will feel threatened."

Eliza's ears perked up. Mr. Wylly was clearly discussing Cleo's manumission.

"I will be careful, but I will not falter in my objective," Charles answered dryly.

The answer did not satisfy.

"Can it not wait until this matter is settled? Until we have a new governor?" Mr. Wylly asked.

Now Charles slowly began to stand up, reaching for his cane.

"No. This enterprise concerns people's lives. It is more than mere politics."

Mr. Wylly watched him limp towards the door, then they all entered the shadowy hallway.

"You are a stubborn man, Charles."

"And yet you admire me," he replied with a laugh.

"I see my own reflection in you at times; it is true. You should have studied the law," Mr. Wylly said.

The men bade farewell to a few lingering guests who interrupted their conversation.

"I could never be civil to my enemies," Charles said, nodding to another gentleman. "Besides, my experiences of late have only taught me that our laws are far from infallible. There is no greater enemy to our rights than those who profess to uphold them. You, my friend, are, of course, exempt from this characterization."

Mr. Wylly smiled, but Eliza could tell he was still troubled. Now he turned to her.

"Lady Sharpe, it is a pleasure to make your acquaintance. Your husband is quite the serious, thinking man."

"I am well aware," she said, then added playfully, "I see no detriment."

"Why, the two of you would make a splendid couple in that white mansion on the hill ..." Mr. Wylly jested.

"Now, I am afraid you have worn out your welcome, William. Be gone from my sight!" Charles said, teasing him.

His laughter was bright and filled the hallway. She could not recall a recent time when she had heard him sound that way. It lifted her spirit and seemed to do the same for that of Mr. Wylly's.

They said their goodbyes and watched the rest of the men file out. The chatter was frenzied and excited. One lone man who had not spoken slowly shuffled his way out the door, taking one last glance at Charles, who raised his hand in acknowledgment. She listened as their horses departed the yard, stirring the dry dust once more. Then the house quietened down in the golden afternoon light.

But Charles' penetrating gaze was solely fixed on her, watching her carefully.

"What did you think?" he asked.

"That was thrilling. Now I understand what goes on in these meetings of yours. I find it refreshing to be seated with likeminded company."

She began to remove his jacket.

"Red suits you. Why do I never see you wear it?" he asked.

Eliza smiled and handed it back to him. He hung it over the banister.

"I apologize for Mr. Rivett," he said in a more serious tone.

"That was part of my amusement."

Charles nodded and looked out into the yard. "And how do you find the leader of our small group?"

"Mr. Wylly is a gifted orator. But I am unsure of how you figure in all of this."

Charles sighed.

"I have set my sights on destroying the governor."

"But he has already endangered your life," she protested, pointing at this leg. "Remember Jean's warning. This man will not stop. Is it truly worth it?"

"I believe so, yes," he said, as he moved towards the open door to the porch. "I have remained passive for as long as my self-preservation would allow. Captain Johnson has agreed to remain here until this trouble dies down. We will be much safer with two pairs of eyes guarding the property."

The addition of the captain's protection did offer

some solace, but she was still stunned by Charles' words.

"This will ruin your career," she said quietly.

She stepped outside into the light, and he followed her. The descending sun had set the sea ablaze in fiery streaks. For a while, he did not answer. His fingers brushed against the violet petals of the bougainvillea, creeping along the porch. It was like he had never noticed its colorful blooms before. Further out, the waves crashed on the shore, seizing forward then retreating in an endless dance.

"It is true," he finally said. "I have long hesitated to place myself in a situation in which my duty and my inclination would be so at odds. But I find myself immune to the intoxications of power now. It comes at too dear a cost. I would rather choose to be a friend to liberty."

His words were reasonable, soothing even. But she still had misgivings. He needed to accomplish much greater things. She feared his efforts to slowly dismantle Pleasant Hall would diminish underneath the weight of politics.

"Pirates once ruled here. Now noble villains have taken up the post. I mean to rid our island of them. No man should stand below the law ... or above it," he said, gazing out at the sea.

Eliza studied Charles with a growing measure of awe. A man who had once let his temper take control of him now used that same defiance in a principled way. His manner was calm, deliberative, and precise. In a word, he was unassailably logical. He displayed no impatience on any front. Instead of a bitter, jaded man she saw one sharpened by muscular reasoning.

He turned and looked at her, a wry grin forming on his face. It no longer mattered to him if she let the sun tan her skin or if she wandered around the yard in her stays. The weightlessness of freedom enveloped her now. She was free to think, free to speak, and free to breathe. Their views were no longer at a variance. At some unknown point, the two of them had merged.

She had never found him more attractive than the way he carried himself in that moment, and it quickened her pulse.

CHAPTER XIX.

The governor's voice was loud, booming against the mahogany paneled walls of the hallway. A timid slave named Abbey showed Captain Hiram Bruin an open door, then curtsied.

"A malignant spirit has them in its grips. There can be no other credible reason for such schemes. They should be carted off to London and tried for their high crimes!"

Bruin immediately tensed up as he entered the room. He irrationally feared that he was the subject of the governor's wrath.

"I will ruin his small fortune!" Lord Dunmore thundered. "That man has betrayed me in the gravest manner!"

Reassurance settled over Bruin's frame. The governor couldn't have possibly intended *him*. His profits had nearly tripled in the last year. He was nowhere near the lofty goals he truly intended, but no one could say he was penniless now. His entrance into the room went without remark, and Lord Dunmore continued his rageful speech.

"If this is not speedily crushed, it will topple the government. We must avoid an insurrection at all costs. This colony has grown brazen. Whitehall cannot intervene quickly enough! The House of Assembly seems to think itself on par with Parliament. Confound them and their cursed meetings! Fools!" His spittle flew across the desk.

Bruin assumed he was speaking of the men in politics who threatened his schemes. It was all he ever complained about now. He wished he would find something else to distract himself with.

The ship captain admitted that he was slightly impressed by Lord Dunmore's resolve. In recent months, he had chastised the House and used measures to prevent their assembly. Taverns grumbled that their licenses were in danger if they accepted business from the men involved. It was all a thinly disguised threat, and that was precisely what the governor specialized in. Now, militia officers were requested to purge miscreants from their ranks, but efforts had slowed in that department. Even Lord Sharpe, the lieutenant colonel, had been targeted. Lord Dunmore's wrath knew no bounds.

The governor had even dispatched an urgent missive to Parliament. He had wildly claimed that, were the king to not intervene, he foresaw the total subversion of government and the very ruin of the colony. Dramatics and deception well suited the man. London would hardly know the difference between truth and fiction at such a distance, and it was plain that he intended to work this angle to his advantage as much as possible.

Dunmore had wicked ambitions, and Bruin had risen

in his esteem. It had already secured him a royal pardon. That was the only reason he tolerated the governor's company. He studied his knuckles, then the gold, jeweled rings that graced his fingers. Brighter boons loomed on the horizon. He could nearly taste it.

The governor had been preoccupied with speaking only to Jennings, a weak underling sort of man, but now he directed his retribution at Bruin as well.

"And I see you have nothing to add, Bruin," Lord Dunmore scoffed. "I accepted this post and expected a quiet administration. This office has become more troublesome and disagreeable than I could have possibly expected. It has served as nothing but a banishment. Why, I am the worst paid of the royal governors!"

"But Your Lordship, your deals with others are rather lucrative if what we profit from is any indicator. And I have no doubt you have a handful more partnerships just like it," Bruin said.

"That is no matter! You couldn't even imagine the wealth the governor of Jamaica has amassed. His parties make my balls look like a simple peasant gathering! How I long to be gone from this worthless base of operation. I wish the cursed place burnt. Let it return to the sand and sea!"

"You require a hurricane, it would seem," Bruin replied with a sly smile.

"Yes. Some force of nature should wipe the entire thing off the map. But not until I have vacated this hill. I simply do not deserve to suffer any more misfortunes."

"Your mood appears very dark today, my lord," Bruin said.

He had been summoned up to the grand house in the stifling heat, and he wished the governor would get to the heart of the matter. Bruin looked out at the vast sea below them. He longed to return to his ship and feel the breeze on his skin. He started to pour himself a drink.

"Yes, yes, how very observant of you, as you help yourself to a hearty share of my wine. You never possessed manners," Lord Dunmore said. He continued his lament. "They have found a detour around me, sending letters to the Marquess of Lansdowne and to an earl! Crying that they are not disloyal, not undutiful. They claim that my letters contained lies! They are totally abandoned to wickedness. My blood boils at their insolence; their actions border on high treason. These men are bankrupt in reputation and will likewise lose their fortunes if I have any hand in the matter! Indeed, some of them will find themselves carted off to prison after I have a talk with their creditors."

Dunmore's nonexistent regard for others never ceased to astound Bruin. Not to mention his sheer hypocrisy. The governor carried the biggest debt out of anyone on the island. Bruin's heart was dark and cold as well, but he was used to men who were more artificial in their dealings. A measure of sympathy, even if borne of contrived measures, was more pleasant to hear than the unfiltered dross that continually poured from this man's pudgy mouth.

"I recall that dissidents were the first to plant a flag on this soil, and I fear the contagion has yet to be rooted out. This rotten constitution must be reformed. These men walk the streets with impunity! That damned attorney Wylly will not prosecute them— nay, indeed, he is one of them! He, too, may be on a French payroll."

Captain Bruin made the slightest smirk as if to confirm the unspoken ludicrousness of such a statement. Dunmore took a breath, dabbing the sweat away from his flabby chin.

"It is very lawlessness! It is a singular display of impudence after the greatest offering of tenderness and leniency I could possibly make towards such offending subjects. Mark me, I will not be hesitant to fulfill directives from London if they would only give them to me!"

Lord Dunmore picked up a gold letter opener and idly spun the blade on the desk. Bruin watched the flash of gold spin again and again. He wondered if the governor would notice if it went missing.

"I believe Whitehall will send a swift response this time, my lord," Mr. Jennings said in a placating tone. "There is no doubt!"

"I am subject to humiliation at home and neglect from abroad. My application for a transfer continually goes unanswered," Lord Dunmore whined.

"It is simply because no one possesses the fine acumen and intelligence you have shown, warranting your replacement nigh impossible, Your Lordship," Mr. Jennings said.

Dunmore was a portentous man. He was likewise greedy with compliments. Flattery was the one reason Jennings was allowed to remain in his company. Bruin could not assess any other capabilities from the man.

The governor's beady eyes darkened, and his lips curved upward in a scheming smile. Then he set his sight on the captain.

"Captain Bruin, I have called you here today to discuss an important matter. The colonel has attempted to raise thousands of men to seize this island."

"My Lord, take care to remember your own plots. You confuse the two," Bruin replied with satisfaction.

"I care not!" Dunmore thundered.

"I meant no affront, Your Lordship."

It was a lie. He enjoyed pointing out his mistakes. Bruin was continually impressed that a man of low intelligence had amassed such a high position of power.

Lord Dunmore glared at him and made a growling exhale.

His eyes darted to the expanse of blue outside the window, and then he smiled as if the view afforded him sudden clarity. "For our purposes, it is that damned Sharpe's fault. And, and the … French soldiers who have escaped from Saint-Domingue. Write that down, Jennings; I want no other record left to permanence."

Mr. Jenning's quill scratched furiously against the parchment.

"Is this not the time for reform? This island practically begs for a flogging. It is like a recalcitrant child, and I will bring it to heel," the governor said with venom.

Just as Lord Dunmore finished speaking, he slammed his hand down on an unsuspecting fly. Two of its conspirators still swirled in languid circles above a pile of overripe fruit that crowded a silver bowl. A hefty pineapple, an orange, and a handful of lemons sat inside it.

Bruin looked at its contents with disgust. What place did the lemons even have? They were purely ornamental, like most of the contents in this mansion. No one ever picked up a lemon and ate it. They had no place in the parlor, but there they were. Everything this house stood for was merely waste and overindulgence, and like the fruit he looked at, it was spoilt and tainted. All the while, the man behind the helm groaned about what he lacked.

Bruin knew plenty of men who would fight over the gleaming silver bowl itself. But a man like Dunmore made decadence look undesirable. Bruin sighed as he pondered what he would do with the governor's wealth if it belonged to him instead.

"I am up against a most dangerous plot," lamented Dunmore.

"But what can we possibly do?" The expression on Jennings' face was distraught.

Bruin cast a disgusted look in his direction. It occurred to him that Jennings actually admired the man and thought him worthy of his position of governor. Nothing could be further from the truth.

"Those men more resemble a mob than a governing body, and yet they hold the colony in their deluded thrall! They all deserve capital punishment and nothing less. But I am not presumptuous enough to think I can accomplish that again. Even with a bought-off executioner." Dunmore rubbed his temples. "No. People will not tolerate it a second time. I was dogged with unrelenting questions for days. It was not worth it."

"I told you to take the Frenchman and toss him from the cliffs. The sharks would have cleaned his body quite nicely, and no one would have been wiser. But you wanted the spectacle," Bruin said.

As soon as the words left his lips, he knew he had hit his target. He inhaled with satisfaction as the governor's face reddened with humiliation.

"Is it your aim to enrage me, Captain Bruin?" Lord Dunmore fumed.

"No, my lord. My apologies, I mean no affront."

"Do not interrupt the governor again!" Mr. Jennings whispered.

"There must be an abridgement of what we call English liberties. No, they will not dispose of me as easily as those rebels did in Virginia," Dunmore said angrily. "I wish I could buy them off with some public office. That is the time-honored method, but it is useless with these men. They have no honor or decency. Sharpe can no more easily be bribed than intimidated. It is a waste of time to reason with such people." He swirled his Madeira. "These Conchs are a rude, depraved, and degenerate lot. It is a mortification that they speak English and can trace themselves from our stock. They hardly act like it. I only realized this far too late."

"You must admit that Lord Sharpe was a wise choice of commander for a brief length of time. He saved you much trouble," Bruin countered.

"Yes, he was. Until he began to think on his own," Lord Dunmore snapped.

"Arrests may trigger anger from the public, my lord,"

Jennings said nervously.

"But it is wiser to strike now before this opposition solidifies. Whitehall should ignore any missives that arrive from these insurgents. Write that down."

"We could employ use of my tactics, my lord. But then again, we both know that my method of handling trouble is not necessarily palatable," Bruin said in a wicked tone.

He purposely stared down Jennings. He enjoyed watching his fear rise. Jennings looked away and pretended to amend something in his notes.

"That is precisely why I called you here today. You are not a stupid man, Captain. Indeed, your ambitions may outmatch my own. How would *you* take care of this problem?"

Bruin leaned forward, twisting his knuckles in the light so the red and blue gems in his rings reflected it.

"For Sharpe in particular? Or all of these men?" he asked.

"Sharpe, that arrogant fool. We have a man named Evans who has attended their last few meetings. His latest report said that not only is Sharpe thriving, but that someone called for him to become governor. There was unanimous support. Is this not a threat to my appointment? It cannot stand! The man should have been dead, and yet he threatens me even more!"

"If you enlisted my services earlier, he would be in the ground."

"I know you take delight in reminding me of my mistakes, but if you continue in that direction, you will find yourself on the wrong side of my temper, Bruin," Dunmore seethed. He looked down, drumming his meaty fingers on the wooden desk. "Evans also reported that the missing captain, that Johnson fellow, has taken up residence at Pleasant Hall. Is that not evidence that Sharpe is actively conspiring to raise his own army? He intends to foment rebellion!"

Captain Bruin readjusted himself in the seat and made his expression more serious.

"The situation is indeed grave, my lord," he said. "Do you want Sharpe dead or alive?"

"Dead, you fool! Have you not heard a word I've said?" the governor thundered.

"You, sir, are wasting Lord Dunmore's time!" Mr. Jennings cried.

Bruin ignored him and retained his composure.

"It is only that killing him publicly may make the man a martyr and his plantation a permanent holy ground for their pathetic meetings ..."

"Do not underestimate their politics," Lord Dunmore warned. "Men like this have ruined me before. That is why I find myself on this damned island. There is no other solution. I want him dead. You are severely testing me, Bruin. I warn you. I will get the garrison to remove him and then order them to come for your head next!"

Bruin did not take kindly to threats, but he let the governor's mistake slip.

"But surely you cannot use the army's help to remove its own commander? That logic seems flawed to me, my lord," Bruin said.

"Perhaps I can bribe another man. There can be an accident at the fort ..."

Lord Dunmore was a fool, and he severely underestimated Lord Sharpe.

"I believe a man like Sharpe will avoid the fort at all costs now."

"And yet you have no other ideas! You sorely test me, Bruin!"

Bruin reached for the decanter and refilled his glass. "The man loves his horses, I hear. Maybe we catch him in the stable?" he said, giving his wine a swirl.

"Do what you must." Lord Dunmore seemed tired of the discussion.

"If that fails, we will need to draw him into the town. Is he a church-going sort of man?" Bruin asked next.

"No, no. He hasn't attended services in quite some time. No," Dunmore said, shaking his head. Giant beads of sweat dropped from his jowls and dampened his white shirt.

"What of his legal proceedings? I heard he's causing quite an uproar with some of the planters in town."

"What of them? He wanted to free an old woman. That is merely a distraction."

"The rumor is that he intends to manumit even more. And I believe that requires multiple appointments in front of the justice in court. It's bad for the island's business, no doubt, but I only see an opportunity."

This finally pleased Dunmore and a grin formed on his awful lips. "Ah, very clever, Captain Bruin. Very clever. We will destroy these malcontents one way or the other! The sooner Sharpe is dead, the better. I can start to feel relief even now."

The matter seemed settled, but Bruin had a lingering need to suggest something.

"My Lord, what if the colonel was not killed but removed?" Bruin asked.

"Your meaning?"

Lord Dunmore shooed a fly away from his face, but the insect was relentless.

"Removed from this island. For good."

"Explain."

"What if he was taken by force away from Nassau? Abducted? I can send him to a place where we will never hear of him again. Then he cannot be made a martyr, for no one will know whether the man is dead or alive. I, of course, would expect a rather large reward for the trouble. But it can be done, I assure you."

Now he had secured the governor's attention. A captured man with a title was worth a great deal in the shadowy, clandestine world Bruin operated in. And he never turned down the opportunity for an extra purse of gold.

"And how would you arrange this? What surety can you offer that he will not return?"

"Where I would deliver him, no one can return," Bruin said. "Allow a vessel of my men to stage an attack on the town. Ensure that the regiment is distracted and that the fort will not defend itself. I will personally see to it that this man is captured, and you will never have to worry about him again."

"I want his bitch dead too. She enrages me to no end.

She foiled our plans last time, and now her attitude to-wards me is unbearable. Can you see to that?"

Bruin was surprised to hear him say that. She must have turned down Lord Dunmore's advances. He was clearly sore at the woman.

"Your thoughts are quite dark, my lord," Bruin said.

"Do they trouble you?"

"Not in the slightest."

This was not a lie. In fact, he felt thrilled by their dis-cussion. Then he heard Jenning's idiotic voice speak up with distress.

"I'm sorry, my lord, do you mean his, his wife? Lady Sharpe?" he said, his voice quaking.

"Yes, I mean his damned wife! Do *not* write that down!"

Bruin had to stifle his laughter as he watched Jen-nings cross something out on his list.

"I want them both gone. And then I will arrange a deal with the creditors to seize his property," Dunmore said. "It sits on a fine piece of land."

Bruin could almost see the governor counting coins in his mind. It was an apt time to remind him that Bruin did not work for free.

"I will require a down payment in advance."

Jennings and Lord Dunmore looked up at him in surprise. This was solely a business transaction to Bruin, and he was irritated to see their reaction. If the governor did not intend to pay Bruin for his endeavors, he was simply wasting his time.

"And my men will not be molested. They will have

free reign in the town and any bounty they see fit to seize when this occurs," Captain Bruin added.

"Yes, yes, I will see to it that the island turns a blind eye. There will be no record of the attack. I will ensure that no colonist files any claim for damage. I will pay off any discontents. It will be like it never occurred. I understand your concerns."

"Excellent, my lord. Then, for fifty thousand pounds, I will do it."

Internally, he felt brazen for even suggesting such an amount. But he ascertained that the governor was desperate indeed, and desperate men made foolish decisions. He meant to capitalize on it.

The governor's eyes bulged in disbelief.

"Are you mad? That is a fortune!"

Bruin expected resistance, but he had wagered high enough to still make out handsomely.

"It depends on how badly you feel the need to remove this … Sharpe. He seems to cause you a terrible amount of trouble," Bruin replied without a flinch.

"Forty thousand."

Bruin smiled. The governor had acted exactly as he hoped.

"Forty-five thousand. And again, my men are allowed to retain whatever spoils they take that day. I expect some security in the form of a payment now, and the rest can be managed the day before. I will not be able to return to the island for quite some time."

Lord Dunmore buried his face in his hands.

"It is not fair. It is simply unfair! How does it always

come to this? That I, an earl, must be reduced to bargaining with Negroes, or savages. Now pirates! To heavens … must I continue to be so tormented?"

Bruin's eyes narrowed. He felt his temper rise, but he gripped the arms of the chair to steel himself. It would be so very easy to kill Lord Dunmore right here in that humid, airless room. He would take care of Jennings too, and then he could rule this damned island.

But he was no fool. He knew a legion of redcoat soldiers would descend upon Nassau the moment they heard the news, and Bruin did not feel like engaging the British in a battle. He no longer had the energy for such daring ventures.

He forced himself to remain calm. If he managed this deal, he would never have to worry about money again. He deserved nothing less at his age. He was only in the middle stage of his life, but a life at sea was crude and short. This would serve as the perfect end to his trials.

"Only great men are worthy of such challenges, Lord Dunmore!" Jennings said in a cheery tone.

Bruin suppressed a grimace. Irritation rose within him. He needed to be clear about one thing. The governor's remark still stung.

"You pardoned me yourself, my lord. We both know I am no longer a pirate," Bruin said with a false tone of confidence. "You called for my help, and that is what I offer. Those are my terms."

"Only a madman would agree to them," quipped Lord Dunmore.

"I do not see the royal governor of Jamaica encountering these types of problems. Perhaps it is this strange island. The sand itself must be cursed. Nature itself seems primed against you," Bruin said.

He knew that any mention of Jamaica's leader would infuriate Lord Dunmore. He viewed the man as his rival, not his comrade.

"Lieutenant-Governor Williamson is a military man; you cannot compare the two! He was even granted discretionary powers to protect the poor people of St. Domingo. He has his garrison under heel," Mr. Jennings said. It seemed as though he had intended the remark to correct Bruin's statement, but he stopped the minute he sensed he had stirred the governor's ire instead. "The hell that has been unleashed over that part of the West Indies is a terrible affair," he added quietly, sinking into his chair.

Lord Dunmore scowled at both men, then looked towards the ceiling as if it could provide a better alternative to his current predicament.

"We have a deal, Bruin. But damn you to hell. This is not an easy decision for me," he started. The fat in his shoulders quivered with fury, but he was not done with his rant. He had a captive audience, and he intended to use it. "I tried to prevent any proposal to recall me by dissolving the House, but they have taken their gatherings elsewhere! It is an entity to which anything that resembles a man may be admitted to without scrutiny. These men are not educated! They have no fortunes!"

"Not all of them are penniless artisans, my lord. Mr. Wylly and Lord Sharpe, in particular, come to mind.

Wylly alone is in possession of what—two or three plantations on the far side of the island?" Bruin said.

His thoughts lingered on the coins Sharpe's woman had stolen from him. He would finally recover his losses. No one ever stole from him without consequence. And she would learn that matters *always* resolved in his favor.

"Well, their fortunes are insignificant at the very least. It makes the destruction of this island a matter of indifference to them. Something must be done! Make the necessary arrangements at once," Lord Dunmore replied.

"The plan we just discussed, my lord?" Bruin inquired.

"Do not make me repeat it," he growled, his temper flaring.

"I simply want to be assured that you understand my terms."

The privateer narrowed his eyes, and for a moment, Lord Dunmore had no words to offer. There was a silent standoff of tempers, then Dunmore relented.

"Yes, dammit. Let me know the day, and the town will be yours."

Bruin nodded. "Perfectly understood."

He stood up and extended his hand, but the governor would not take it.

"Lord Dunmore does not shake hands with men like you," Mr. Jennings hissed.

Bruin turned towards him, and the small man shied away, clutching his paper and quill. He wanted to punch him in the face, but he restrained himself. This was his most lucrative deal, and he did not want his anger to spoil it.

Besides, these aristocrats expected a reaction like that from him. He wanted nothing more than to prove them both wrong. He would build himself a small kingdom on this side of the world, even if it meant stealing and making wicked deals with the ones who currently ruled the seas. All empires came to an end, and Bruin would be there, ready and waiting to seize his chance when the moment finally came.

"You can deliver payment to my ship. You know where it is. I expect it tonight," he said. He walked to the doorway, leaving both men silent, the heat of how boldly he had spoken to a royal governor still hot on his back. One wrong word could have sent him to the gallows, but he had mastered reading Lord Dunmore's emotions a long time ago. Still, he felt the slightest surprise to find that he retained some form of shame with how he procured his fortune.

He strode down the silent mahogany hallway, past more silver bowls of near-rotting fruit that no one would touch. These rich men always created spectacles in their hallways. It was not merely a passage from one place in the house to another. It was a grand display of the homeowner's wealth, a place to show off an expensive hue of verdigris paint, silk damask wall coverings, and sterling candlesticks. It made Bruin sick, and he prayed the governor would not change his mind. He wanted to leave this place and never step foot in this house again.

"It is a misfortune that Your Lordship must deal with degenerates like that. Why, that man is no better than the lawless banditti we are trying to apprehend! There is simply no civility to be found on this small island," Mr. Jennings said.

What a stupid, insolent fool to utter that near an open door, Bruin thought with disgust.

He felt himself lose control. As Bruin passed another bowl of vibrant lemons, he struck a hand at the yellow pyramid of fruit, and they toppled to the red runner on the floor beneath him. A servant entered the hallway and gasped, but Bruin did not look back. He stepped out into the blinding sunlight and sauntered back towards the harbor. He had good news to share with his men.

CHAPTER XX.

The silence surrounding the dinner table at Pleasant Hall was sharply punctuated by a series of yells from the front yard. It was only a matter of moments until footsteps bounded up the porch stairs and they were joined in the dining room by an unusual guest. Josiah half-stepped into the room, fully aware he was not allowed inside the house. His large eyes were wide, and there was a streak of sweat marking his shirt.

"Lord Sharpe!"

"What is the meaning of this?" Charles asked.

"The stable is on fire! Captain Johnson said to send for you straight away! Me and Julius is trying—"

Charles did not need further explanation. He shot up from his chair, and the two men ran out of the house, with Eliza slowly following behind them. Once she saw the conflagration from the porch steps, she stood back in awe. The entire stable was engulfed in flames. She immediately thought of the horses inside and took off running as well.

The heat from the building was already scorching the air before she even reached it. She saw some horses, including her mare, tethered to the trees next to the house. A wary slave held them at bay, trying to calm them in the commotion. But she knew there weren't enough horses. She did not see Alastor.

Charles was shouting to Josiah and Julius while the captain directed other men to fetch buckets of sand and water. The front entrance was impassable. Visibly blocked with fallen debris and flames, the men did not need to explain the problem. They raced towards the back. The flames had not reached that portion of the building yet, but the smoke was billowing out of it. The men were so absorbed by the spectacle they did not notice Eliza behind them.

"The path is blocked. We got the others out, but the path is blocked now!" Julius shouted, pointing to a crooked timber that had come loose from the glowing ceiling. The heat was nearly unbearable, but they edged their way further into the building, trying to keep a clear view of the trapped horse. A loud pop sounded towards the front of the stable as the fire consumed more of the wooden building. An orange glow greedily expanded over the thick straw.

Charles attempted to duck underneath the beam, but the wound in his thigh stopped him. He could not bend or crouch his way inside. He and the men seized upon the beam of wood and immediately began trying to push it. Eliza watched helplessly. In between patches of smoke, she saw Alastor, and the fear in the animal's eyes was painful to behold.

They were running out of time. If it was this hot in the rear of the stable, she knew Alastor could not survive an even more intense heat much longer. Without thinking, Eliza ducked underneath them and ran towards the horse.

"Eliza! No! Eliza!" Charles shouted over the roaring fire.

She felt his hand grasp the material of her dress, but it slipped through his hold. She fell forward, skidding her knee on the hot brick pathway that lined the building. She could not tell if it was from the force of his grasp or from the billowing heat. It felt nearly impossible to stand the further she ventured inside, and she began to crawl, identifying her path only by touch as the smoke obfuscated her vision. She heard Alastor snort in panicked fury, and she knew she was nearly upon his box.

Her surroundings were utter disorientation. The smoke made it nearly impossible to see past her hand, let alone free the poor animal. She started to cough, struggling to breathe in the heat. All she could hear was the roar of the fire and the horse's breaths. She refused to think about the crumbling structure above her head. It could completely collapse at any moment, but she only focused on powerless Alastor.

Fumbling around next to her, she realized the box's door was open, but something else was blocking him from escaping. Her mind raced for some explanation, trying to remember the interior of the stable on a better day. She recalled seeing a chain blocking the box when the door was open, and she blindly patted the air next to her to see if she could find it. When her hand struck against something hard, she grasped it without thinking and yanked it upwards. She screamed out in pain as the metal blistered against her skin.

A force surged towards her, and she knew it was Alastor. She ducked and turned her face to the side in case the horse panicked and kicked her, trying to move as far away as possible from its path. She prayed the horse would not trample her in the chaos. Only then did she realize there might not be an open exit. She turned back to the direction she had entered, or at least she thought the opening was that way. Her heart sank when she did not see the horse or a clear path out.

Her coughs became uncontrollable, and she struggled to move as she choked on the fumes. The little clarity she had finally began to fade, and her head pounded. Then a rough hand grabbed hers and yanked her forward. In moments, they were back outside, and she was lying on top of Charles.

He was panting, staring at her incredulously. They exchanged words between bouts of coughing.

"That was utterly stupid of you."

"Where is the horse?" she asked, casting a panicked look around the yard.

"You are a fool! You could have died, Eliza! You—"

"Where is the horse?"

"…could have died! And for what … a horse? Damn you!"

Slaves were running with buckets of sloshing sea water from the beach, and an acrid brew of smoke and steam now assaulted the humid air. Charles stood up and pulled her with him.

She wouldn't stop asking about the horse, fearing he was dead.

"Where is he? Where is—"

Charles sighed, looking at her with frustration.

"He is alive. Thanks to you. Thank you, Eliza."

Eliza thought she saw a trace of emotion in his hardened eyes, but it was most likely from the smoke. Her eyes were also uncontrollably moist.

"Come, let's return inside. Your wound needs tending to," he said, steering her towards the white house. "Forgive my anger, but I value your life more than any horse."

Only then did she realize how seriously she had injured her right hand. She gingerly spread her palm open, seeing two red lines arc across it. Slight blisters were forming near the top of her palm. She looked back at the burning stable and wondered that she had been inside and made it out alive.

The wind picked up the remaining flames at an angle. A coconut tree caught fire and made a wonderous sight in the darkness. The ball of flame at the top was blindingly bright, and shards of palm fell to the ground as it mixed with embers like a shower of molten snow. They all watched the tree, and Eliza began to panic that the fire would spread further, but a light rain began to fall. Its faint, fresh scent mingled with the burning wood, and Charles led her back inside the house.

The plants beyond the porch rustled in the darkness as the window casements trembled with every new approach of wind. The rain had stopped nearly an hour ago, but Eliza and Charles remained in the dining room. Neither sought sleep, both disturbed and on edge after what they had witnessed in the stable. All the horses had miraculously survived the blaze, but the building had not. It sat in a sullen, collapsed heap, still smoking with troubled embers.

Cleo had come and tended to her hand, wrapping it in a strip of linen. The food on their plates was now cold. A cup of hot water to soothe Eliza's throat had lost its warmth, and the servants had been dismissed. A slave's work started before dawn, and with the chaos that unfolded tonight, it had been an especially taxing day.

Charles pensively stared into a void, and Eliza became engrossed by the candle flame before her. She pushed the undesirable plate away and steered the candle in its place. Keeping an open flame in such close proximity seemed a dangerous irony now. But this flame was different. It was tamed, contained, gracefully bending to the curves in the air.

"What could cause such a ferocious fire?" she finally asked.

"I suspect its origins were not natural but rather manmade. Yet no one saw anything suspicious. I spoke with the slaves. It remains a mystery."

"Who would do such a thing? Why not set fire to the house instead?"

"To serve as a warning," Charles said. "I suspect those

who are displeased with my latest legal proceedings have some dark hand in this."

Now she recognized the cause of his sullen demeanor. She had fully expected him to leave the property and get help, but he had remained in the dining room with her. There was no recourse to be had and, therefore, no reason to request assistance. Many islanders felt that he was indeed in the wrong, but it made little sense to her.

"What would killing your horses figure in any of this?"

"Those horses are my prized possessions. I am threatening their property so they see it fit to tamper with mine," he answered in a detached tone.

It was clear he had expected a reaction like this. One could not threaten the established order on this island, one which ran off of the toil of the enslaved without dire consequences. The ongoing slave rebellion in Saint-Domingue did not help settle such heightened emotions. Now there were even rumors that the French had abolished slavery on the island as a desperate bid to quell the violence and regain control.

Manumitting slaves at a time like this was nearly akin to some form of treason, either to the British nation itself or to the fragile sensibilities of enraged planters. Eliza did not fully comprehend the events unfolding on that island, but she recognized the familiar hatred of anything French. It made men in this colony insecure, infecting them with a kind of unhinged madness. If it were not the threat of malignant disease, tropical storms, or famine, the idea of French invaders was enough to make even the most even-tempered Englishman take up his musket.

"You must tell the authorities! This is unlawful!" Eliza exclaimed.

"And what use would it serve under a governor like this?" he scoffed. "I wouldn't be surprised if this was not some ruse from that quarter. I can no longer trust anyone on this island."

"Someone could have been killed tonight! This cannot go unpunished!"

He leaned forward now, stirred by her words.

"Indeed. You shouldn't ever go near such strong flames. I wonder that you would do that for me."

An awkward silence followed his words. His green eyes flashed with a nameless wave of emotion.

"I simply did it for the horse. I carried no other motivation," she finally answered.

She returned to her fixation with the candle.

"For an animal that terrifies you," he countered.

"He is an animal, as you say. But he does not know his effect on me."

With a crash on the roof, the rain returned, filling the room with the sudden violence of the storm. They sat quietly for a few moments, adrenaline refusing to release either of their minds to rest.

Eliza's voice broke through the noise.

"I remember when I arrived here. I feared time would pass by slowly. The first month seemed to confirm my dread. It was such a torturous length. But now, three summers have passed, nearly four. I wonder what is still to come ..."

She watched him, remembering the conversation

they had had inside the governor's mansion the very first day she arrived.

"This beauty ... it is unimaginable," Eliza said, toying with a jasmine flower.

"Perhaps you will reconsider when we continue our journey. It is a paradise, to be sure, but a dangerous one. I daresay I'd go so far as to describe it as deadly. Aha! Our drinks are ready!" Charles said, stepping back into the room.

Eliza sighed. She wondered what could be so threatening on a barely inhabited island. The intrigue of what could make Charles possess that kind of attitude to a place he had grown up in fascinated her. He appeared a robust and thriving man, and she saw nothing but beauty and flowers around her.

That day felt like a decade ago. Neither Charles nor Eliza were the same people who had stepped off *The Albany* that sweltering day in July 1791. The events that followed their arrival consumed her thoughts in a torturous sequence.

"Do you realize what we've done?" she asked, so very tired of it all.

Charles did not immediately reply.

"We've taken ourselves away from the noise, the destitution, the squalor ... *civilization* ... and brought ourselves here to a place where nature still reigns. Where everything that surrounds us is black and white, life and death ..." She did not look up as she spoke, gazing only at the edge of the candle flame. "Or peace and terror. Where men can come in the middle of the night, set fire to your property, and remain unscathed. It seems a continual nightmare to me."

Now her dark eyes met his. She was unsurprised to find them locked on her countenance.

"Do you not see it so?" she asked.

He did not venture an answer for several moments. Then he reached across the table and clasped his hand over her bare one.

"I only see you."

She looked at their hands intertwined on the cool mahogany table. There was a time when her instincts would have pulled away from his touch. Instead, there was only something comforting to be found from the warmth of his steady grip. Even the freshly cut flesh on the side of his wrist did not make her recoil. She looked at his injury, then at her bandaged free hand. When she glanced up again, she was arrested by the urgency strained across his features. And then he spoke.

"I know we are attached by ties stronger than reason alone. That nothing on this earth could break the cord that binds us. You once said love comes when you are not even looking. Indeed, it is true. I had given up. Finding a wife had become inconceivable. I had never met anyone who seemed a commensurate match. And in truth, I still have not. For you are above me, Eliza. In every conceivable way. You challenge me to be a better man."

She was going to interrupt him, but she had no words to say. He squeezed her hand for emphasis as he continued.

"I accepted the invitation of my friend to go to Bleinhall Manor. I was his guest, and I could not decline the offer. And just when my tolerance for the niceties of society was eclipsed, a flash of brilliant fuchsia distracted me. I followed behind you, straining to see what you were pursuing. I briefly saw the moth, but I was more taken by you, Eliza. And with every word you uttered, it had never become more apparent to me that you should be my wife. That you were the woman God had been saving me for."

Eliza turned towards the window, staring at the darkness outside. The man before her was too intense. She wanted to quit the room, but his hold on her tightened.

"Eliza, I had seen you before. When I was near death on a battlefield in America. I cannot explain or make sense of it. I do not expect you to comprehend what I myself still, to this day, cannot. But I saw you. It was a fleeting vision, but it was unmistakably you. That is why I never questioned asking for your hand in marriage. When I saw you running across the lawn that fair summer day, I knew. The angel I had once beheld on a distant battlefield was a living, breathing woman. I can see things like this at times, but my mind rarely connects the events together. It tortures me. And what's more, I know *you* can see such things too. You possess unearthly knowledge of my past."

Her lip began to quiver, and the weight of what he had said coursed through her. She nodded in agreement but could not look at him directly. She thought of the strange thunderstorm she had experienced when Jean had stayed with them. The night she had met Shango, a spirit she could only understand as the king of the *orishas*, on the beach. And the disturbing dream she had had of a battle on distant shores with a young, horrified man.

It was more than an ordinary dream, and like everything else she had seen on this island, she knew it was unquestionably real.

"You did something that day you still regret. It made you question war for the first time. There was a strategy, a plan ... but it failed. You feign glory in battle now, but you were terrified. You nearly died that day—" Her tone was one of frustration.

"Yes. Do you want the truth, Eliza? War is hell. It is *hell.*" Charles sharply exhaled, gazing down at the table. "There was a soldier my age. My opponent. He refused to die. It felt like I was tasked with killing him, again and again, and then right before the last time I struck his body, a part of me wished for him to live. But I knew it was impossible. We were too far gone. The only reason I had the upper hand was because his pistol failed to fire. An error, a simple mechanical error, and fortuitous timing was all that separated me from him."

Eliza's mind reeled from this sudden reversal. This was not the usual tone of their conversations about the war in the American colonies. Older words bubbled to the surface, past evenings where he had gloried in tales from the battlefield. Hindsight now made those words seem nothing more than a drunken bluster, a false show of bravado.

Indeed, Charles had never spoken of any regrets from the war. She recalled how Jean had interrupted him and tried to cease his deceptive version of events. Had Jean been right that sultry evening? What were Charles' intentions in revealing the truth now? Eliza's thoughts spun in maddening circles. A part of her could not bear the sight of their hands intertwined, resting as one, but another part of her relished it.

"What else have you seen in this house? Why did you ever keep such things from me?" The words tumbled out of her in a half-forced whisper.

"I can ask the same of you." Charles steeled himself for what he would say next. "I have seen your death. In the water. That is why I was sick with fear on the boat. That is why I forbade you to swim. I once had a continual nightmare of you drowning, wearing nothing but your stays and skirt. But it has ceased to continue. I understand why now. By your own choice, it nearly became true."

His grip on her hand tightened further. They had not spoken of her jump from the Black Reef, and she did not want to start a second distressing conversation now.

Eliza watched him in awe, finally beginning to understand the worst aspects of his personality. It had not been for control alone. He had tried to protect her.

"I cannot die in the water. Cleo tells me that I am protected," she hastily said.

As the words left her lips, she swore she saw a shadow cross her line of vision on the other side of the room. It was as if merely discussing otherworldly experiences conjured the beings to attention.

"It is this house. This cursed house. It is making us mad," she said, shaking her head.

She tried ignoring the shadow to her left. Only the man in front of her deserved her full attention.

"You are a rare soul. You see the war within my eyes, and you do not flinch." He looked down at the table. "I thought the army would mold me into the man I wanted to become. But it did not. Only you did," Charles said, the softness in his voice unmistakable.

"We cannot change the past. It is done. It is too late," she quickly replied.

"I will wait for you, Eliza. I was too eager to love you, but I now know that one day spent with you in friendship is greater than I deserve."

He was urging her to focus on the present, but her mind was fixed on events from the past. She recalled the night she had tried to poison him. The evening he had nearly strangled her. Even as time progressed, the sight of him lunging across the table, squeezing the very life from her, still flashed before her. Something like that could not be erased from memory.

The world was quickly being reduced to a small circle, darkness encroaching on all sides until she could only see his eye, animalistic in its rage, boring down on her.

"Do you know how many lives I have taken?" he fumed. "I can destroy you! I can kill you with my bare hands! I could squeeze the very life out of your body!"

Her breath caught in her throat as the scene played before her. They sat in the very same room, but the energy between them had shifted into something incomprehensible. She did not know whether she fully trusted such a change.

"The only way this ends is if one of us dies," she muttered to herself, watching the wavering candle flame again.

She finally managed to free her hand from his. It would be the height of absurdity to act as if their conflict had never happened.

"No, do not utter such a thing!" Charles urged. His voice broke with his next sentence. "I cannot lose you; the cost would be too dear!"

Eliza glared at him.

"I am surrounded by light when I am at your side. You stir—" he began to say.

He was beginning to speak from his passions again. Passions that seemed unbreakable, pursuant to their undaunted aim, no matter how many barriers she constructed before him. Eliza did not possess the energy to tolerate such hope-filled discussions tonight. She dismally wondered if he would ever wake from his frenzied delusion.

"I do not know you now. You reside in a place that is neither love nor hate," she stated quietly.

She began to crease the folds of her skirt with anxiety. Charles' chair scraped against the floor as he stood up and walked around the table. His steps were slow and careful. He kneeled before her, claiming her hand again. For once, she not only endured his proximity but welcomed it. She was unsure of what to think about the novelty of it all. She had been blunt with him, and for once, it had not caused anger within him. That alone changed the entire interaction between them.

"So long as I am removed from your hate. I deserve nothing more from you, and indeed, I expect nothing," he said, as he surveyed her expression. "Do not torment yourself with these thoughts. They weigh on you, I can see it in the way you look at me. Be still."

He pressed her hand, but his closeness only stirred a deep sadness within her. Tears began to well up in her eyes, then stream down her cheeks. She wiped them away with disgust. She knew what he truly wanted. The very air around them seemed to urge her to say something, to please the man crouching before her. To finally yield to him.

"I cannot love again. I do not possess such an ability within me."

"Shh ..." Charles stroked her cheek, wiping away a tear.

He hovered near the ground to be close to her. An unwelcome warmth, an animal type of heat, began to encircle her ears and rise on her chest. If he was aware of the effect he was having on her, he gave no sign.

"I do not seek to erase his memory. Jean has claimed a power over you that I never could. No, I do not wish for that. I only want to see your happiness."

A sudden sob escaped from her lips.

"I begged him," she said as she cried. "I begged him to tell you the information he knew. He wanted nothing but to quit this place. He grew angry with me that night because he found duplicity in my concern. He saw no reason in it, and now that time has passed, I confess I find very little in it myself."

She covered her eyes with her hands as she began to weep, her cries racking her entire frame.

"Eliza ..." His voice was astonished. "Why?"

"Yes … *why* did I ever make such a mistake? I do not know. It maddens me—that night is relentless in haunting me. I dream about it and every time I see a different outcome, anything other than the truth. That I sought mercy for my captor. The villain in my life. My tormentor."

Neither party spoke. Eliza had used her words carefully so far, and for the first time, she worried she had spoken too harshly. The moment dangled before them, threatening to tilt to its usual angle of discord. But she also felt the smallest opportunity that an argument could be avoided this time. It was a singular occurrence, a chance that had slowly evolved as the span of days without disagreement lengthened between them.

"You taught me to brave the future," she continued.

"I do not understand your meaning."

"When you used me so cruelly … I was afraid because I understood that I would suffer for days. You taught me to dread the darkness that comes once the sun leaves the land, and you taught me that I could survive whatever the next day brought in its wake." Now her hand sought his, and she held it with an air of curiosity as she moved his fingers. "But I also saw that you gleamed. You shined … ever so briefly. I saw it when you rode your horse on the beach with abandon when we first arrived. I saw the real you, free of the burdens of the ship. You were a marvel. And the conversation we had that first night, before … before—"

A strange sound issued out of him, and she witnessed his resolve slowly unravel. He was now crying as well.

"You *did* feel that ..." he whispered.

He looked down and shook his head in disbelief, cupping his free hand over his mouth. He appeared as a man who had seen a ghost, some specter of hope in a callous life that had seemed irresolutely unattainable until now.

She continued without acknowledgment, desperate to release the emotions roiling inside her. It was as if the act of pronouncing such thoughts into the air caused her necessary pain and subsequent relief in one stroke.

"I saw it when you used your weapon to take down the overseer. You had no reason ... no man, no thinking, feeling man would have reacted so. You frighten me, Charles; you frighten me with the depth of your feelings. And how could I not harbor such sentiments with my knowledge of you and your treatment? Yet, how could I interpret recent events other than what they truly were? You saved our ... you saved *his* child. *My* child. Philippe. And you saved me, on the rocks, and those poor men in the sea. But my heart rages like these storms. Those same hands destroyed so much. You destroyed me, Charles. You broke my faith, my trust, my innocence ... I am burdened by my thoughts. I fear myself mad ..."

Her gaze shot upwards in disbelief, and she laughed.

"No, no ..." Charles replied, reaching for her face again. "Shh ... no ..."

A pause in the conversation settled over them until he spoke again.

"May I confess once more?"

He sat on the hard wooden floor before her as her focus traced the barely perceptible, curving lines of sand left from their mingled footsteps.

"Can I confess that my head is so burdened by thoughts … endless thoughts, broken thoughts, that I fear to speak at times lest I make no sense? That the inconsistencies I see, the imbalances you so recently describe, are a spur in my side? They drive me to madness because I cannot act. I cannot resolve them. But this flood of thoughts, this anguish, is only silenced by a single look from you. *You*, Eliza.

"I love you more than you will ever know, and the blame for all of this lays with me. It is not with you. For too many days, I have squandered any chance of sharing happiness together. You suffered ill-treatment from my hands, and I cursed you when you recoiled from me. But I heard you speak some small miracle just now. I feel hope like I have not felt since I first brought you here."

Charles looked forlornly into her damp eyes.

"May I hold you?" he asked quietly.

She initially shook her head but then became absorbed in brushing away fresh tears.

"Eliza …"

His voice was an earnest and pained remark.

She felt his arms slowly encircle her as he rose up to her. She buried her face in his broad shoulder and released a torrent of anguish into him. From the heaves of his back and broken breaths, she could tell he was likewise crying. Then his body convulsed in a violent jerk.

"I beg your forgiveness."

The sentence came out in a gnarled twist of fury and fear. The words were few in number, but the sincerity of them was unquestionable. Words could perhaps never be adequate to the task.

She squeezed him, steadying him. Eliza left the chair, and they both stood.

"*Why* did you do that? What could we have been if not for those wretched first days ..."

She comforted her enemy, only he resembled such a description less and less. Was this what reconciliation looked like? Was such a thing possible between them? Were they capable of truly understanding one another?

"I wanted to trust you. I accepted you. You said you would be my protector in this world." Her voice came out like daggers, and she hurled them willingly at the sobbing, broken man before her. "But you failed to protect me from yourself."

"I failed you; it is true. I am not worthy of such a charge ..."

Eliza and Charles held each other in a strange mixture of grief and anger, of tenuous love and withering hatred. She had wondered if they would ever reconcile, but now that the moment was in front of her, it seemed surreal. She did not know if such a feeling could constitute forgiveness.

A few minutes passed, and they finally pulled apart, still looking at each other's faces. She could feel the pulsing emotion between them, the raw pain, the unremitting grip of a shared history. The vulnerability she beheld in his face was making her question the things she once held inviolate. She surely could never love *this* man. But one thing was abundantly clear: her fear had left. The threat between them had somehow been extinguished.

Instead, *she* felt powerful. What happened next in that room was her decision. She knew she could break the man before her with one careless word, yet the urge to hurt him had left her completely.

"I have never seen your countenance so vulnerable," she said softly.

"You did not see my face the moment I realized you had met Jean that night. You did not see me the night I tended your wounds after your fall ... or tonight when you saved my horse."

"Why was it hidden?" Eliza stroked his face, watching him as if a new man had emerged in his place.

He swallowed, breathless, closing his eyes.

"It is foreign to me. I had not felt it as intensely since I lost my mother. The days of my childhood feel ancient to me now. I learned to feel again, Eliza. Can you comprehend my meaning? I fear you cannot. I fear so many things. I fear I have lost you. I fear ..."

Eliza stopped him, her lips nearly touching his. And then she kissed him, slowly, cautiously. His grip at her lower back trembled in response. She kissed him again, deeper, frenetically, with desperation. She so badly wanted for this to be true, but prudence urged her to linger between stages, to still tread carefully.

"I fear this is the commencement of delirium. It surely is. From the smoke. Or the heat. It has racked my mind," she said as she took a breath.

An equally dangerous suggestion was his response.

"No, we are both tired. We should sleep. Let us retire to bed."

He held her in his arms, and they did not step apart. He had a strange, joyful glitter in his eyes that altered his entire countenance. As she watched him now, she recognized the man she had seen that very first night when they had conversed by the fireplace. They were both exhausted, but his lips pursued hers with an unwearied hunger.

"I fear I am already asleep. This is some kind of unnatural dream," she uttered in between kisses.

A warning slowly curled its way inside her mind. If they continued in this way, if she gave herself to him, she would be fulfilling some cruel obligation. She would be proving that she indeed owed this man a great deal, but the way he touched her now beckoned her mind to distraction.

But he had never asked to lie with her since the changes they had passed through together. What if it wasn't a repeat of the past but a blessed release? He lavished the kindest caresses on her now, and she recognized a grand difference in the way he moved. It was where his hands did not wander. He was hesitant and careful. He was holding back as if he was completely aware that she had only granted permission for him to access her lips.

She turned her neck towards him, craving more of the touch that she once feared, and when she finally felt his lips trail there, the unexpected pleasure was nearly unbearable. They moved slowly, savoring every point of connection. They had not met for the first time on that sunny afternoon in Somerset, now more than two years ago. They had become acquainted only tonight on this small, vulnerable island fraught with danger.

She pressed her forehead against his chest.

"It is incredible; it cannot be. What accounts for such a change within a man? My heart can feel it, but my mind rebels. Reason alone cannot dictate such a conversion. If it is not from these meetings, from some political discourse, is it from God? Has your soul found God?"

"I have found *you*. And I lost you. In doing so, it awakened a part of me that has long been buried, a part of my soul that has slumbered for nearly three decades. You, Eliza, were the impetus, the being of change, an angel cast down from the clouds. You must have merited some punishment to be paired with me ... I cannot explain a thing I do not fully understand. I only know what I feel. What you do to me."

"The only punishment is that we squandered so much time in bitter argument and disagreement. We cannot possibly recover from it."

"Shh ..." he whispered in her ear. "Look to tomorrow instead. To this very moment. The words we have just exchanged ..."

"You are caught between two ways of life. Between two modes of being. I fear I cannot yet trust the man you are becoming. The wound from before is too deep."

"I love you, Eliza. Please, let me *show* you."

He stepped back from her, slowly taking her forearm and studying her injured hand.

"You are my soul, my director, my conscience," he said, his eyes connecting with hers.

He pressed his lips against the pale inner skin of her

arm, kissing her slowly until he reached the soot-covered fabric near her elbow. The sensation of his warm breath gave her chills, and she converged with him. It seemed inconceivable that the very same man had hurt her so deeply. The heat she felt from his body against hers made her head spin. The man who had once hunted her, served as her enemy, could now be a lover. A true husband in every sense of the word.

But only if *she* allowed their relations to progress. Eliza had made him wait so long she knew he would worship her body now. She recognized it from the way he touched her tonight and the words he had spoken. His lips returned to hers, and she acquiesced in their silent, slow dance.

"Will you …" he suddenly asked.

His directness confused her until she looked down and realized she had curled a leg around his, pulling him even closer to her. He did not finish the sentence, but she understood him perfectly. Their mouths met again in a bout of explosive kisses, and he moved her towards the wall. When his touch was not distracting her, the words he had yelled from other nights echoed through her mind.

"You will bear me children. Whether it pleases you or not—that is not my intent. I would carry it out in the hallway this very moment for all to see just to reduce the height of your pride," he said, pressing her to the wall. *"You have no reason for your bold conceit. Your blood and background have done nothing in the way of improving you into a decent wife."*

She pushed them away to the side, merging with him as if every move could undo her misgivings. That night was in the past—it all felt so long ago.

An odd smell became apparent as if the fire had started anew outside. It was like wood burning but reminded her more of pork roasting. She ignored it, inhaling the scent of Charles instead. Could they make new memories? She wanted to be cleansed, to move forward. And if she had to walk through fire, she would do it.

Feeling him harden against her seemed like a natural confirmation. This was the only recourse. She charged headlong at dizzying speeds, refusing to pause, to think. She only wanted to *feel*, but more worries flowed in. There might be pain of both mind and body. Where was her loyalty? To her body? To her heart?

They kissed and kissed, fingers racing to undress one another. She felt the air hit her back as it was exposed. Her chest was flushed, the sensitive skin there prickling with redness. Only his lips could soothe her fraying nerves now.

No.

Her stomach dropped, then calm was restored. No, this was the new path. She was overthinking. Her fear was wrong. It was all wrong. Jean had been mistaken. She had been mistaken. She had always belonged here with Charles, the man she had willingly married. She couldn't remove his shirt fast enough. He was laughing, his joy palpable like the muscles that moved against her as his large hands ran along the sides of her waist. His mouth caught hers again, and she was reminded of his sheer strength as he lifted her upwards with the slightest movement. A humming began in her ears, and her heart was beginning to pound madly. She could no longer tell if it was some strange form of desire or a burgeoning madness.

NO!

This time, there was no mistaking it when the voice sounded. Only she had heard it, but it was not the voice of her conscience. It had originated from outside of her—a firm, unyielding disagreement. A contradiction to the way she felt inside her heart. She opened her mouth one more time, her tongue clashing against his, as she held his face, pulling him to her.

A burst of noise sounded behind them as the door to the porch blew open, pushed by a gust of wind. A loud clang slammed against the table, and the candle she had stared so intently at was now on its side, tendrils of smoke wafting upwards. Charles stopped as well, turning slowly around. The wax oozed onto the surface, but neither of them moved to wipe it away. There was the faintest scent of wood, burning from the heat.

Eliza recognized a change in the air. The room itself seemed to clash with some eerie, unseen force. She looked from the table to Charles and then froze in horror. A fine, translucent flicker of a man with dark hair stood directly behind Charles' shoulder. His blue eyes were familiar, but the feeling he imparted was not. His anger was discernible, like a weight on her chest. It made him unrecognizable to her senses. He looked directly through her, and it felt like the floor was swallowing her whole.

"Eliza? What did you see? Your face grows pale," Charles said, his voice heavy with concern.

He whipped around again, scanning the room for an answer that was not forthcoming.

"It is nothing. It is the wind ..." she said slowly, her dark eyes fixated on the same spot. She was transfixed by Jean, by the manner in which he presented himself and the way it was making her stomach turn. It felt like an intrusion, a disruption. Why did Charles not witness him as well? Why did Jean only choose to terrify her?

She would receive no answer. As quickly as he had appeared, he was gone. But her horror lingered.

"There is something here. I can feel it," Charles insisted. He turned away from her, and she took the opportunity to step away.

"Eliza, what did you see?" Charles asked again, his voice nervous. "What are you thinking?"

She dared not say. Mysteries between them had been revealed only moments before, but this felt like a secret she was bound to keep. Something about this felt wrong, terribly wrong. Charles wrapped an arm around her back. Her sense of the way matters worked felt inverted. She had wanted to be with her husband for the very first time, and there had been an ungodly interruption. She needed to seek out Cleo.

The floorboards creaked above their heads ever so slightly, and Philippe woke up with a cry.

A very different feeling now awakened in her. The guilt poured over her like a summer deluge. What had she almost done? Jean had vanished so quickly. He had been disappointed in her. She had betrayed him in some unfathomable way. This was a mistake. It was all a mistake. She was a mother now and a mother first and foremost. And she was the mother to Jean's child.

They were overtired and not thinking clearly. There existed something between her and Charles that had been newly formed, but its origins were unnatural. It was certainly not love, and an otherworldly visit had mercifully stopped her from committing a grave error.

Charles returned to her, holding her cheek.

"We will have to wait," she said, looking down at the floor. "It is enough."

His voice was steady, reassuring. He leaned forward and gently kissed her forehead. She hastily disengaged herself, heading upstairs to the baby. She felt torn between the two men, though one was no longer walking the earth. But perhaps in a place like Pleasant Hall that did not matter.

Her heart had softened to Charles. She had even desired him. This alone was a great enough change for one evening. And while she sat mired in conflicting emotion, pulled in one direction, then another, she recognized that it was a blessing to pause. To stop and to take account of what she really wanted was surely the proper course. She did not know what tomorrow would bring, but she knew that she would have one more night unscathed. She had worked so very hard to heal parts of her, some of which she had not even realized existed, and she refused to throw that healing away in a hasty decision. She savored knowing that she was still fully in control, that she was still free to choose.

No. She would not get burnt twice by this man. The potential of losing her peace was too high a cost. There was merit in staying cautious and reserved.

She needed to rest. Her body ached from the day's exertions, her reasoning was not clear, and she was tired of the pain of this life.

She reached Philippe and picked him up, soothing away his cries. The child was so innocent, so very ignorant of everything around him. She prayed the world would change soon, for his sake. She envied him. Eliza had lost her innocence a long time ago. It lay crumpled on the floor with the dress Charles had once ripped off of her on a very different night. It had drifted away from her fingers on the wild currents of the sea surrounding Nassau.

The fatigue returned to her in waves, and she gently placed Philippe back down in his bassinet. Eliza threw herself on her bed, and all she could see was the vision of Jean's face. What did it all mean? She was aware of a sensation at her lower back as if the sheets had fallen and twisted into a strange shape, one that nearly resembled a form holding on to her. As if something was stubbornly clinging to her, breathing alongside her troubled breaths. It was familiar and foreign in the same instant, filtering over her like a forgotten remembrance.

"Why did you leave me ..." she whispered into her pillow.

Her body flushed with a sudden warmth. There was no doubt that there was a sacred link between her and

Jean, and some distorted wonder, some slip in the natural order of things, had fostered a new connection between them. Death had been defeated. Like Tabitha, Jean was somehow able to transcend time and space to claim her and even be greedy in his possessiveness. It disturbed her, but she could not deny that it made her feel unbelievably loved. She felt comforted knowing she was protected by an invisible force. One that was not some lofty divinity but one that intimately knew her.

It was a love that was profound, nearly ancient in feel. A love that had never been dangerous, like the shaky beginnings of the one she had fled from downstairs. A love that conquered death and a communion that should not be defiled. She now regretted how dangerously close she had come to doing just that. Perhaps she and Charles were fated to be together, to be linked by invisible chains. But he had pushed her into Jean's arms, and he had no right to expect her to return.

Yet she burned with questions. Her natural tendency had at first been to reject it. To fight off any traces of the once dormant desire towards him. She had not immediately agreed to stopping what Charles and she had started. It was clear to her that it would have been foolish to lie with him, but why did Jean appear only now? Or when she had thrown herself off the Black Reef? Why did he come so selectively? How dare he not answer her desperate pleas: the countless nights she had cried herself to sleep, or when she had begged for some message, for some dream she could remember when she awoke in the morning? She had quickly understood that there was an afterlife when she arrived on the island, but in the early hours of this morning, she now also remembered it could actively meddle in her affairs.

And while so many answers remained unclear, she knew one thing. Eliza treasured it in a helpless, confused way. She loved the very force that threatened to disturb her because she could not help but love any fragment of the man who had once changed her life.

CHAPTER XXI.

Cleo lay down on her bed. It was on the ground and not raised like the other beds she made in the stately white house, but she had a pad made from old quilts that soothed her aching joints. She watched the shifting coconut trees moving against the blue afternoon sky, and the weight of her exhaustion crept over her. A story unfolded underneath her closed eyes. It was not her own, but it called her attention and played out like the ripples of a puddle, expanding, gathering clarity in its detail.

The hall is crowded with soldiers and women. Philadelphia celebrates a victory after Brandywine. The town is excited to welcome the British and enjoy some levity; it is the first time since the war has started a year ago. This moment is a break from stagnant misery. Charles speaks to a woman who is shy and reserved. She has finally smiled after a few minutes of conversation. He is younger; this afternoon is from his time in America. The woman likes to converse with him, perhaps even more than he realizes. Her father is a Methodist preacher in the city, and he can gather that she holds abolitionist sympathies. His voice falters, doubting his next statement.

"Don't be dishonest, brother," someone says next to him.

He turns and sees Jean, resplendent in his red uniform. He has listened to the conversation, and Charles fears that he is eyeing the same dark-haired woman.

"My friend has failed to mention that his father owns one of the largest plantations in the West Indies," Jean continues. He steps closer, and Charles notices his polished boot is strategically placed between him and the girl.

"I, for one, am completely against the trade," Jean says with a gleaming smile.

The fear is confirmed. Heat seizes Charles' face, and he rushes to another room. He does not know which stings worse: the mortification or the betrayal. This has not been the first time Jean has planted himself between him and a potential lover. He fears the woman thinks ill of him now.

A few hours later, and after more drinks than Charles can keep count of, Jean enters his space again.

"Why so sour, brother?" he asks, as he throws himself into an empty chair.

His shirt is rumpled, and his black hair is disheveled. Charles no longer sees the woman at the gathering. He turns to Jean now, anger flaring in his eyes.

"You lied. You failed to mention that you are a trader's son," Charles said as he tosses back his drink. "You sullied my character. And for what?"

Jean's face pales, and he grows more serious.

"Yes ... forgive me," Jean says quietly. "I wanted the girl. I suppose I am competitive in that regard. But do not trouble *yourself; you will always best me on the battlefield."*

The jest fails to lighten Charles' mood. He wants a friend who is loyal. Who does not lie, cheat at cards, and scheme to take advantage of him. Charles stands and moves towards the window, pensively watching the passers-by.

"I am sorry," Jean says once more, joining him.

A young girl with flaxen hair walks underneath the window, arm in arm with her mother.

"Now why isn't one like that here in this room tonight? Here we are arguing over a modest maid. A preacher's daughter!" Jean scoffs. *"Look at this one."*

Charles sighs and moves from the window. Jean grabs hold of his arm and steers him towards the open door.

"Come, the night is young. Let me find you a girl."

The half-moon outside is bold and yellow as it rises in the navy sky. It is a different night than what passed before. The two men trot quietly in the woods, the fallen leaves cast in an eerie glow from the moonlight.

"What is this about?" Charles asks him. *"What official business can this be? It is past midnight!"*

"We have orders from Colonel Agnew to complete a reconnaissance around Cresheim Creek."

But they approach the creek, a gleaming silver ribbon that meanders past a bend, and continue past it. Charles' suspicions grow.

"It seems highly irregular. Why would he give you the order and not me?"

"You were fast asleep. Night patrols are devastating the area. They want to keep it hushed."

Charles and Jean stop by a line of trees, dismounting from

their horses. There is a white barn and a house alongside them. Jean is cautious and quiet. He urges Charles to follow suit.

"To heavens, Jean, why are we stopping here?" Charles demands.

"Because this is the mission." Jean's reply is smooth and crowned with a mischievous smile.

Charles does not see any levity in the situation. They have broken curfew, and he fears Jean has played a ruse on him. He does not want to face trouble from his superiors again because of another's foolish mistakes. Charles follows Jean's careful footsteps, his sense of foreboding growing the further they encroach on the property.

The house is a modest size, and there is no light coming from any window. The family inside is sleeping because of the late hour. Unseen crickets chirp slowly in the early autumn chill.

"What does this really concern, Jean?"

"I have a rendezvous. A second one, I might add. With the most ethereal nymph!" Jean says, amused by Charles' confusion. "Our girl from the window. I tracked her down, but her father is a terror. I barely escaped the last time. Tonight, you can stand guard," he explains as they walk around the barn.

Charles pauses, anger rising in him.

"You lie again! Do you know nothing else? You are impudent!"

Jean smiles as he reaches the barn door. It is slightly ajar, a secret invitation.

"I am simply opposite of you. You are too honest, Charles. It can be a detriment."

Jean moves the door further apart, peering inside. Then he enters with a laugh.

"*This is madness! We are in enemy territory!*" *Charles snaps. Then he adds in a forced whisper,* "*We left camp without orders; they will skin our hides.*"

He is reluctant to go inside the building. He looks at the door and curses.

Jean reappears in the shadows. "*Shh! You must be quiet!*" *he says in a disarming tone.* "*The officers adore you; you're soon to be promoted! The powers that be could care less about my career. But Captain Sharpe? One of His Majesty's finest? Nothing will happen. Especially to you.*"

Jean is dismissive, but Charles is stubborn.

"*Jean, I refuse.*"

Charles stands up straight, reminding Jean of their difference in size. He has let him trample over him many times, but tonight, he will not tolerate it.

Jean does not like the challenge. He leaves the barn and takes him by the arm.

"*Maybe you are envious, brother. You wax poetical about finding the ideal woman as if she'll be dropped on your lap by cherubs from above.*" *Jean shakes his head.* "*You have to go out and find them. Mingle and sample a wide variety. The sampling is the most essential part. And in truth, there is no ideal woman. Just many, many fine ones.*"

Jean squeezes his arm and disappears back inside the barn. Charles feels awkward standing by the door, so he retreats to the side. He begins to pace and pulls out his pistol, fingering the trigger nervously. He never stops monitoring the trees before him. Every whisper of a branch could signal a threat.

A feminine giggle and the noise of hay disturbed issue out from the barn. Charles releases an exasperated sigh. It is sim-

ply too quiet in this field to mask the noise of their lovemaking. When they grow even louder, he marches back to the front of the barn. Now he is in view of the quiet house, but he cannot spend another minute within earshot of Jean and his lover.

An owl makes a single hoot in the distance, and then Charles hears the slightest creak, followed by the more definitive snap of a branch.

He looks up and sees a figure rushing towards him with a hunting knife.

"You are ravishing my sister! You fiend! You bloody redcoat!" the man shouts.

Time speeds into a blur. Charles tries to fight off his knife, but the assailant slashes his jacket. He sees the opportunity of space between their bodies, and Charles aims his pistol at his chest and fires.

The hidden girl in the barn screams, and everything is silent. The man stops, shock coursing through his body. He looks down at the hole inside him, blooming scarlet through his nightshirt, and he staggers towards Charles, collapsing on him.

New noise sounds by the house now. A door flies open, and the swinging golden light of a lantern arcs across the grass.

"What was that?" an older, gruff man's voice asks.

"Jacob! Pray be careful! Thieves could be looting the barn!" his wife, in a pale cap, answers.

A third voice sounds behind them, younger, feminine.

"Mary and Ethan are missing! They are not in their beds!"

The woman in view puts her hand over her mouth when she looks over and sees Charles. Her husband pushes her back in the house.

"Get inside, Emily!"

Charles looks down at the man who attacked him. Now that the frenzy has died away, he can see he is young. Much younger than he suspected moments ago. He is barely past boyhood. Charles moves away, covering his mouth in horror.

Jean appears from the back of the barn with the blonde girl who answers to the name Mary, the same they spotted from the window days before. She screams again and runs to her fallen brother, kneeling beside him.

"Ethan! Ethan!" Mary cries, shaking.

She looks up at Charles, who stands frozen.

"You monster! You've slain an innocent boy! You evil man!"

Charles begins to apologize, clumsy words tumbling from his lips.

The father is closer now, and as he peers with his lantern, he can see his son, but he also notices his daughter in her shift and Jean's half undone uniform.

"You have killed my only son and have lain with my daughter?" he thunders. He raises his rifle and levels it at Jean. "This is what the king's noble soldiers do for us!"

His daughter starts weeping earnestly, crying desperate lies. Her innocence matters more than her brother lying on the ground.

"He took me in the barn, Papa; he took me by force!"

Jean looks at her in shock. "You lie!" he says defensively.

The father charges into him, but Jean manages to bend his weapon away and out of his hands. But the man's rage is not satisfied. He throws Jean against the barn wall, slewing him with punch after punch. The deceptive girl shrieks and runs back to the house.

Charles knows Jean isn't strong enough. He watches the

father assault him, then he is moved to intervene. He tugs the man's jacket and pulls him off Jean. The man wheels around, eager to attack him as well, but a second shot erupts in the yard. Charles is astounded and watches the man drop like a sack to the ground.

Jean is trembling, his hands barely keeping the smoking pistol straight.

"This was a mistake," he finally utters.

"You've killed him!" Charles wrings his hands through his hair, looking at the two bodies on the lawn. Jean rushes towards him, his hands raised in reconciliation.

"You don't understand fathers. He wouldn't have stopped. It was me or him," he starts to say. But he sees that it does not soothe Charles. "These people are ruthless. You don't understand our enemy. They hate us, Charles."

"Look what you've done!" Charles exclaims.

Jean shakes his head and dashes to the back of the barn. The front entrance creaks open a moment later. He begins dragging the boy inside next to a tumbled bale of hay, then repeats the same with the father. He is calm, methodical, the opposite of Charles. Charles is moving frenetically, his blood-soaked hands covering his face.

"I am your captain. I will be held responsible. I will be court martialed! I could be hung! Who are these people? Do you even know their names? Who are they to the community? I cannot—" He watches Jean take the lantern and chuck it into barn, setting the dry hay ablaze. "Are you ... Jean! No!"

Charles steps forward, but the flames spread out of control.

"Because of your poor judgment, two men lie dead, Jean ..." he says in shock.

"I saved your life," Jean answers.

Charles laughs in disbelief. "You endangered it by dragging me here under false pretenses! Do you not think before you act?"

"Enough of your complaints," Jean mutters.

He stands back and watches the flames, a fiery portrait on display.

"You are desecrating the bodies! They deserve a proper burial. Have you gone mad? I order you to stop!" But Charles' voice holds no confidence in tone. In fact, it breaks, and Jean looks at him.

"Every life I take weighs on me; it hangs on my back like a shadow. I can feel it. This is wrong," Charles whispers.

"Are you crying?" Jean sneers. "Charles, what did I tell you? Tears are wasted in men. They do not suit our constitutions. That is a woman's trait. You cannot picture him as a young, sprightly boy or that man as a devoted father. You have to see them as weapons, as the gun or the knife, charging at you." Jean places a hand on his shoulder. "He saw our faces. The risk was too great. Remember what I told you? It is always you or them. There can only be one victor."

But his words do not have the intended effect this time. Charles wipes his face with his sleeve and clears his throat.

"I order you to turn in your pistol and dagger."

Jean steps back and watches the blaze grow even higher. He turns to the house, still quiet, now with fear instead of sleep. The women will not come outside. Charles can feel them watching from the windows. They will never forget their faces after tonight.

"Jean, listen to me."

He does not answer.

"I can say you fled the camp, and I apprehended you," Charles says to himself, thinking aloud. Jean pays him no heed.

They watch the flames grow wild. Charles squats on the ground, covering his face.

"You're destroying their crop! The women will have nothing to barter with now. They will starve when winter comes …"

"It is only hay," Jean says carelessly.

Charles stands up and grabs Jean by the collar.

"You understand nothing. I should have never believed you. You are a liar. Hand over your weapons," he seethes.

Jean's eyes narrow, and he reluctantly shoves his pistol at him. He keeps his knife, and Charles does not repeat the order. Instead, it is Jean who speaks cruelly.

"You will say nothing of this," he threatens. "Perhaps some other male relatives will seek vengeance, but without bodies, they have no proof."

He walks towards the horses, but his unaffected manner infuriates Charles. Charles pursues him, making him turn around.

"Where is your honor?" he says. "Jean, I believed better of you."

His disappointment is palpable in the air. He will never look at Jean the same way again. Golden memories of their childhood and their adventures in the woods wither under the weight of his disappointment.

"You know what Agnew says—"

"Colonel, Jean. Colonel, dammit, for the love of God, follow an order. I order you to use our proper titles, including mine."

"Very well, Captain Sharpe. I am not an officer. You are a mere captain. We are not Agnew … we would hang. He *would not. Do you not see how this system works?" Jean sighs. "There is no honor in war. And this is a war," he says darkly.*

Grey smoke billows high into the sky, and Charles surveys the land around them.

Jean mounts his horse. "Let us leave. We have overstayed our welcome."

The vision gathered in motion and swirled into blackness as the dream shifted into something much more lucid, but Cleo remained on the border of wakefulness. There was something interfering with her rest, and she knew the mystery would be resolved when she looked in front of her.

It was a familiar scene. A plain, unadorned table sat in the center of a dark room, and a row of thick candles provided shifting bursts of light. Cleo sat at one end of the table, and she waited for the guest to reveal his face.

Jean moved into the wavering light. It was not surprising to see him. He was, after all, the subject of the vision she had just seen. But the sight of him was shocking.

He looked worse than the last time she had encountered him. His eyes were smaller, beady, and full of cruel anger. The ligature mark from the rope remained across his neck, a lifeless hue of blue bruises.

"Death does not become you," Cleo observed. "You carry too much anger."

The man refused to transition. She knew this moment would come, but it never arrived when she expected it. That was not how spirits worked.

"The child is safe," she said in an attempt to reassure him.

She had to maintain a fine line between seeking information and not directly asking the spirit questions. If they wanted to talk, it was difficult to make them stop. A single question could turn into a deluge of information, of stale memories, and past regrets. The more he spoke, the more rapidly her energy would be consumed.

"She is *mine*," he said.

A ripple of an image of Eliza walking alone on the beach surfaced in Cleo's mind. So, he was not here to discuss his son.

Cleo looked at him and through him, seeing his memories flash before her as if they were her own. It left her dizzy, but her grip on the table steadied her. She would not fail to send him where he belonged this time. Jean had crossed a line, and there would be severe consequences.

"You let her see you," Cleo said breathlessly.

"Of course I did," came his answer, brimming with arrogance. "She confuses me for that slave, that woman that roams in the house. A slave! Can you believe it? I cannot endure it any longer."

"Watch your tongue," Cleo snapped.

She refused to let him demean Tabitha in such a way. His memories continued to flit before her in a silent parade.

"You saw her leave the ship that day. The day she first arrived. You had already known about her. You watched her swim. You heard them arguing, and you saw an opportunity. You waited for her at the rich man's ball; you knew she would be desperate to escape," Cleo said as she observed these scenes. She raised a hand as if to shoo them away from her. She had witnessed enough. "Leave her now."

Jean said nothing. He stared at her. He was furious that she could read his intentions so clearly, but he needed Cleo to relay a message. Or that was what she assumed of this encounter. He wanted something from her. She would not give it to him.

"You are a gifted liar," Cleo said, still studying his thoughts.

He leaned forward and slammed his fist down on the table. Cleo grew tense, but she would not allow him to gain the upper hand. He did not frighten her.

"Why is she allowed to continue without me? Why is she allowed to let that man raise my child?" he cried.

"You would wish her harm?"

"No, you fool," he spat. "I ache with misery. My body has died, but my feelings have not. No one speaks of this cursed state. There is no peace here. And now … now I can feel everything. I can *see* everything. I can feel how badly he desires her. I can feel how she yearns for it. I will not allow it. This would not happen if I was still alive."

He was obnoxious and insufferable. He was nothing like she remembered when he was living, but he had always carried a dark shadow behind him. In death, that shadow had only intensified, wiping away any grace that he may have once carried.

"Exactly. You are a dead man. It is not your place. You cannot meddle in their affairs."

"Has she forgotten me? I sleep beside her at night,

but it is not the same. I send her dreams, and she forgets them by morning." He turned his head in the direction of Pleasant Hall. "I will destroy that house. I will make her notice me. If I cannot have her love, I will take her fear …"

Cleo could sense tendrils of his energy lengthening and leaving the space they occupied. That was the tricky thing about spirits; they could be in more than one place in a single moment. It was difficult to summon them, but if they wanted to leave, they could depart in a single breath.

"No. You will do no such thing," she commanded. Cleo raised a hand and cut the air with it. She felt his energy return to the form she now addressed. His rage simmered like a low flame. He did not appreciate her skills.

"You yourself did not want him to see the child. Why? Answer me that," he said smugly.

He sat with his chin resting in his hand as if he was interrogating her.

"We all have free will. I did not know if Charles would choose the right path."

Jean shook his head with disgust. "And now he has given *my* child his name."

"You linger over Eliza and the boy. I will say it again. It is no longer your place."

"You did not warn him," Jean scoffed. "I was the first to warn him, but he did not listen."

He spread his cold fingers on the table, staring at them absentmindedly.

"No, he would not listen to a liar," Cleo replied.

His once bright eyes rocketed up to her, cold, hollow, and defiant.

"Listen, woman. I will not leave her side. She is intelligent. I will find some way to communicate with her. She will understand it."

"You must leave. She should not be carrying your weight on her shoulders."

"I love Eliza."

His words echoed around them.

"And so do I. Leave her alone." Cleo's voice was short and final.

"You cannot love those who enslave you. I am no fool," Jean hissed.

"You know nothing of love, even now in death."

"That man owns you."

He spoke to her like she was an idiot.

"Do not talk to me like that. He has freed me," Cleo said, her eyes not leaving his. "You were a trader's son. I have seen it. Your family made misery for my people. Tell me, do you see your father where you are?"

"No, and I do not care."

"I am not surprised. Where he is, *you* belong as well."

"I almost had her. I lured her to those cliffs. I convinced her to leave. A few moments longer, and she would have been at my side. But then he came."

"You want her dead?" she asked with surprise. Cleo began to cough as if the churning sea water that had assaulted Eliza before had now found a way down her throat as well.

The information he had just shared took her off guard. His influence on Eliza was stronger than Cleo had realized. He was manipulative and a master of deception, much like in his waking life. Cleo almost felt saddened; he was a tortured spirit. She sometimes helped heal the darkness in spirits so they could return to where they belonged, but she could not heal someone who did not want it. And her desire to protect Eliza and Philippe was stronger.

"No, but she would have been with me," he said.

Even now he could bend an awful statement with a twisted reasoning that suited his selfish needs. But his time in between worlds was running thin.

Cleo saw a light emerge from behind him. She knew it was the doorway to the next realm he was destined for. He ignored it entirely and glared at her. Its brightness no longer caught his eye. His next strategy was to insult her and distract her.

"Have you ever wondered why you have such an ability? No one wants to be cursed like you."

"It is not a curse. It is a birthright," Cleo said as she stood up. "I do not like you. Your energy is low. It makes me feel dirty."

"I will never let that man seek happiness. He is not worthy of it. He did this to me. He sent me to this accursed place! A *brother*. What could he possibly do for Eliza and my child? I will not have it. She is no better … she is choosing him over me. I need to remind her. I need her to feel me around her. I must—"

"You want to control her."

Now his eyes gleamed with a sickening light.

"I can see more than I ever could before. I can see how very weak she is. I will be that whisper in her ear, I will tell her what to do. She will listen to me. If she does not, I will rouse terror in her."

"She has already felt your presence and seen you in the house. How did you manage that?"

"I can siphon off her energy; she gives it to me willingly in her sleep. I am like a bee drinking nectar from a flower. I can see her true self now, the marvelous colors around her. It is so very beautiful."

Cleo shook her head. "She cannot give it willingly. She does not understand. You are no bee. You are a roach, feeding off any scraps you can find."

"I will be the wedge that drives them apart," Jean insisted. "I can see a path forward. I will make them cross with each other. I will send her dreams so vivid she'll have to recall them. I will sing poetry in her ear as she's falling asleep in my arms. I *will* make her remember me. And I will throw obstacles in their path like they have never imagined. I alone will be the cause of their ruin."

"You seek revenge when you should seek forgiveness."

"She will have no other lover than me. I will be the last man who takes her."

"She does not belong to you," Cleo insisted. "Their reconciliation angers you? She is his wife. God has blessed their union, not yours."

"God sent me to her himself."

"Do you think you are some kind of prophecy? You were not meant to stay by her side."

"And I will be here waiting when the time comes for her to leave," he said smugly, pointing at the table. "To join me."

"You will not be in the same place. That is a mistake." This vexed him.

"I no longer wish to be perceived by someone like you."

His energy began to seep away, but Cleo also felt him begin to drain her light. His presence was heavy, like the chain on an anchor. This was taxing on her. She hated to admit it, but she required help.

"You cannot hide from my sight like you do with the others," she reminded him.

"I will not watch my child grow from afar," he threatened.

"The boy loves Charles. I think you have seen that. The pink hue that lingers between the two of them will only grow stronger as the years pass."

"Damn you to hell," Jean shouted.

His wrath distorted his voice, but still Cleo did not flinch.

"Turn now and go through the door behind you," she ordered.

Jean ignored her. He flashed a disturbed grin, and the candles blew out on the table. An unearthly thunder emanated from the ground. He was trying to scare Cleo, but it only irritated her. He was stealing her energy to make this dramatic show. She began to pray to Papa Legba, the gatekeeper of the spirit world. He would help restore order.

"You do not know what is coming. Because if you did, you would stop it," Jean said.

Spirits often used fear to their advantage. She ignored his comment. He continued speaking as she felt even more of his presence leave the space. She needed to send him away now before he disappeared entirely.

"She should have listened to me. She is as wrong as he is. We could have left this island. We should have left! I never listened to women before, and I never will again."

Cleo smiled for the first time.

"You will listen to *this* woman."

"Why?" Jean asked rudely.

He foolishly thought he was in control.

"You leave me no choice. I banish you from this land, Jean Charles de Longchamp. You do not pay rent; you must leave," Cleo said as she closed her eyes. She gripped her temples to fight off the piercing headache she felt as he resisted.

Now she heard disjointed voices around her, swirling louder and louder. The interruption was a warning. This spirit was wasting her time. Others wanted to speak with her, others needed help from her.

Then, a bony hand emerged from the shadows. Jean whipped around and saw a thin older man wearing a coat with tails and a tall hat. He began to protest, but the man ignored his words, pulling him backward into the shadowy void. Cleo's view shifted, and she opened her eyes.

She lay on her bed, her brow drenched in sweat. At first, she worriedly searched her dwelling for any sign of Jean. But he was not there. Then she felt a sudden rush of peace. It had finally worked. She tried sending him away once before, and she had failed. Now she had succeeded, but her chest ached, and her back was sore from lying still in such a tense position. This act had weakened her considerably. It had taken a significant amount of stamina to accomplish. She worried about the toll it would take on her. She was older now, and every encounter with a spirit stole a little piece of her.

Cleo would never speak of it. She did not do this to be thanked or acknowledged. She did this to restore the balance. It was an ill-omen to bring up the dead once they had been sent away. His absence would be strengthened if she remained silent and silent she would stay. Now Charles and Eliza would face a future free from interference.

Cleo felt sleep calling her again, and she knew she would not rise from the bed for hours. But the deed had been done, and for that, she was relieved.

CHAPTER XXII.

The water was rough and choppy, as if it warned of an approaching storm. Eliza did not want to linger in the ocean today. It was too difficult to look for shells when the sand swirled and clouded up the water. She walked up the porch stairs and squeezed her hair out, then entered the house. But as she crossed the threshold, she felt like something was terribly wrong. She moved further into the house but stopped in the hallway.

The house had been ransacked. Furniture was tipped over in the parlor, spilling into the entry. Papers from Charles' study were loose and flying like giant leaves in the breeze. Gilt frames on the walls tilted at crooked angles. The sunlight from outside had vanished.

Eliza looked back, expecting to see dark clouds, but the sky remained the same. Her ears began to buzz, and the more she noticed objects in disorder, her panic grew. She crunched on broken glass and proceeded inside even more slowly. It was like a silent explosion had rent through the house.

"Cleo?" she called out. "Lucy? Celia?"

There was no answer.

She was seemingly alone, but she did not feel alone. Eliza stopped. She thought of robbers and vandals, of men like Captain Bruin. Maybe he had come looking for the coins again. Paranoia crept up her spine like a chill. She should have never been so reckless when she first arrived on this island. Where was Charles? Was this some kind of attack against him? Was it Lord Dunmore's doing?

"Charles? Charles!" she shouted, afraid to move further into the house.

Then she heard a humming. Her breath caught in her throat, then the noise grew louder in her ears. Familiar. Haunting. She recognized Tabitha before she even saw her.

Eliza looked up and everything was restored to normal order. She walked around in shock, her face pale. To see everything returned to its place so effortlessly was even more jarring. She could think of no name for the disturbance that had transpired. It was beyond reason.

"Lady Sharpe! What is the matter?" Lucy called out as she and Celia ran down the stairs.

"The house, the house ... someone had broken in. The furniture was all in disarray. The chair, the chair in the parlor was half in this hallway. The frames were tilted, there was broken ... broken glass ..." Eliza stopped when she recognized confusion in their glances.

"Lady Sharpe ... ain't nothing moved here," Celia replied.

This was not Eliza's normal experience with Tabitha. Tabitha visited her at night as she lay sleeping, waiting for her at the foot of her bed when she awoke. She had yet to experience something so unexplainable in broad daylight as this. It was beyond reason; she was wide awake. It was more than merely seeing a person who should not be in the room; it was a violent upheaval. It felt like a dire warning. Like the world of the living and that of the dead had suddenly overlapped and had brought on disturbing consequences.

As she looked at Celia and Lucy's concerned faces, she saw a third figure standing behind them. It was impossible to decipher fully; it was more a breathing shadow than an apparition. It somehow did not seem familiar like Tabitha, but she could think of no other explanation. She felt Lucy latch on to her arm as she steered her into the parlor. She sat her down in the now undisturbed chair, but Eliza hardly moved.

"It's just the heat, Lady Sharpe. Celia gonna fetch you something to cool you down," Lucy said.

"This room was destroyed, Lucy, I saw it … I saw it …"

Eliza could not get the image out of her mind. She grabbed the frame of the chair, fearing it would topple over of its own accord.

"Did you check the house? Are you certain we are alone?" Eliza stammered.

The shadow-covered figure had disappeared from view, but she could still feel something in the air around them.

"We were upstairs this whole last hour. I didn't hear

no one and I would have," Lucy said, trying her best to soothe Eliza.

Celia handed her a glass of water. She said nothing but watched the corners of the room as if she noticed something strange as well.

"Lord Sharpe says you grow faint when you're frightened. How do you feel, Lady Sharpe?" Lucy asked nervously, wringing her hands.

Then, in an instant, the invisible heaviness that had crowded around them left. The room was restored to a brightly lit space, with columns of warm sunlight crossing their feet on the oriental rug. Celia locked eyes with Eliza, and they communicated an unspoken knowing that whatever had just occurred was not only unnatural but undeniably real.

"I will be fine, Lucy; I just need to sit for a moment. Thank you," Eliza said slowly.

She released a deep breath and relaxed her legs. The longer she sat there, the more her sense of ease returned. She felt safe once again, but she couldn't erase what she had just seen and how it had made her feel. Her ever-curious mind raced with ideas. She wanted to know what had just occurred.

She thought of Tabitha with dread. She had not witnessed her sitting on the edge of her bed in some time now, but she had not forgotten her. She pictured the brass hoop under the waves that had once fit in Tabitha's ear, of the red and white checkered fabric that flowed underneath the ceaseless current. She had to tell Charles. The lies his father had told him as a child were a nightmarish reality.

Yet something about this had *not* felt familiar. Tabitha always revealed herself, bright and bold, like any living person. The shape she had seen had remained an elusive shadow. She did not know what it all meant.

"Where is Cleo? I must speak with her," Eliza asked the women.

"My mama is not feeling well. She resting now," Lucy said, turning in the hallway. Her voice bordered on the edge of nervousness. "Would it please your lady for me to go and fetch her?"

Cleo would have an answer as to what had happened just now, but Eliza did not want to disturb her on this hot afternoon. She would ask her the next time she saw her. Only Cleo could make sense of the wild and terrifying things she experienced, and she was grateful for her.

"No, I will wait until I see her again. Thank you, Lucy," Eliza answered.

"My pleasure." Lucy nodded and bounded back up the stairs.

Eliza sighed. She needed to clear her mind, and staying a moment longer in the house would not improve matters. She could tell the women wanted space to finish their tasks for the day. So, she took Philippe and returned outside to the beach. She was determined to distract herself and shake the strange occurrence far away from her thoughts. She could think of no better cure.

Eliza walked down the shoreline with the boy in her arms and the setting sun alongside them. Yesterday he had finally uttered the word "mama," and she had cried to hear him speak a recognizable word. He looked at her with two small eyes, full of love, as she carried him further down the beach, humming a nameless song. He was nearly one year old now with a full head of black wavy hair. She had never realized how fast time sped forward until she had watched something she created grow. Eliza savored these moments alone, realizing that one day, the child would no longer fit in her cradled arms.

"Eliza!"

She heard Charles' voice and turned around. He dashed barefoot through the sand towards her.

"May I join you?" he asked. "The weather is pleasant today."

She nodded without speaking, and they continued walking together. A few days had passed since their amorous encounter, and she was unsure what could inspire such a reaction between them again. They had grown closer to one another, but she felt that they now occupied unknown territory. It frightened her, but she would be false to deny that it did not also excite her. Hearing his voice close behind her back was enough to quicken her heart.

"Let me take him. Here," Charles said. "Your back is surely sore; I can see the way you're moving."

"No, he will cry if he leaves me," she replied. "He is content now."

A few more steps later, she realized Charles was still intent on holding Philippe. She slowly handed him over to Charles with reluctance. She straightened her back, not realizing how heavy a weight the baby was. Philippe began to fuss, just as she anticipated. But to her surprise,

Charles soothed him at once.

"He can walk now ... with some assistance," she said, watching the two of them interact.

She had never realized how well they responded to one another. Philippe did not passively sit in his strong arms. He looked up at him and smiled, reaching for his face.

"He is growing fast. Yes, you are," Charles said, bowing his head towards Philippe.

They continued walking in silence, the gold tinted waves murmuring softly against the sand by their steps. The sea was placid and calm today.

"He so reminds me of Elias," Charles said in a soft tone. "Not for looks ... but to hold a babe in my arms again. I had to raise him, you know. Cleo was there to supervise us, but my father tended to his whiskey more than his children."

Eliza glanced at him with an astonished look. Charles hardly spoke about his brother. She assumed it was too painful a topic to discuss.

"But all the care and devotion I showed him when he was a youth wasn't enough to save him as a man. I thought he would follow in my direction. I secured a military post for him, but he gambled it all away in the London clubs. He was more like our father than I care to admit."

Eliza felt a lingering sadness as she observed the difference between the raw words that left his mouth and the gentleness he now showed to Philippe. They lapsed into silence once more, but it was not tense or awkward.

She felt at ease by his side. It was as if his lips had communicated some measure of trust to her that night despite countless such exchanges before. But in the past, he had forced his passion onto her. Their relationship had transformed, and she welcomed it.

Time had wrought change on Charles' appearance. His strained features were now shaped into something much more temperate, and their softness made his profile more handsome. His face resembled the man she had encountered that day in the garden of her childhood home, as she had chased a curious moth and they had spoken on the iron bench. With each passing day, he was more like the person she had agreed to wed, and their troubled past seemed more a bygone nightmare to her mind.

"It is something wonderous to witness such a change in you, Charles," she finally said. "I do wonder what has caused it."

"I hope the answer is obvious," he said, his green eyes gazing deeply into hers.

She colored under such direct scrutiny. Eliza did not know if she was capable of charging headlong into a more intimate future with him. She did not yet know whether she could embrace him unconditionally, if she could truly give him her heart and live as his wife. But she understood one thing about the turn between them, this burgeoning chance to heal; she was willing to take steps she had never dared to before.

"But you did not respond to my ideas in such a way before," she said, looking away. "Even you must admit that."

"Too many events have altered my world. I am no longer the man I once was," he said, looking ahead of their path.

"It seems to me that you have returned to the man you once were," Eliza said. "Before you left this island."

Charles shook his head, and she laughed when she saw Philippe attempt to imitate his gesture. He looked down at him and kissed his forehead. Perhaps she was looking at the entire affair with too serious a mind. She needed to simplify things. She desperately wanted the peace Philippe exuded as he absorbed the world around him, to return to a childlike sense of wonder and innocence.

"No," he said, still gazing at the child. "That man was afraid to challenge his problems. He ran away from them instead."

Eliza took in his words, envisioning him in his regimentals, chasing after glory in the chaotic haze of distant battlefields. When they had first arrived on this island nearly three years ago, he had never taken off his scarlet jacket. Now she hardly saw him wear it.

"Indeed ... now you confront them," she said with a slight smile.

"Military life continually hardened me. But then something remarkable undid it all."

When Eliza looked up at him again, he was staring at her. She recognized his longing, but the usual disgust that accompanied it did not surface this time. She dug her feet into the wet sand, conscious of every forward step she took with him. He had promised to progress slowly with her. She would hold him to his word.

"Sometimes when you are not around, I take Phillipe here, and I rock him on my knee. Then I sing him a song or two. The child has a gift to quieten my mind like no other," Charles said, his face full of joy as he looked at the boy.

Eliza felt her ears turn red. She was mistaken. He was merely speaking of the child, another man's baby that he had agreed to raise in their strange arrangement. No, it was foolish to try to make such a complicated relationship into something simple. Their marriage was anything but.

"Eliza, I pray that this child is a new chapter for us," he added.

That look returned on his face, and she took a deep breath, pretending to be more engaged with the incoming roll of the waves. She had read him correctly the first time. The heat of the sun felt stronger on her chest, and she feared it was burning. But she also wondered if it was a different kind of heat. She did not answer him, and her blush deepened.

"I believe my society is obviously less desirable than his," Charles said with a laugh as he made a comical face at Philippe.

When she looked at her son's face she found a measure of strength, of confidence in knowing their darkest days were past them now.

"I should conjecture such a thing to be so," Eliza quickly replied. "He is more charming than you. It would seem you require more practice. It cannot be helped."

She was relieved that the conversation had taken a less serious tone. Their stroll on the beach was restored into a modest walk once more.

"No, it certainly cannot. I can hardly blame Philippe." Charles bounced him up and down as the child giggled. "He did not ask to be here, after all."

She looked at her husband carrying the child, and a peculiar softness settled over her shoulders. A year ago, she would not have been able to cast such a scene in her mind. It filled her with joyful thoughts of the future.

"Soon we will need toys for him. Tops and hoops. A shuttlecock. The days pass by so quickly now."

"You cannot forget some pewter soldiers. And a rocking horse. I will make him the finest rider this side of the Atlantic."

"He will have an excellent teacher," she replied. "A former member of the British Legion. Oh, the stories he will be regaled with …"

"I will ready what is required at once, my lady," he said with an outstretched wave of his arm.

They passed by three male slaves carrying firewood. The lighthearted effect of their last words quickly dwindled.

"I do not relish the task before me, Eliza," Charles said, his tone somber. "I will auction off the very furniture and carpets if I must.

"I fear you have gone mad."

"Does my plan displease you?"

"No, but I fear such a turn is simply too good to be true. I fear you will regret your current thoughts. And I fear you will change your mind."

"How very little you know me. Once I have my mind set on an object, I never fail to achieve it."

She could not deny the verity of such a statement.

"I welcome each sunrise now because it is another measure of the time that has passed since my decision. I find myself detached from my former life more and more. I only despair the obstacles I may encounter. For one, I fear I will run out of money. This plantation oftentimes seems a burden. My wealth is the land itself and the slaves that occupy it. I have very little profit coming in. It is no easy task to conjure funds in order to free them. I must deliberate my next steps very carefully."

Eliza's words left her lips before she could even process the thought further.

"I want you to take the gold coins I found in the water. I can think of no greater use for them than this—"

"What do you speak of? You have money?"

"Yes," she said quickly. "I found them when I first came here. In the water, not too far from the shore."

Charles appeared mired deep in thought.

"You know ... my father would taunt us at times and say he buried gold out in the water. He claimed he did not trust us, and he was greedy with his coin. He used to say many tall tales of how he buried ... things ... in the sea." Charles shook his head, his face troubled. "When I was younger, I would go look for it myself. I never found it. But you ... you spend all day in the ocean. It is no wonder."

Eliza shuddered and immediately thought of Tabitha's

bones resting beneath the wavering surface of the water. She did not want to distract him by changing the topic. The matter of manumission for those slaves still alive and suffering was tantamount to the sins of his father in that moment. She would tell him soon enough.

She felt her mind ease when he did not question the coins further. She was certain they belonged to Bruin; the height of his confidence knew no limits. Why would a great privateer like him trouble her over the coins if they were not truly his? Why did he have a scout patrolling that area of the beach if there was nothing of value to guard? She feared explaining the entire situation to Charles. It could only bring old troubles to the surface.

"If that is still not enough, I will sell my dresses. I will sell my jewelry, the pearls you have given me," she said emphatically, pausing in the sand. "Charles, I will support you in this endeavor in any way I can."

He stopped walking now, and they looked at each other, Philippe cooing in oblivion to the gravity of the situation.

"There are people who think like us, Charles. They may not be found on this island or the islands around us, but the women in England abstained from drinking tea for some time to save this country from the ruin of slavery. You are not alone in your sentiments."

"England remains the world's best hope," he said with a sigh.

They started to walk again, and he switched Philippe's weight to the other side of his body.

"I thought France had declared the slaves in Saint-

Domingue free this summer ..." she said with confusion.

"That is nothing but the vagaries of war. They can retract it. They have no government. As far as I am concerned, France is no longer a country but a disarray of blood-soaked shambles. The monarchy is gone, and so is the idea of France as we recognize it."

She thought of the words Jean had once uttered at Lord Dunmore's ball, where they had first met; her mind recalling the glow of candle flame and the muffled verve of the string quartet.

Jean looked down at the patterns on the rug.

"I quite enjoy your company, sir, if I may be so bold as to say. Perhaps I belong in France with like minds."

"Not these days, madame. It is no place for people like us."

Now, events in France had only worsened. A violent radical named Robespierre led an aptly named *La Terreur,* where all order was upended. Instead of doling out law and justice, the new French state called for arrests and executions of its citizens. Once accused of treason, no one was spared, not even the queen. Some said the streets of Paris ran dark with blood.

"I fear whoever is bold enough to stop this and seize power in such chaos. No ordinary man can accomplish the deed. The madness will spread like a contagion throughout Europe. Mark me, Eliza ... we have never seen anything like this in our days."

They turned and began to walk back towards the gleaming white house above the sand dune. Celia and Lucy were now on the porch sweeping.

"I have not seen Cleo today. Have you?" Charles asked.

"No. Lucy told me she was not feeling well."

"It is a marvel. I told her to rest, and yet yesterday I caught her sweeping the porch," he said as he shook his head.

"Well, she no longer wakes me in the morning. Now it has fallen to Celia, and that is quite a different experience," Eliza replied.

As she watched the women on the porch, something stirred in Eliza's memory.

"You say you left one island for this colony. Why do you remain here?" she had asked her once.

"I am waiting on two things: a little one and my freedom. A baby boy," Cleo had replied with a laugh. "Oh, I'll get my freedom. I did enough for this family. It's coming to me. And then I will be gone."

"You know," Eliza said after a few moments, "Cleo said something strange to me once before she was freed. She is past child-bearing age, isn't she? Or do you not know how old she is?"

Charles understood her intended meaning. It was rare to know the true age of a slave one purchased at the market.

"I wager she is past child-bearing years, yes. Why?"

"She told me once a long time ago that she was waiting on a little one and her freedom. Now that you have manumitted her, my mind is curious. I wonder what she will do now that she is freed."

"Perhaps she meant when Lucy bears a child," he said.

"No, she is a child herself! She is what ... sixteen years of age?" Eliza exclaimed.

"Nearly seventeen, I should think. I can peruse my records."

"I hope Lucy bears a free child. I pray for this monstrous cycle to break," she added quietly.

"I have another appointment before the magistrate next week. The matter of Lucy's manumission will be settled soon."

"I will give you my aid in whatever way you require it."

"I thank you, Eliza. I answer to a single judge. I have already wasted half my life in utter disregard of that fact. I refuse to spend another day in shame. But when I look into your eyes and see the joy contained within, I know that heaven is on my side."

His eyes seized up with sadness, and they stopped walking. Eliza was unsure of what to say. She wanted to wrap her arms around him. She wanted to feel the heat of his chest pressed up against hers, but she remained stoic, watching him struggle to contain his emotions. He looked to Philippe for relief, holding him up in his arms and laughing when the child did.

Philippe uttered something that sounded like the half-fragment of a word. Eliza moved in closer to them so she could hear better.

"Shh ... he is telling me an important secret, Eliza," Charles said in a serious manner.

Philippe repeated the babbling sound again, but this time he matched his tone to the way Charles had spoken.

"See?" Charles added with emphasis.

He pressed his ear towards the baby and pretended

to be engaged in a deep conversation. Then he took a sweeping survey of the beach and the water, and they both turned towards Eliza. She looked down and smiled, continuing her walk towards the house.

"Your mother is a mermaid. That's right. You're an observant boy," Charles said. "Her skin turns to shimmering scales in the night, covering her legs and her arms. Like gold in the sun."

Eliza laughed and heard his footsteps catch up to hers.

"That is why she is so very pretty. She bewitched me in a garden. I caught her talking to a fairy, but to my mortal eyes, it looked more like a moth."

She was surprised to hear him bring up the day they had first met, a thought that had just pressed upon her memory on this short walk. But Charles was not finished with his tale.

"And like other mermaids, your mother has a beautiful voice. I cannot sing; you yourself can testify to this. But your mother is different. She can talk to all the creatures, all the fish in the sea. The sharks, the whales, the crabs. But one creature she cannot abide ..." he said with a mischievous pause.

"He cannot understand a word you say, and I am thankful for it," she muttered.

"A man! Like me. But all manner of men are drawn to her. It is her beauty, her charm. And she will be sad one day when you become a man because you'll no longer fit in her arms. But you see, I tricked her in return, Philippe. I brought her to this sea. And this is no ordinary sea. No.

Do you see how it sparkles in the sunlight? And because this sea is filled with magic, if she gets her feet wet while walking beside me, it means she will fall in love …"

As if on cue, the surf rushed up higher than anticipated. It sprang up around her ankles, and Eliza shrieked and sprang to a safer distance. She bowed down, erupting into laughter.

"It's just a story, my dear Philippe. Your mother is silly," he whispered to the child, who smiled as he watched his mother's antics. "But now you know. It is too late for her; she cannot outrun magic."

Eliza linked up with Charles and the baby once more, and the undisguised delight she saw in Philippe as he gazed into Charles' eyes melted something inside her. She reached for her husband's hand, and he squeezed hers, his grip full of warmth and steadiness.

"You make me forget that I am not ready for love. For the sweeter things to return to my life," she said softly.

He leaned over and kissed the top of her forehead.

"If tomorrow does not bring us a better world, let us make our own," Charles replied with a smile.

CHAPTER XXIII.

"Is it any good?"

Eliza looked up from her book to see Cleo standing below her, pausing before she ascended the porch stairs. She was out of breath from wherever she had come from, but the sight of her was a delightful surprise. She had started to miss her warm presence in the house.

Eliza smiled. "Beg pardon?"

A rooster cawed out on the side of the yard.

"The book, Miss Ellie. The book you are reading."

"Oh," Eliza said with a laugh. "Marcus Aurelius Antoninus. Yes, it is. It's his *Meditations*."

"I have never heard of him."

"He was a great man. A philosopher of Ancient Rome. I think you'd rather like him."

Cleo looked at her and then the book as if its presence was equal to the philosopher himself.

"Why's that?"

"Here," Eliza replied, holding her place in the book with a strip of dried palm. She flipped a handful of pages back. "There was a line I passed a while ago. *And thou wilt give thyself relief, if thou doest every act of thy life as if it were the last, laying aside all carelessness*

and passionate aversion from the commands of reason ... ' Surely, you would agree with a statement like that?"

"I would, Miss Ellie. I suppose I would. Although he uses a lot of words for one simple thought."

Cleo was clearly feeling better. Her quick wit had resumed its rapid-fire pace.

"I found it in Charles' personal library. It's quite an old copy," Eliza said.

A few days had passed since Eliza had experienced the alarming vision in the house, but now, as she looked at Cleo, she decided to wait to bring it up. Eliza noticed she was sweating profusely, even with today's mild temperature.

Cleo put her hands on her hips. "I told you he was a good boy. I have a saying, although I doubt it will ever make it into any book. It is good to be underestimated, Miss Ellie. Remember that. It is an opportunity. The truth will always come out."

Her wide eyes expanded as she spoke, then she nodded with satisfaction. Eliza wondered to herself if her remark was a mere quip or something deeper. One never knew with Cleo. She often disguised profound messages in plain speech.

"You do not need this book, Cleo. You're full of wisdom enough," Eliza said with a smile.

Cleo winked and slowly started up the stairs, joining Celia on the porch, who was already sweeping. Charles had told her once again that it was no longer necessary to do any housework, but Cleo took great pride in ignoring him. A new, hushed conversation began, their words filtering between the loud cooing of a dove that had nestled on the roof.

"I'm nearly done, Cleo," Celia said. "You shouldn't be up here."

"It makes the time go."

"Are you doing this side?" Celia asked, an edge to her tone.

"Yes, Celia."

"Once I'm done with mine, I don't want to go back. There's always sand in this damned house. Someone doesn't know how to walk on the path."

Eliza was in earshot, but Celia never cared to disguise her feelings. It was a dynamic Eliza was more than used to.

"Some of us are not meant to walk on the path," Cleo answered calmly.

Eliza suppressed a laugh and tried to focus on her book. Cleo began to hum some nameless tune, and it was one that Eliza found pleasant to listen to. The sound of her voice, the distant thundering of the shoreline, the brisk sweeping, and the occasional clank of broom handle against the porch railing made for a soothing melody.

A nimble black butterfly with curved white stripes landed on a burst of fuchsia bougainvillea flowers. Its elongated wings wavered up and down, and Eliza marveled at it. Usually, she spotted them with a yellow tint in their stripes, but this one had a perfectly balanced contrast of black and white hues. It drank from the flower and then flew nimbly through the porch, above the two women's heads as they swept the sand away.

Her exchange with Cleo had sharpened her curiosity, and Eliza desperately wanted to tell her about the occurrence in the house, but she would wait until they finished. She wanted to speak with her privately, without Celia's judgmental presence.

"Here you go again, Cleo," Celia sighed as her brush strokes grew more agitated. "I'm tired. My back is aching. And I still have to set the table for supper."

But Cleo did not respond. She continued sweeping until a moment later when she paused. She was distracted by something in the distance, and she stared out at the beach.

"Why are you still doing this anyway? You're a free woman now. And Lord Sharpe gives you money. That must be something," Celia muttered in a low tone.

Cleo did not resume her sweeping, leaving most of her portion of the porch untouched. Celia grew more agitated by the minute. But Cleo raised her hand in the authoritative way she always did, keeping her gaze locked on the water.

"Tell Lucy I will come get her."

"All right," Celia said quickly. Then she paused in confusion. "For what?"

"Tell her that. For me, Celia. Please tell her."

Cleo's voice was solemn and urgent. Something about it made Eliza look up from her book once more.

"Yes, Cleo, whatever you say."

Cleo walked towards the other set of stairs that led down to the beach and started walking towards the water. Celia shook her head.

"I know that woman has a gift, but I swear she's mad sometimes. Two things can be true at once. Getting paid and still sweeping this damned porch. She didn't even get it all. She made it worse! She shouldn't be working. Said so herself the other day. She should leave well enough alone now. It only makes double the work for me …" Celia said aloud to herself, banging the broom every chance she had.

Cleo was slowly walking on the sand, and the porch quietened down except for Celia's low utterances.

"I'm telling you. It's not right. It's just not right …"

Eliza was growing agitated, but then she regained her focus on the page. She was nearly finished with this section of the book.

'And, to say all in a word, everything which belongs to the body is a stream, and what belongs to the soul is a dream and vapor, and life is a warfare and a stranger's sojourn, and after-fame is oblivion. What then is that which is able to conduct a man? One thing and only one …' she read.

Eliza looked up again when a breeze whistled through the palms. Cleo was talking to a man and a woman on the sand. It looked like there was a small group gathering on the beach, but the other people were harder to discern. The man at the front almost looked familiar.

"Celia, who are they?" she asked, not caring if she irritated her.

"Who?"

"The slaves on the beach. The ones Cleo is speaking with. They are not from here. I do not recognize them."

"Don't know."

But Celia hadn't even bothered to look up once. Eliza stood and walked closer to the beach side.

"Whoever they are, they do seem happy," Eliza said.

The man now looked up at her, and it felt like the sun was shining directly upon her. There was something kind and gentle about him. She smiled in turn despite her present confusion. A sense of misgiving started to surface, but she pushed it to the side and continued watching them. Their encounter was fascinating to watch. It warmed her heart.

"They must know Cleo. They must be glad to hear the news!"

Cleo laughed in the distance, raising her hands. Now Celia stopped cleaning and joined her, looking from the beach back to Eliza.

"There is no one there, Lady Sharpe."

Eliza turned to her and stopped when she saw the concern on her face.

"There is. There are people on the—"

She didn't finish her sentence because she could not. Now that she looked again, she saw Cleo by herself. She was alone. The others had gone. She was no longer moving or speaking, only gazing out ahead at the setting sun on the water. Her body started to tilt to one side, then she tumbled to the ground.

The women on the porch screamed out her name in unison. Celia's broom crashed against the wooden beams.

"Oh my God … Cleo!" a blend of their voices cried.

As they ran down to the beach, Charles appeared from the back and rushed towards her. He reached Cleo's side first and started to talk to her. Her eyes were closed and serene. He knelt down, touching her arm. But no response came.

"What happened?" Charles demanded of them. "I saw her fall. She was standing, and then she just fell …"

Eliza stared at Cleo's lifeless body in shock. Charles took her and laid her flat on her back, and as he moved her, Eliza swore she witnessed Cleo's lips crease into the faintest smile.

"She has no pulse. I feel nothing. She has no …" Charles said, panic overtaking him. He pressed his ear to her still chest. Celia reached down and grabbed one of her hands, then her face paled. She looked at Cleo and then at the water as if the rolling waves held some clue. She glanced up at Eliza next, who stood immovable, transfixed with horror.

"She's … dead, Lord Sharpe," Celia said flatly.

Charles' face wavered with emotion, and he covered his hands with his mouth. A small cry escaped his mouth despite his best efforts to mask his unstable feelings. Then he began to weep and shake.

"She was just standing here. What … why?"

He reached for Cleo again with a shaking hand.

"She is still warm. She is—" he argued.

"She is gone."

Celia's voice was toneless and devoid of sympathy.

Charles shook his head in refusal and began to say her

name, over and over again, as if it was a half-whispered prayer. His breathing grew uncontrolled and hysterical, and he retched air.

Eliza dared not speak. She carefully touched his shoulder, but he balked at her touch. She could not bring up what she had just seen. The man who had looked so familiar reminded her of Cleo. Could it have been her father? And the other woman beside him, her mother? The idea was too overwhelming. Nuances of feeling hit her in passing waves, each one quicker than the last. Denial filtered over her first, then a terrible, overwhelming helplessness. Sadness came last, a sadness she had tried hard to refute. She finally began to cry as she realized the scene before her would not change. Cleo would never wake up.

A coldness seeped into her; waves of sorrow grew from the top of her head, swirling behind her ears, with a tense chill that settled around her shoulders. The immensity of what had just occurred bore down on her and was followed by regret and confusion. Could any of them have done something? Could they have helped her in some way?

The slyest whisper of doubt came: perhaps this was some trick of nature. Perhaps her heart was still beating, undetectable to them. But Eliza understood that it was a false hope. It was stubborn to refuse to acknowledge something so obvious as death, and she could not delay her reaction any longer.

But it was so unbelievable. She had just spoken with her. There had been no sign, no warning. Only that strange request, what she had asked Celia to do for her.

She felt an urge to join Charles and Celia on the ground. Celia was staring at Charles now, her face flabbergasted. It was as if she had never witnessed the depth of their connection before.

"Charles ..." Eliza started to say, the weight of uncertainty never more evident. She could not finish the sentence; she could not find the right words to comfort him. The more she watched him unravel she thought that nothing could truly help him.

"She's free now, her spirit is free," Celia said quietly. Tears had fallen across her cheeks, but her crying was more controlled, more subtle, as if she was waiting to reveal her true reaction in private. She kept an outstretched hand covering her nose and mouth, her pale palm facing outward.

But the weeping man took the remark as an insult. He looked up at her with fury in his glance and then stalked off, rushing to the beach.

Both women watched him with astonishment as he disappeared, wiping his wet face with his arm.

"Aren't you going to tend to him?" Celia asked.

Eliza hesitated to answer, unsure of how to proceed in any of this. She sullenly looked down at Cleo, whose face resembled sleep more than death. She would know. She always had the answers.

"No," Eliza finally said, "I think it would be best to leave him. He should be alone with his thoughts for now. I will speak with him when he comes back."

She took Cleo's lifeless hand and squeezed it, wiping

her cheek with a free hand.

"Do you have a way of mourning the dead? A way that would be known to Cleo?"

Celia's eyes grew wide. Eliza could not tell if it was from watching her cry so openly or from her question.

"Lady Sharpe, she a slave. We don't have no rituals. We're not allowed to."

Eliza's stomach twisted in a mix of disgust and rage.

"She is a free woman. Charles freed her right before she—" Her voice faltered, and she paused to steady herself. "Celia, you know my true meaning," she said in between breaths. "How would Cleo mourn a loved one?"

"I only know how white people mourn. Nothing else. I only know what I did for the old Lord Sharpe, and that was nothing much at all."

"I'm not talking about that way; I'm speaking of *your* way."

Celia only gazed at her, and in the darkness of her eyes, she could feel the smallest flame burning. She wondered what caused her such anger. If it was for Cleo's sake alone, for the cruel timing of her life's journey, or for the seeming silence Celia experienced regarding her own freedom and the injustice of it all. But now was not the time or place to explain what Charles ultimately intended to do with this land.

"You must make all the necessary arrangements. Do not worry about the cost; it will be paid for. Only do what should be done. What she would have done. Whatever prayers, whatever offerings need to be made. Find a carpenter to make a casket. We will bury her in the back where Charles' mother lies."

"You mean … with a stone? A tombstone?"

"Yes, Celia."

Her face grew pale, and she looked off to the side, standing up slowly.

"Go and get the others. I will stay with her. And someone … someone must tell Lucy," Eliza said in a softer tone.

The way Celia walked towards the back of the house, rigid with shock, as if her tall, erect form would suddenly fall from the slightest stir of wind, made Eliza recall a conversation they had once had in the yard a long time ago. Of how slaves were not afforded the luxury of a grave marker. How the brutality of slavery ran deeper than the breath of life itself; even in death, distinctions were made and kept, and the enslaved regarded as a creature lesser than human in a cold refashioning of the afterlife.

"When you a slave, there ain't no difference between you and his cattle. You ain't no person. You ain't no one. You are nothing but dirt, and one fine day, you gonna return to it, and that's the only time your constant troubles are gonna come to an end. And when you die, ain't no one gonna know you walked this earth. That your tears and blood stained this ground. Won't be a trace of it left except some fine white house," Celia had said that day.

Now Eliza watched as she neared the back of the house, not seeing a small black child who eagerly waved to her. She was looking for Cleo's daughter, and she would not stop until she found her. Eliza could almost feel the weight of the responsibility on her shoulders, the unwantedness of bearing such a grievous message.

Eliza turned back to Cleo. A feeling of wrongness, a lasting sadness, and a permeating, hollow feeling trickled into her. Cleo was now at peace, but the living she had left behind would not be. Eliza's dark eyes scanned the shoreline, looking for Charles again, but he was out of sight now.

Cleo was the thread holding all of the chaos at Pleasant Hall taut in a single line. Now that thread had been broken. She was shocked that Charles had grieved so openly, even more so in front of Celia. He had finally revealed a part of himself that he had long kept hidden. Charles had seen so much death on a battlefield, but the way he had cried marked this encounter as if it was his first. Eliza understood why, perhaps more than anyone else. The trauma of losing a loved one without warning, without explanation, was a greater torture than the violence of war. She did not judge him. She feared she would be inadequate in the following days. No one could soothe away troubles like Cleo.

Cleo's body was nothing but a shell now, a husk of the person who once existed. Her brilliant energy was displaced, surrounding Eliza in the air, on the warmth of the breeze, on each glimmer of light that rolled on the top of every wave. She was everywhere and, at the same time, nowhere. In leaving her body, she joined the ranks of the countless spirits and ancestors. Cleo's eyes looked out at nothingness, but she knew she had seen something beautiful as her last vision, because Eliza had seen it too.

She smiled as she thought of it: her father and mother,

and others covered by shadow, standing there and greeting her. And then Eliza remembered Cleo's last wish that she had spoken to Celia.

"Tell Lucy I will come get her."

Her words echoed on the roar of the tide. When Lucy's journey halted on this earth, Cleo would be there, ready, standing, and waiting.

More tears crowded Eliza's face, and she laughed. She wondered if she would see her own parents when her time came. If they were not there, she knew who would undoubtedly take their place. She looked down at her, squeezing her hand, and thanked her in silence.

One final memory flashed, vivid and bright in her mind.

"I am waiting on two things: a little one and my freedom. A baby boy," Cleo had replied with a laugh. *"Oh, I'll get my freedom. I did enough for this family. It's coming to me. And then I will be gone."*

It had never made any sense to Eliza, but then again, many of Cleo's sayings were lost on her. But now it settled upon her with increasing clarity. She had known. She had always known. She had seen Philippe's birth, and she had seen her own manumission. She had helped Charles and Eliza in every way she could, and now her time with them had ended. Now it was up to them, and them alone, to see it through. To bring something good to this situation; to make what Cleo had seen in her visions become a beautiful reality.

More sadness consumed Eliza as she realized that Philippe would never remember Cleo. She would never again hear her voice on the porch, sweeping away, a sound she only recently decided sounded like serenity itself. Cleo was peace; she alone brought calm to the chaos around her. Her wide hands and her dark eyes, eyes that could see beyond the physical space they occupied, had brought light to a shadow-filled time.

The sun continued setting, oblivious to what had unfolded and relentless in its timing. Eliza closed her eyes, saying a silent prayer and dreading the sound of the men as they approached. Soon the three of them would no longer be the sole witnesses to Cleo's passing, and the reality of what happened would be undeniable. She felt the warmth of the sun on her face, and the softness of Cleo's unfeeling hand, and she brought it to her lips in a final act of gratitude.

CHAPTER XXIV.

C harles helped Eliza descend from her mare, then he hitched both of their horses to a post.

"I do not need these miscreants spotting me from horseback a quarter of a mile away. I prefer to blend in with the crowd," he said as he surveyed the area before them.

A week had passed since Cleo's death, and today, they had come to town to continue the legal proceedings to finally manumit Lucy. Eliza had wanted to join him, half out of curiosity and half out of obligation. She wanted to be more supportive of him. The tenderness she felt growing towards him no longer surprised her. The last few nights, they had held more than a few difficult conversations, but it seemed as though Charles had finally tempered his emotions. He did not take to drink, and he did not lose himself in fits of rage. After his long walk on the beach, he had come to Eliza, and she had held him.

Their relationship was in a delicate state, but it was no longer founded on hatred. He was still subdued, mourning the woman who had acted as his mother, but now he wanted to continue with his plan. Freeing Cleo's daughter was the next priority. Eliza, naturally, was more than willing to help.

"I had a doctor look at Cleo. He couldn't find any cause for such a sudden death. He concluded it was apoplexy. He has heard of such cases before. But while he studied her, he found a tumor near her stomach. If it had already seeded there, who knows how much longer she was meant to live," Charles said. "I am glad she was spared an agonizing death."

It was so very strange to live at Pleasant Hall without her presence. It was surreal, like a half-interrupted dream. A future that had loomed so unknowable only days before seemed like an urgent, pressing weight now.

"I promised her that Lucy was next. So that is what we must do." Charles' voice from last night rang out in her mind.

There was work to be done. Charles had made a life-altering decision, and he would not change course. If anything, Cleo's unexpected death had stirred an even greater passion in him. It had reminded him of the fragility of life, of the senselessness of waiting a moment longer.

"And you are sure you did not want Captain Johnson to accompany us?" she asked.

"No, I need him to guard the house," he replied. "I can manage your protection myself, my dear."

They continued walking but hardly encountered any other people.

"Thank you for joining me today, Eliza," Charles said, glancing at her as they walked. The sun made his green eyes translucent like glass. "It means more than you know."

"I confess I am proud of you, Charles," she said quietly.

The town of Nassau appeared empty as they pressed on, and Eliza found it odd. On a hot afternoon like this, it was usually bustling. Only stray dogs greeted them today as they approached. It was just past noon, and it was usually difficult to see a block away, let alone observe the bare limestone ground for so great a distance. She distantly wondered whether they had made a mistake and made the journey on a Sunday. But the absence of church bells told her it was decidedly not the sabbath. There were only two churches in the town, and their pealing bells could be heard for miles.

Soon they reached the green hill where the newly christened Fort Charlotte stood. To the unobserving eye it looked completed, but something about the view made Charles stop in his tracks. He squinted up at the imposing structure and cursed.

"Where is the flag? To think an English fort could stand without flying the standard. I have not been absent for long, but it seems a fool has replaced me," he snapped as he scanned the battlements.

"Perhaps they are changing it? Do the guards not generally change positions at this time of day?" Eliza asked.

Now Charles took off, his strides long and furious.

"This colony is going to hell. Instead of carving their bloody initials into the walls, perhaps they could learn some decency and proper soldiering."

She rushed to catch up with him. As they began to pass the open harborside, she spotted two hulking ships at a close distance. One looked distinctly familiar, but she couldn't place it in her memory. The searing heat was too distracting.

Ships were a common enough sight in these waters, but something about these two vessels made her feel uneasy. Charles was watching them as well.

"There is a strange air floating about this town today. Let us hurry and do our business. I do not wish to tarry here," he remarked uneasily.

Three or four longboats bobbed up and down on the glowing water. Eliza expected to see wares removed from the vessels in preparation to be sold in town, but she only saw men crowding in them. That seemed to catch Charles' notice, and he paused to take a longer look. Waves of a fragmented sound drifted in pieces on the breeze, and Eliza heard the men shouting on the water. A peculiar combination of noises followed: one high-pitched and shrieking, the other the low murmuration of voices, growing in volume, swelling as the moving mass grew nearer.

Then a cannonball whistled over them and lodged itself into the hill with a thunderous pound. The sound was so loud she could feel the vibration trembling in her gut. The blast echoed around them, and she could not move. Charles ducked and braced himself for a second impact. It reminded her of the night she had seen the French ship torn to pieces, and her fear returned without hesitation. Iguanas that had mindlessly perched on the limestone rocks to sun themselves scattered into the undergrowth. Then a curious noise followed, first like a whisper, then growing louder like a violent roar.

When she turned away from the fort to discover its source, a more disturbing sight arrested her. A group of men, their faces hidden under black soot, were scaling up the beach closest to them. Now she could clearly hear their maddened frenzy. They stumbled upwards to town, their swords clanking and withdrawn and their pistols shooting into the air for effect.

It worked on Eliza. She stood in shock, awed by the spectacle racing towards them. There was no time to return to the horses. Charles grabbed her and pulled her behind him as he withdrew his pistol. The impetus to scream left Eliza's body. She was rigidly fixed to the place where she stood. A hard push hit her arm.

"Eliza! Run! Seek cover! Go!" Charles shouted as he fired his gun. It found its mark, but another attacker soon replaced the fallen man. She heard the ringing of his blade next as he pulled it from its sheath. Charles lunged forward into the crowd as it hurtled into him. There was a mixture of shouting and the clang of metal and gunshot.

Eliza picked up her skirts and took off running back to the horses. The invading men blocked the path, and their faces were all uniformly covered and indistinguishable. She whirled in a circle, unsure of where to race to or if, indeed, any shelter could be had. Her fleeing steps took her to a one-story wooden building, and with a pull, she flung the door open and threw herself down on the floor. The wooden planks dug hard into her knees, and she tried to steady her panicked breaths. Brown jugs of spirits lined the haphazardly made shelves. She wondered where the owner of the shop was, but then she heard the harsh breath of someone unseen on the other side of the room. Another boom roared through the air. Eliza instinctively ducked and covered her ears, unsure of its ultimate target.

The door behind her kicked open, and she became aware of two men.

"Here we are. I told you this would be worth our while, Simon. While the others run around and cause terror, we can take some bottles for ourselves, load the boat up with them. John said we could have anything we wanted. Better to make the most of it, I say," one gruff voice said.

A large fly buzzed loudly near the corner of the ceiling, repeatedly hitting it, adding to Eliza's agony. She, too, was trapped here against her will. She feared the insect would draw attention to her hiding spot. The men's footsteps were too fast and loud for her to remain where she was. As the sound grew closer, Eliza scrambled the other way. A gun fired, and she screamed, expecting to feel a burning hole in her back.

But she remained intact. She whipped around to face her opponents. The sweat was beginning to erase their clever disguises. They were certainly not soldiers. They were ruffians. Thieves. Pirates. She had been in their company once before, and she did not hesitate in her assessment. There was no doubt of their identity. Their eyes grew huge at the unexpectedness of her presence. Her attention fell to the floor, and she saw a lifeless hand behind a counter. She assumed it belonged to the unfortunate shopkeeper.

But now neither man was interested in the rum that lined the shelves around them. One of the men slightly narrowed his eyes at her, and she knew he would charge. She flew back outside, her hands nervously fumbling with the knob, and threw her back against it. With the first determined push, she knew her body weight was not enough to hold them inside. She ran, but she was not quick enough. She felt a sweaty hand grab the back of her hair, and it slammed her into the shop's outer wall. Her back ached from the force.

"There's other spoils to be had first in this town, I think," her captor said.

He was heavyset with a wide head. His entire frame threatened aggression. She looked into his hazel eyes and spit at him. She tried to kick him, but he moved away in time. Her weak exertions only amused him.

Eliza no longer saw his accomplice. Her entire field of vision had shrunk to the threat holding her against her will. He grabbed her by the chin while his free hand caressed her side, and then a sudden force pushed him up against her further. His eyes were confused, then horrified as a thin sliver of blood gathered in the corner of his mouth. Then she heard a sword leaving his body. The man fell to the side, and she screamed.

Charles stood before her, his face already streaked with other people's blood. With the briefest glance, he swung his left arm up and fired into the other man. Eliza turned, finally looking at her would-be tormentors, and shrieked as the second man collapsed on the ground. She raised her hands in horror and looked from the fallen men back to Charles.

"Pirates are attacking the town; you need to flee. To horse!" Charles said roughly as if she was a soldier in his company.

"The French pirates? The ones in the cave?"

Her legs were tense but quaking with fear. She refused to move.

"No, they are not French. I do not know who they are or why they're attacking. You have to leave now. Now, Eliza!" Charles shouted.

Her shaking head shot a glance towards the horses, and she saw more men gathered in the spot. Charles reloaded his pistol and charged forward. Eliza reluctantly followed him, ducking from every unwarranted noise and shout around her. She looked back towards the pandemonium of the main street. A handful of people appeared now, screaming and running from the pirates while the invaders looted the stores. The meticulously ordered orange and green piles of fruit toppled to the ground, and chickens were scattered around, their white feathers hovering in the air. The sound of glass from shattered windows sounded further down, and she could smell the acrid smoke from indiscriminate fires. Why were they attacking Nassau? Why was no one stopping them?

She saw no soldiers in the mix, and she gaped at the

disorder around them. There was not one single red coat to be found. What played before her terrified eyes was surreal, made of more nightmare than ordinary afternoon. Charles took her hand and dragged her forward into another unwanted encounter. He fired into the group of men by their horses, loaded, and fired again. He rushed to the enemy and unleashed his sword to finish the rest. Eliza stalled joining him as she watched some of them continue to quiver on the ground.

Time crept along at a slowed rhythm. Charles saw her terror and altered his stance, holding out a hand, beckoning her forward. His voice was gentle, reassuring, but she hesitated to move. She took a slight step toward him, and he latched on to her, lifting her atop Alastor. She protested, looking at her mare, waiting and silent.

"He is quicker. He will deliver you to safety," Charles said as he untied the horse.

He gave Alastor a slap and stepped back as the horse took off. She screamed again and desperately grabbed hold of the reins.

No sooner had Charles helped her on the horse than a fresh group of men appeared. His escape was blocked. Events tumbled so quickly after one another that he had barely any time to think since the first cannon was fired. His mind was wracked over the strange emptiness of the town center, of the lack of response from the fort. Was it indeed deserted? Not a single shot had been fired from its ramparts in response to the attack. Something sinister and planned surrounded this.

But the most important matter was to secure Eliza's safety in the tumult. Having accomplished that task, he was beginning to feel his muscles ache, but he did not have the luxury of stopping now. He eyed the men who rocked back and forth in anticipation of his next move.

A tall, lanky man nearly his height, with his face half draped in a dark cloth, sauntered into the group, watching in amusement. The sunlight glinted off of a garnet ring he wore on one hand, but there was nothing else distinguishable about him. That was the most frustrating part of this entire assault. All of their identities had carefully been covered by some kind of soot, and they wore no uniforms. Nothing around Charles was rational. Reason would not be found in this fight.

"I am your opponent," the man said boldly.

Charles looked up at him for a moment, and then refocused his gaze on a new man who encroached on his space to the left. With one swing he felled him, but another soon replaced him. Charles eyes scanned side to side, attempting to keep track of the men advancing towards him.

"I told you; *I* am your opponent."

The man sneered and continued walking through the carnage.

Charles lost focus, then felt a pair of large hands wrap around his throat, strangling him. He cursed. He hadn't seen this one approach. He had let his guard down.

"Distractions, distractions …" the man chided him. "You're taking down too many of my men. You'll have to pay for that."

Painful moments followed as Charles' eyes teared up from the pressure. His head felt as if it would explode. The heat of the sun streaming down on his face only intensified the discomfort.

The tall man moved from view, and Charles felt the grip suddenly loosened. But a new danger fast replaced it. The barrel of a pistol lodged firmly next to his aching spine. He raised his hands in quiet surrender immediately.

These were not ordinary attackers. They were unorthodox and unpredictable. He was pushed to face a new angle and could now clearly see Eliza on Alastor.

"Do not resist. I have my other pistol fixed squarely on the small of her back. And when she evades my range, I have men waiting in the shadows of the trees. All it would take is one signal from my hand. Would you like to test it?" the man whispered menacingly in his ear.

Fear stopped Charles' ragged breath. It was not an emotion he generally allowed to consume him, but in this instance, where he clearly could no longer protect her fast-dwindling figure, he could not will it away. He began a silent prayer, repeating endlessly that Alastor would carry her away to safety, that she would not stop for any reason, that the horse would not fail. His eyes darted from tree to tree, looking for some tell-tale sign of a man's shadow or the gleam of a weapon. He saw none, but it did not count for much reassurance.

"On whose orders are you here?" Charles asked, his voice strained and hoarse.

With a drop in his stomach, he already knew the answer, but he wanted it said aloud.

"A man who paid dearly for your life," the lanky man answered.

"Am I to understand that the entire meaning of this raid is to seize me?"

"You flatter yourself. You always were an arrogant man."

Charles could feel more men gathering around them.

"I will admit, we didn't quite finish the job in February, now did we?"

A new face loomed into view, and a dirt-covered hand raced down his thigh. Charles was about to struggle when an arm clutched him in a chokehold. A punch to his leg came next, precise and targeted. He doubled over from the pain.

"You were once a powerful man. My, the tables have turned."

Then Charles was seized with a new bout of energy. He rose, and his face lightened. Eliza had reached a point of safety. The tree line had receded, and fields opened up on either side of her. A smile crossed his lips, crusted in blood. Her welfare was the sole matter that concerned him.

He heard the man sigh and begin to speak again. "I am desperate to have this over. I need to return home."

Alastor continued to gain speed as they passed underneath the silk cotton trees that lined the exit of the town. Eliza managed to turn around once to look back at Charles.

He stood, a lone figure in the haze of gunpowder, anxiously watching her retreat into safety. He seemed pleased as if her escape afforded him some measure of peace in the noisy chaos. As if the threatening men that surrounded him no longer held any danger.

Then as the horse shifted, she noticed a masked man standing behind him, his arm raised in the air. He was nearly the same height as Charles but with a slighter build. Now he moved swiftly, wasting no time. The blow came down hard on the back of Charles' head, and the once formidable soldier collapsed. His body lay crumpled on the dusty ground, and the man signaled for others to come to his aid. They surrounded Charles and grabbed his limp arms as if surveying their prize.

Alastor took a bend in the road, and Eliza could see nothing more.

TO BE CONTINUED …

Author's Note

If you are reading this, I would like to thank you for choosing to spend time in the historical world I recreated and with the characters I have made. But, if you are anything like me and you enjoy skipping ahead in books, please wait to read this until the end, as I have included some spoilers here. History is one of my biggest passions, and the eighteenth century has fascinated me since childhood. While I love the more light-hearted Regency era romances, I also wanted to create a story that showed the darker side of the late eighteenth century.

The Regency period officially spans the years 1811 to 1820 when the Prince Regent ruled in his father, King George III's stead, after the king's notorious decline in mental health. However, some writers and historians like to refer to a longer Regency period, ranging from the years 1795 to 1837. This covers the last 25 years of King George III's reign, as well as the reigns of George IV and William IV, up until Queen Victoria's accession in June 1837. To simplify things, we can lump *The Strange Eden* series into this longer Regency timeframe. For even more exactness, this part of the eighteenth century is known as the Georgian era. I wanted to clarify this before using these terms in depth.

There are many Regency romances, though delightful to read, which may be misleading when they paint a picture of the late 1700s as one made up of pretty dresses, blooming rose gardens, and dainty tea cups. While there was a tremendous cultural explosion in the arts, especially in the field of writing with Jane Austen, Lord Byron, and Walter Scott, there was a dark undercurrent beneath this flowering of the arts. For you see, that is not the aspect of the Georgian era I'm focusing on. I love researching the darker periods of history, and I find the uglier and more brutal aspects fascinating to unpack.

When I think of the Regency time period, I think of a time of chaos, revolution, inequality, and bloodshed, brightened only by the optimism of Enlightenment ideals. We see the first organized questioning of the morality of slavery with the rise of the abolition movement in England led by Granville Sharp and Thomas Clarkson. But life on the edges of the empire was still dominated by the slave trade, and The Bahamas, while more forgiving than the more brutal sugar islands to the south, was no different.

Georgian England, with its colonies strewn across the globe, was rife with contradictions. So, while there are splendid balls happening in palatial homes, there are also documented cases of poor children who were executed for the pettiest of crimes. Women were still considered the property of their husbands, and love matches in marriages were not readily encouraged. The reality for many women of the time period was not a rosy one, and you could argue that the beauty so often portrayed in novels and movies ends the moment one strays from the path of those perfectly manicured gardens.

I deliberately show Eliza as a character who questions the world around her. Raised as an aristocrat's daughter, she would have led an educated albeit extremely sheltered life. She enjoys reading the works of Voltaire, Rosseau, and others, but before she journeys to The Bahamas, she lacks real world experience. She is naive and doesn't understand that the world beyond her childhood home is very different than the one she imagined from her books. In my writing, I love to use the metaphor of a teacup for this. In Chapter X of *Strange Eden*, we encounter Eliza right before Lord Dunmore attempts to seduce her by force:

> "She studied her teacup, noticing for the first time new details previously undetected, like the mistakes the painter had left behind on the fine bone china. The swirls of ivy and arabesques that didn't quite align with one another left her feeling disappointed. It rivaled the superficiality of her current environment."

By the time we encounter Eliza in the second book you have just read, we read the teacup imagery again, but with added tension. "Charlotte's teacup clattered in the saucer. Eliza gripped her cup so tightly she wondered it did not crack." (Chapter XIII, *The Island King*) By this time, Eliza is fully acquainted with the dark side of her world, and she rebels against it. Unlike the other aristocratic women around her, she is not wooed by the wealth Lord Dunmore displays. She is fully aware of how corrupt and rotten the island colony is, and in writing these books, I hope I've helped shed a light on the uglier side of the Regency time period.

One aspect I would like to bring up is Charles' decision to raise another man's child as his own. As modern readers, we sometimes like to assume that the past is steeped in perfection and propriety, but people in the Regency were just as flawed as we are today. (If you don't believe me, read *Lascivious Bodies* by Julie Peakman. You may require the use of smelling salts.) I think this attitude is partly derived from the repressive society that followed in the Victorian period of the 19th century, but the Victorians acted in such a way as a response to what they viewed as the excesses of the Regency years. Nuance is very important to my writing, and nothing I depict is ever cleanly portrayed as black and white. I love to dive headlong into the more uncomfortable aspects of everyday life in the Regency and how these people viewed the greater world around them. To do that, we need to understand honor and how it shaped everyday lives.

Honor was an extremely important concept to Georgians, and during this time period, it transitioned into something more about relations between men than the chivalry showcased between men and women in centuries past. This is why duels evolved into such an important feature between gentlemen in disagreement, and Charles and Jean would have certainly engaged in one had Jean not been arrested and executed in *Strange Eden*.

But as this book opens up, we are immediately thrown into Charles' pathos about Jean's death. For an eighteenth-century man, the idea that an innocent friend had been executed, one close enough to figure as a brother, would have been horrifying. But for Charles to finally realize the mistake he made after reading Jean's papers, to know he had helped to not only destroy his character but take his life—now that would have been devastating. Charles was responsible for ruining Jean's honor in a century where one's reputation, whether dead or alive, was paramount.

On the other side of honor, Charles has vowed to protect Eliza. Beyond his understandable feelings of betrayal and hurt, he would have felt duty-bound to protect her reputation, as well as the result of her illicit affair, baby Philippe. Divorces were extremely difficult to attain in this age, and he would have known that the chance of the baby's survival would have been slim to none if the child was sent off into the world. The way marriages worked during the Regency period was like a double-edged sword. On one hand, women faced more restrictions and less freedom than we are used to today. But on the other, a good and dutiful husband would have protected his wife and her honor to the ends of the earth, fully aware of the societal ramifications she would face should he publicly abandon her.

When Charles is finally confronted by Philippe's existence, he is unsure of what action to take but knows without a doubt what *should not* be done. The baby must remain on the property at Pleasant Hall if it is to live, and Charles cannot have a second innocent life on his hands. The pain he feels about Eliza's infidelity is eclipsed by his sense of honor. Of course, as revealed by an intimate conversation he and Cleo have later in Chapter VII, he also secretly hopes the child will finally mend the broken relationship with Eliza. He is desperate to prove his love to her, and protecting this marital secret helps both assuage his guilt over Jean's demise and build the family he yearns for.

You might think that people in Georgian times followed strict codes of etiquette. While this is true to some extent, I've also found from my research that illegitimate heirs were not entirely uncommon in the British upper classes. Ian Mortimer has an excellent quote about this revelation in his book *The Time Traveller's Guide to Regency Britain*, where he says, "You can depict the extent of sexual immorality in society in the shape of an hourglass: ample to overflowing at the top, narrowing around the middle, and burgeoning again among the lower classes." Simply put, the wealthiest of society often acted the most scandalously because their power gave them public immunity. A married woman's child was legally regarded as the husband's, whether a biological relation existed or not, and Charles is ensuring Philippe's survival by choosing to rear him as his own. A lesser man could have easily sent the child away to die in poverty or live with some distant relations. He could have even been excused for actively disowning the "natural" child, as the 18th century would have termed it, by taking legal steps, but he chooses a different path. Charles is on a mission to restore his sense of honor, and he will stop at nothing to protect those he has wronged.

And I would be remiss to forget Charles' other stunning decision: to gradually free all of his slaves at Pleasant Hall. It is easy to assume that all slave holders thought the same way or that it was simply impossible to emancipate large numbers of enslaved people. But history once again corrects that assumption. While it was extremely difficult to achieve, it was not entirely impossible. In Chapter XV, Charles remarks, "In my legal queries, I have come across the case of an American in Virginia who has formed a method that unfolds gradually. He is still involved with the local courts." The person I have referenced was Robert Carter III, a real man who was a contemporary of America's founding fathers like George Washington and Thomas Jefferson. But unlike Washington, who freed his slaves upon his death, and Jefferson, who only freed a handful for personal reasons, Carter worked tirelessly at the cost of his own fortune and reputation to free all 450 of his slaves while he was alive. He was a fascinating man, and if you are interested in learning more about his life, I highly recommend the book *The First Emancipator: Slavery, Religion, and the Quiet Revolution of Robert Carter* by Andrew Levy.

This leads me to talk about my style of writing historical fiction. History doesn't always occur with the great thundering of cannons; in fact, it happens every day, even in the smallest of moments. We are all connected with each other in one way or another, and what impacts one group eventually spreads outwards in a ripple to touch us all. That is why I am particularly fascinated by incidents leading up to and after great world events. While I love studying the American Revolution, I am equally fascinated by its fallout and what happened to many of the Loyalists who fled from the colonies. A great number of them ended up in The Bahamas, where they encountered a familiar figure: Lord Dunmore, the failed governor of Virginia. There, much to his dismay, a microcosm of the troubles and grievances that eventually led to revolution began to play out a second time.

I prefer to center my stories around fictional characters, who are still painstakingly researched but flawed enough to resemble actual people. But of course, I like to make them encounter real historical figures, and this series is peppered with them. Lord Dunmore, the corrupt governor; Hiram Bruin, the crooked privateer; William Wylly, the outspoken attorney; and Lord Grenville, Jean's spy master, were all once living people. In fact, you can still visit Lord Dunmore's Virginian home today, at the Governor's Palace in Colonial Williamsburg, and see the result of his extravagant spending at Fort Charlotte in Nassau, Bahamas.

I have also visited the Bahama islands extensively for research for this project in the past few years. If anything, I hope you could feel the love I have for The Bahamas as you flipped through these pages, and I hope you enjoyed learning more about its history. The Bahamas is a beautiful jewel in the Caribbean, but it is more than a cruise stop, and I hope *The Strange Eden* series has convinced you of that.

I could go on and on because I'm a history nerd, but I'll leave you here. I am grateful you chose to read this novel. All the books I write are a labor of love, and as an independent author, every reader and every review is so, so important to me. The final installment of *The Strange Eden* series is in the works, and it will be on its way to you soon.

The past is a very different place, and it may not always be palatable. But it serves as an invaluable lesson to us all. Thank you for taking the journey with me.

Acknowledgments

I dedicated this novel to my mother, and this book would not be here without her constant love and encouragement. She has always supported my creative endeavors, and made it a priority in our lives. Thank you for your feedback, for all of your help marketing this project, and for every little thing you do. You are the best mother I could have ever asked for.

Thank you to Michael, my husband, for loving these books as much as I do. I love hearing your opinions, and I feel so honored that you love reading them multiple times. Thank you for keeping me sane, and thank you for all the freshly made midnight Nutella crepes.

As always, I would like to thank God, my Circle, and all of my ancestors. I would also like to thank Elizabeth Daisy Williams. When I wrote this book I never imagined that I would find my soul sister across the sea. Thank you for your friendship. I literally could not have survived my first year as an independent author without you grounding me and encouraging me. And thank you once again to Norimasa Suzuki for helping me manage my chronic pain so I could continue writing.

I had the pleasure of working with two wonderful editors on this book. Cath Lauria, you completely understand my vision for this series, and you make editing these books fun. Barbara Bowen, I am so glad we connected. Thank you for helping me and for being a perfectionist. I have less anxiety after you look over my work, which is no easy feat! Finally, I am incredibly grateful for C-Allyssa Reckley. She is without a doubt the best photographer in The Bahamas. Thank you for crafting such beautiful headshots and product photography!

Thank you to the Bahamian people for their generous hospitality and beautiful, vibrant culture. A special thanks to Perry Claire for providing rides for all of my research trips. Finally, I would like to thank Gail Saunders for a lifetime of historical work. Your contributions to the preservation of Bahamian history were unmatched, and I have consulted your research many, many times in the making of these novels. With your passing last year, The Bahamas has lost its premier historian, and I was very saddened to hear the news.

Last, but not least, I would like to thank my assistants, Goonie and Tippy Bouvier. Goonie, you understand book marketing like no one else. Thank you for driving engagement to my social media pages. Tippy, keep listening to your brother's advice. Also, it is now permissible to gallop inside the kitchen.

Bibliography

Adkins, Lesley, and Roy Adkins. Jane Austen's England: Daily Life in the Georgian and Regency Periods. New York: Penguin Books, 2013.

Aron, Paul. Founding Feuds: The Rivalries, Clashes, and Conflicts That Forged a Nation. Naperville: Sourcebooks, Inc., 2016.

Benezet, Anthony. Some Historical Account of Guinea, Its Situation, Produce, and the General Disposition of Its Inhabitants with an Inquiry into the Rise and Progress of the Slave Trade, Its Nature, and Lamentable Effects. Project Gutenberg eBook, 2004. https://www.gutenberg.org/files/11489/11489-h/11489-h.htm

Bethell, Arnold Talbot. *The Early Settlers of the Bahamas and Colonists of North America.* Third ed. Westminister, MD: Heritage, 2008.

Block, Sharon. Rape and Sexual Power in Early America. Chapel Hill: The University of North Carolina Press, 2006.

Burstein, Andrew. Jefferson's Secrets: Death and Desire at Monticello. New York, NY: Basic Books, 2006.

Byrne, Paula. Belle: The Slave Daughter and the Lord Chief Justice. New York: Harper Perennial, 2014.

Carpentier, Alejo. The Kingdom of This World: A Novel. 1949. Reprint. New York: Farrar, Straus and Giroux, 2006.

Cavendish, Georgiana. The Sylph. Edited by Jonathan Gross. Evanston, Illinois: Northwestern University Press, 2007.

Chambers, Douglas B. "Runaway Slaves in the Bahama Islands, 1784-1819," February 2014, 1–97.

Davis, Graeme, ed. Colonial Horrors: Sleepy Hollow and Beyond. New York: Pegasus Books Ltd, 2017.

Deren, Maya. Divine Horsemen: The Living Gods of Haiti. New York: McPherson & Company, 1953.

Equiano, Olaudah. The Interesting Narrative and Other Writings. 1789. Reprint. New York: Penguin Books, 2003.

Flavell, Julie. The Howe Dynasty: The Untold Story of a Military Family and the Women Behind Britain's

Wars for America. New York, NY:
Liveright Publishing Corporation, a division
of W.W. Norton & Company, Inc., 2021.

Handley, Sasha. Visions of an Unseen World:
Ghost Beliefs and Ghost Stories
in Eighteenth-Century England.
New York: Routledge, 2015.

Heyer, Georgette. April Lady. 1957.
Reprint. Naperville: Sourcebooks Casablanca, 2011.

Hochschild, Adam. Bury the Chains: Prophets
and Rebels in the Fight to Free an Empire's Slaves.
Boston: Mariner Books, 2006.

Hoock, Holger. Scars of Independence: America's
Violent Birth. New York: Crown, 2017.

Howard, Martin R. Death before Glory!
The British Soldier in the West Indies in the
French Revolutionary and Napoleonic
Wars 1793–1815. Barnsley:
Pen and Sword Military, 2015.

Jackson, Christopher C. "Preservation and the
Future of the Bahamian Past: A Case Study of
San Salvador Island's Historic Resources"
(master's thesis, University of Georgia, 2018).

James, Erica Moriah. The Awakening Landscape:
The Nassau Watercolours
of Gaspard Le Marchant Tupper.
National Art Gallery of the Bahamas, 2004.

Jasanoff, Maya. Liberty's Exiles: American Loyalists
in the Revolutionary War. New York:
Vintage Books, 2012.

Kemble, Frances Anne. Journal of a Residence
on a Georgian Plantation in 1838-1839.
Edited by John A. Scott. Athens:
University of Georgia Press, 1984.

Knight, John. War at Saber Point: Banastre Tarleton
and the British Legion. Yardley:
Westholme Publishing, 2020.

Levy, Andrew. The First Emancipator: Slavery,
Religion, and the Quiet Revolution of Robert Carter.
New York: Random House, 2005.

Mackenzie, Henry. The Man of Feeling. Oxford:
Oxford University Press, 2009.

Mortimer, Ian. The Time Traveler's Guide to
Regency Britain: A Handbook
for Visitors to 1789-1830.
New York, NY: Pegasus Books, 2023.

Nedervelt, Ross Michael. "A Tumultuous Upheaval and Transformation: The Impact of the American Revolution on the Bahama Islands" (master's thesis, University of New Hampshire, 2012).

O'Shaughnessy, Andrew Jackson. The Men Who Lost America: British Leadership, the American Revolution, and the Fate of the Empire. New Haven: Yale University Press, 2013.

Peakman, Julie. Lascivious Bodies: A Sexual History of the Eighteenth Century. London: Atlantic Books, 2004.

Peters, Thelma. "The American Loyalists in the Bahama Islands: Who They Were," Florida Historical Society 40, no. 3 (January 1962): 226–40. https://www.jstor.org/stable/30139824.

Reddie, Richard S. Abolition! The Struggle to Abolish Slavery in the British Colonies. Oxford, England: Lion, 2007.

Richardson, Samuel. Pamela. Oxford: Oxford University Press, 2008.

Ronald, D.A.B. The Life of John André. Havertown: Casemate Publishers, 2019.

Saunders, Gail. Bahamian Loyalists and Their Slaves. Nassau, Bahamas: Media Enterprises Ltd., 2011.

Saunders, Gail. Slavery in the Bahamas: 1648-1838. Nassau, Bahamas: Media Enterprises Ltd., 2015.

Schiff, Stacy. The Revolutionary: Samuel Adams. Little Brown & Co, 2023.

Schoepf, Johann David. Travels in the Confederation [1783-1784]. Translated by Alfred J. Morrison. Baltimore: The Lord Baltimore Press, 1911.

Schwartz, Marie Jenkins. Ties That Bound: Founding First Ladies and Slaves. Chicago: The University of Chicago Press, 2017.

Shirley, Paul Daniel. "Migration, Freedom and Enslavement in the Revolutionary Atlantic: The Bahamas, 1783–c. 1800" (PhD thesis, UCL, 2011).

Tanner, Lynette Ater, ed. Chained to the Land: Voices from Cotton & Cane Plantations. Winston-Salem: John F. Blair, 2014.

Vanhorn, Kellie Michelle. "Eighteenth-Century Colonial American Merchant Ship Construction" (master's thesis, Texas A&M University, 2004).

Washington, George. George Washington's
Barbados Diary: 1751-52. Edited by Alicia K.
Anderson and Lynn A. Price. Charlottesville:
University of Virginia Press, 2018.

Weingast, Barry R. "Adam Smith's Theory of the
Persistence of Slavery and Its Abolition in Western
Europe," (Stanford University, July 2015): 1–28.
https://doi.org/10.13140/RG.2.1.1354.9924.

Winters, Lisa Ze. The Mulatta Concubine:
Terror, Intimacy, Freedom, and Desire in the Black
Transatlantic. Athens:
The University of Georgia Press, 2018.

Wolfram, Sybil. "Divorce in England 1700-1857,"
Oxford Journal of Legal Studies 5, no. 2 (1985):
155–86. https://www.jstor.org/stable/764190.

Worsley, Lucy. If Walls Could Talk:
An Intimate History of the Home. New York:
Bloomsbury USA, 2011.

About the author

Gina Giordano always had an insatiable curiosity and a penchant for history. Born in New York City, she is a writer, artist, and a conjurer of the past. She holds a BA in history and a master's degree in historical fiction from New York University, and has traveled to over fifty-five countries across the globe. When she is not climbing ancient ruins or exploring forgotten palaces, she enjoys swimming with sharks in remote pristine waters. Her debut novel, *Strange Eden*, was longlisted for the 2023 Bath Novel Award.

You can find Gina on Instagram under the handle **@ginagiordanobooks.**
Her website is **www.ginagiordanobooks.com.**

If you enjoyed reading this book, please consider leaving a review on either Goodreads or Amazon. Positive reviews are extremely crucial for independent authors, and helps readers like you discover us.